HIDDEN MICKEY

By

Nancy Temple Rodrigue
David W. Smith

2009

Double-R Books

DOUBLE-R BOOKS

Cover Design by Jeremy Bartic
HTTP://MYTDUCK.DEVIANTART.COM
Back Cover Photo by Xochitl Rodrigue
HTTP://THEXGALLERY.COM

1st Edition , Volume 1 in the Hidden Mickey series – 2009
Volume 2, Hidden Mickey 2 coming Sept. 2010

ISBN: 978-0-9749026-2-3
ISBN: 0-9749026-2-4

Published by:
DOUBLE-R BOOKS
A Division of
Rodrigue & Sons Company
244 Fifth Avenue, Suite # 1457
New York, New York 10001
HTTP://DOUBLE-RBOOKS.COM

Printed in the United States of America

"Sometimes Dead Men Do Tell Tales"

While running the spirited Mouse Adventure road rally through Disneyland, best friends Adam & Lance stumble across a long-lost diary of Walt Disney's. The diary hints of hidden treasure and leads them on a wild cross-country search filled with discoveries – about the famous man, his life, and about themselves.

Beth, Adam's former girlfriend, was fired from her beloved job at Disneyland thanks to Adam. Now he needs her help in untangling a web of clues that Walt left behind. Can she put their past aside and work with him again? Can the three friends decipher the eccentric clues that Disney himself may have ingeniously devised? Is someone else sniffing the same trail of clues and seeking the Disney cache for themselves?

As the clues lead them closer to their goal – and deeper in the legacy of Walt Disney himself – will they find some long-lost treasure? Or is this one final illusion by the World's Greatest Storyteller?

Anyone who loves all-things Disney will be swept up in the intrigue of the sometimes subtle, sometimes obscure, and always amazing facts surrounding one of the most recognized, beloved and ingenious men of all time. Walk in the shoes of our intrepid treasure hunters as they scavenge historical records and discover amazing connections, while they seek out what Walt may have left behind.

Hidden Mickey takes readers on a wild ride; consider it Mr. Toad's Wild Ride on steroids

For Chayad Bruce,
Enjoy the
Grand
adventure!
Nancy
2012

I would like to dedicate my part in this joint venture to my own General Contractor, my husband Russ Rodrigue. His support, assistance, advice, patience, and even more patience have been invaluable to me.
Nancy Temple Rodrigue

I dedicate my efforts in this book to the two women most important in my life: My wife, Dr. Kerri Smith, who has provided the means for me to do what I enjoy doing, and my Mother, Donna Winchester who has always faithfully supported me and my projects. In addition, thanks go to Virginia Naifeh for her help in editing and proofreading our early draft.
David W. Smith

Disclaimer

PROLOGUE

DECEMBER 14, 1966

"It all started with a moose."

The words were mumbled, faint. It took too much effort to chuckle at his own private joke, but the corners of his eyes crinkled as a smile passed over his pale lips.

The only other person in the room glanced up from the paperwork in front of him, a wave of sympathy and grief flooded his face before he could say anything to the man lying on the hospital bed. He self-consciously coughed to clear the lump in his throat. *How am I ever going to be able to carry this off?* he thought to himself before speaking. "You say something, Walt?" he managed to ask out loud.

Walt's eyes drifted back to the present and rested on the man peering anxiously at him. He gave a dismissive wave of his hand, a gesture that rose only two inches off his bed. Energy spent, the hand dropped soundlessly to the covers. "Oh, just having some fun reminiscing."

His idea of fun was doing the impossible...doing what everyone else said was foolhardy. Over the years, he had not only proven the naysayers wrong, he was now considered a living legend. However, he now labored to breathe, catching himself as if having spent the day breathing in the heavy smog often found in the Los Angeles basin. He came to the same conclusion his doctors had come to several days prior: He was soon to become a non-living legend. He gave a slight, resigned sigh. There was so much left to do. So many projects going. So many ideas still waiting in his active mind.

"I think I have everything I need, Walt," the young man who looked to be in his early thirties concluded, standing, straightening the small stack of papers and carefully placing them into a manila folder. "I'll make sure your instructions are followed to the letter," he promised. He then reached over to a black, leather-bound book that had been sitting on the small table next to him. "You're positive about this?" the man asked, referring to the book he held up in his hand.

Walt, in his weakened state, issued a nearly imperceptible smile. "Yes," he was able to say. It was said with such a breathy sigh that it resonated with the man as absolute finality, as if it were to be the last word ever to be spoken by this individual. The man nodded, and then turned to open the door to leave. He would have turned back to say good bye but he didn't want Walt to see the tears welling up in his eyes.

Walt's secretary, Louise, slowly walked down the hospital hallway carrying a painting under her arm. It was Walt's favorite tree, a smoke tree, painted by artist Peter Ellenshaw…something that would end up being Peter's farewell gift to his long-time friend. As she approached the room that she knew would be littered with more get well cards and flowers than the previous day, she saw a young man come through Walt's door and then close it quietly behind himself. She watched the man quickly dab at the corners of his eyes with a white handkerchief before turning to walk down the hallway towards her.

Dressed in a freshly pressed suit, the man carried a manila folder in his hands along with a little black book. His fingers were curled underneath, holding everything firm, his other hand grasping the top of the items as if he was in fear of dropping something. The short-cropped blonde-haired man nodded in Louise's direction. She had never seen this man before, but she noticed his eyes. There was grief in them – the same look that haunted everyone who left that room. But there was something else in this man's eyes. There was a soft – almost con-spiratorial – look, one that seemed out of place here in this hospital and especially coming from the room where one of the most famous men in the world was clinging to life.

Louise watched the man until he went around a corner out of her sight as he headed towards the exit of the hospital. She turned back to the door, drawing a deep breath as she prepared herself emotionally to enter her boss's room.

Walt smiled when Louise stepped into the empty room. She glanced around and marveled at the color and fragrance of the dozens of bouquets of flowers that lined nearly every flat surface of the room. She looked at Walt; his color contrasted the vibrancy that the flowers around him offered. His pallor was ashen, his cheeks sunken more than the day before. A full glass of V-8 tomato juice sat next to a plate of uneaten breakfast items. A small mound of scrambled eggs and a square of hash browns made the plate look larger than it was. None of it looked like it had been touched.

"Walt, you really need to eat," Louise said sliding onto the edge of the bed next to her boss.

Walt gave a weak smile, closed his eyes and shook his head back and forth very slowly. "Can't eat anything right now," he whispered in an even weaker sounding voice. He glanced at Louise's side. "What did you bring me?" he asked, his face momentarily lighting up at the thought of a present.

"Peter Ellenshaw painted this for you," Louise said as she turned the small 10-inch square painting toward Walt revealing a perfect smoke tree with its lavender leaves spreading out among narrow branches centered within an open field. She then stood it up against a water pitcher that sat next to his plate of untouched food so he could see it.

"That's terrific," Walt said, stifling a deep-throated cough.

"Walt, who was that man who was in here a moment ago?" Louise asked, trying to sound nonchalant.

Walt closed his eyes. Louise thought his illness had taken his memory for a moment. His eyes suddenly opened with a strange gleam. It was the same twinkle Louise had seen hundreds of times when Walt had a new dream.

"He is going to help keep me alive," Walt finally told her.

Louise was puzzled as the man she had seen looked nothing like a doctor. She glanced back at the door picturing the man whom she had passed outside moments before. Just as she was going to ask Walt about the man's profession, she turned back and noticed his eyes were closed again. He was breathing in easy, but short, shallow breaths. Louise knew Walt needed rest, so she quietly rose to the side of the bed and gave her boss a gentle kiss on his forehead.

As she silently opened the door, she took a "Patient Sleeping" card from inside the door and placed it on the outer handle. Struggling with the emotion tightening her throat, Louise took one last look at the man who she knew would live forever in the hearts of anyone and everyone who had ever heard the name Walt Disney.

WINTER, 2040

"It all started with a moose."

That's how Adam would always start his explanation when anyone would ask him how he got to where he was today. One needed only to see the mahogany-accented coffered ceilings or exquisite granite countertops set on finely crafted teak cabinets of his expansive home to know that Adam Michaels had gotten pretty far in his 68 years.

If Adam happened to be at home relaxing in his living room – as he was on this chilly winter day - he would chuckle appreciatively at the confused expression on his interviewer's face. "Yes, I said 'moose', not mouse." Before explaining further, Adam would settle back into his overstuffed chair and stare into the flickering fire blazing in his fireplace for a moment. Eight animation cels, each framed in deep rust-colored polished champak, adorned the mantle above the fireplace; the detail within each drew Adam's attention, his eyes lingering upon them, remembering just how he came to own the rare pieces. Dopey, Doc and, of course, the Little Princess, all played a part in Adam's history; the eight celluloid caricatures, authentic and easily recognized, added an eclectic accent of gaiety within the ornate walls of the living room.

Adam took in a deliberate breath followed by a long sigh. It was then that he would begin his story:

"No, I said that right. It did all start with a moose – for me. Lance Brentwood and I were double-dating at Disneyland one hot afternoon in August. Now, this was a long time ago…probably around 1995 or 1996. We didn't usually double like that, but I did it as a favor for him. There were these two blondes, and he asked me along to help him with one of them. Can't even remember which one was supposed to be mine. They were both glued to his side the whole day." Adam looked back into the fire and chuckled to himself, adding for his listener's benefit, "Those girls probably no more remembered I was there than any of the other thousands of guests at the Park that day!

"Lance got hungry, as Lance always did," Michaels continued, leaning forward in his chair as he warmed up to his story. "We decided to go to the Hungry Bear Restaurant there in Critter Country for lunch. I was getting kinda bored by that time, bored of being ignored by my so-called date. We sat up on the upper terrace and had our hamburgers and hot dogs. The girls were busy feeding Lance French fries. I occupied my time by watching the canoes start out on their journey, pulling away from the canoe dock down below and to the right of where we were sitting." Adam tilted his head in thought, then continued, "Of course the Mark Twain passed by. I remember seeing its three decks and white-washed rails lined with guests, many waving to those of us eating at the restaurant. Not too long after the Mark Twain had passed by, I could hear the sound of banjo music coming from a Keel Boat that was approaching beyond the canoe dock. She was a little too far around the bend to see just yet. But I could kind of hear the pilot poking fun at the canoe guides who must have been coming in for a landing at that point. Oh, I could tell she was ripping into them even though I couldn't hear exactly what she was saying." Adam paused, knowing the question that was forming in his listener's mind. "Yes, I said 'she'. She was a female Keel Boat pilot. The only pilot that was a girl, I found out later…"

Adam picked up his drink and took a sip of the fine Single Malt that had been sitting on the burlwood end table at his side. He swirled the amber liquid around inside the Wedgwood tumbler and then held it up to the firelight. A dazzling array of fireworks exploded from the finely-cut crystal. Nodding appreciatively at the fine color, Adam took another sip and then continued. "I didn't pay too much attention right then because the blondes were arguing about which ride to go on next. Then I could hear the banjo music getting louder as the Keel Boat got closer to the restaurant. I could hear the pilot telling the passengers: 'As we leave the last outpost of civilization, and head deep into the back woods, keep a sharp hunter's eye out for wild game. You never know what you will see'. This gal suddenly says, 'oh, hey, look over there on your right. That's old Bruce the Moose. Did y'all know that Bruce the Moose runs footloose through the spruce after his girlfriend, Lucy Moose?'"

Adam stopped while his companion, who had been listening intently, laughed a little at his recitation of the spiel he had heard that fateful day. "Yeah, I thought it was cute too. The Keel Boat – the Gullywhumper on that particular trip around Tom Sawyer's Island – slid by and I saw this little brown haired gal steering the Keel Boat literally with her rear end, holding a microphone up to her mouth with one hand, and using her hat as a pointer with her other." Adam paused here for a moment. "You knew the Keel Boats weren't on a track, didn't you? Well, they weren't. The pilots had to actually steer the double-deck boat with that long rudder that extended out the stern. Well, this little gal steers that boat over towards the canoes that were just leaving the dock and started telling the passengers who didn't know what they were in for yet that the guide in the back had a little motor under his seat, and if they didn't feel like paddling, don't worry, he can just turn it on and they can sit back and enjoy the ride!" Adam chuckled a bit, picturing the episode in his mind. "The canoe guides didn't like that much. There was no motor and if the guests didn't paddle, the guides had to provide the muscle!"

Adam took another sip of his drink, smiling at his memories. His eyes were far away. "I tell you, she kept in on them as the Keel Boat and the canoe continued down the river and out of sight around that first big bend. I never heard anything so funny from off those boats before. And, that's all it took." Adam chuckled again with a wry smile. "Well, it didn't hurt that she had a cute little figure to go with that voice I was drawn to. I had to meet her. I turned to Lance, but he hadn't even seen the Keel Boat go by. He was just basking in the attention of his blondes. I asked if they wanted to ride the Keel Boats next. Well, my blonde looked at me as if she couldn't remember who exactly I was. But, Lance agreed. He didn't mind where we went. He was like that. Pretty easy going.

"Well, I led them down to the Keel Boat dock. I figured it had to be about the time for the Gullywhumper to be coming back. We didn't have to wait too long. I could hear the banjo music and the pilot asking everyone to remain seated while she tried to get the boat into the dock without it 'keeling over so nobody got keeled'. Then she added something about women drivers and 'why do you think they call them Keel Boats anyway' which had everybody laughing even harder. Well, the boat barely nudged the dock as she landed it just as soft as anyone could with a boat that size, then she got the rope over the end of the rudder to hold the boat firmly against the dock. Next she had to help people exit safely." Adam picked up his Scotch again but held it without taking a drink. "She reminded the guests on board, 'Those of you comin' up from the bottom, watch yer top. And those of you comin' down from the top watch yer….uh…watch yer step, yeah, watch yer step.' When the last person was off the boat, she took off her hat to wipe her brow on her sleeve. I saw two things at that moment: the prettiest brown eyes I have ever seen…and her nametag told me her name was Beth." Adam stared into the fire for a moment, the corners of his mouth turned up in a private smile, finally taking a sip of his drink before he continued.

"She must have noticed me standing there staring at her, because she gave me a cute little smile. She told me later they were trained to do that, smile sweetly to the guests." He broke off and laughed. He didn't mention it felt like a bolt of lightning had hit him square in the chest when she had smiled at him.

"Well," he continued, "the blondes and Lance and I took the next boat, but it was Beth's turn to be on the dock. I was still looking at her as we pulled away, but she was too busy with the ropes. Our new guide wasn't near as funny as Beth had been. But, I didn't care. As the boat made its way past the Hungry Bear Restaurant where I first spotted Beth, I gave a subtle wave to Bruce the Moose as we passed him by at the bend of the River. When we got back, Beth wasn't on the dock. Talk about disappointment! One of the blondes had to go 'fix her face' as she put it, so we headed for the restrooms in New Orleans Square over by the train station where Lance said he had to use the facilities too. Well, I was standing outside waiting for Lance and the girls to finish up and who do you think walks out of the ladies room? It was Beth. Now, I'm not usually forward with women, but I had to say something. Her head was down, so I stepped in front of her so she would have to run into me. She turned all red and said 'I'm sorry. I didn't see you.' I said 'Obviously' or something stupid like that. She tried to go around me, but I stepped in front of her again. Before she kicked me or called security, I quickly explained how much I had liked her spiel. That perked her right up. She gave me that cute little smile again and thanked me and told me to come back and see her again some time."

"And you did, didn't you?" was asked by Adam's audience.

Adam gave a sigh. "Well, the blondes wanted a little more of Lance and a lot less of me, so they wanted to go on the Haunted Mansion. I knew I would be left in a doom buggy all by myself while both of them rode with Lance, so I wished them a good ride and I headed back to the Keel Boats."

"Was she glad to see you?"

"Well, I asked her out for the following night and she said yes. And the rest is, as they say, history."

"So, what happened to Lance and his blondes?"

Adam shrugged. "Never saw those two girls again. It was a couple of days before I saw Lance. He never said a word about it. But, that's Lance."

"How did he like Beth?"

"Totally smitten. They started bantering like an old married couple. Had me worried there for a while until I saw they would always be good friends and nothing more."

"Not what you hoped for yourself, correct?"

"Hell no! Did I ever tell you about the time she stole a canoe and we went on a picnic on the uninhabited backside of Tom Sawyer's Island?" Adam raised his eyebrows, nodding his head as if validating this incredulous part of his story. "And that, my friend, was only the beginning!"

CHAPTER 1

THE RACE

SUNDAY MORNING, 9:30A.M.
APRIL 21ST, 2002

The crowd sitting eagerly in the Fantasyland Theater early Sunday morning was a lot smaller in number than the usual 1500 or so that came to see the "Mickey's Detective School" stage show. The regular show, one that is performed every two hours at Disneyland, had been canceled for the day to make room for this year's edition of Mouse Adventure; a unique and typically wild rambunctious romp through Disneyland by dozens of teams in what is fondly described as a cross between a scavenger hunt and a car rally – only on foot. The participants arrived already divided into seventy teams that totaled two hundred and twenty players for this spring 2002 running of the race. Their enthusiasm more than made up for the relatively low numbers this year. The vast majority of runners were Disney aficionados, people who immersed themselves in all things Disney. While most had full-time jobs, from professionals to homemakers, all of these participants made it a hobby – an obsession for many – to learn and know as much as they could about Walt Disney and his Magic Kingdoms. The Mouse Adventure was sort of a proving ground for all to tout their knowledge – and subsequent bragging rights for those who won their divisions. The majority of the teams were made up of people from Southern California. However, the event drew many avid Disney fans from all corners of the country.

The teams had begun gathering in the Theater right after Disneyland opened at 8 a.m., sitting with their team members of two, three, or four people per team, scoping out the competition around them and eagerly, impatiently waiting for the race to begin. Some members recognized other teams and players from previous years, giving camaraderie 'high-fives' and welcome-back hugs to familiar faces. It was not uncommon for relationships to emerge with several weddings as a direct result from the event. Off to the left side of the stage, individual team photos were shot in front of a huge picture of Mickey Mouse dressed in safari gear. A group picture was attempted at 9 a.m. And at 9:15. It proved to be difficult to get two hundred and twenty people all facing in the same direction at the same time and not talking. Then, at 9:30, the emcee, Steve, welcomed them as quest packets were passed out amid much stomping and clapping. The quests were divided into two levels: Beginner and Advanced. First time questers were encouraged to start at the Beginner level until they got used to way the race was run. Returning questers would usually go to the more difficult Advanced level.

Steve quickly ran down the rules of the Mouse Adventure, reminding the teams that they had from 10 a.m. until 3 p.m. to run as many of the quests as they could. For reference material the teams could only use the Disneyland Park souvenir map given to all the guests entering at the main entrance turnstiles. No hand-held devices, notes or cell phones could be used. Purses and backpacks had already been searched for contraband devices, notes, trivia books, and reference guides. Team members had to stay within ten feet of each other at all times. There would be no asking the Park's cast members for help — as they have been known to give out wrong answers to the questers. Yes, there were Mouse Adventure people throughout the Park to watch for any breach in the rules. And yes, there would be penalties given for those breaches. Steve reminded them to have their answer sheets turned in at the Opera House on Main Street before the 3 p.m. deadline. At 3:01 the doors to the Opera House would be closed and no one would be admitted with their papers.

From his position at the podium on stage, Steve had a good view of the groups sitting below him. Most teams were already leafing through the twelve pages of quests, plotting their strategy for the game. He could tell this would be a good, competitive year. However, his eyes kept going back to a certain team off to the side. Teams were only allowed four people maximum. Here were a group of five people — four women and one man. The women, recognized as a returning group, had on identical bright blue T-shirts with their team name screen-printed over the fronts — Team Bad News Canoes. The man was in a brown polo shirt. Obviously not one of their team members. Steve made one last announcement:

"Just a reminder, people, that there is no fraternizing between the teams, either…. That means you, Team Pecos Bills. Last warning."

When he heard his team's name mentioned, Adam Michaels' head shot up from the quest he was reading through. "What the……" His race partner, Lance Brentwood, was not sitting next to him. The pile of papers Adam had given him to look over sat on the bench untouched. Half-standing from his bench, Adam tried frantically to locate his partner. He finally spotted Lance as he was ambling back to his seat.

"What do you think you're doing!?" Adam growled at him when Lance was close enough to hear over the dull noise of teams talking to each other within the theater.

Lance looked totally unrepentant. He grinned over at the group of four women who were still blushing furiously. Whether at being singled out for the warning from Steve or from whatever Lance had just said to them, Adam had no idea. Lance gave them a wave as he sat back down and picked up the Trivia Section page. He mentioned, offhandedly, "Did you see that redhead?"

Adam cut him off. "Are you trying to get us kicked out of the race before it even gets started? Sheesh, Lance, I..." Adam paused as he glanced back at the group of women Lance had been talking to, and more specifically, the redhead who easily stood out. "Wow, she is cute," Adam said almost apologetically.

"Got her number," Lance told him, reaching for the paper he had stuffed in his shirt pocket.

Adam stopped his arm. "Leave it there. We're still being watched."

Lance shrugged, unconcerned, his focus already back on the race. "Hey, it looks like we get to go into Club 33 and Walt's apartment this year." In almost the same breath, he changed the subject. "Do you know how many carrousel horses there are?"

"We do? Wow, I've never been in either of them!" Adam's head jerked up to look towards the stage. "Wait a minute, what did Steve just say?"

"'Have fun'." Lance quoted, eyes focused now on one of the word jumbles he picked out of his pack.

"No, before that. I think he mentioned something about Walt's apartment."

"Dunno. Hey Adam, look at this," Lance said, pointing to a two-word scramble on one of the sheets he was holding: "'Trust Sora'. That has to be Star Tours."

The two men looked up as a rousing cheer broke from everyone around them. It was 10 a.m. The Race was on!

There was no set pattern for the runners to accomplish their quests. They could take any quest in any order. As the excited, focused crowd surged out of the Fantasyland Theater, some turned left and headed for either ToonTown or the Disneyland Railroad station just behind them. The rest, the majority, turned right and headed towards Matterhorn Mountain. The mountain would be the dividing place for the rest of the Park. Those going to locations in Tomorrowland would go left around the mountain. Fantasyland was off to the right. Main Street was straight ahead. Frontierland and Adventureland would veer off to the right from the Main Street Hub.

Adam sorted the quest papers as he and Lance speed-walked towards the back of Sleeping Beauty's Castle. "How about Critter Country first? There is a multiple choice question set there. Plus there's the Canoe Quest where we have to ride the canoes and collect a token afterwards. It says to keep the token and turn it in with the answer sheets. This quest is worth eighty points. It might be a good idea to get the canoes out of the way early and not have to go that far into the Park later in the day."

They came around the side of the Castle, past Ariel's Grotto, into the Main Street Hub. "Want to do Walt's Apartment before we head to the canoes?" Lance watched a particular group of bright blue shirts as they headed down Main Street.

It looked as if they weren't the only ones excited about getting into Walt's Apartment. There were a lot of questers heading in that direction, moving in groups against the grain of regular Disneyland guests who were coming down Main Street from the park's entrance. Adam shuffled quickly through the papers and looked over that particular quest. He grunted and shook his head. "Well, it says they only let in two teams at a time. We'd probably have to wait in line a while. Let's come back later."

With a good-natured shrug, Lance took the Canoe Quest sheet from Adam's hands and looked it over, reading out loud the questions: "How many seats in a canoe? How many riders can a canoe hold? The canoes have been in how many different lands since they started running? Name them."

"So, do you count the canoe guides in the rider count, or is it just passengers?" Adam asked as they entered the Frontierland stockade gate and walked past the Shootin' Exposition.

"Probably a trick question. I'd include the guides." They were passing the Golden Horseshoe now. Unlike the thousands of guests who visited the Park, Adam and Lance barely took notice of their surroundings. They ignored the perfectly manicured planters, themed within the rich, western landscape of Frontierland; the intricate detailed scrollwork of carved letters in gold leaf paint that welcomed guests to the Golden Horseshoe Review. To their right, the Mark Twain Riverboat was busy loading passengers for her trip around Tom Sawyer's Island. The large white Disney icon sat pristine at her dock, paddlewheel rotating slowly to maintain the mooring ropes tight as people embarked across the gangplank. The Sailing Ship Columbia, with her three tall masts and authentic rigging, was still berthed just beyond the old Keel Boat dock and due to come out and join the Mark Twain later in the day as the Park became busier. The full-scale replica of the first ship to carry the American flag around the world was an afterthought of Walt's, Adam remembered reading; something about Walt seeing a busy river one day as he looked over it with his Frontierland manager. The manager thought Walt was going to criticize the number of objects that moved people around Tom Sawyer's Island; the Mark Twain, two keel boats, six canoes, and three Tom Sawyer Island rafts. Instead, Walt had insisted that what the river needed was "another BIG boat." Adam hoped that there might be a trivia question about the Columbia or its history on this quest.

Adam and Lance moved quickly along the riverfront,

avoiding the growing line in front of Pirates of the Caribbean and dodging families taking pictures along the river-walk. The smell of popcorn permeated the air as the men passed by the brightly-painted cart just past the French Quarter restaurant. Lance was tempted to stop and buy some, wanting to feed his often voracious appetite. His well-built frame was a front for a seemingly never-ending need to eat. Adam often wondered how Lance kept such a great build while eating at almost all hours.

To their right, a canoe half full of sporadic-paddling guests splashed by on the Frontierland river – also known as Rivers of America, as it was printed in their Disneyland guidebook – but something most Disney aficionados already knew. He could hear laughter coming from the canoe. Four of the passengers, two seated in front of the other two, all teenage girls, were engaged in a water fight with their paddles.   Smiling to himself, Adam glanced at the sky. It was a beautiful spring day. The low morning coastal clouds were in the process of burning off. The temperature would probably set around a warm eighty-degree high; perfect weather for a Sunday at the Park.

Bringing his mind back to the quest, Adam thought about one portion of the question regarding the canoes. "What about the different lands?" he asked Lance who was looking over a different quest page. "The canoes are in Critter Country now. It was called Bear Country before that," Adam ticked off on his fingers. "That's two. What was it before Bear Country?"

Having just passed the Haunted Mansion, Lance's attention was drawn upward by the screamers on Splash Mountain. A log was just starting its plunge down the fifty-two-foot long chute with the riders in various positions of holding their hands up in the air or holding on for dear life. He watched until it hit bottom and a huge splash of water went up.   "I'm not sure. Did the Indian Village count as a land?" Lance answered Adam, not taking his eyes off the mist of spray that still permeated the air above the splash zone at the base of the steep log flume.

"No, that was just part of Frontierland," Adam said, oblivious to the steep, plunging log of screaming guests, his head focused only on the papers in his hand. "Oh, I guess that's the answer. Frontierland would be the first actual location. I'll write down 3."

The entrance into Critter Country was striking with the reddish orange rockwork of Splash Mountain on their left, and the granite façade separating Fowler's Harbor where the Columbia sailing ship was docked, on the right, which officially was still in New Orleans Square. (But, to Adam, it more resembled a dock he had seen in a New England tourist guidebook.) Years ago, Adam knew, this area was the entrance to what was called Bear Country. Before Splash Mountain, the area had been the low-key area of the Park with most guests only entering the land out of curiosity, by mistake, or for the love/hate musical attraction, The Country Bear Jamboree. Now closed and boarded up with a new attraction being built there, Adam knew that the Jamboree was still a popular attraction at Walt Disney World on the east coast, but had only marginal popularity here at Disneyland. Adam felt a wave of nostalgia as he was one in the camp of those who enjoyed the attraction when it was operating. He would laugh to himself remembering the Jamboree when it was retooled as the "Country Bear Vacation Hoedown"…and the huge lead bear, Jasper, would look down at the tiny tee-shirt he had on saying, "Still have on my camp tee-shirt. Still fits…kinda!"

Adam and Lance hadn't seen any other teams as they came into Critter Country. As they entered the ramp going down to the canoe dock, Lance looked over longingly at the two-story Hungry Bear Restaurant just beyond the exit to the ride.   "Fries?" he asked Adam, hopeful.

"No time. Didn't you eat breakfast?"

To Adam, Lance always seemed hungry. "Yes, but I might give out on the trip around the island. Paddling's a lot of work, you know," he tried beseechingly, all the time knowing his big brown eyes had no chance of swaying Adam away from his determined path. That tactic usually only worked on his female friends.

"Poor baby," Adam crooned, unimpressed. "You're taller than me. Look over the guests in line and see if you can count the number of seats in the canoes."

While they waited in the short line for Davy Crockett's Explorer Canoes, Lance counted the number of seats: twelve. When the full canoe in front of them pulled out of the dock, there were eighteen guests and two cast members or ride operators. Lance totaled the three lines and filled in the final answer as twenty riders in a canoe before he grabbed a paddle and got into his assigned seat. Because of his 6' 2" height, he was positioned in the back near the cast member in charge of steering the canoe. Adam was a few rows in front of him. The race papers had been stashed inside the protective cover that had been given them when they received all the race documents, although Lance was currently sitting on the sheets he had rather than putting them inside his backpack.

Using the tow ropes, the two guides pulled their canoe to the end of the loading dock and gave the passengers a quick lesson in paddling. "Raise your paddle over your head, flat end over the water…not over your partner's face…" the front guide said, drawing a few laughs. The guide demonstrated how to cup the end of the paddle with one hand and where to place the other hand near the business end of the paddle. "On the count of three, reach forward, pulling the water towards the back of the canoe…and not into the lap of the person behind you!" he continued. Like most of the canoe guides, this one had large arms, biceps bulging out from the rolled-up sleeves of the mustard-colored, fringed canoe shirt; this guide was certainly not a rookie, Adam thought, leaning forward and to his side to take a stroke, careful not to collide with the paddle of the young boy in front of him.

Now away from the canoe dock, they were floating slowly past the lower level of the Hungry Bear Restaurant where families and others were sitting, enjoying an early lunch. When a French fry flew over his head, Adam looked over at the tables. Three laughing young women were hurling French fries to the smiling, encouraging Lance. Adam guessed their ages to be in their late teens, probably young college girls out for a sorority event at the Park. Lance had the ability to attract women of all ages: from early on, Adam observed how women seemed to be consumed with Lance. About half of the fries hit their intended destination; those which fell short of the canoe were being eagerly fought over by the flock of well-fed black mud hens and a number of mallard ducks that always hovered around the restaurant. Kids hanging over the rope railing were enamored of the various ducks that would watch the fries carom off the canoe. The three women were more interested in watching Lance. Adam just shook his head. He had to admit Lance had his ways.

Once they got out of throwing range of the women, and Lance remembered they were on a race and not a sight-seeing trip, the satisfied Lance dug in with his own paddle. The canoe shot forward. Mike, the guide in the back, chuckled to Lance, "I like it when you Mouse Adventure guys ride. Less work for us!"

They rounded the first bend and were nearing the Settler's Cabin. Tony, the guide in front, was standing now, facing the guests. "Off to our left", pointing out a solitary Native American sitting on a spotted horse, "is Chief Auto Parts. Looks like he traded in his old bronco and got himself a new mustang." As they slid past the Settler's Cabin, he told them, "We are now approaching the dangerous Keel Boat Rapids." Adam gave a sigh at the name of the rapids. *Don't go there. Don't look at the cabin*, his mind warned him. *Focus!* Guide Tony continued, with dead-panned, mock seriousness, "Careful we don't hit any rocks 'cause we might just keel over and somebody might get keeled! Ooh, look at the white water rapids splashing over the rocks! Treacherous!" He splashed some water on the rocks with his paddle as the canoe glided past; a nearby mallard duck swam away at the small splash. They rounded the bend in the river away from the Pinewood Indian Village – "because that's what they are made of – Pine Wood" and the riders were given a break from paddling. Right after floating past the wrecked Mine Train on their left, they dug in again – much to the delight of the people on Tom Sawyer's Island who were shouting out helpful suggestions. "Stroke!" one teenage guy yelled. "You're going to have a Stroke!" His buddy next to him, standing on the bank of the River, added, "Take the Mark Twain next time! You see the same stuff!"

As the canoe rounded the final bend, going past New Orleans Square, Adam marveled at the panorama that spread across the bank of the river. Within the wide walkways that lined the River, from the Mark Twain dock to the entrance of Adventureland, from the queue area in front of Pirates of the Caribbean to the Haunted Mansion, people moved like a colony of ants, walking in different directions each with different destinations within the Park. It was a mass of humanity enjoying the beautiful day. Adam thought about the vista and believed that this was what Walt Disney had intended for his park: *A happy place for all who come.* Adam looked at the families all around, each having a different type of fun. He knew this was what Walt had meant as to the reason he built Disneyland.

The canoe turned towards the canoe dock, passing the rafts crisscrossing each other, taking and returning groups of people to and from Tom Sawyer's Island. On the left, the massive, three-masted sailing ship, Columbia, was still docked in Fowler's Harbor. There were a number of employees on the ship. Adam recognized that the ship was getting ready to be backed out into the River to join its counterpart, the Mark Twain, in taking guests around Tom Sawyer's Island.

"Paddles up!" Tony called as the back guide steered the canoe towards the narrow entrance of the canoe dock. "Watch your hands and fingers; please keep your hands inside the canoe as we approach the dock. We don't want our pretty dock scratched up," Tony advised the guests, keeping an eye on the younger ones who might not heed his warning.

They climbed out and Adam pulled his wet shirt away from his chest. He had been placed behind an eight-year old who, he felt, had left more water on him than in the river.

After collecting their race token, Lance grinned at Adam's soaked shirt. "Well, that was invigorating, wasn't it?"

With a snort, Adam replied, "I see you don't have a drop on you."

"I know how to paddle."

Adam didn't bother replying. The two exited the canoe dock with the others who had been on their canoe. Adam took the plastic pouch; Lance began looking over the various sheets he had protected by sitting on them. Adam was sorting through the quests, looking for the Multiple Choice section. "Here it is. Thought I had these in order... Oh, we also need to ride Pirates and Indiana Jones – unless we know the answers. Listen up." He started reading the questions:

1. In Critter Country, which wooden animal can NOT be found?

a. Tortoise

b. Porcupine
c. Coyote
d. Moose

2. How many rubies are on the Golden Horseshoe Sign?
a. 39
b. 40
c. 41
d. 42

3. As you sail through the Bayou, what creature do you see?
a. Possum
b. Swamp Cat
c. Raccoon
d. Alligator

4. What two animals did the Pirates NOT set free?
a. Cat and Dog
b. Duck and Geese
c. Donkey and Chickens
d. Pigs and Parrots

5. What do the Pirates offer the dog for the key?
a. Bone, Rope, Mug
b. Mug, Ball, Bone
c. Bone, Cat, Rope
d. Ball, Rope, Meat

6. What is Indy's truck license plate?
a. THX1168
b. NDYJNS
c. WH11204

7. Which bad end does not come to those who stare at Mara?

a. Eaten by rats
b. Stung by scorpion
c. Impaled on stakes
d. Bitten by snake

8. Which pair has wandered into Adventureland?
a. Snow White & Prince Charming
b. Bernard & Bianca
c. Buzz & Woody
d. Mrs. Potts & Chip"

To answer question one, they started looking around for the wooden animals. They found carved wooden statues and wooden seats. There was also the large entry sign to Critter Country to consider. They finally arrived at 'Coyote' by process of elimination and Adam circled that answer.

"Should you work on 'Horsing Around' while we figure out these multiple choice questions?" Lance asked, looking over at Adam as they stopped at the entrance to Critter Country. The two moved over to the side of the walkway next to a wooden railing, away from the wave of people coming in or leaving the area. "We have some travel time before going back to Fantasyland," he pointed out as they turned and started walking towards Frontierland. "You are good at the movie trivia."

"Yeah, it's worth 100 points total.

' • Name the horse from each of these movies:

1. Sleeping Beauty
2. Hercules
3. Mulan
4. Beauty & the Beast
5. Cinderella
6. Aristocats
7. Mr. Toad

Bonus question – 20 points
• Name the Lead Horse on King Arthur's Carrousel

Bonus question – 10 points
• How many horses are on the Carrousel?'"

Listening to Adam without looking where he was going, Lance had stopped right in front of the entrance to the Golden Horseshoe. People had to walk around the pair as they came to a halt in the middle of the traffic flow of people. "I didn't know there was a 'Lead Horse', did you, Adam?"

"Yeah, I read about it in a magazine a while back. It's a real pretty white one," Adam added lightly with a grin.

"They are all white," Lance reminded him dryly.

"Just seeing if you're paying attention," Adam said with a sly smile. "Ok, then, how many rubies are on the sign?"

Adam and Lance looked up at the Golden Horseshoe's ornate sign that stood above them, attached to a second floor balcony that surrounded the front and sides of the western food and comedy review saloon. The balcony was sometimes used for mock gunfights before the actual stage show started inside the building. The balcony was now quiet as strains of fiddle music drifted out of the open doors of the saloon. Red rubies were imbedded within the large gold letters spelling The Golden Horseshoe.

They both silently counted. Adam came up with forty. Lance said it was forty-one. Adam said to count again. Adam again arrived at forty rubies. Lance was now talking to a group of girls who asked him what time it was. Rolling his eyes, Adam circled the '40' on the answer sheet. He knew Lance wasn't wearing a watch. Trying to be helpful, Adam told them it was almost eleven o'clock. He was completely ignored while the girls, the oldest not much older looking than eighteen, continued to look to Lance for the correct time. "Lance, we need to go. Yo, Lance? Pirates or Indiana Jones?"

Lance smiled his good-bye to the girls. The girls moved about ten paces away, waiting to see which direction Lance was going. "Well, we probably should get a FastPass for Indy and go on Pirates. I don't think I know any of those answers," Lance said as he focused back on his partner.

Adam and Lance retraced their steps along the Frontierland River towards Adventureland. They turned left at Tarzan's Treehouse, went past the entrance to the Indiana Jones Ride, and headed for the kiosks that give out FastPasses. The kiosks were positioned right next to the entry of the Jungle Cruise.

The passes were designed to move people through the lines faster. The guests are allowed to bypass most of the queue and it usually saves quite a bit of wait time on the more popular rides. Guests can get one FastPass for each entry ticket but cannot get another FastPass until they have used the one they already had. For the Mouse Adventure racers, any extra time saved can mean a lot more time finishing quests. Adam and Lance's Fast-Passes gave them an entry time in another hour and were good for a window of two hours. Lance stuffed their passes into his shirt pocket along with the phone numbers he had been collecting.

They turned back towards Tarzan's Treehouse and followed the crowd heading under the bridge into the line for Pirates of the Caribbean. The line was moving pretty quickly around the chain maze. Adam waited for his eyes to adjust to the dim interior as they entered the building and walked past the squawking parrot. "Let's see. What animal is in the bayou?" Adam recounted as they approached the loading area. "What animals are either still in cages or not in the ride at all? And what do the pirates have in the jail scene? That is basically it," he finished as they waited their turn to tell the pirate "host" how many in their party and then find out which boat row they should stand in to wait their turn to board.

"I know you can hear frogs in the bayou, but you can't see them. Didn't they add an alligator a while back?" Lance asked, thinking out loud.

Adam nodded. "Yeah, that was my first thought, too. Help me figure out the animals on the ride. I know the jail scene is towards the end, and we know there is a dog there."

The men didn't pay much attention to the actual ride. They were marking off animals as they were seen and Adam was also thinking about the 'Horsing Around' quest. "Did you see that goat?" "Is that a donkey or a horse?" "You're kidding, right?" "Did you see a cat?" "Yeah, back in the beginning of the ride." "What's left?" "I don't know." As they neared the end of the attraction, Adam studied the jail scene with the dog holding an old key that dangled around a metal ring that hung from its mouth. "Oh, look, a rope, then a bone, and the last guy is holding a cup," Adam said looking at the menagerie of audio-animatronic pirates standing or kneeling behind the iron bars; each one begging for the dog to bring them the key to their freedom.

"Is it just me or does that dog have a grin on his face?" Adam said as they passed the mangy mutt, his tail wagging, seemingly keeping time with the music and singing pirates like a fur-covered metronome.

"Yeah, kinda," Lance said, looking back as their boat passed by the scene just before the shoot-out between the drunken pirates at the end of the ride. He turned forward again as their boat lurched and pitched at a steep incline as it started to climb the up-ramp that resembled a waterfall and marked the end of the ride.

They could see the answer sheet better now as sunlight streamed in through the ride entrance after their boat leveled out at the top of the up-ramp and settled softly in the ride flume that curved out in front of the line of guests waiting for their turn to ride. Adam circled answer 'a' for question #5, and marked off the animals they saw. He was left with 'Ducks & Geese', so he chose answer 'b' as their boat drifted around the curve just before Lafitte's Landing where the boats would be guided to the unload dock on conveyor belts. A brief, "Please exit this way," was directed to the guests in the boat by the pirate hostess on the exit side of the boat. Her vest and scalloped beige blouse did little to hide the young lady's attractive figure. Lance caught the eye of this worker, who smiled in his direction before having to divert her attention towards the new group of passengers stepping into the now-empty boat. Adam was amazed that Lance wasn't able to somehow capture her phone number, or at least, find out what time she might get off work.

After the cool, dark interior of the ride, Adam had to squint his eyes from bright sun filtering in from the "French Quarter" of New Orleans Square as they exited Pirates. People pooled around the narrow Royal Street that created a convergence from the ride and the shops and restaurants in the immediate area. Adam pushed a hand through his blonde hair wishing he had remembered his sunglasses. "What do we have, thirty minutes before we can use our FastPass? Want to go to Fantasyland and finish the Horse quest?"

"Sounds good. Let's take the short cut behind Big Thunder Mountain. Miss the crowd on Main Street."

The Mark Twain sounded its whistle as it neared the dock. White steam rose from its contrasting black smokestacks. People crowded the ornate white railings on all three decks as they got ready to disembark and continue their adventures in the Park. Further on, a Big Thunder Mountain runaway mine car went screaming past on its roller coaster rails that were fashioned to appear as dilapidated train tracks. The train disappeared into a dark tunnel carved into the red rock mountain and rumbled out the other side. The passengers, some with their hands held high in the air, were laughing and getting ready for the next hairpin turn. As the two men walked past the mining equipment on the right, Lance looked over at the still mountain lake on the left. The screams coming from the Big Thunder roller coaster seemed a sharp contrast across from the placid lake scene complete with jumping fish and white birch trees. "This used to be part of the old Mine Train ride, didn't it? Weren't there fishing bears in here?"

Lance's question brought up Adam's head from the quest he was filling in. "Bears? Oh, right. Yeah, that tunnel up there in the rocks," he pointed to a large beam-encased hole carved into the barren hill above the lake, "lead into Nature's Wonderland. Old Unfaithful Geyser and all that. I think it was taken out in the late '70's. I don't remember the ride, but my parents used to love it."

They left Frontierland through a huge stockade gate made out of logs and entered into brightly-colored Fantasyland. They noticed an immediate crush of people and noise as more families with small children were getting in line for the rides here in Fantasyland. Walking past Dumbo the Flying Elephant, they veered around a jungle of strollers as they made their way to King Arthur's Carrousel located about in the center of the land. Adam noticed another group of girls staring in their direction after they spotted Lance. His tall frame and good looks, as usual, created a stir. Not that Lance noticed. It wasn't that he was aloof. His good nature attested to that. He was just totally unaware of the effect he had on the ladies. He had no idea women found his looks 'devastating' as one once described to Adam.

"I'll count the horses, you fill in the blanks," Lance offered. He moved away from Adam, counting as he went, the Carrousel still loading passengers. Adam saw some of the girls following him.

Smiling to himself, Adam filled in what he remembered regarding the horses named in various Disney movies:

1. Samson
2. Pegasus
3. Khan
4. Phillipe
5. No Idea (he wrote)
6. No Clue
7. Cyril Proud Bottom
8. Lead Horse – Jingles

Lance came back and stuffed a piece of paper in his pocket.

"What was that?" Adam asked, suspicious.

"Nothing. I came up with seventy-five."

"Seventy-five? You sure? Shouldn't it be an even number? Or were you distracted," as an attractive woman with a man at her side gave Lance a knowing smile as she walked past and got in line for Mr. Toad.

"We could count again. There are four horses in a row. Just count the rows and see."

Adam came up with eighteen rows on the moving Carrousel. "Eighteen times four equals seventy-two. You agree?"

"Sounds good. So which horse is the Lead? You never said."

Adam watched the Carrousel as it traveled in its circle. "There, that one on the end of the row, just behind the bench seat. It has flowers in its mane, and has bells all over...Glad we didn't have to count the bells... Anyway, the 'lead horse' is always the most elaborately decorated horse on a carrousel. They named that one Jingles," Adam said, pointing to the outside horse as it swung past them for another go-around.

"Fascinating. You really need to get a life," Lance said, amazed and amused at the same time by his friend's depth of Disney knowledge. "You really need to go on *Jeopardy*...the host of the show needs some competition!" Lance added with a chuckle. They both heard his stomach growl. "You hungry? We could get something to eat and work on the Jumbles."

Adam glanced at his watch. Amazed, he saw it was lunchtime already. "Ok, I'll have to stand in line with you, but that works. You are better at those word puzzles than I am. Let's see if we can knock these off while waiting," Adam suggested as they walked over to get in line for the fast food at the Vilage Haus Restaurant across from the Dumbo the Flying Elephant ride. After grabbing a couple of burger and fry combos, Adam and Lance took a seat inside the Danish-themed eatery, grabbing a corner table away from some rather loud groups of families with young kids.

At ten points each, they worked as fast as they could while they ate:

'All Jumbled Up'
Unscramble the mixed-up attractions:
1. rigid handlebar tour
2. landslide radio yarn
3. troll was dismal
4. yell troll joy
5. sure uncle jig
6. faint scam
7. ten inhuman soda
8. briar soot rot
9. trust sora
10. mansion teacup
11. dinnertime cook hat
12. repeat bicarbonate fish
13. sandy door millennia
14. teamwork trivia barn

By the time they were finished with lunch, it was already after noon. They had less than three hours left and eight more quests to work on. They had only the following answers to the "All Jumbled Up" attraction names:

1.
2.
3. It's a Small World
4. Jolly Trolley
5. Jungle Cruise
6. Fantasmic
7.
8.
9. Star Tours
10. Space Mountain
11.
12.
13. Disneyland Monorail
14.

Now they turned their attention to "The Road Rally" that would earn them fifty points.

Total up the following:

1. Address of Pieces of Eight Shop
2. Number of pillows in Walt's Apartment
3. Number of Teacups
4. Number of Fire Engines
5. Number of Flying Elephants
6. Number of Astro Orbitor Rockets
7. Maximum number of guests in a StarSpeeder
8. Number of seats around the large dining table in the main dining room at 33 Royal Street
9. Number of stairs in the first flight of steps around the golden elevator

While they were still in Fantasyland, they counted sixteen Flying Elephants, and eighteen Teacups. "Let's head past the Tomorrowland entrance and get the number of rocket jets," Adam said, referring to the Astro Orbitor but using the name that the jets went by for decades when Adam was young. "Wow! We actually get to go in Walt's Apartment!" Adam exclaimed, still excited by the prospect of going through Walt's original living quarters that he used when spending many days, weeks, and months at Disneyland. "Hopefully the other teams already scoped it out and are gone."

There were twelve Rockets circling as they went by. The StarTours entrance was right there, but they didn't want to take the time to ride it now even though the line was fairly short for that popular attraction. "After Walt's Apartment, we can head to New Orleans Square and hit Club 33 and find the Pieces of Eight shop's address. I think it is on the same street. Then we can ride Indiana Jones."

Adam and Lance headed around the Main Street Hub, with its detailed bronze sculptures of famous Disney characters perched on short, white pillars among meticulously manicured shrubs, flower beds and lawns. Guests were meandering around the hub taking pictures of each other with the iconic Sleeping Beauty's Castle poised in the background to the north. The two men headed south down Main Street towards the Park's entrance, passing shops constructed to match Walt Disney's idea of what 'main street' in any American city should resemble at the turn of the century…the nineteenth century, that is. Hence the name he had given the main thoroughfare: Main Street U.S.A.

"Did you write down '1' for the fire engine?" Lance asked as they passed the Candy Kitchen on Main Street. They could smell the butter toffee that could be seen being made through the window display. Adam put a restraining hand on Lance's arm to keep him from going in the candy store. "Don't have time," Adam reminded him as he pulled Lance past the candy shop's red and white awnings that were hung overhead, shading the interior of the shop through their plate-glass windows. A few steps farther, they had to pause, avoiding a group of kids who darted out of the Penny Arcade.

"One fire engine, Lance? Are you sure?" Adam gave him a smug smile. "Now you see why I am the superior partner. There are two fire engines. That one," he pointed at the red engine chugging down Main Street with a load of guests, "and the one that sits *inside* the Fire House," Adam added, pointing up ahead where the Main Street Fire House sat, directly below Walt Disney's private apartment. "That's two."

"I bow to your greatness," Lance kidded back.

They rounded the street corner in front of the Emporium – one of the largest souvenir shops in the Park - and saw the little side gate next to the Fire House was opened. They knew the gate led to the steps heading up to Walt's original apartment that sat above the Fire House. The stairway was guarded by a cast member who asked to see their race papers as Adam and Lance approached.

They excitedly climbed the steps on the north side of the Fire House to enter Walt's apartment. Neither of them had been in before. In fact, few people outside specific employees and supervisors were ever allowed inside. This was actually the first year the Race had allowed the Advanced Teams to enter. The men took a couple of moments to look around. The room had been furnished in early 1900's to match the theme of Main Street below. They took in the brilliant white walls and dark red accents of the draperies and floral carpet. The seating area was arranged around a red throw-covered pull-out bed, with antique lights and pictures for accent. Six upholstered chairs, with the exception of one red velvet armless seat, were floral-on-white tapestry material. The apartment had two hallways: the entry hallway through which they had just come, and a second hallway leading to the small Victorian bathroom on one side and the private balcony on the other. There was a large standing music box between two windows looking over the back area. The small kitchen, usually behind bi-fold louvered doors, was open for all to see with its small chrome toaster and white mini-fridge. The pictures hanging on the walls had been changed since Walt's time. The hand-painted lamps were the originals. The ivory French Provencal telephone was still there with its rotary dial.

Wendy, the cast member assigned to guard duty all day, had long been inured to the opulent surroundings and the privilege of being allowed in that special place. She was now completely bored by her assignment and had been looking out the front window at the more exciting goings-on of Main Street. After a fleeting glance at yet another set of wide-eyed, hush voiced Adventurers, she did a double-take at Lance. Even though her face turned a bright pink, she never took her eyes off him. Always unmindful of his looks, Lance gave her his devastating smile as he and Adam turned their minds back to the race and their quest. They quickly counted the pillows in the living area, and then Lance moved towards the bathroom to see if there were any pillows hidden in there. Adam noticed his shoe had come untied, and decided to take a moment to lace up. He figured Lance wouldn't have any problem identifying a pillow, and began thinking of their next destination. Momentarily forgetting the Dire Warnings issued orally and in print, subliminally and etched in stone, he plopped down on the nearest chair, which turned out to be the tallest, the Victorian tapestry wingchair. Sitting on the edge, crushing the cushion as he bent over, he felt something poke him in the behind. He adjusted his position a little, ignoring it. His movement only made the object prod him sharper. Glancing back at Wendy, who was, of course, still staring wistfully after Lance, he felt gently through the fabric. He could make out a hard, squarish shape. Before he could further his investigation, he heard a startled gasp. Wendy, after tearing her eyes away from where Lance had disappeared, made a cursory glance around the room to see where that other guy was. What she saw was his two feet from below the back of the chair. She was frantic as she ran over, "Oh my god! What are you doing!!?? You can't sit on Walt's chairs! Get off of there!"

Startled, his hand between his legs, Adam shot to his feet, dropping his pencil in the process. "Sorry. I was just tying my shoe." He tried to charm her with his smile. But, he wasn't Lance. When the smile failed, he stepped away from the chair as Lance came back to see what was keeping him. He took another step, turning away from the angry cast member. He said quietly to his partner, "Lance, I need a diversion. I need to check something out," as another team, Team Yeti, entered the apartment and started their count of the pillows in each room. They looked over, curious at the other team member who obviously had gotten in some kind of trouble. Hands on her hips, Wendy never took her glaring eyes off him as he pretended to be studying his race papers. *Great*, Adam thought, *now she watches me.*

Lance said nothing; he just looked around, pretending he was doing his count again. He sauntered off past the music box, down the hallway. In another five seconds, a piercing alarm went off as he opened the patio door and stepped out onto what was Walt's private balcony. Wendy turned pale and raced down the hall, followed by the other team who looked greatly amused by this turn of events. Adam dropped in front of the chair as he heard Wendy on her walkie-talkie explaining that 'some idiot on the race opened the patio door'. She paused, stammered, and then added, "No, sir, they can't hear me." The walkie-talkie squawked again. She started to say something to

Lance, but stopped. Adam knew Lance was probably smiling at her again, more than likely writing down her phone number.

In Adam's position, he was temporarily out of sight of the other people. Crouching down in front of the chair, he pulled the cushion away from the back and felt underneath. He could hear Wendy getting a code to disarm the alarm. Pretty soon the other team would get bored of the little comedy episode and move from the hallway into the little bathroom to continue their count. He was about out of time when Lance yelled, "Hey, look at that!" He was obviously still on the balcony. Over the protest of Wendy, the Yetis now piled out on the balcony with him. *Atta boy, Lance.* Adam vaguely wondered how many fit on the balcony as his hand worked over the floral pattern. His breath caught as he found something hard. Broken backing? A small box? A book? He couldn't tell. He only knew it shouldn't be there.

Mouth dry, he now did the unthinkable. He defaced The Sacred. Finding a couple of loose stitches in the back of the cushion, he tugged them apart. *Oh, god. I'm going to hell for this.* He slipped his clammy hand through the layers of cotton batting. Hearing everyone coming back in from the balcony, laughing at something Lance was saying, his fingers closed around the stiff object. It felt like leather and he barely saw it was a book as he jammed it down the front of his shorts. Heart pounding, he pulled his shirt down and got the cushion back in place just as Wendy herded everyone back into the living room with a stern warning about boundaries and rules. Standing very close to Lance, she seemed to be directing the entire warning to the innocent Team Yeti, who was nevertheless still vastly entertained by all this. She broke off her tirade when she saw Adam stand up from in front of the wingchair. Her eyes narrowed at the white lint all over the front of his brown shirt.

"Dropped my pencil," he tried, holding it up for everyone

to see as he brushed the cotton lint from his shirt with his other hand. "Dandruff," he explained, managing to look embarrassed.

Exasperated, Wendy told them to finish with their clue and get out. She must have worked on the Jungle Cruise at one time because she amended, "Oh, I'm sorry. That was rude. *Please*, get out."

As they headed down the stairs and back out onto Main Street, Lance asked him, "Why are you walking funny? She wasn't that cute."

Adam ignored the question and the crack. "I have to go to the bathroom."

As he veered off to the Men's Room that was right next to the Fire Station, he heard Lance's parting, "need more fiber," as Lance leaned against a post to wait. He waved at the departing Team Yeti. "Maybe she *was* that cute," Lance grinned to himself and checked where he had written Wendy's phone number.

Adam unnecessarily washed his hands, stalling until the only other man in the restroom finished at the sink and left. Adam ducked into an empty stall, locking the door behind him. Silently apologizing for the ruined cushion and his impromptu hiding place, he pulled the leather-bound book out of his shorts. It was old leather, cracked with age, the black color having faded to a dark gray. There was no embossing or any markings on the outside cover, front or back. The binding was about three quarters of an inch thick, but the way the front edges came together showed some of the pages were missing.

His heart – which still hadn't returned to its normal beat – pounded harder as he opened the stiff cover. Immediately he saw that what he had guessed was correct: There were numerous pages that had been ripped out of the front of the book. The first four yellowed pages proved to be blank. He slowly turned through these empty pages until he found writing. His eyes widened as he began reading the first page.

"Holy Crap."

CHAPTER 2

THE ADVENTURE BEGINS

SUNDAY AFTERNOON, 12:30P.M.
APRIL 21ST, 2002

Hands shaking, Adam reread through the diary. For that was what it had to be – a long-lost diary. It couldn't be anything else. And it was written in Walt Disney's own handwriting. Adam felt as if a weight was resting on his chest; he was having trouble catching his breath. He unconsciously tried to swallow and he became aware of how dry his mouth and throat were. He even tried to lick his lips; his tongue felt as dry as the yellowed paper he was looking at between the dark leather bindings.

Adam slumped down onto the commode as he stared at the words written in the worn leather book. What the book told him, what it hinted at was lost to him at that moment. All he could think about was the fact that he had found Walt Disney's personal diary and that he was holding it right there in his hands. His hands. Adam Michaels, a thirty-year old General Contractor from the city of Orange, California, was holding in his hands something written by the Grand Master himself. Right here. In Disneyland. In the men's room…*Oh hell*.

With a guilty look, he sprang up from his impromptu seat and frantically looked around the small stall. By any public restroom standards, Disney restrooms were exceptionally clean, even after thousands of uses each day. But, no, this won't do at all. This is wrong. He had to find a more appropriate place to read and handle the book. This was… this was exciting. This was big! Adam felt that he held the Holy Grail of lost literature. Well, not the Dead Sea Scrolls big, certainly, but a modern-day's version of something that simply was not known to exist, at least not to any Disney historian or collector.

He tried to open the stall door as quietly as he could and peered cautiously around the edge. He found the restroom was occupied by only a few men and youngsters, so he…well, what *was* he going to do? Adam's pants pocket proved too small for the book. The same for the breast pocket on his shirt. Lance had the backpack they had been allowed to carry for the race. But Lance was outside. In public. In broad daylight. Adam felt he couldn't just walk out of there with such a valuable item in his hands. What if someone saw him? What if they asked him what it was? What if they tried to take it away from him? He started breathing fast again. He knew he was being paranoid; he was almost hyperventilating. *Slow down, Michaels*, he told himself. *Calm down. Think. Think. Think. Great… now I sound like Winnie the Pooh,* Adam said, not trying to be funny, even to himself.

Adam closed the stall door again, turning the latch. He eyed the small locking mechanism with disdain. *There should be a padlock on this door,* Adam thought to himself as he stood there facing the door and coat hook attached near the top. Adam couldn't bring himself to face the commode, and he didn't want to face out towards the poorly locked door. So, he turned sideways, facing the side wall, away from the rolls of toilet paper, of course. Maybe if he just stayed in here long enough Lance would start to worry about him and come looking to see what was wrong. Okay, that's a good idea. That will work…Well, that would work if it was anyone other than

Lance. He knew Lance would lean against that lamppost all day long watching people go by and thoroughly enjoy himself. No, he had to come up with something else.

Holding the black, leather-bound book with both hands, Adam willed his pounding heart to slow. He noticed he was almost hyperventilating again. With a deep, deliberate inhale and exhale, Adam finally opened the stall door. Surprisingly, the restroom was now vacant. Adam knew that would change in a matter of moments. He looked at himself in the large floor-to-ceiling mirror that was next to a row of sinks. In his polo shirt and khaki shorts, he looked unworthy of holding something of such significance. He knew the book was something Walt Disney himself had penned.

"What should I do?" Adam muttered as he glared at himself in the mirror, shaking his head self-consciously. Just then, voices echoed among the tiled walls from just outside the men's room entrance. With a startled gasp, Adam did exactly the same thing he did the last time he had to make a hasty decision. He crammed the book down his shorts and pulled his shirt down to cover it. He then walked over to the sink and lathered up his hands with soap just as the voices became attached to actual bodies entering the restroom. Adam tried again to relax, rinsing his hands off in the basin.

A harried father muttering, "hang in there, buddy, few more seconds," herded his five-year old son into the open stall without even a glance at Adam. Adam let out a breath he didn't realize he had been holding. He happened to look into the smaller mirror hanging over the sink in front of him. He realized this was how he would have appeared if that man had bothered to look at him: Guilty. With a disgusted shake of his head, Adam rinsed his hands one more time, ran the cool water across his face, and walked over to the paper towel dispenser where he took several of the sheets to dry off his hands and face. *Relax, man! Sheesh, you're as jumpy as a cat.*

With another silent apology for his hasty hiding place, he pushed through the door and walked hurriedly over to Lance, who was, as he had expected, still standing exactly where he had been left.

"So, how'd it go?" Lance teased when Adam finally showed up next to him. Chuckling at his own joke, he glanced at Adam's face. Adam was flushed, his eyes were wide, he looked ready to bolt and run, and for some reason his hair was wet. "What'd you do? Miss?" Lance continued to tease, looking at Adam with a big grin.

Adam snapped out of his silent meditation on what he should do next. "What?" Then he reddened when he understood what Lance had asked. "No! Something's come up."

Lance gave him a guy's look. "Oh, really?" Lance tossed back his head and gave a full-throated laugh. His deep voice usually carried pretty far and now his laughter drew unwanted attention to the two men. Well, unwanted to Adam. Lance didn't notice several ladies who looked over appreciatively at the sound and its good-looking owner.

Adam grumbled for him to knock it off; they had to go.

Still chuckling, Lance figured Adam meant he wanted to resume the race. "Okay, okay, I'm sorry. We can head for New Orleans Square and do the count in Club 33. Wish we could have dinner there. The food is superb." He strode off to retrace their steps up Main Street. After about five steps, he realized Adam wasn't with him. Looking back, he saw Adam hadn't moved from the spot next to the men's room. He went back. "Adam, we need to stay within ten feet of each other or we lose points. You with me here?" When he received no answer, he became a little concerned. "You okay, Adam? What's wrong?"

Adam was silent as people walked past them. He looked nervous. Adam eyed the excited kids and even the excited parents as they strode up Main Street towards the heart of the Park. His eyes darted back to see if there was anyone coming towards them. To Lance, Adam seemed almost paranoid. When Adam saw there was a break in the foot traffic around them, he said quietly to Lance, "I found something."

Lance was confused. "In the men's room? Like what? A wallet or something?" He motioned over to the left at the tall white building that dominated that side of Main Street. "City Hall is right here if you want to turn it in to Lost and Found."

"No, not like that," Adam whispered, making Lance even more confused. "I found it…someplace else," he stopped mysteriously. A couple of moms pushing strollers walked slowly up the ramp towards the restrooms. Adam's eyes followed them until they were inside, but he didn't continue his explanation to Lance.

Lance gave an impatient sigh. "Adam, listen, we are losing time standing here chatting. Tell me all about it while we head to New Orleans Square. First, what did you find?" Lance strode off again, still talking, only to find Adam did not follow him. Again. Rolling his eyes, he returned to his increasingly odd-acting race partner. "Okay, first, I am getting tired of talking to you only to find you are not actually walking next to me. Now, while it is entertaining to those to whom I end up talking, it is frustrating to me. Second, you need to get your ass in gear and move from this spot. We have a race to finish. And third, well, I don't have a third. But you need to tell me what's going on."

He wondered if Adam even listened to anything he said. Adam just stared across Main Street, apparently at the Opera House. Looking towards the Opera House himself, Lance could see nothing that held any particular interest…outside of that devastating blonde buying popcorn. But Adam didn't seem to be looking at her. He knew Adam preferred brunettes. Himself? Yeah, blondes were good. He looked the woman over again. Too bad they were already losing so much time. And, too bad she was handing the popcorn to her three children..."Adam. Earth to Adam."

Adam turned his distracted eyes back to Lance. "Sorry, man. I think we need to leave the Park."

"What?" Lance came as close as he ever did to becoming angry. "We've waited six months for this race! And we're doing…well, we're doing pretty good. We've lost a lot of time with you farting around for some unknown reason in the men's room. Are you going to tell me *why* you want to leave?"

"No," Adam stated shortly. He shifted uneasily on his spot. "You'll have to trust me on this. I think it may be worth it to leave right now. I can't concentrate on the race. Let me have the backpack a minute." Adam held out his hand to the surprised Lance.

Lance stared at his friend. He knew Adam loved running the Mouse Adventure races. Adam even considered himself a Disney expert. For Adam to willingly leave the race in the middle - well, something major had to have happened. And he knew Adam was not going to tell him anything, whatever the reason, right now. With a shrug, Lance took off the pack and silently handed it to Adam. Frowning, he watched as Adam turned without a word and reentered the men's room. "Must not be fiber," he mumbled to himself as he crossed his arms to wait.

In less than a minute, Adam was back outside. "Do you want to turn in the answer sheets we have done already?" he asked as a way of apology for leaving early.

"What's the point? We didn't finish enough to make any difference," Lance said sullenly.

Adam knew he was being unfair to Lance, but he just had to leave and examine this exciting find. He did not want to look it over here – in the shadow of the building in which he found it. He needed to get it away from the Park. He had to put some distance between them.

"But we will get the credit for having run it for the next time," he offered.

"Will there be a next time?" At Adam's vague shrug, Lance just shook his head and followed Adam over to the ornate Opera House.

The Mouse Adventure people were surprised a team had finished all the quests so quickly. Usually teams burst through the door at the last possible second, still filling in answers. They weren't really ready for teams to arrive yet and were just sitting around, chatting together. Adam handed in their quest packet. There were some pages they had completed, even though most of their quests were only partially filled-in or completely blank. Sometimes they were awarded points for each correct answer. However, there was so much that was not done that it wouldn't make much difference for Team Pecos Bills final score. When this was pointed out to Adam, he just answered, "Something came up and we have to leave." From the look on Lance's face, the race people could tell his partner didn't agree with Adam's decision, but there was nothing they could do. If a team wanted to drop out early, they were allowed to. Adam and Lance were told, "All right. Scores will be posted on the website in a few days. Hope to see you in the fall. Here is your participation certificate. Thanks for trying."

Lance took the brightly colored paper and attached it to the now-empty clipboard they had used as a writing table for their quests. Without actually shoving him, he got Adam to turn around and Lance thrust the clipboard into the backpack.

Adam now added 'guilt' to his jumbled feelings. He hoped his discovery would make it up to Lance. Lance would then understand that the race wasn't important right now. With an inaudible sigh, he silently led them under the Entry arch and out of Disneyland. Moving against the flow of tourists coming into the Park, Adam led the way, parting the sea of guests like a ship's bow. It was now Lance trying to keep pace with Adam as he pushed through the exit turnstile a step behind his friend. Without a word spoken between them, the two men caught the next tram to the parking structure.

Still Adam said not one word to explain the 'why' or the 'what' of this mystery. Lance figured he would be told when Adam was ready to tell him.

And, it had better be a darn good explanation, too.

Adam was silent all the way to his apartment in Orange. Lance just bided his time by playing with the radio and changing all of Adam's favorite settings. Rap music blared into the cab of the Silverado. Adam didn't even notice. "I'm thinking," was Adam's only words while the two drove, answering Lance's question, "So, what is this all about, Adam?"

Arriving at his apartment, Adam grabbed Lance's backpack from behind the driver's seat where he had stashed it and motioned for Lance to follow him. When Adam unlocked the door to his apartment, he indicated that Lance should sit on the sofa.

"Yes, sir." Lance goose-stepped over to the sofa and stiffly sat on the edge of the cushion, pushing two throw pillows to the other side of the sectional.

Adam didn't notice the sarcasm. Frowning, Lance watched as Adam unzipped the backpack and threw the various items they had been allowed to bring on the race all over the coffee table and the floor. Then Adam paused, and then slowly pulled out something Lance didn't recognize. It looked like a small book.

"Is that what you found in the men's room? What is it? A book?" His irritation receded a little as his curiosity took over. Lance leaned forward, looking closer at what he could tell was a fairly old book in Adam's hands.

Adam ran his fingers lightly over the cover. He seemed mesmerized by the object. His eyes were wide and excited when he finally raised them to answer Lance. "This is a book. And…," Adam paused, "I believe this is a very special book." He looked back down at the book and added, "And no, I didn't find it in the men's room." He broke off and swallowed, thinking back on what he had done. A little more nervous now, he took a deep breath and continued, "I found it in Walt's Apartment. Remember when I asked you to make that diversion?"

Lance's eyes narrowed. "What did you do? Steal one of the antiques? Do you know how much trouble we could get into for that??" he demanded, standing. This was too much. First Adam made them lose valuable race time. Then he demanded they quit early and leave. And now he does something that could get them banned from the Park and probably thrown in jail!

Before he could voice his misgivings, Adam threw up his hands. "No! It wasn't like that!" Adam declared, instantly irritated. He then calmed himself and added, "I would never do something like that. You should know that." At Lance's silence and condemning glare, he felt he had better get to the point. "Well, I wouldn't steal anything outright like that."

Lance didn't seem too convinced. "Then what is it?"

Adam brought it over to the sofa and offered it to the frowning Lance. "Why don't you read it for yourself and tell me what you think it is," he stated quietly.

When Lance sat back down with the book, Adam went to his refrigerator and got them each a beer. He popped Lance's and set it in front of him. He took his beer over to his desk. Throwing himself back in his chair, Adam propped his feet up on the edge of the desk and watched his friend's face as he read. He saw what he expected to see; what he himself had gone through: He saw Lance's face go from angry to suspicious to confused to interested to excited.

Lance read the book through again before he looked up from the yellow-edged pages. His eyes were wide, just like Adam's had been when he first came out of the men's room. "Do you know what this is?"

"I know what I think it is. What do you think it is?"

Lance didn't want to voice his opinion yet. This was extraordinary. "Tell me again where you found it and how."

Adam reiterated how he had unthinkingly sat in the first chair he came to and felt something poke him in the behind. After getting Lance to create a diversion, he had ripped open the back of the cushion and found this crammed inside between all the stuffing. How he had jammed it down his shorts when everyone had suddenly come back into the room.

Lance's eyes were as big as Adam's now. "You found this hidden in Walt's private apartment. In one of his chairs. Do you recognize the handwriting?"

Adam nodded slowly. He considered himself an expert on Walt and all things Disney. He even had a prized autographed picture of Walt he had won in an auction. Yes, he knew the handwriting. He knew it was written by Walt himself.

Lance just stared at him. "So, you think this is legit? You think he means it?"

Adam knew Lance was referring to what was written inside. He continued to nod slowly. It was all he seemed capable of doing at the moment. This was big. This was monumental for them. It would take planning. It would take work. It would take time.

"Me, too," Lance mumbled, understanding Adam's nod. He gave a slow smile. "Now I know why I hang around with you. You always come up with the damnedest things!" He stared back down at the book for a moment before adding, "But this....THIS!" Lance was, for once, at a loss for words.

Adam walked back over to the sofa and reached out his hand for the book. He had to touch it again. Had to make sure it was real. He had to read it again. Falling back into his armchair, ignoring the cloud of dust that billowed out, he read through the book again.

Here is what it said:

"*To all who come to this happy place – welcome. Disneyland is your land. Here age relives fond memories of the past and here youth may savor the challenge and promise of the future. Disneyland is dedicated to the ideals, the dreams, and the hard facts that have created America with the hope that it will be a source of joy and inspiration to all the world.*

And, to you who found my little black book - welcome.

People still think of me as a cartoonist, but the only thing I lift a pen or pencil for these days is to sign a contract, a check, or an autograph. That is not the case now.

I don't know who it is who will find this legacy that I am leaving behind. Now, I'm not getting maudlin here. Facts are facts. This damn cough of mine is getting worse. And those doctors can't seem to do a damn thing about it.

Maybe I'm wrong. I hope so. I'm going to continue working as I always have. There's so much to be done. Hey, I might even pop in on you going through this little book of mine and we can have a big laugh together! Wouldn't that be keen?

Now, considering that you did find my book and considering where you found it, hopefully you love Disneyland as much as I do. If that is true, you no doubt recognize the first words I wrote up there. I said them on a proud occasion. Maybe you were there. I was! I said then that we would relive fond memories of the past. Well, that is what we are going to do together. This is important to me. It was important to me when it all happened and it is important to me now.

I only hope that we don't lose sight of one thing – that it all started with a moose.

No, I didn't get that wrong. My hand might be a lit-

tle shaky with all this coughing, but you read it right. No, I'm not talking about Mickey. There is a Mouse and there is a Moose. I'm talking about Morris the Midget Moose. Now that was a good cartoon! If you aren't familiar with it, <u>go watch it</u>. But, anyway, the whole plot came down to one thing: Two heads are better than one.

Why am I telling you this? Well, you might need some help on the journey I'm sending you on. Choose your partner well. I always tried to.

I know. I'm rambling. I'm entitled. This is <u>my</u> life.

You want a hint at what lies ahead? Okay. There is more treasure in books than in all the pirate's loot on Treasure Island. But you aren't going after any book. You already found that.

Curious? When you are curious, you find lots of interesting things to do. We keep moving forward, opening new doors, and doing new things, because we're curious and curiosity keeps leading us down new paths. I hope you find your new paths interesting.   You are going to find a lot of different ones.

I just got in late last night after getting the last piece situated and I'm tired. It has taken me a few years to get all this in place for you. I've been planning it for a long time. Today I reviewed everything I set up and I think I got it right. I did everything I could to make sure it was secure. Now it is up to you. I want you to know here and now that I'm going to make you work for it – whatever <u>it</u> is.

There are three things you need to do on this Quest I am sending you on. You could call it a Quest for Hidden Mickey's: (Hey! That would be a good title for a cartoon! I'll have to remember that.)

1. I want you to appreciate where you are going,
2. I want you to appreciate what happened there, and,
3. I want you to appreciate whatever you might find.
  Look around and learn. Never stop learning. Never

*get too busy to learn from what you do. And, whatever
you find, put it to good use. Remember me. Maybe this
is my way of living forever. I've always wanted to outlive
my dreams. Perhaps you can help me do just that!*

*So, here is what I want you to figure out first. This
is your first clue:* **Do some belly botany under the
Dreaming Tree. From where I stand, it's down 2 feet.
Bring a shovel.**

*I always said the way to get started is to quit talking
and begin doing.*

<u>*So begin doing.*</u>"

Adam finished reading the diary again. There were
some more pages after the clue, but they were all blank.
He flipped through a few of them. He then saw something he hadn't noticed before. Quite a few of the last
pages looked like they were glued together. Running his
fingers over the top sheet, he felt that there was a soft
spot in the middle.

Lance was still waiting for Adam to finish with the
book so they could start discussing it. He saw Adam an-
alyzing the last pages that he, too, thought were blank.
He came over to the chair at the odd look on Adam's face.
"What is it? Did you find something?" Lance watched as
Adam ran his finger along something near the center of
the page.

Adam was still lightly pressing around the edges of
the soft spot. He found a hollow opening about two and
a half inches wide by a little over one and a half inches high.
Not sure if he should do this or not, he brought the book up
to his ear and lightly shook it. There was a dull thud inside.
He handed the book to Lance for his opinion. "What do you
make of that?"

Lance did the same maneuvers Adam had done.
"Feels like the pages are cut out inside and there is something in there. Whatever it is isn't very big. Want to open it?"

"Yes. No." Adam was undecided. He wanted to

know what was in there, but he didn't want to rip open Walt's diary. He didn't want to damage anything else. He voiced his concern and then asked Lance, "Any suggestions?"

"Well, we can stand here guessing about it all day, but that won't tell us anything. How about if we made a small slit and use a flashlight to try and see what's in there?"

Nodding, glad to have the decision made for him, Adam went to his desk and opened the top drawer. He pulled out a pocketknife. "There's a Mag light in my toolbox in the closet."

Lance was back quickly in time to see Adam make a small incision in the middle of the page. Using the light, and carefully pulling up the edge of the slit, they could see the glint of gold inside. That did it. The two men looked at each other with eager smiles on their faces. "Okay, we open it." Adam said with authority. Lance was more cautious, still uncertain. Adam made the instant decision and didn't wait for Lance's vote. He extended the cut across the width of the false bottom and made a cross cut the other way.

It wasn't gold that Adam pulled out of the diary, but an oval piece of bronze metal. It was two inches wide by one and a quarter inches high. The bronze was thick and stamped *Disneyland* in raised letters across the middle. Embossed stars extended around the edges all the way up to a little round plate attached to the top that had the number 1 stamped on it. On the back was a hinged straight pin so it could be worn.

"Oh wow oh wow!" Adam exhaled in hushed excitement. "Do you know what this is, Lance?!" Adam's eyes danced over the object. He turned it over and over in his hands. "Do you know what this is!?" Adam repeated adamantly this time, holding the brass object out to Lance.

Lance took the gold-colored object into his hand and

looked it over. Considering the probable age of the diary, it was still very bright, no scratches, no sign of age. "It's the shape of a cast member nametag, but it doesn't have a name on it. Just a number 1. It is in great shape, whatever it is." He handed it back to Adam.

Adam took it over to a trophy case he had on the wall. It held a number of items from Disneyland and some of them were cast member nametags he had collected from different years at the Park. He held up the new item to compare it in size. It was somewhat smaller than the ones he had.

"Lance," Adam said, turning back to his friend, his eyes shining with excitement. "This *is* a cast member nametag." Adam paused, falling back on an accumulation of trivia based on a near twenty-year obsession of learning about Walt Disney: "When Disneyland first opened, the employees didn't wear their names and hometowns like they do now. They wore a badge with a number on it. This is one of those first nametags. And, if I am guessing right, this was Walt's own nametag. Who else would possibly wear Number 1?" He sat heavily on the sofa next to Lance. "This is amazing! I read that the Disney Archives doesn't even have one of these nametags! What a find!"

Lance looked impressed. "That is a pretty rare piece of Disney memorabilia, then. Pretty cool. Do you think…." He broke off, unsure of voicing it.

Adam was looking steadily at him. He knew where Lance was heading. "Do I think what?" Let Lance say it.

"Do you think this is an example of what the 'treasure' is that Walt wrote about in his diary? Do you think this will be a treasure hunt of sorts?"

Adam thought for a moment, then nodded with pursed lips. "That's exactly what I think. He talked about the 'past' and a 'legacy' he was leaving behind." Adam then sobered for a moment. "He must have realized he wasn't going to be around as long as he would have liked.

Maybe he had a premonition about the cough he alluded to in the diary." Adam felt his heart suddenly pound in his chest. He again looked at the worn black book sitting on the coffee table between them and suddenly wondered if they now had a long-lost treasure map to something like Blackbeard's fabled treasure...or the Lost Dutchman's gold mine of Disney Artifacts! "Lance," Adam shuddered at his thoughts. "Lance, this could be big."

Lance picked up the diary and looked at the worn cover. "Who do you think this was written for?" Lance asked hesitantly, not sure if he wanted to explore that aspect of their find too deeply.

Adam took the diary from him and looked back through the wording. "He doesn't name anyone specific. Doesn't mention family or employees or stockholders. Nobody. He even says he doesn't know who will find it.... I think it is fair game for whoever finds the book, don't you?" His voice resonated with hope that he was accurate in his assessment.

Lance looked wary, but excited. "I'm no lawyer, but it sounds that way to me, too." He hesitated even longer before he asked, "Do you think we should run it by someone who might know?"

Not liking the sound of that, Adam shook his head slowly. "That might open up a whole set of problems and questions..." Adam paused, setting the diary back on the coffee table. "Questions that I don't think we want to answer regarding how we came to possess this book." He started pacing his living room, still holding the nametag tightly in his hand. If he had looked, he would have seen the word 'Disneyland' imprinted in his palm from the raised letters of the tag. "We would have to explain where I found it and how I found it. I'm not inclined to think that would go over very well. Do you?"

Lance almost thought that was rhetorical, but realized Adam wanted his input and his help with the decision. "Well, you did rip open the chair cushion...."

"Five stitches, man, five stitches! It's not like I took a butcher knife to it…"

Lance threw up a calming hand. "Hey, I know that, but I doubt the Powers That Be would agree. I do see your point, however. Think we should keep this to ourselves for the time being and see where this clue leads? We could always tell someone later."

"Much later," Adam mumbled, thinking that he would tell someone in his will after he was dead and gone. He looked at the diary again. He looked up to meet Lance's eyes. They silently studied each other's face for a moment. "Partners, then? We follow Walt's Hidden Mickey Quest and find what there is to find and go from there?" He extended his empty right hand.

Lance met his hand and they solemnly shook on it. "Partners." After the firm handshake, the two picked up their beers and simultaneously chugged. They smiled and tilted their bottles towards each other in a silent toast to their find.

"So, I get to keep the nametag, right?" Adam asked immediately. At Lance's skeptical look, he added, "Hey, I do have a collection already… Fine, we will divvy it up whenever this is over." Adam looked disappointed, but tried not to show it. "Let's keep these in my safe," Adam continued, walking towards a cupboard under his kitchen counter top. He opened a concealed latch which revealed a compact safe; pale green steel door with a black tumbler lock and a chrome handle which Adam opened with a few turns of the combination lock. "I don't keep much in here, but it will at least keep the diary and nametag safe from fire and theft…Not that I've ever been robbed…and I don't smoke..." Adam broke off from his rambling, looking at the nametag with a smile; a triumphant smile that revealed how he felt about holding history in the palm of his hand.

Watching Adam, Lance silently chuckled to himself. He didn't care about the nametag. He knew Adam would appreciate that tag far more than he ever would. He had a feeling there was a lot more at stake here than a simple nametag. He just liked messing with Adam's mind now and then.

Before Lance handed over the leather-bound diary to Adam for safe keeping, he read through the last part of the diary again – the part that said it was their first clue. "So, Partner, what the hell is 'belly botany' and what in the world is a 'dreaming tree'?"

Adam looked up from the safe after setting the nametag carefully on the small top shelf inside. The nametag was an incredible find, even to a small-time collector of Disney memorabilia like himself. He pulled his mind from the valuable piece of bronze to what Lance had asked. Adam gave him the 'no clue' look and shrug.

Lance handed Adam the diary which he placed on the bottom section of the safe and slowly shut the steel door. He gave the tumbler dial a spin and said, "I guess now we follow Walt's advice and get to work."

CHAPTER 3

BEGIN DOING

JULY 21ST,1962
12:18P.M.

He stood in the shade of a huge cottonwood tree. That tree had to be over a hundred years old. It was in full leaf now that summer was here. The heat was oppressive, the humidity high. After wiping the pieces of bark off the blade, he slid his worn pocketknife back into his slacks pocket. *Had it been this hot before?*, he asked himself as he fanned his flushed face with his beat-up old Fedora. *Probably*, he decided. But you don't remember the heat or the humidity or the chiggers. You remember *things*. Things like this tree and the wooden swing that used to hang from a lower branch, the barn that was tilting precariously to the left, the dusty lane leading out to the main road, the farmhouse, the orchards of apples and peaches and plums, Yellow Creek, the white gazebo in town, the Santa Fe trains. And, more importantly, you remember *people*. People, so many people. The visions of their faces so strong, so vivid, your heart still aches for the ones who are gone. Ruth, Roy, Mom, Dad, Herbert, Raymond, Uncle Mike, Uncle Martin, Uncle Ed, Uncle Robert, Aunt Maggie, Grandma Disney, Doc Sherwood, Erastus Taylor.

Looking up through the leaves at the dappled sunlight filtering through, he continued to fan the perspiration across his forehead. *It changes.* That was his thought at that moment. If he had been pressed for more of an explanation, he probably would have added the word *everything.* Even this tree had changed in the fifty years since he had first seen it. It was difficult for him to admit to those changes – that they weren't always for the best. This tree, for example, wasn't as full and lush. Some of the bigger branches had fallen, victim of old age or lightning. There used to be more trees, more animals, more everything. But, he could still see it as it used to be. His mind was clear and sharp.

He sat under the tree – as he and Ruth had done so many times before – letting the sounds of nature and peace drift over him. *Yes, everybody should have a tree like this,* he decided; to sit under; to watch the clouds; to simply dream.

Closing his eyes, he stood quietly and listened. There it was – the birdcalls from the thickets and the berry patches. Now that he had quit moving around so much and the coughing fit subsided for the moment, the birds came back. Bees buzzed around the little white flowers dotted here and there on the overgrown path. The breeze rustled the tall weeds around him, making a light *sh sh sh* sound. The leaves overhead flashed light green to dark green to light green again as the breeze turned them this way and that.

He quit fanning now as the breeze picked up. His hat was placed negligently off to the side, next to the shovel and the odd, grey, elongated capsule he had brought in the rented car. A few clouds began drifting by. He knew his Midwest. There would be a few more clouds, blindingly white at first. After a while, the white underside would darken. The formations would get taller, bumping into each other, crowding the blue sky. The breeze would pick up. The sun would come and go and, finally, just disappear. The heat would remain, but the first few drops would feel refreshing. More drops would follow. Within minutes, a gigantic bucket would be overturned from the sky. A brilliant white flash of jagged light would be followed almost immediately by a loud *BOOM*! There was no need to count after the lightning to see how far away it was. It was there.

With a wistful sigh for the now and for the past, he got stiffly to his feet. He wouldn't have much time before the storm hit. Enough, though. The rain was good. It would cover what he was about to do very nicely. *Just what I would have written into the plot*, he chuckled to himself as he marked off the distance and the shovel bit into the soft soil.

MONDAY, APRIL 22ND, 2002
2:00P.M.

By Monday afternoon there was a stack of library books on Adam's coffee table. They were all about Walt Disney and his life. Lance was speed-reading through his second book. Adam, holding a book in his left hand, was making notes with his right hand. He glanced up, disgusted and jealous, as Lance turned yet another page. As he watched, Lance's finger trailed back and forth across the rows of print, down one side, back upwards to check a certain word, then down again, and over to the next page. Estimated time of arrival at next page: twenty seconds.

Adam shook his head. "How do you get anything out of it when you read like that?" he demanded. He was only on the fourth chapter of his first book. "And you aren't taking any notes!"

"Just a sec," Lance mumbled, his finger slowing down a split second, then finishing a page. "End of chapter. Sorry, what?" His concentration was broken now with Adam's interruption. He rubbed the bridge of his nose. They had been at it for hours.

Adam was frustrated at his own lack of progress at this point. He had expected to find the answer to the riddle quickly. True, the notes he was taking would probably come in handy later, whether for this treasure hunt or just for his own edification. But he was taking it seriously. And he expected his partner in this enterprise to be equally serious. Speed reading did not equal serious in his book. But, his mind tried to justify, Lance was here and Lance was doing research. He was helping. He had a vested interest in this too…Not that Lance needed the money….

"What did you ask?" Lance broke into Adam's thoughts now.

"Do you really get anything out of the book when you read like that?" Adam didn't mean to sound snippy, but it still came out that way.

Lance was taken back by the tone of voice. He knew what he was doing, what he was capable of understanding. He slowly closed the book, holding his finger in the pages to mark his place. "Yes," he answered shortly. He could see by the look on Adam's face that he hadn't meant it that way. "Would you like a quick rundown of what I have found out?" Without waiting for Adam to answer or recant, he launched into a dissertation in vivid detail of Walt's early studio beginnings in Kansas City in 1920 up to and including the move to Hollywood in 1923, adding the names of the projects worked on during that time, the key animators, actors, failures, successes, backers, and opponents.

Stunned, Adam just sat there. It was more than he had in his notes so far. It was a different time period than he was studying, but it was still good information.

Lance was just showing off. Still, he also knew he was, and would be, contributing to this joint effort. It would be counterproductive to have his methods questioned over and over. "Satisfied?" he asked calmly.

"Uhm, yeah, I…that was impressive," Adam finished lamely. He knew he had been out of line.

Lance let him off the hook. "Well, it got me through Harvard," as he picked up his book to continue.

"Wait, wait, wait," Adam held up a hand. "You went to Harvard? Then what were you doing at Cal State when I met you?"

The book dropped again. "I was finally enjoying life," he explained, taking the last question first. "I didn't care for law school. It wasn't what I wanted to do."

More news. "Law school?" Adam's eyes narrowed. "How far did you get?"

"Far enough to know that wasn't how I wanted to spend my life." *And Father hasn't forgiven me yet,* he thought. *And he never will*, he reminded himself. Breaking 'Sacred Tradition' was not a family honor. "Cal State suited."

Adam didn't want to let this go that easily. He had known Lance for what? Close to eight years now? And he had never had a hint of his life before California. Adam was intrigued. Oh, he knew Lance had "money". That was obvious from his, well, everything about him. His townhouse. His car. The way he wore his clothes. The way he carried himself. All this had been pointed out to Adam by an ex-girlfriend of his. He, of course, hadn't thought much about Lance or where he came from before he suddenly appeared in California in their fraternity house. Guys don't do that. But his girl had been intrigued by Adam's tall, handsome friend. She had pointed out the traits she saw in Lance, and now, after this revelation, they made sense. What she had called him – to his face no less – 'Sir Lancelot' and 'Frat Boy' and 'Pampered Poodle' made sense, too, in a twisted sort of way. Man, how those two had loved to verbally spar at each other! When Lance threw a 'Gold Digger' or a 'Grudge' right back at her, the repartee had reduced both of them into a laughing heap.

Adam's face had changed while Lance watched,

waiting for the next onslaught of questions he was sure were coming. But now Adam seemed to be on a different mental track. Lance didn't mind. He didn't really want to delve into his past and his problems with his father. Lance had made his choice and he was happy and satisfied. His father would have to learn…well, he doubted his father would ever learn anything about his 'wayward' son. *Time wounds all heels.* He smiled at the revised saying.

"'Pampered Poodle'," came out of Adam's memory.

"Excuse me?" Lance's eye narrowed, not sure he heard his friend right. There were limits within friendships.

Bad reaction. Crap "I was just remembering a verbal war you used to have with someone. You used to enjoy it," Adam defended himself.

Lance now realized where Adam's mind had taken him. Adam wasn't making a slur about him. He was treading on dangerous personal ground for himself, though. Lance relaxed. "I enjoyed bantering with her, yes. She was allowed. You are not." Lance thought back to the missing one of their previous trio. He really missed the feisty little brunette. Adam was such an ass sometimes… "You sure you want to go to Memoryland?" Lance pointedly asked. Adam's break-up had been difficult on a lot of people.

Adam shook his head. Too many memories had flooded back just at the remembrance of those soft-sided insults she and Lance used to fling at each other so often. No, he didn't want to go there. It was bad enough every time he went to Disneyland. That was where he felt her the most… He had to stop. That was the past. He had made it that way and he was stuck with it. Mooning around wouldn't help. He had a 'Dreaming Tree' to find.

"Sorry," mumbled Adam as he picked up his book again. "One thing just led to another. I take it you didn't find anything about botany or a tree, then?"

Also mollified that the personal questions seemed to have come to an end, Lance let his good nature take over. "No, not yet. I don't think I'm studying the right time frame. This might all come in handy later, but I don't see it leading to where we need to go."

"What are you thinking? Earlier or later in his life?"

Lance slowly shook his head. "Not sure. It kind of sounds like a cartoon plot, but I couldn't find a reference anywhere that sounded right. If he wants us to go on a journey, do you think we should start at the very beginning?"

"But you are researching the early studio days. I am in the early days of Disneyland, but coming up empty too."

"Then we must be on the wrong track," Lance said, a little disappointed with their lack of progress. Then he added, "The diary did say we would have to 'work for it'."

Adam gave a little chuckle. "Maybe the shovel he mentioned was both figurative and literal. Well, we know we have to keep the focus on dates before 1966 when he died. Still, there is a lot of ground to cover."

"Probably also both figurative and literal," Lance smiled. "And two feet down. Maybe we should choose the book two feet down in your huge pile here."

Adam shrugged. It was as good an idea as any they had followed already. "Which book would that be?" He eyeballed the pile. Being a General Contractor, he was used to looking at something and knowing how long or how tall or how wide it was. He rarely ever missed, and then it was only by an inch or two. "Try the red-covered book, under those," Adam said, pointing to a stack of books in the middle of the coffee table.

Lance pulled it out. It was a history of the Disneyland Park, full of glossy pictures of all the rides. "Don't think that will do it," as he thumbed through it. "Back to what we were doing before I was so rudely interrupted?"

Adam was glad to see the good-humored smile on

Lance's face. Last thing he needed was to be left alone with this mountain of books to go through. "Sure thing, boss. Hey, are there any fries left in that bag?" He should have known better.

"No, I ate them all. I could heat up this catsup packet for you and make soup."

"Thanks, no," was all Adam replied as he got back into his book. He knew Walt wasn't a scientific person, so a reference to botany was unusual. Still, nature did play a big part in Walt's work – all the way back to the Silly Symphonies and *Flowers and Trees*. That was around 1932. It would be the first Silly Symphony to be made in color and it would go on to win an Academy Award. He switched his reading to write-ups about that era.

Still, no luck, Adam thought as he read paragraph after paragraph about Walt. While he knew a lot of Walt's history, this in-depth study was far more enlightening to Adam then his previous interest in Walt. It was fascinating reading about the change from black and white cartoons to color and the problems Walt had both within and outside his company trying to convince everyone that the change was a good idea. But, it was pure Walt. He went ahead with his idea and just did it. It was well known that when Walt met with resistance to an idea, he honestly believed that those who resisted the idea simply couldn't see it from his perspective. He left financing his idea to his brother, Roy, who was not only responsible with money, he communicated the financing situations so that Walt had a reasonable understanding of limitations due to the lack of funds. However, even such understandings often were scoffed at by Walt as minor issues. Roy shouldered such questions as: Should the company go public? Should they accept a loan from the company that invented the color process for fifty percent interest in the studio? An investment banker in New York? It was exciting reading. Adam felt, however, that he was discovering more about Walt than the vast majority of Disney fanatics knew about him.

When he realized he was reading just to read the story, Adam had to pull back. He knew what he was looking for wasn't there. Back farther in time or forward? That seemed to be the question both he and Lance had asked. Lance had started at 1920 and the garage studio in Kansas City, Missouri. That was pretty far back. That was the beginning of the studio where Walt would practice his cartooning. Farther back than Kansas City? That would bring them to Marceline, Missouri, Walt's boyhood home he loved so dearly that it colored his perspective of hometown life forever. What years would that be? Adam thumbed back through his book. 1906 to 1911. Can't get much farther back than that. Walt had been born in 1901.

Might as well begin at the beginning, Adam told himself, closing the book he had been reading and reaching for a different one. With a fresh page of notepaper, Adam settled back and began reading.

TUESDAY, APRIL 23RD, 2002
9:30A.M.

Tuesday morning began with problems on a remodel that Adam had to handle in person. As a General Contractor, he found his business was full of frustrating situations. Just when Adam wanted time to spend on this new, exciting adventure, he got pulled away to deal with a homeowner who had changed her mind once again.

Lance let himself into Adam's apartment with the key Adam had given him. After a quick raid of the refrigerator, Lance sat back on the familiar sofa and picked up yet another book. He sat there looking at it, his eyes starting to throb from just reading the cover. He felt they were getting closer but couldn't bring himself to open the book at that moment. Glancing around the living room, his eyes stopped at Adam's computer. They hadn't done any research on the computer yet. Might be worth it, he figured.

Not familiar with Adam's computer, he allowed himself some 'getting acquainted' time seeing what programs were loaded and what might be of help. He found Adam's Organizer. Grinning, he went through Adam's appointments, resisting the urge to cancel a few for fun. Instead, he added a daily reminder alarm that would go off at 7 p.m. every day: "Feed Lance." Pulling up the Phone-Book, Lance noticed the shortage of women listed inside. He added a few of his girl friends from memory, wondering if Adam would even notice. Surprised there was no password needed, Lance did a quick run-through of Adam's business records. He gave a mild grunt of surprise. Adam was doing very well. Again resisting the impulse to rearrange some invoices, Lance closed the books. The CADD blueprint drawing program was of no interest. Being the good friend that he was, Lance left the virus killers in place. And, being the friend that he was, he turned off the spam filter.

Now refreshed, Lance settled back in Adam's leather computer chair to get to work. He brought up his favorite search engine and typed in 'belly botany'. The first listing was from Arkansas and described 'belly botany' as "the study of belly flowers that are plants with a full height of one to four inches. To fully appreciate these tiny wonders, one must get down to their level by lying on your stomach." *Charming,* Lance muttered to himself. Further links were full of flowers photographed from a low level. Next were encyclopedia listings, prayer meetings for botanists, and universities that offered degrees in botany. Travel sites proclaimed to be the best in 'belly botany' adventures. There was an exhibition two years earlier they missed there in California, and a photo competition upcoming in Colorado. Lance groaned, wondering if this computer searching was such a good idea after all.

It wasn't until page eight of those search pages that he spotted a reference to Walt. He almost missed it as it scrolled by with all the other listings. With a sense of excitement, he pulled up the article. It had been written by someone who had made a pilgrimage to Walt's hometown of Marceline, Missouri. She had been thrilled to find that Walt's "Dreaming Tree" was still standing and described in flowery prose how Walt and his little sister Ruth had spent hours and hours of their childhood sitting and dreaming under this particular cottonwood tree. As an adult, Walt himself had used the term 'belly botany' to describe their pleasant musings under that tree; how they would watch the insects and animals around them and later he would use this as the inspirations in his animated films.

Alert now, Lance wanted to make sure this article defined the tree and the cipher Walt was referring to. It sure sounded right, but Lance wasn't one to rest on one laurel. He now typed in 'dreaming tree' and added 'Disney' to the search. He came up with the same link, plus many more describing the same events and, most importantly, the same place in Walt's early life. He even found a picture of the huge cottonwood tree. It was taken from a great distance away barely showing two people standing nearby. The text said this was a picture of both Walt and Roy when they had visited their hometown in the early 1960's for the dedication of the town's swimming pool.

Bingo. Without waiting for Adam, Lance brought up his favorite travel site and booked flights for two to Marceline, Missouri the next day. Adam would have to work out his construction problem today. He was flying out tomorrow. They would be back late Friday afternoon. That should give them plenty of time.

He left a note for Adam taped to his refrigerator: "You are out of beer. Be ready 6 a.m. tomorrow. We fly to MO. Will be home Fri. Love, Lance."

WEDNESDAY, APRIL 24TH, 2002
5:45A.M.

Lance ignored his ringing phone all afternoon and evening. Around midnight Adam gave up trying to reach him so he could get some kind of explanation for the note. At 5:45 a.m. Wednesday, Adam threw open his apartment door just to stop the constant ringing of his doorbell.

"You packed?" Lance asked, looking well-rested and ready to go.

"Packed for what? You wouldn't answer your damned phone! Unlike some of the idle rich, I have work to do!"

Lance walked into Adam's bedroom, ignoring the outburst and sarcasm. "We really need to be on the road in five minutes. The freeways can be brutal filled with you 'working class' slobs," his voice was muffled from inside Adam's closet. He found a gym bag buried in there and tossed it to the boxer short-wearing Adam. "You might want to put something on that's a little warmer," Lance suggested, adding, "Though that look would probably get you through security a lot faster."

Adam caught the gym bag and tossed it on his rumpled bed. "What are you talking about?" Adam ran a hand through his mussed blonde hair. He had only gotten about five hours of sleep and was in no mood for Lance's games.

"Our flight to Missouri leaves at 8:45. Didn't you get my note?"

"Didn't you hear your phone ringing?" Adam shot back.

"I thought you would understand." Before Adam could explode, Lance held up a restraining hand. "I found the answer to the clue. We are going to Marceline, Missouri by way of LAX, Denver, and Kansas City. There is a rental car waiting for us this afternoon. We will drive approximately 125 miles from Kansas City to Marceline.

Now, you really need to get going." Lance leaned against the wall and let his news sink in. He knew Adam wouldn't let this opportunity pass by. He just waited.

Grumbling, Adam literally threw clothes and a toothbrush into the gym bag. "You could have told me all this yesterday," running a hand over his unshaved face knowing he didn't have time to shave.

Lance herded him into his Mercedes and tossed Adam's gym bag on top of his own carefully packed carry-on in the trunk. "Yes, I could have given you more of a heads-up..." Lance admitted as he sped away from Adam's apartment and headed for the 405 Freeway, "but this is a lot more fun."

While Lance was casually weaving in and out of traffic on the freeway, Adam called his foreman, Scott, at 6:30 a.m. and gave him some instructions for the next two days, telling him that he would probably be able to reach his cell phone if something important came up. By 7:30, they had parked at the Los Angeles International Airport and were sprinting for the entrance to the terminal. Coming to a screeching halt, they were stuck in the newly-formed Security check line as the minutes until their flight left ticked by. At 8:40, they ran into an almost empty terminal. Their plane had been loaded and the terminal door was shut. It took a wink and Lance's special persuasion for the flight attendant to let them onto the plane. The door of the plane was sealed shut behind them. At 8:50, the seatbelt lights came on. At 12:05 p.m., they were in Denver, racing for the terminal at the opposite end of the building. At 12:45, they were in the air again heading towards Missouri. At 4:30, Lance was driving northeast out of Kansas City towards Marceline with Adam slumped in the passenger seat. Around 6:45 that evening, they spotted the tall silver water tower proclaiming Marceline and headed down Kansas Avenue...a street many would recognize as Main Street USA if they were walking into Disneyland towards Sleeping Beauty's

Castle. It was here that Disneyland's Main Street was etched into the memory of Walt Disney who wanted to preserve the essence of his small-town experience and share it with the millions who would visit his Park.

There were plenty of references to Walt and his family ties there on Main Street, from antique stores to metal plaques at the local movie theatre. The small town aura was obvious in this well-kept town of 2500 residents. In Walt's time here, the railroad had been a big focus. But, in time, the town became an agricultural and industrial center and home to a large publishing industry. The railroad is still active in town and part of the new Disney museum under construction would be dedicated to the Santa Fe Railroad. Many of the business façades in town are either the old Western-influence wood or painted-over original brickwork. As in a lot of small towns, stores can cater to more than one type of customer. Here, the local appliance center boasted a soda fountain complete with padded chrome stools. Over on California Street is the Walt Disney Elementary School. Walt himself, arriving by train, had come back in October of 1960 for the christening of the new school. At the northern end of Main Street is Ripley Park that was named after E. P. Ripley, the past president of the Santa Fe Railroad. Sitting in the park for inspection is a huge engine, coal car and caboose from that same railroad. The beautiful white gazebo in Ripley Park had been built in 1898. Walt and his family had attended Sunday band concerts there. Sometimes his father, Elias, would join in with his fiddle. So deep were the memories of this time and place that Walt named one of his first steam locomotives at Disneyland the *E. P. Ripley*.

Lance pulled in front of the Uptown Theatre and got out, stretching to relieve his travel-induced aches and stiffness. Adam sat in the car for a minute, still somewhat stunned at this turn of events, yet excited to be in a place he had read about and had wanted to visit. And now, he was here.

As Lance pulled the luggage out of the trunk, Adam came out of his stupor and got out into the warm sunshine. "We're going to see a movie?" he asked, confused, looking up at the three-story tall theater's old-fashioned brick façade and ticket booth.

"There is a bed-and-breakfast upstairs," Lance explained. "I booked the Walt Disney Suite for us. I was going to get the Winnie the Pooh Room for you, but it was already booked."

Adam just shook his head, looking around. "This is amazing. I can't believe I'm in Walt's hometown!"

They checked in and were shown up to the two-bedroom suite with a sitting room, small kitchenette, and dining room. Lance claimed the bedroom with the king-sized bed for his 'superior' height. Adam, not caring, tossed his almost empty gym bag in the other bedroom, on his queen-sized bed. He wandered through the quaint suite with its clean white walls and maple furniture. In the dining room, dishes and glasses were encased in a glass-fronted chest set into a wall. Discreet pictures of Walt dotted the walls here and there. A directory on the small table next to the phone gave them a historical run-down of the Uptown Theatre and apartments that had been opened in 1930. Walt and Roy had been there in 1956 to host the premiere of the Disney movie *The Great Locomotive Chase*. Walt had told the children in the audience that "they were lucky to live here" in Marceline. There were ads from other businesses in town and even a preview of a new Walt Disney Hometown Museum that would open soon in May 2002. They were directed to the Zurcher Building and its original Coke mural that inspired Coke Corner, the outdoor restaurant with red and white awnings found at the end of Main Street in Disneyland.

They found a diner and had a home-cooked meatloaf dinner complete with flaky biscuits, mashed potatoes, fresh-cut green beans, and a blueberry cobbler for dessert. After dinner, while walking down the sidewalk, they found the hardware store. It was difficult to buy a shovel discreetly. Adam picked out a sufficient one – it actually folded which made it easier to hide – while Lance chatted with the clerk. Adam just hoped she didn't remember too much about 'the other guy' who bought a shovel. Usually the girls just remembered Lance. That could work out well to their advantage this time.

Travel fatigue on top of a wonderful meal caught up with Adam. He managed to get his teeth brushed, mumbled something that could have been 'good night' to Lance, and shut his room's door. He noticed fresh-smelling floral sheets right before he fell asleep in the silent room.

Thursday, April 25th, 2002
2:45p.m.

"You can't miss it," they had been told by nearly everyone they asked about Walt's special tree.

"Go north," a senior gentleman walking an equally senior-looking Springer spaniel said, pointing up the street. He then added, "Then go left on Broadway. You'll see a bank on the left. The tree is across from it."

That should have been simple enough. The bank was easy enough to spot. They knew what the tree looked like from that old picture. How difficult would it be to spot a one hundred-year old huge cottonwood?

More difficult than you might expect, they found. They passed it three times. They didn't account for the growth of the weeds or for the current shape of the tree.

Time and old age had affected the tree as it does humans. Huge branches had fallen and been hauled away. It looked like half a tree as the men walked around it. The re-creation of Walt's barn stood back even farther from the main road. There were little signs posted here and there describing the events that happened in the history of the tree, the barn, and the site.

Remembering that the diary had told them to look around and appreciate wherever they found themselves, the two men did just that. They took a moment to wander through the barn. The signs had told them this barn had been Walt and Ruth's favorite place to play. They had performed a 'barn circus' with the animals, including a pig and a goat, dressed in Ruth's doll clothes. The admission price had been refunded by Flora, their mother. The barn had shown up in the movie *So Dear My Heart* and another re-creation had been built in Walt's backyard in California in 1950 to become his personal workshop and his own 'Happy Place'. Inside this Missouri version, they found that guests were encouraged to leave a personal message. These messages were written on the boards of the barn and came from all over the United States and around the world. Adam and Lance went to different sides of the barn and left their own message. It seemed like the thing to do.

The land is privately owned now. There are no parking lots or signs indicating a 'roadside attraction'. But visitors are welcome at any time to wander the site. Nobody even looks twice at strangers walking through the high weeds or sitting under the fading tree. Everyone who visits there comes for their own reasons. They are encouraged, respected, and left alone.

Adam and Lance found themselves alone on that Thursday afternoon. The folding shovel Adam had chosen was tucked under Lance's lightweight jacket. Adam hadn't had time to pack any jacket. After their time in the barn and reading some of the messages left by others, they wandered back to the tree. As Walt had written, it was time to 'begin doing'.

Lance had set down the shovel and put his jacket over it. They silently contemplated the tree. "I don't suppose there is any big, red arrow, is there?" Lance asked, his head leaning back to see the topmost branches.

"That would be nice," Adam admitted with a smile. He walked around the tree. "Nope, don't see one. Tell me again what you found 'belly botany' to mean."

Lance recited the close examination of bugs and plants from the on-your-stomach perspective.

"Okay," Adam started, "Walt was about my height, maybe a little shorter, but not much. If he was lying here on his stomach, like this," as he demonstrated with his own body, "would you go by where my feet are now?"

Lance came and stood at the place where Adam's feet had been as Adam got up. "Or, since the clue says 'from where I stand', would be it where you are now that you are standing?"

"It isn't that much of a difference in distance."

"It is if you are digging," Lance pointed out. "Think we could find a backhoe and do it all at once?"

That got a smile out of Adam. "Well, I think a two-foot deep trench all around the tree might be noticed. I think we need to find one particular place to dig. Where that is, I'm not sure."

"Well, mark both distances and we will see if we can get any inspiration on where to start."

They stood at the trunk of the old tree and looked at the view from different positions. Because they didn't know what had stood in the distance over ninety years ago, they didn't get any answer. Looking up into the tree didn't help as so much of the tree was gone. They just hoped their reference point hadn't been burned for fire-wood years ago.

"How about in relation to the barn?" Lance suggested. "Between the tree and the barn?"

Adam shrugged. "You want to try first? Sounds good to me."

Not realizing he was going to be on the business end of the shovel, Lance paused for a moment. Adam knew him well enough to know exactly what Lance was thinking. Adam kept quiet. If there was more digging that had to be done after this, he would do the next hole. Lance now knew he was going to get down and dirty. He gave a sigh as the shovel bit into the weedy soil.

Adam kept his smile to himself and sat back under the tree facing the road. He would alert Lance to stop if anyone else came. This was a place to reflect, not dig up. He wasn't exactly sure what he would say to anyone who questioned them, but he would think of something. He heard some mumbled cursing, but saw no other cars or people.

Within ten minutes Lance had his two-foot deep hole dug. He had examined the dirt as he threw it out but only saw rocks and more rocks. Unless Walt left them a special rock, he didn't find anything. Calling Adam around, Lance asked his opinion. Adam looked through the pile of dirt and the hole. He shrugged. "Fill it back in. We'll try another one. Oh, and be sure to leave a patch of weeds to put back on top."

With Lance muttering about his hands, his back, his favorite shirt, and various places Adam could stick the patch of weeds, Adam wandered around the tree trunk again. It was only about three feet in diameter. He studied the trunk at the height he thought a five- to eight-year old boy would be, allowing for some growth of the tree. Nothing. Then he tried again at his own height, as if Walt were looking at the tree as an adult.

He almost missed it, it was so faint. There was some crude carving in the tree trunk. It might have been passed over as some harmless prank by a kid. But as Adam pulled away a little more of the bark, he saw it was initials. They weren't very deep, but they were legible.

W.E.D.

Walter Elias Disney. As Disney aficionados know, those three initials were a cipher for many things Disney. The acronym was used to create WED Enterprises, the design and development organization Walt founded in

1952 to help him create Disneyland. And here they were, most likely carved by Walt himself so many years ago.

Adam traced the letters with his fingers to make sure they really were letters, not random scars left in the tree. Lance was almost done with filling in the hole. Adam turned his back to the carving and looked out over the land. There was nothing he could see that would inspire that particular spot. He lay down directly under the letters and dug his heels in to mark the spot. Lance came over while he was still prone.

"Having a nice nap?" He tossed the shovel next to Adam, and sat with his back to the tree. His face was lined with sweat. He ran his hand through his tousled hair in a way that usually made the ladies want to reach up and smooth it back in place, and then run their hand down his high cheekbones and dimple. But, there were no ladies here to see him. Only Adam, who had no such inclinations. Adam, who didn't seem to notice he had finished with his manual exertions in record-setting time. His eyes narrowed at Adam who turned a smiling face at him. Adam indicated 'up' with his chin. Lance was in no mood for guessing games. "What?"

"Look up above my head, if you can drag your weary body over here," Adam told him.

Barely stifling a curse, Lance got to his feet and eyed the trunk.

"About six feet up from here," Adam added, tilting his head straight up so his eyes led Lance to the spot.

Lance ran his fingers over the carved initials. "How'd we miss that?"

Adam stood up and reached for the shovel. "I guess we weren't looking for it. Didn't know what to look for." As the shovel took its first bite, Adam asked, "Will you watch for incoming?"

Lance barely nodded as he looked at the initials again. "Incredible," was all he said.

"Hey, mister, whatcha doing?"

The squeaky voice took them both by surprise. Adam's shovelful of dirt was lowered back into the hole as he stopped what he was doing. He was only about ten inches deep. Lance spun around and his eyes dropped lower than he expected. A young boy stood, hands held behind him, watching. He looked about six years old to Lance, who was not a good judge of children's ages.

The boy was curious. "Whatcha doin' to Walt's tree?" he wanted to know.

Adam kept his back to the boy and let Lance handle it. Lance smiled and said to the boy, "I'm Bob and this is my friend Ernie."

"I'm Timmy. I live over there," with a vague wave off to the east somewhere.

Lance tried to keep him talking as Adam got back to digging. "You come here a lot, Timmy? We're new."

"You probably shouldn't be digging up Walt's tree," Timmy said, sounding somewhat doubtful as he was curious about what was down there.

"Oh, we're not digging up the tree," Lance assured him. "See how far we are away from it? Ernie dropped a contact lens. We're trying to find it."

Timmy edged closer to the hole. "It's going to be really dirty," he muttered. Adults did the stupidest things.

"Well, we will just have to wash it off real good if we find it. How are you coming, Ernie?"

'Ernie' just felt the tip of his shovel hit something. It could be another rock. There were plenty of those in this soil. He scraped a little dirt to the side and saw something gray. He felt the length of it with the shovel blade. He knew he could scoop it out in one throw. Seeing Timmy eyeing him, he covered it over and made a small trench around the item. "Say, Lance…"

"Bob."

"Bob, show Timmy what we found on the tree. It is really cool."

Lance saw the outline Adam had made in the dirt.

He knew he had found something and had to distract Timmy. "Oh, that's right! Look at this! Bet you didn't see this before."

As they turned to face the tree, Adam dug in and tossed the big clump of dirt off to the side. He jumped up out of the hole, grabbing Lance's discarded jacket. As Timmy was complaining he was too short and 'can't see nothin',' Adam uncovered a gray plastic capsule and threw the jacket over it. He turned back to the hole and started filling it in as fast as he could.

Lance lifted the boy up to see the initials. "Oh, wow, cool, wait until I show my friends! We never seen that before!" Lance put him back on the ground. Adam was just about finished. He nodded to Lance that it was all right. "I'm going to go get Tony!"

They watched the boy run off across the foot bridge and down street. He seemed so excited to show his friends something new that hopefully he would forget about the hole. As Adam tamped the weeds back in place, he hoped they were long gone if Timmy did remember.

They folded up the shovel and stashed it with the long, gray plastic tube Adam had dug up under Lance's jacket. Both dirt-stained and sweaty, they hoped they could get up to their suite without too much notice or any questions. Excited with their discovery, Lance still drove sedately through town. "What do we do with the shovel?" Lance wanted to know.

"Take it back for a refund?" Adam kidded. "I think the clerk would do it for you," he batted his eyes.

Lance ignored him. "I was just wondering if we should dump it in case Timmy tells his parents someone was digging up Walt's tree."

Adam glanced at the sky. It was late afternoon now. He hoped it was dinnertime for Timmy and his friends and they would be too busy to tell anyone anything. "You might be right. Maybe there's a dumpster behind these stores."

Lance drove around the block until they found a city dumpster. Adam tossed in the shovel, trying not to make too much noise. Other than a cat he disturbed, no one seemed to be around. Lance drove back to the Bed and Breakfast. They beat off as much dust as they could before they went inside. The front desk was busy with another guest as they took the stairs to their suite.

They closed the cheery curtains in the front window and set the capsule on the kitchen table. It was about a foot long and six inches around. They didn't know for sure exactly how long it had been buried in that field. It had to have been before 1966 – assuming Walt himself put it there – so it had to have been in the ground at least thirty-six years. The scratches on the plastic must have been from the dirt going in and coming out. There were no dents, no ravages from time. One end had a cap screwed on. Adam tried the lid and found it wouldn't budge. He gently tapped it on the edge of the kitchen table, the way he would try to loosen the lid off a pickle jar. Even then, it took all of Adam's strength to weaken the hold on the cap. They found it had been sealed with double neoprene seals, so everything inside was well protected from the elements.

They found they were both holding their breath as the cap came off. Adam tilted the case and a piece of wood fell out into Lance's waiting hands. They looked at the size of the case and that small piece of wood, and looked at each other. "Is that it?" Lance was the one to voice it.

Adam shrugged and tilted the case again. They heard a soft scraping inside. Peering in, they found paper loosely rolled to fit the sides snugly. Reaching in, Adam could feel the texture of parchment paper and lightly eased the edge towards the lip of the capsule. Before he could grasp the edge, Lance suggested they wash the dirt off their hands first. "You never know," he pointed out.

The majority of the dirt was left on the dishtowel as they eased the paper out of its resting place. Lance unrolled the red-bordered sheets. There were two of them rolled together, eleven inches wide by about seventeen inches long. At the top of the sheets, there was a highly detailed picture of a steam train – much like the one sitting in Ripley Park that they hadn't explored yet - a coal car and passenger cars. A woman passenger was holding her hat against the onrushing wind of the train. In the background, a mid-1920's car was seen parked near the wooden terminal. The writing covering the entire page was flowery with the words Atchison, Topeka, and Santa Fe Railroad Company in bold, shaded letters. They were stock certificates proclaiming ten shares each, numbered, signed, embossed. The paper had that unusual quality Lance had only seen – and felt – in old historical documents.

With Adam peering over his shoulder, Lance looked them over. He had more experience in that area than Adam. His eyes were wide when he finished his examination. "Congratulations, buddy. We are now shareholders in the railroad!"

They simultaneously high-fived each other.

"Thank you, Walt!" Adam walked over to Walt's picture on the wall and saluted their benefactor.

Lance stopped in mid-stride with a sobering thought. "What if someone comes looking for whoever dug up the ground out at the tree?"

Suddenly deflated, Adam sunk into the floral chair. "Whoa, you're right. That kid could possibly tell his parents. This is a small town. It wouldn't be too much of a stretch to find the two new guys who bought a shovel this morning."

"Think we should get out of here?"

Adam nodded. His elation was turning into neurosis - just like it had done when he found Walt's diary at Disneyland. Someone could burst in here at any minute and demand to know what they were doing out at the Dreaming Tree. "We're paid up through the night, though, aren't we?"

Lance was in his room gathering up his clothes. "I don't care. We'll head back to Kansas City and find a place to stay there. It is only a two hour drive. We'll have dinner once we get there."

Thinking ahead to the airline and the gray capsule, Adam asked, "What do we do with this case? Would it be searched at the airport?"

"Probably. Just make sure it is empty and we will dump it somewhere in Kansas City. What do you think that wood block is?"

Adam shrugged. "Our next clue? Did you look at it?"

They picked up the neglected piece of wood. It looked like it was broken off from a bigger piece of wood. It had the number **1127** embedded on it.

"Toss it in your bag. It has to be a clue of some kind. Kinda vague…You packed?"

Lance nodded and looked around the room. He would have liked to have stayed and explored more of the town tomorrow. He bet he could have talked their way into that new museum that was about a month away from being open. Oh, well, nothing could be done. They both felt it best to put some distance between themselves and those holes they had dug. He glanced down at his shirt. "I'd like to take a shower. No, let's get on the road. I'll talk to the front desk."

They regretfully shut the door and headed to their rental car. On the way back to Kansas City, they decided to put all metal items into Lance's carry-on for Security at the airport to go through. The paper and wood in Adam's gym bag would go through the X-ray machine without any problem. There was no need for anyone to see the stock certificates. They felt they were home clear.

Now all they had to do was find out what in the world – and where in the world - the number **1127** stood for.

CHAPTER 4

1127

**Monday, April 29th, 2002
3:15p.m.**

"**W**hat do you mean 'we have to go back to Missouri'??"

Adam had wondered why the sleek, black Mercedes pulled up in front of his bathroom remodeling job in the Anaheim Hills. He set down the blueprints he was going over with his foreman, Scott, then watched Lance amble over, saying hi to his workmen, calling several of them by name. Lance picked his way around the lumber scraps and power cords. A Skill saw whined in the background as a two-by-four was sized for a wall. After shaking hands with Lance, Scott headed back inside the house, leaving Adam and Lance standing over the blueprints half rolled up on the impromptu table made of two saw horses and a four-by-six piece of plywood.

When he received no answer, Adam asked Lance, "What did we miss in Missouri?"

Before Lance could elaborate, the homeowner, Mrs. Anderson, came around from the back of her house, wrapped in a silky, transparent sarong after a dip in her pool. She looked Lance over appreciatively. "I thought I heard a Mercedes," she purred, her eyes unabashedly taking in Lance's well-built body. "Aren't you going to introduce us, Adam?" she asked, not even looking at Adam.

With his devastating grin, Lance leaned across Adam, pushing him back. "How do you do? I'm Mr. Brentwood, Adam's lawyer. My friends call me Lance." He ignored Adam's muffled choke as he extended his hand.

Adam ceased to exist. Grasping his outstretched hand, Mrs. Anderson gave Lance another slower look over. "His lawyer? My, I might just have to sue him." Still holding his hand firmly, she gave him a wink and a conspiratorial chuckle. The soft clinking of the gold and platinum bangles on her wrist blended with the sexy sound of her feminine voice.

Lance knew he would probably have to break his wrist to get his hand back at that moment. He smiled at the fifty-something who was trying desperately to look forty-something and wishing she was thirty-something. "Oh, you don't want to do that. My boy Adam here is a fine contractor. You have a lovely home, Mrs…..?"

"Just call me Rose. Can I show you around? I don't think Adam would mind if I steal you away." Without a word or glance at Adam, she tucked her arm through Lance's and led him off.

Mutely, Adam stood where he was, watching them wander off to the back of the house, Mrs. Anderson chatting amicably to Lance, a death grip still on his arm. Scott came back, walking up to Adam. He was grinning, obviously amused, watching Rose and Lance meander around the corner of the house. Scott turned to Adam. "Rose, is it? You haven't been able to call her anything but Mrs. Anderson for the two months we've been working here. Didn't know Lance was your lawyer. Jacobs might be interested to hear that." He was trying very hard not to start laughing. He wasn't sure he would be able to stop.

Oblivious to Scott's amusement, Adam just shook his head. "He isn't. I don't know how he got her purring like a kitten. Well, I guess I do," he amended with a dry laugh. "It's been that way ever since I knew him. Oh well, as long as he keeps her off our backs, we might actually get something accomplished today. She didn't mention any other 'new revelation' she had about the design of the bathroom, did she?"

"Nope, not yet. What did you tell her about the glass block window she wanted?" Scott knew the design was impractical for the room and the house. They would have to redesign the whole room around the window, repositioning the Jacuzzi tub and the three-sided glass shower. It *could* be done. It just wouldn't look right for the house.

Adam grinned, "Twenty-three thousand dollars and a four week delay."

"Ooh, good one! What did she say?"

"She wanted to think about it. I wish she would quit looking through those celebrity home magazines." Adam gave a sigh. It was part of the job, he knew. Part Fashion Designer. Part Contractor. Part Listening Ear. Part Babysitter. Part Troubleshooter.

Scott hedged, "Speaking of delays…"

Eyes closed, Adam groaned. "What happened?"

"You know that special beam you ordered for the ceiling?"

Adam just stared at him. Twenty-four foot 'Distressed' beam. It had taken two weeks for it to come in.

"Ben cut it short."

Adam swallowed his curse. 'Measure twice. Cut once. Measure twice. Cut once.' He drilled that into every man he hired. And, if they were worth their tool belt, they already knew it.

"It might fit a gazebo," Scott added helpfully. "Don't know if we have one coming up, though…."

"Call the lumber mill."

"Already did," Scott told him. "Two more weeks for them to bring another one in."

"What's Ben doing now?"

Scott chuckled. "Besides hiding from you? I put him

shoring up the floor. Not too much he can screw up there."

"Wouldn't be too sure on that," Adam mumbled as he headed inside to see Ben.

The sound of laughter came through the missing bathroom windows. Adam didn't know why he was surprised to see a swimsuit-clad Lance floating on an umbrella-shaded life raft, drink in hand. Mrs. Anderson – he wouldn't dare call her Rose – was floating next to him on an identical raft. The fountain had been turned on in the middle of the pool. Apparently the swimmers had just drifted through the fine mist of spray emerging out of the top of the fountain and found it vastly amusing

Looking at the swimmers, Adam just then remembered what Lance had told him when he arrived. "We have to go back to Missouri." It had to be the clue '1127'. Adam had had no time to look into the meaning. After they got back from Marceline late Friday, he had come out here on the job Saturday, worked all day by himself, and then spent Sunday running estimates on what Mrs. Anderson had wanted changed. A quick trip to the grocery store and the weekend was gone. He hadn't even thought about the stock certificates they had found. Apparently Lance had been busy. That was good. If he found the meaning of the clue, Adam would let him have his dip in the pool. Maybe if Lance came out every day with him, he might actually get the job finished and signed off…

"We're invited to a barbecue tonight. Well, I was invited…I insisted you come, too," Lance was telling Adam.

Keep calm, Adam told himself. *Keep calm. Deep breath.* "We, and I mean you too, are not going to Mrs. Anderson's for a barbecue tonight or any other night, Lance. I think you know there is no Mr. Anderson. Yet," he mumbled. "It is not appropriate."

Lance waved off his objections. "I told her there was some wording in your contract...."

"You what!!??" Adam exploded, coming out of his desk chair and storming over to the sofa where Lance was currently lounging. "Might I remind you that you are *not* a lawyer? I've been tap dancing around that woman for two months now. Keep out of my business!!"

Again he was waved off. Lance put his feet up on the coffee table, nudging aside the reference books Adam had neglected. "Now, now. I just pulled a random line out of the contract – which is very well-written, I might add – and told her how much of a tremendous benefit it was for her to have you as her contractor. She was very appreciative," he finished, taking a sip of his Scotch.

"Don't want to hear it. Don't want to hear it," Adam mumbled. "So, did you or didn't you bring up a hornet's nest with my contract?"

"No, no. She was sighing with relief that she is so well protected. She might even want you do redo her kitchen next."

"Hope you're not expecting a finder's fee for that little gem," Adam sighed. He didn't know if Lance was a blessing or a curse. Time would tell.

"My treat," Lance finished magnanimously.

"I don't suppose it would do any good to tell you not to go around telling people you are my lawyer or anyone else's for that matter, would it?"

"Only in special cases. So, the barbecue is really out? Rose will be so disappointed," Lance added as he casually flipped through a remodel magazine that Adam subscribed to. He held up a page showing an all-chrome and glass kitchen. "Think this would look good in Rose's house?"

Adam glanced at the picture. "Only if she never planned on actually doing any cooking in there."

Lance gave a laugh at that and finished thumbing through the magazine. "Well, she did say she had something cooking. Not sure if she meant in the kitchen or not…" he drifted off. Looking around Adam's apartment that had been new in the early '70's, he wondered out loud why a contractor with Adam's ability lived in a green shag carpet wonder like this.

"Give me time," Adam sighed. He had wondered that, too, on many occasions. He had plans once to build his own home. Had the blueprints designed in his head. Two-story country French. Four bedrooms. Three baths. Formal dining room. Huge playroom in the loft for the pool table and a jukebox. Oak kitchen. Covered patio stretching the length of the house in back. He even had picked out the lot. He had picked out the woman too. But…

"Want me to call Rose, or do you want to do the honors?" Lance's voice broke through his thoughts.

Glad for the disruption from where his mind had taken him, he snorted. "You made the plans. You break them."

"I could go without you."

"Ah, but you won't," Adam told him pointedly.

With a good-natured shrug, Lance pulled his cell phone out of his slacks and the phone number out of his shirt pocket. Truth be told, he didn't mind canceling all that much. Being friendly and gregarious, he liked the company of all women. He found something interesting in everyone he met. But, he hadn't been born yesterday – as he knew Adam liked to think. He knew trouble when he saw it. And Mrs. Rose Anderson was trouble with a capital T.

Even from where he was standing, Adam could hear the shrill of disappointment in the voice on the other end. But, Lance being Lance, he managed to turn it around; she had ended the conversation being 'so glad' that he had called. "What were you doing on the job site anyway?" Adam wanted to know when the phone call was finished.

"I was already in Anaheim, so thought I would stop by for a chat and tell you the news."

"Just can't keep away from Disneyland, huh?" Adam kidded.

An odd look passed over Lance's face that quickly dissipated. Wary? Suspicious? Adam wasn't even sure he saw it, let alone analyze it. "Yeah, well, you know me," Lance said a little too lightly. Then, turning the conversation to a different channel, "No, I wanted to tell you about our flight to Missouri this Wednesday."

Calm. Calm. God, it would take the Dalai Lama's patience to be friends with Lance and not kill him. Shaking his head, Adam pinched the bridge of his nose. "I cannot leave the job again so soon, Lance! I have responsibilities there."

"I could go without you," Lance repeated his earlier statement, and then added, "but I think I will need your expert skills on this one."

Stifling the instant objection he was ready to voice, Adam realized he didn't even know what Lance had found. He had been so wrapped up in work and his frustrating customer that he hadn't even asked. He dropped into the overstuffed chair next to the sofa. "Maybe you'd better tell me what you discovered."

Already knowing that Adam was going to object, Lance had just waited for Adam to mentally work it out himself. "That might be a good idea," Lance agreed, picking up one of the books on the coffee table. He thumbed through about a third of the book and handed it, open, to Adam. There was a black and white picture of a large brick building in the center of the page. A smaller picture showed men in white shirts and black suspenders hunched over drafting tables, racks of paper stacked on the walls behind them. The caption proclaimed the 'animators hard at work'. The title of the chapter was "Laugh-O-Grams Era".

"That was Walt's first big job," Adam muttered more

to himself than to Lance. "Their offices were rented upstairs in a huge building with skylights. Ah," he read, "the McConahy Building. That's right. This was in Kansas City," he finished, looking at Lance. "This is what you found? What does the number have to do with it? 1127?"

"That, my friend, is the address of the building. 1127 East 31st Street, Kansas City, Missouri. Sorry, I don't know the zip code," Lance grinned.

Adam didn't hear the last part. He would have ignored it anyway, just on general principle. An address. What a sly dog! "How long did it take you to find it?"

"About two days more than it should," Lance sighed. "I wasn't being 'literal' enough when I started looking. I was trying numerology, dates, safety deposit boxes, phone numbers, you name it."

Adam was impressed. "Good job. What did you mean when you said you would need my 'expert skills'?"

Lance indicated the picture of the building in the book. "You see what the building looks like there." Adam nodded, waiting. "Well, that building was pretty new when the animators moved in and started work. As you probably know, that was in 1920 after Walt got back from France the year before. So, to put a fine point on it, the building is approximately eighty-two years old now."

"There are plenty of old buildings from that era that not only survived, but thrived and are the focal part of many cities," Adam pointed out, not seeing any significance in Lance's point.

Lance reached over and turned a few more pages in the book. "But not this one." He held open a page to Adam. The picture showed a devastated building. Shoring held up the outside brickwork. The roof, if it could still be called a roof, was either sagging badly or gone completely. They couldn't tell from the angle of the picture. "I think this is what you contractors would call a real 'fixer-upper'," Lance said as he watched

Adam frown at the dilapidated structure in the photograph.

Adam's contracting skills took over and he mentally evaluated the time, cost, and effort needed to fix the problem. "It would take hundreds of thousands to fix it up to its former glory. I'd have to see the condition of the roof and the flooring…"

Lance chuckled. "Adam, we aren't assigned to fix it. We just have to find whatever it is Walt left for us. I would guess it would be inside – where his office used to be."

Adam was silent as he thought about Lance's words. If the conditions of the building were as bad as this undated photo showed – or worse – it would be dangerous for someone not familiar with construction to poke around inside. It would be bad enough for Adam – and he knew what he was doing. He still looked at the photo as his mind went over the possibilities. "You would probably break that pretty neck of yours if you went in there alone," Adam remarked, handing the book back to Lance.

"Rose would be very irritated at you if I did. And, Rose aside, I am quite attached to my neck just as it is," he finished with a smile. He knew Adam would go with him. He knew it all along. He had even told Rose not to expect either Adam or him back for a few days. She pouted rather prettily, but agreed if it had to be done, it had to be done. She would be waiting when he got back.

Lance handed Adam his cell phone. Adam noticed his foreman Scott's number was already punched in.

1127 EAST 31ST STREET
KANSAS CITY, MISSOURI

WEDNESDAY, MAY 1ST, 2002
7:12P.M.

Lance drove slowly around the dilapidated neighborhood. No matter which angle they looked at it, the building looked bad. The picture they had seen must have been taken years earlier. Even the braces looked wobbly. They sat across from the red brick front. There were no "Keep Out" signs posted. The owners probably figured no one would be dumb enough to risk their lives going inside anyway. And now these two were planning on doing just that.

"The front doors are all blocked with boards. Most of the windows are broken and boarded. Did you see anything around back?"

Lance backed the car and drove around back again. "I think those two windows are about the only access. They are low enough even for your tiny legs."

"Five eleven, buddy, is not short," Adam muttered, distracted by what he saw in front of them. How in the world would they find anything inside that mess?

"What do you think we will need? We will have to go somewhere else to get some tools. This area doesn't seem likely to have a home-improvement store on the next corner," Lance frowned, looking down the street, seeing nothing but litter-strewn empty lots and other old, run-down structures.

"A bulldozer comes to mind, but that isn't exactly helpful…Wow, what a mess," Adam said, punctuating his words with a heavy sigh. "Do you want to try to go inside now? We still have some daylight left."

Lance hit the door lock of the rental car before they

moved away from the vehicle. It seemed prudent, especially in the given neighborhood. They walked along the cracked sidewalk that bordered the sides of the building, coming up to a large rectangular section of heavy plywood that would have been the main entrance of the building decades earlier.

Adam tugged on the boards blocking the doors. He could probably rip them off, but didn't want to do that yet. He would rather find another, more non-intrusive method to get inside. He hoisted himself up onto the first window sill. The glass was long gone, so he brought a leg up and pushed himself inside. Lance followed and they both ignored the scurrying noises in the debris littering the floor. From the dim light they could make out a few walls still standing. Most of them had holes knocked in them – whether from fists or from a sledgehammer didn't really make any difference at this point. A few tatters of posters, and some old newspaper articles were tacked to what walls were left. Without a flashlight, Adam didn't want to venture too far from the light of the window. Holes in flooring could be hidden under the plaster pieces that had fallen from the ceiling. There were remnants of a staircase leading up into darkness.

Lance's voice seemed overly loud. "What do you think we'll need?"

Shaking his head, Adam thought out loud, "Flashlights, broom, snakebite kit, hammer, ladder, rope?"

"Rats, maybe, but not snakes."

"Then a ratbite kit," he amended. "Let's get out of here and come back early tomorrow." Retracing their steps, the two men climbed back out the broken window.

Once outside, after drawing in deep breaths of fresh air, they looked back at the building. "Do you know where Walt's office would have been?"

Lance nodded and pointed upwards. "That wall for sure. Exactly where inside is a little vague."

A voice startled them. They had been so concentrated on their endeavor they hadn't seen the man as he came down the street towards them. "You boys going to fix this place up?" The old man stopped his daily walk, glad at the chance to talk to somebody. A little black and white Boston terrier obediently sat at his feet and waited, looking up expectantly at her owner.

Always quick on his feet, Lance gave him a friendly grin and extended his hand. "Nice to see you, sir. Quite an old building, eh?"

"Nice to see some interest in it," the old man said, returning the smile. "Been that way a long time."

"It's all right if we poke around inside, isn't it?" Lance asked him as if the old man was the owner.

The old man just chuckled. "Well, considering I just saw you two come out of that there window, I guess you don't need my permission. Hey, it's okay with me. Probably okay with everyone around here as long as something gets done. Fine old building in its time. Fine old building. You just do what you need to. Nobody will bother you." He gave a gentle tug on the dog's leash. "Come on, Mazie, we've kept these young men long enough. Y'all be good now, ya hear?" he waved as he walked off.

Flashlights didn't help much. At least the brooms cleared the area. And Adam had been right. On the bottom floor, there were holes in the flooring here and there opening up to the sub-floor supports and concrete support columns holding up the floor trusses. They cleared a path to the stairs, the brooms causing a cloud of dust to rise. Their eyes watered; both were glad to wear the protective masks that Adam had suggested. The use of asbestos was common in those days and who knew how much lead paint was floating around in that dust. When the way had been cleared, Adam started up the stairs first, testing each board before putting his full weight on it. Waiting below with the ladder, Lance let him get all the way up before he followed Adam's dusty footprints. The upper floor was even more ravaged. The skylights, once such a help for the animators, had been neglected and had leaked for years. Some had fallen in. The roof sagged badly. Adam didn't think it would last many more years – not with the snowfall Missouri usually got. Actually, he was surprised there was any roof left at all.

With part of the roof open, it was lighter than they thought it would be, so they shut off the flashlights. Adam was even more careful with each step he took. Wood rot could be hidden under any normal-looking board. One false step could take them all the way down to the first floor the hard way.

Lance pointed out the side for Walt's old office and they made their way slowly over to that section. Any remaining lath on the walls was long gone. The flooring seemed more stable the closer to the outer wall they got. Adam's broom cleared away the birds' nests, paper litter, and moldy somethings they didn't want to explore too deeply. He declared the floor safe and they walked over to the brick wall. He jumped back when one of the floor boards squeaked. Testing it with his broom, and then his foot, he ignored the squeak as he put his weight on it again.

"Ok, now what?" They both had the same thought, but Lance voiced it first.

Adam just shook his head as he surveyed what had been an animator's office eighty years earlier. "No clue. But then, we didn't really have much of a clue when we were in Marceline, either. He would have to have left us something to go by. There is no tree growing here – yet – so that is out." He broke off as Lance went over to the window opening and looked out. "Anything?"

Lance shook his head. "I doubt the view is the same. It would have to be somewhere inside. We have walls, ceiling and floor to work with. Which one do you want?"

Adam was setting up the ladder Lance had carried

up. "I'll take the ceiling. What's left of it," he muttered as he climbed up the first three rungs.

Lance backed up a few paces and stood on the squeaky board. He bounced up and down a few times on it. Adam warned him that might not be a good idea. The squeaking stopped as Lance went over to examine the brick wall. They were silent as they each went about their business. Starting at the far edge of the wall, Lance was running his hands over every brick and checking the condition of the mortar. Adam started at the opposite end of the wall, doing side to side sweeps with his eyes. After finishing one section, Adam came down and moved the ladder to the next spot. They slowly made their way to the center of the room.

Adam was about to move the ladder again when Lance called to him. "Adam, come and see this."

He climbed down and went to where Lance had his fingers on one of the bricks under the window. "What did you find?"

Lance moved his hand to the side. Adam got down on his knees to look at it better. It was faint, but he could make out the **WED** chipped out of the brick. It was like the Dreaming Tree in Marceline. Walt had given them a starting point.

"Do you think we should remove the brick?" Lance asked, sounding doubtful at his own thought. The mortar around that particular brick was just the same as all the other. It didn't look like it had been removed and repaired. He wasn't an expert, but it looked identical. He voiced his thoughts to Adam.

After his own examination, and chipping away a little of the mortar there and over a few bricks, Adam agreed with him. "No, I don't think it is the brick itself. Look at the way the letters were formed. To me, it looks as if the initials were put in after the brick was already in place. The 'D' looks too awkward to have been done on a level surface. I think we need to use it as an indicator."

Lance backed up a little to look the wall over. He bounced up and down again. Adam wondered what it was about squeaking floors little boys liked so much. Lance didn't ask Adam about his sudden grin. He was wondering which direction they needed to go. Up or down?

1964

He stood on the sidewalk outside the familiar red brick building. *Have I been gone that long?* he wondered to himself. The crisp painted trim was gone. Some of the windows were blocked up with wood. Awnings, signs of occupants, hustle and bustle of a busy intersection were all gone. The photographer's studio was gone. The Forest Inn Café was gone. *No lunch on credit today,* he chuckled in spite of the feeling of loss that swept over him.

He lit another cigarette while standing there. Looking up and down the street, there was no one else to be seen. He looked at the entry door marked "Pool Hall". *Guess that means the drug store is gone too. Well, let's get doing*, he reminded himself.

Pushing open the door, he paused for a moment, allowing his eyes to get accustomed to the dim, nondescript interior lighting. His hesitation allowed the patrons within to accustom themselves to a visitor, something they didn't exactly relish. They looked over the old man, cigarette held negligently in his fingers, an indication of someone long used to the habit. Gray hair, thin mustache, slightly slouched shoulders. His clothes were unremarkable; from his dusty black shoes up to his old Fedora. Non-threatening. Still, he was trespassing on their turf.

The old man wasn't aware of their scrutiny. He didn't see the smoky interior of the pool hall, or hear the soft clink of the pool balls as a shot was made, or smell the alcohol being served. He didn't see the nervous owner trying surreptitiously to get his attention. He was seeing the Café, the soda fountain, and the photographers and the artists and the messenger boys running in and out. He was hearing the ideas being bandied around the office; he could smell the black India and Iron Gold ink. He envisioned the permanently stained fingers of his artists.

Forty years. Has it really been forty years? So much time. So much has happened since. So much progress and so much hope for the future. And this had been a starting place. He fondly remembered the little pet mouse he had fed. Who would have guessed that mouse would lead them to where they were today? He smiled at the memory. That little mouse had built a great empire. And now he had something he had to do to preserve that memory and continue the legacy.

His eyes came back to the present and focused on the now. He began to realize it would take a little more planning than what he had already come up with to do. Too much had changed. Too much was gone. What would be left...

"Hey, mister, you in the wrong place?"

The sound of the pool balls had stopped. The players had leaned against the beat-up tables to watch, their faces eerily lit by the table lights hanging just inches over their heads. Some of those faces were smirking. Others looked on, irritated by the interruption to their games. Some didn't care.

"You hear me, old man? You lost *and* deaf?" The apparent leader leaned against the table closest to the entry door. He seemed to think he had made an incredibly funny joke. Two of his followers laughed obediently.

Walt looked at the three young men in front of him with the eye of a storyteller. He already had them categorized as the 'toughs' in the story that automatically started to form in his head. They would be angry young men, unable to find work. All they needed was a job and some encouragement. There would be a cute leading girl in this story. She would find the leader charming when nobody else gave him a second thought. Her father, on the other hand…

"Well?" the youth demanded, not liking the fact that he was being ignored. The old man was looking at him oddly. He felt he was being scrutinized. He didn't like it at all.

"Hey, there, young fella," Walt smiled pleasantly. "How are you?"

Not receiving the reaction he usually got, Kevin stammered, years of training hammered in by his mother pushed against the rebelliousness he was honing to perfection. Still, the guys were watching. Mom was not. "I…I asked you a question, old man." His flunkies snickered. This old man was toast.

"Sorry, I guess I didn't hear it. I used to work here," he told them cheerfully. "Well, not here," indicating the pool hall. "Upstairs."

"There ain't nothing upstairs now."

Walt looked deflated at the news. "Aww, now that's too bad. How long has it been empty?"

Kevin didn't know what to do. He was used to pushing his way around people. It boosted his ego when they turned and fled. Now this harmless old man wanted to chat about the old days. As he watched, the man walked past him and went to the front window. Kevin doubted he could see much. The window was filthy. He knew the man was still waiting for an answer. He looked at his two friends. They shrugged. "Uhm, I don't know. It's a mess up there." Even more so after he and his friends had torn it up just for something to do.

The bar owner edged over to where Walt was standing. He talked quietly so the wanna-be thugs wouldn't hear him. "Mr. Disney…" he swallowed. "I know who you are. I love Mickey Mouse," the old proprietor said in an awestruck whisper. "You probably shouldn't be here, sir.

This ain't so nice a place anymore."

Walt smiled at him and shook his hand. "Aww, they're just having some fun. Boys will be boys."

"Well, these boys…well, they like to cause trouble. Is there anything I can help you with? If not, you might not want to stay too long." His eyes darted nervously to the youths and then back to his honored guest. He didn't want to upset Mr. Disney, but he wouldn't be able to do much to protect him if trouble started.

Walt looked over at the young men. They were glaring at the owner's interference and trying to look tough. Walt lit another cigarette, taking his time, opening, lighting and closing his cigarette lighter. He took a long drag on the lit cigarette. Ignoring the silent plea of the owner, he ambled over to the pool table where the gang had stationed themselves. Standing on the opposite side, he mimicked their stance of leaning on the table, the smoke from his cigarette rising and mingling with their own. There was a seven-ball in front of his hands. He took it up and looked at the number, then put it back on the table, rolling it towards the far end of the table. All eyes watched the trail of that burgundy ball as it banked around the corner pocket and returned to the old man. He caught the ball and sent it on its way again.

"Did you boys ever hear the story of Pinocchio?"

That caught all of them by surprise. They looked at each other open-mouthed. Here this old man was supposed to be afraid of them and now he was going to tell them a bedtime story?

Before the surprise of the moment fled, Walt stood back from the table and began telling them the story of the puppet who wanted to be a real boy. He changed the sound of his voice for Geppetto and Pinocchio and, if they had known who he was, they would have recognized Mickey's voice being used for the Blue Fairy and Jiminy Cricket. When he described Cleo the goldfish, he puffed out his cheeks and 'swam' around the room. He slouched and winked for Honest John and Stromboli and rolled his eyes and slurred for Gideon. When he described the attack of Monstro the Whale, the boys leaned back from the table, so wrapped up were they in the tale by the Master Storyteller. As Geppetto, he held up a lantern as he searched and called piteously for the little lost boy. Pleasure Island came alive for them with cigarettes and pool balls and beer bottles for props.

Mesmerized. That was the word that would have described Walt's audience – much the same as it had been during the storyboard years when he would act out the movie or the cartoon or the Disneyland ride that was in his head and not on paper yet. Only these weren't his artists or his storymen. Still, they were his audience just the same as the others had been. And they were in the story with him. There was no animosity now – only the voice of the storyteller flowing over them, painting the scenes with his voice, illuminating them with his actions.

When he finished and Geppetto had realized his little puppet was a real boy and Pinocchio had realized he needed to listen to his conscience, Walt walked slowly up the rickety stairs to the second floor. There was silence below him. The young men looked at each other. They weren't sure what had just happened, but they knew it was something special.

They left the old man alone as they watched the red-orange glowing tip of his cigarette dangling from his fingertips disappear as he stepped with a knowing stride up to the second floor.

Walt breathed deeply. He was tired. Acting out a story like that took a lot out of him these days. He used to be able to go on all day long with a story like that. He used to… Well, he used to be a younger man, he reminded himself with a grin.

He looked around the desolation that used to be their offices. No chairs. No tables. In some places, no walls. The skylights – those wonderful skylights that had been the boon of every artist and photographer in the building – apparently leaked, if the stains on the floor were any indication. A lot of the windows were broken out and replaced haphazardly with boards. He looked out the window that used to be his. He shook his head with a sigh. So different. The skyline was different. The neighborhood was different.

Time to get to work, he told himself. *But how? It has all changed.*

He examined what was left of the walls. His wall was gone and the brickwork of the exterior was all that was left. The ceiling sagged towards the middle of the room. He wished he could bring in his Disneyland construction crew. They could fix this up in no time flat! But, they were two thousand miles away. And he didn't need a crew for what he wanted to do.

He ran his hand over the brickwork. It was solid. The floor squeaked as he walked over to the window again. He paced off how large his office used to be. *That's right. Table over here. Papers stored there. Chair was here.* The floor seemed pretty sturdy in spite of the shape of the roof, and there was just that one floorboard that squeaked.

Looking at the brick wall and the floor, seeing in his mind the layout of what used to be, he decided what he needed to do. He would need a hammer, probably a screwdriver would be enough instead of a chisel, a couple of nails, and about twenty less years on his back, he chuckled to himself. He would come back tomorrow and fix it up just fine.

He patted the little capsule in his pocket. *Almost home. Almost home.*

WEDNESDAY, MAY 1ST, 2002
8:10 P.M.

"So, up or down?" Lance asked when he tired of bouncing. It was no fun when Adam ignored it.

Adam glanced back up at the ceiling. "I did a pretty thorough search. I didn't see any indication something had been taken down and put back. Going by the assumption Walt did it himself, I don't see him ripping off part of the ceiling."

"That leaves the floor. You said it was pretty solid here. Think it was further back in the room?"

Before Adam answered that, he asked, "Show me again the dimensions the office would have been."

Lance let out a breath. "It was kind of vague." He walked off a portion of the floor. "I would guess about this size, from what I read."

Adam checked it in relation to the window. Lance was making the floor squeak again. Good thing Adam had nieces and nephews and could block out irritating noise. "I need to check where the floor joists are." He used his hammer to sound out the floor. He found the joists were eighteen inches apart running perpendicular to the window. He marked the two closest to the brick. "Okay, now that I have that, now what? The boards aren't warped. Which would he choose? Is there a cross beam?" Talking quietly to himself, Adam sounded the floor in the opposite direction. Lance whistled a drinking song in time to the hammer hits. Again, he was ignored. Asking Lance to move from his favorite spot on the floor, Adam kept moving. He found the cross beam just behind where Lance had been playing. He marked it with the claws of the hammer. "Here is the cross section of the strongest part of the floor. If we are looking for another capsule, it might be placed near the cross. Looks like we have a choice of four boards to try first. What do you think?"

Lance shrugged. He hadn't been listening. The words of the song were still going through his mind. "Whatever you say, boss. Do you think that part of the floor always squeaked?"

"Hard to tell. Would have been easy enough to fix. Want to start there?"

"Be my guest," Lance bowed.

Adam rolled his eyes and hammered the wood around the old nails. This action compressed the wood and lifted the nail heads higher. Once that was done, it was easier to get the claw of the hammer under the nails. With a squeal of protest the nails pulled out. Adam repeated the motions on the other end of the board. He set the floorboard aside and reached for the flashlight.

Mold. That was the first thing that greeted his eyes. He ran the light along the subfloor as far as the beam would reach. The light caught a few items that had fallen through some crack years ago, but they looked more like pencils than anything else.

"Do we need to pull up another board?" Lance asked, peering over his shoulder.

"That might be a good idea. I don't think anyone would mind."

Lance looked around the devastated room. "Nope, nobody said a word."

The next board proved a little stickier. Adam had to bang it from below to loosen the nails. "That's interesting," he muttered. "The first board came up a lot easier."

With the second board removed, there was more light – and more mold. "Hope you don't want to go crawling around down there," Lance grimaced.

"Well, if we don't find anything this way, we just might have to."

"You're shorter," Lance was quick to point out, smiling. There was no way he was going down in that mess.

"Aww, you too delicate?"

Lance refused to be baited as Adam put his mask

back in place and stuck his head into the larger opening, flashing the light back towards the beams. "Delicate has nothing to do with it. You are used to such conditions. I am not."

"I could get you used to them…wait, give me the other flashlight. No, you shine it over here. What's that on the cross beam? No, the other side…Lance, can you see where my light is shining? Over there…What does that look like to you?"

"You think that's it? It's a lot smaller than the last one we found."

"Nothing said they have to be the same size," Adam muttered, thinking. "Back out of the way. I think I can reach it from over here. Hold the light so I can use the hammer. I think it is nailed to the brace." Adam grunted at the effort to loosen the two nails holding the capsule. "Walt had quite a grip," as he got the final nail out and caught the capsule before it fell onto the moldy subfloor. He handed it over to Lance and nailed the two floor boards back into place. Might as well not leave any more holes in that poor old floor.

Lance looked back out the window. "Want to get out of here and look at this in our room?" He had noticed the same black Camero go slowly past their rental car again and watched as it disappeared down the street. "What about the tools?"

"Let's leave them. Can't take them back to California anyway. Maybe someone will put them to good use inside here."

Lance nodded and made his way carefully back to the stairs. It was pretty easy to see their footprints, but they didn't need to hurry. He hoped…

Lance was tense until they pulled into their hotel and turned the car over to the valet. He had constantly checked the rearview mirror, but didn't think they were followed. He had seen the Camero again once they had turned off of 31st Street. It didn't reappear as they put distance between themselves and the McConahy Building.

They had a suite at the Hilton President in downtown Kansas City. It was only three miles from the old building, and about twenty-five miles from the airport. The lobby was an elegant blend of gold and burgundy with marble pillars reaching up to the second balcony. Seating areas were comfortable and plush and were arranged on green and gold Persian rugs. The hotel was located just blocks from the Crossroads Art District. There were also two sports arenas in the area.

Chatting to cover his nervousness, Lance filled Adam in on some of the history of Kansas City that Adam didn't know. Close to the Missouri River and the Kansas River, the city had been the launching point for travelers in the Old West. Along with the nearby towns of Independence and Westport, the Santa Fe Trail, the Oregon Trail, and even the California Trail had all originated from here. Kansas City is now known as the City of Fountains, boasting two hundred fountains and claims to be second only to Rome in the number of fountains. Kansas City also claims to be one of the 'world's capitals of barbecue', something Lance was much more interested in than fountains, shopping districts and architecture.

If Adam had wondered why Lance was so chatty on the short drive to their hotel, he didn't ask. He was looking at the beautiful buildings of the downtown area, including their hotel. It would be nice to do some exploring if they had the time.

On this trip, Lance had brought his laptop computer. They didn't need to be flying back again in another three days. They could research the next clue – if there was one – and see if they needed to stay longer. They were quiet in the ornate elevator up to their floor. Dusty from their excursion into the old building, they didn't want to draw any more attention than necessary. They could always tell people they were prospecting along the Missouri River.

When they got to their suite, Lance handed Adam the capsule. "I have to take a shower. I can still smell that mold."

Adam set the plastic container on the coffee table and took up the hotel directory. He looked over the extensive room service menu and ordered a couple of Kansas City Strip Steaks for their dinner. Having had more time to pack for this trip, he took his own shower in his room and changed into a clean set of clothes. Lance was already sitting down to eat when he came out. "I'm glad to see you waited for me," he commented dryly as he saw Lance tearing into his steak.

Lance didn't even look up. "Like one pig waits for another."

"You do realize one of those dinners is mine, right?"

Lance dipped his bite of steak in the deep red barbecue sauce. Closing his eyes, he savored the rich flavor. "Then you had better hurry and eat it," he mumbled between bites.

As Adam started on his meal, he asked, "You open the capsule yet?"

Lance shook his head. "For that, I did wait for you."

"I never did ask. Did you find out what the Santa Fe train stocks are worth?"

Lance grinned over his last bite. "Yes, I did. Called a stock broker friend. He took down the year – 1929 – and the stock numbers, etc. They are each worth about $1000."

Adam's face fell a little. "Oh. I thought, since they were so old..." He stopped and bit back his disappointment. He didn't want to sound either greedy or unappreciative.

Lance shrugged and speared Adam's last bite of steak. "Still, it is a nice, well-preserved piece of history. Just the paper itself can go for a couple hundred. He said he could move them for us if we wanted. If trains make a huge comeback in years to come, they could be worth more."

"Hmmm," was all Adam said to that. If airline travel hadn't become so prevalent, who knew what they could have been worth? But, as Lance said, historically they are interesting and worth keeping.

Now they had another piece of history to consider. And it was sitting there on the coffee table waiting for them.

Lance let Adam do the honors again in opening the capsule. This one was about six inches long and three inches around. The seal was just as tough to get open as the first one they found.

Adam set the cap aside, and, heart pounding, tilted the plastic. Nothing fell out. Looking inside, he saw paper rolled, hugging the rounded sides of the container. Making sure there was no barbecue sauce anywhere on his fingers, he reached inside and caught an edge.

There were three pieces of paper in all. The largest piece, the one that had been carefully wrapped around the others, was yellowed plain stationery covered with writing. There was a business card, and a piece of paper with a torn side.

Adam handed the largest piece to Lance and he examined the business card. He recognized it from his research. It was yellowed with age, but still very clear and distinct. The middle of the card proclaimed in black letters 'Laugh-O-Gram Films Inc.' Behind the dark wording were the words Laugh-O-Gram, again in faint color, but inside the oversized 'O' was the picture of a cartoonist at work on an easel, pictures flying off left and right. The bottom left corner had 'Walt Disney, Cartoonist', and the right corner had the address of the building in which they had just found this capsule. He knew Walt had drawn the cartoonist himself. There was a later business card, with that picture prominent on the front. However, this card he was holding had been made first.

Lance was reading through the sheet he had been

handed. It was all done in Walt's own handwriting. From the words, he could tell it was a script for an 'Alice's Wonderland' episode. At the bottom were drawings of Julius the Cat with directions on the actions he was to take in a certain scene. Lance wasn't familiar with all fifty-six Alice episodes, but he thought this might be one that never got produced. The hand-drawn pictures of Julius the Cat were fascinating. Lance knew there was a succession from Julius the Cat to Oswald the Lucky Rabbit to Mickey Mouse as Walt's studio – and life – progressed. Lance fingered the writing and the drawings, knowing that Walt Disney himself had written and drawn the words and images he was holding. Like the diary, the page felt electric.

The third paper looked familiar to the men. After having spent so much time reading and re-reading the diary, Adam knew this page had been ripped out of the little black book. It was the right size and paper quality. Had Walt brought the diary with him when he hid the clues? Had it all been written ahead of time and concealed when opportunity presented itself? There were so many questions and absolutely no way to get any answers. That is, unless Walt himself left them something more to find.

Well, there was only one way to find out. They had to keep following the clues and see where they led.

They just hoped it would start getting closer to home…

When they read the next clue they were pretty sure they needn't have brought Lance's computer. They knew where Walt – and now they themselves – were headed after his time in Kansas City was finished – California. The note told them:

**"You ready for some prospecting?
Triple R
Just sing Mario part of the campfire song."**

Well, at least they *hoped* it was back in California.

CHAPTER 5

THE TRIPLE R

FRIDAY, MAY 3RD, 2002
3:00P.M.

"**Y**ou have no sense of adventure," Lance sniffed at Adam.

Adam was tossing the empty gym bag back into his closet. "Hey, I ain't singing nothin' to nobody! You sing. You're the one with no inhibitions," he grumbled, heading back into his living room. "And why is my computer reminding me to feed you?? I can't get the damned thing to shut off!"

"Well, be that as it may, we still need to find the particulars before we know what there is to sing and to whom," Lance pointed out, ignoring the outburst. He could hear the soft chime coming from Adam's computer. It would keep doing that until Adam canceled the reminder Lance had programmed. Maybe he shouldn't have used a password-protected command….

"Why in the world am I getting all this spam?? I paid good money for that program. Look at this! Two hundred messages in the three days we were gone!" Adam took up his mouse to rid his computer of all the unwanted junk mail, still mumbling and cursing at the Internet.

Lance could have told Adam his spam program was

temporarily turned off….Maybe later. "You have any idea what the Triple R stands for?" he asked instead.

"Reading, writing and 'rithmetic?'"

"Isn't that usually written as 'The Three R's'? No, I don't think that would be it. Where should we start? The 'Triple R' or the 'Mario' Walt named?"

Adam was still deleting emails. He had to go one at a time as they were mixed in with vendor quotes, personal mail, and about fifteen messages from Mrs. Anderson with new ideas for her bathroom.

In a moment of weakness Lance tried to be considerate. "You know, you can set up filters to send different types of email to different folders. One for business, one for pleasure, one for Mrs. Anderson," as he read over Adam's shoulder some of the messages. "That way you know what you have in your inbox and what you need to read."

"Now you're being helpful?" Adam glanced up as he deleted another twenty spams in a row.

"I'll admit that watching you work at your computer is fascinating, but we really need to start on the clues. At the speed you're going, we will be here all week."

Adam knew when he was beat. He got up from his office chair. "Show me."

Stifling his grin, Lance sat at the computer.   He brought up the Organize section, made a few folders, created some instant filters, and – nice guy that he was – turned the spam filter back on. After highlighting all the messages left in Adam's inbox, he hit the Reorganize button and everything went to its new home. "Any other folders you need, make them here," Lance pointed with the mouse, "and then the computer will do the rest."

"What is that flashing yellow thing?" Adam indicated an icon on the bottom of his screen.

Lance was all innocence. "That? That looks like your spam filter."

Eyes narrowed, Adam was starting to get the picture. "Where was it before? Hey, were you messing with my computer?"

"Now when would I have had the time to do that?" Lance asked, not a trace of guile on his face. "I've been with you either in Missouri or on the job with that delightful Rose."

"Then where did that reminder to 'Feed Lance' come from and why can't I get rid of it?"

Lance shrugged and got up from the chair. "I have a different type of computer than your dinosaur. How would I know?"

Adam knew there was no use pointing out that Lance had, in just two minutes, fixed a problem on Adam's computer that would have taken him hours. "Fine, I'll figure it out myself." As Lance walked back to the sofa, Adam could have sworn he heard a mumbled "password", but wasn't about to ask.

Lance turned his attention to the clue that was sitting on the table along with the Alice script and business card. "Think the key words are 'prospecting' and 'campfire song'? They kinda go together."

"In what way?" His attention was on those flashing, pinging 'Feed Lance' reminders. There were three of them – one for each day they were gone.

Lance raised one shoulder and thought out loud. "Oh, prospecting to me means looking for gold and campfire would be cowboys sitting around after supper swapping stories, or, in this case, a song. Did you read anything about Walt doing any prospecting or being interested in it?"

Not finding an obvious turn-off button for the flashing messages, Adam sat back in his chair, hands folded on his flat stomach. The chair creaked as he rocked it back and forth, thinking. "No, I can't say I have read anything like that. I know Lillian's family was into prospecting, but I don't know if that would apply to this clue now. Their money dried up years ago."

Lance thought about it a while. "Think it is worth following up? Or do you think we should take a different approach?"

"Well, think about the diary," Adam suggested. "Walt indicated our search would be about things that were important to him when they first happened and were important to him at the time he wrote the diary. I'm not sure if he would go into Lillian's ancestors, do you?"

"Maybe we should leave that for later, in case we come up dry with other tactics."

Adam nodded, thoughtful. "Okay with me. You think the main clue would be about gold, huh? The only thing I can think of that would remotely relate is the Mineral King Ski area in the Sequoias that he was very interested in developing."

"But it never got finished, did it?"

Adam thought back to the revolutionary development Walt had been planning. Working with the environment, he would have turned the skiing industry on its ear – much like he did with the amusement park industry. Unfortunately, cancer had caught up with Walt before any plans had been firmed and finalized. After his death, the momentum on the project slowly faded until a few, vocal opponents kept the project tied up in court. The project was finally dropped in the early 1970's. "No, it never made it. It would have been something though. Not only for skiers in the winter, but hikers in the summer. It would have been a year-around destination."

"I didn't think you skied," Lance questioned. "It sounds like you regret the project was never finished."

"Nope…you're right. I don't ski, but I sure would have gone there to see it. Who knows? Maybe I would have taken lessons."

"Well," Lance settled back onto the cushions of the sofa, "it doesn't sound like that is the place we should do our research. I think the term 'bonfire' would relate to a ski resort rather than a 'campfire'. 'Campfire' is more rustic and Westerny."

"'Westerny'? Is that a word?" Adam grinned. "Thought you minored in Literature."

"And Art...and Psychology," he muttered under his breath. He heard Adam's computer chime again. "So, are you going to feed me or let me starve to death?"

At the sound of the chime, Adam glanced at his computer. 'Feed Lance' was flashing in the middle of his screen again. Adam groaned and ran a hand over his tired eyes. "You want to fix that for me?"

Lance was already on his feet. "Nope. I need to go eat. You want to get a fresh start tomorrow morning?"

Bringing up his Organizer, Adam checked his schedule for Saturday. "I need to check in with Scott and see how the Anderson job is going. And, no, you can't go with me, so don't ask. Give me a call tomorrow afternoon and we'll compare notes."

Lance just nodded his farewell and left, heading for the nearest restaurant. Adam went over and stared into his almost-empty refrigerator.

SATURDAY, MAY 4TH, 2002
7:00P.M.

Lance didn't get back to Adam's until Saturday evening at almost 7:00 – just in time for another ringing on Adam's computer as a reminder to feed him. He sat tiredly on the sofa and put his feet up as if he had been on them all day. Adam noticed his face looked like he had been in the sun a lot.

"You spend the day at the beach?" Adam asked, half joking, half curious.

"No," Lance replied shortly, his head back against the cushions. "*That* would have been enjoyable."

When he said no more, Adam knew that was all the

information he was going to get. He knew Lance hadn't been on the Anderson job as he had been there all day with Scott fending off suggestions. Lance looked beat. That was the word for it – beat. "You too tired to work on the clues?"

He thought Lance was already asleep. His eyes were closed and he hadn't moved a muscle – not that that was too unusual for Lance…

"No, I'm fine," came the non-enthused reply. "You have any cola? I could use some caffeine." Lance issued a tired "Thanks" when Adam came in from the kitchen and handed him the cold drink. He ran the can over his warm face first. He knew Adam's eyes were on him, watching and curious, but he gave no explanation for his current condition. This wasn't something he was going to share. But, he did have news that would take Adam's mind off his personal life: "I think I found the answer to the 'Triple R' thing."

That worked. Adam's face lit up. "You did? Wow, that's great! I haven't had any time to even start on it. What did you find?"

With a mild grunt of effort, Lance sat up on the sofa. He opened one of Adam's reference books to the back and did a quick search in the Index. Not finding what he needed, he tried another. In the second book he found what he wanted and opened to the specified page. He handed the book to Adam and pointed. It seemed too much effort for him to talk.

Adam gave him another curious glance, and then read what Lance indicated. "Who the heck are Spin and Marty?"

Lance gave a little smile. "Seems we are too young for this particular clue. I asked around some today while I was…uhm, out. I mentioned the words 'Triple R' to a few people. Our age group and younger had no idea what it meant. Then I asked some women who must have been in their late 40's. I didn't ask their age…just that they looked older than you and me. Anyway, they said immediately, 'oh you mean the Triple R Ranch? I loved Spin and Marty!'" He took another swig of the cola. The caffeine seemed to be taking effect. He was getting more animated.

"Did you ask what that meant?" Adam interrupted. His finger was still in the book, but he would rather hear it from Lance.

Lance nodded. "You've heard of the Mickey Mouse Club." It was more of a statement than a question.

"Of course."

"Well, *Spin and Marty* was an episodic show that appeared regularly on the original Mickey Mouse Club. The Triple R Ranch was where the boys lived. It was kind of a cowboy camp for boys. It apparently was very popular. Possibly the Davy Crockett fad helped. Anyway, later I asked a few more people who looked about the same age group and they all made the same reference."

"That's great." Adam thought for a minute. "It was something you could ask about without arousing suspicion as to why." Adam pursed his lips in an unconscious smile. "Very good. Was it filmed at the studio? Think we need to do some 'prospecting' around there, a figurative digging for clues, maybe?"

Lance didn't answer those questions. He had something else on his mind. "There is one thing that bothers me," he brought out, "the time frame of this show. This is a lot later than the time period we just left in Kansas City. Walt didn't come to Hollywood until 1923. This show came out around 1955. That is a jump of more than thirty years. What we have found so far has kept to the timeline of Walt's life story."

Adam considered what Lance had just said. "I see what you mean." Then he got the diary. After reading through it again, he remarked: "It doesn't actually say we would follow his life exactly. Just going to important events. Maybe mixing them up makes it more of a challenge."

"Or," Lance paused. "Perhaps we are on the wrong track," Lance suggested, holding his hand out for the diary. "But it doesn't feel like the wrong track, though. That's my problem."

"Did you have any time to look for a 'Mario' who was connected with the show?"

"Yes, I tried that right before I came over. I came up blank. I think we need to read more about the show itself and see if there is some campfire song that was popular back then. You keep reading in that book and I'll see what I can find on your computer."

Adam watched warily as Lance sat in his chair and picked up the mouse. He wasn't sure he wanted Lance near his computer again. Lance caught Adam's look and waved him off. "I'm too tired to play," was how Lance put it. Lance began a search and clicked on a couple of high-lighted results.

Appeased, Adam started reading about Spin and Marty and their adventures on the Triple R Ranch in the book Lance had handed him earlier that he was still hold-ing.

"Where's Newhall?" Lance's question broke into his concentration.

"I don't know. About an hour, hour and a half north of here. Why?" Adam answered without looking up from the pages of his book.

"I found the ranch."

Adam dropped his book and bounded over to the com-puter. He looked at his computer monitor as Lance rolled the office chair to the side so Adam could see what he had found. "Golden Oak Ranch?" he read on the screen. "I thought it was the Triple R," said Adam, a little puzzled.

"It was called the Triple R on the show. The actual lo-cation was at the Golden Oak Ranch," explained Lance.

"I still don't see what this all has to do with prospect-ing. The Triple R was kind of a dude ranch, wasn't it? Or am I missing something?"

Lance must have been tired. He let an obvious chance to say something smart to Adam go by. "No, there is some history to the Golden Oak Ranch we don't know about. Look at this picture."

It was a historical marker plaque that declared that 'on this site in 1842 gold was discovered by Francisco Lopez'. The marker was planted next to a huge old oak tree. Further reading revealed this tree was located on the outskirts of the Western town that was built – and still used – by movie companies.

"So we get to dig for real gold?" Adam murmured, confused as to where all this was leading. "Wait. Look at this sign."

'Keep Out! No Trespassing!' was posted all over the entry gate to the ranch.

"Think that means us?" Lance asked with a grin.

"That never stopped you before," Adam said under his breath. "We need to look into this some more. You keep reading here and I will see if any mention is made in my books."

"Will do." Lance finished his cola and dropped the can somewhere near the waste basket.

"What did you find?"

Adam looked over his notes. "Before 1959, when *Spin and Marty* was being filmed, the ranch was leased. Then Walt bought the original 315 acres in 1959 for $300,000. Over the next several years, the size of the ranch was enlarged to over seven hundred acres. The Disney movie *Toby Tyler* was filmed there in 1960. The ranch is still in use today and is off limits to the general public. What did you find?"

"Similar stuff. There is a green guest house where Walt stayed when he visited the site. One thing I found you might be interested in. There's an assistant on the ranch who has been there since 1964. Guess what his nickname is?"

"Walt?"

"Funny. No. Mario."

Adam was surprised. "No way! Is he still there? It's been thirty-eight years!"

"Yep. He is also very knowledgeable on the history of the ranch and all the movies that have been filmed there, one report said," Lance recited.

"I don't suppose you found out how to contact him?"

Being more rested now and the caffeine having done its trick, Lance was more himself again. He gave Adam a wide grin. "Of course I did. There's a phone number for movie companies who want to rent out the ranch."

Adam looked deflated. "Is that the only way to get in? We have to rent the place?"

"I didn't say that. We haven't tried the number yet. It's too late today, and tomorrow is Sunday. I would guess bright and early Monday morning would be the best time to try."

"So, are we supposed to sing to him over the phone or something?" Adam still found that part of the clue unsettling.

Lance had forgotten. "Oh. You might be right. You find any campfire song yet?"

Adam shook his head and indicated his books. "There's hardly any mention of the show at all, let alone some song out of it. You seem to be having more success with my computer. Want to keep at it a while longer?"

"Before I log off here, do you want to see the layout of the ranch?"

"The Triple R?"

"No, the Golden Oak. It says it isn't to scale, but that isn't too important."

Adam came over. "You really need to show me how you find so much in my computer. I just use it for business."

"Oh, I can find all kinds of things on your computer,"

Lance remarked with a hidden grin. Adam was too busy looking at the map to challenge him.

The map showed a long, narrow strip of land off the Antelope Valley Freeway, Highway 14. The ranch was broken into different regions – Central Region, Placerita Creek Region, Lake Region, Canyon Region, and Bottom Region. Each section had its own merits – and pictures – so film companies would know which would suit their needs. Besides the full Western Town, there were also different style cabins by the lakes and creeks, a white pillared mansion, a covered bridge, different style barns, meadows, dusty trails, corrals, a waterfall, river, and a guest house for the crews if they didn't bring their own accommodations. The names of the locations were just as colorful as the map: 'Moonshine Meadow'. 'Cherokee Trail Set'. 'Outlaw Shack'. 'Toby Tyler Bridge'. 'Big West Meadow'. The men found the Western/Ghost Town and the titled oak tree to be located in the Lake Region. They also noticed the main clusters of buildings were far enough away from the Highway that there would be no encroaching noise at all. It was perfect for movies set over a hundred years ago…provided airplanes or jets with vapor trails didn't fly overhead during filming.

Both men hoped they would be allowed on the ranch, and not just for the clue, either. It sounded like a fascinating place to poke around. On horseback would be nice…

TUESDAY, MAY 7TH, 2002
10:50A.M.

Tuesday morning Lance showed up on the Anderson job. Fortunately for all concerned, Mrs. Anderson was at a spa for the day. Going up to Adam without any preamble, he asked, "Do you want to drive, or do you want me to?"

Adam and Scott were checking the newly-delivered

Jacuzzi tub for any possible visible damage. It was pink and large enough to comfortably bathe four people. Needless to say, the pink color had been a special order, as had everything else on this job. Adam wasn't going to let Ben the Beam Destroyer anywhere near it. "Drive what?" he asked distractedly. "Wait a minute, is that a scratch or just delivery dust?"

"Either your work truck which declares 'Michaels Construction' to the world, or my elegant little Mercedes?"

"Even though I know I am going to regret asking, what are you talking about?" Adam got up from examining the tub. Before Lance could respond, Adam turned to his foreman. "It was just dust. It looks perfect. Now if it just stays this way for four or five days while the plumber finishes his underground connections. Scott, can you please build the platform for the spa personally?"

"Okay, boss, you got it."

"We have a two-o'clock appointment with Mario at the Golden Oak Ranch today," Lance informed him with the same inflection he would have used to say they were going two blocks away for lunch.

Frowning, Adam glanced at his watch. "It's already 11:00."

"That's why I came early," Lance grinned. His attention switched to the tub. "So, can I try out the Jacuzzi?"

"Keep away from it!" Adam warned, blocking his path. "We need to get it around to the back for safe-keeping. After it's installed, then your use of it is between you and Mrs. Anderson."

Lance just rocked back and forth on his feet. He wouldn't get anywhere near this house after it was installed. "Well?"

Adam started to measure the lip of the tub and checked it against his blueprint. "Well what?"

"Unless you want to go to the ranch on an empty stomach, we really need to get going."

Adam seemed to be counting silently to himself. By the time he got to ten, something else had caught Lance's wandering attention. He had gone inside to say hello to the crew. Adam was now apparently chanting. *'Calm. Calm. Calm.'*

"Didn't know you took up yoga, boss," Scott remarked with an amused look on his face. These two were more fun to watch than Laurel and Hardy.

"Only way I can keep from killing him," Adam said dryly, looking from his watch to the blueprints to the tub and using an interesting choice of swear words under his breath.

"You need to take off?"

Adam nodded slowly. "Again." He gave a sigh. "Everything's going pretty smoothly right now. Double check the measurements of the tub. They aren't quite what we were told by the manufacturer. The plumber might have to move the drain and the faucet a little. I don't know if there is cell phone reception out where we're going, but give a call if you need something."

"Will do. See you tomorrow?"

"Yes, hopefully this won't take more than the afternoon. Thanks again, Scott."

With a nod, Scott took the set of blueprints from Adam and started measuring the tub.

Lance came back out to the front. He was holding a bottle of cold water. Adam wasn't sure if he got it from the crew cooler or from Mrs. Anderson's refrigerator. *Not going to ask. Not going to ask.* He knew the crew wouldn't mind. Lance had had four large pizzas delivered to them one Friday afternoon right before shut-down. They would do anything for him. "Ready?"

Adam looked down at his dusty jeans and sweat-stained T-shirt. Well, they were going to a ranch out in the country. Adam's work boots were more suited than Lance's spotless loafers. Lance was dressed as if he were going to a country club social. Adam smiled for the first time since Lance showed up. "Yep, ready. Follow me to my place and we'll go in your car." Yes, the 'elegant, little' black Mercedes would look good covered with ranch dust.

Adam didn't bother changing clothes. He just parked his truck in his assigned spot at the apartments and got in Lance's car. They stopped at a drive-thru for lunch. Thankfully traffic was light as they headed north on the I-5. Lance bit into his hamburger, steering with his left knee.

After he finished his own mouthful, Adam asked, "So, how did you get us into the ranch?"

Lance checked his side mirror and banked into the right lane. "It wasn't too difficult. Mario answered the phone himself. I told him 'Walt sent me'. And before he could hang up, I crooned a little 'Yippi-A, Yippi-I, Yippi-O' to him. I think I stunned him."

"Not surprising," Adam mumbled. "I am guessing that is part of the campfire song the clue mentioned?"

Lance ignored him. "Mario was silent for a long time on the other end of the line. He finally told me he never expected to hear that song after all these years. Then *he* asked *me* when we could come out."

"Wow, it really worked!" Now Adam was stunned. He thought they were going to have to somehow sneak onto the ranch, dodging a hail of bullets and snarling dogs.

"He wants to see the note, of course. He watched Walt write it. I think he wants to see it as much for old times sake as anything else."

"So what do we do once we get there?"

Lance shrugged and swerved back into the fast lane. "He said he will tell us. Watch for Highway 14. Then we need the Placerita Canyon exit."

They were quiet with their own thoughts the rest of the way. They found the entrance to the ranch which looked just like it did in the pictures – forbidding. There were more signs posted warning people away. One, as Adam feared, warned of the guard dogs. The dire warnings were a sharp contrast to the warm greeting that awaited them. Lance had the clue paper in his wallet. Stepping between Mario and Adam, he had opened his wallet so only their host could see it. Mario looked at something Lance slid out of a pocket in the wallet, nodded once, and then took the diary page in his hands. As he read, a smile slowly crept over Mario's face. He handed the clue back to Lance with a far-away look in his eyes. "Yes, that was from Mr. Walt. Pull forward through the gates, and then follow me in your car, please." He climbed back into his pickup after he shut the gates behind the Mercedes.

Heading north, they drove on a well-maintained road through a thick stand of trees. These same impenetrable trees lined the entire border of the property, shielding the fascinating contents from passers-by. It wouldn't do for drivers to see a shoot-out in a meadow as they were navigating the winding outer road. The trees also hid the vistas from the guys in the car as they drove on; their tires produced a low cloud of dust that dissipated in the breeze behind them. Disappointed they were seeing nothing of the ranch, the two friends were glad when they came suddenly to an open meadow. There was a huge parking lot, a cavernous barn, and a couple of outbuildings. After parking, Lance and Adam climbed into Mario's pickup and were given a brief, but very detailed history of the ranch. They caught glimpses of some of the cabins and buildings they had read about as they drove north towards the Lake Region. Their earlier disappointment dissipated as they were driven through the main street of the empty Western set. There was no shooting going on that week, but a crew was expected next week to shoot a commercial. Mario stopped the truck and pointed out the legendary oak tree. Lance was going to open the truck's door, but was stopped by Mario.

"That is not for you," Mario stated in a soft but clear statement. "It is protected by the Historical Society. I just thought you would like to see it." He took his foot off the brake and continued to drive past the lake and went up a ridge. The little green wooden guest house with the rectangle of a pool out front was sitting there just like they had seen in the pictures from the website Lance had found. Mario pulled up near it and stopped. They looked at him expectantly. He gave them a little smile. "Yes, this is where you get out." He met them at the back of the truck. Rummaging through the tools, he reluctantly handed them a flashlight and a hammer and then pulled out a ladder. "This is what I was told to give you."

"Do you know what it is we're supposed to find?"

He shook his head. "No. It is not for me to know. I was entrusted with this much only. It was important to Mr. Walt, and I would do whatever he asked of me." He sighed and looked out over the pool. "He is very much missed. I will be back in two hours." He stared at the hammer as if he would like to take it back.

Adam thought he understood the reason for Mario's reluctance to leave them with tools. "I am a General Contractor. I won't do any damage." Adam then indicated Lance with a movement of his chin. Lance was busy wiping dust off of his shoes with the back of his pant legs. "And neither will he."

Adam was scrutinized with dark eyes. The older man just nodded once and got back in his truck. Mario felt better now leaving them at the guest house. Besides, there was work he needed to do. The pristine condition of the grounds required his constant care.

Setting the ladder down near the entry, Adam and Lance turned to face the rectangular house. They wondered how many people had slept there since Walt's time. Leaving the door ajar and pulling open the curtains for light, they came to the conclusion it hadn't been very many. It didn't have the feel of a frequently used house. There was a faint sheen of dust on the few pieces of furniture and the air was stale – a condition that the open door, and now windows, was alleviating.

Nothing obvious jumped out at Adam and Lance. But, then, when it came to the clues Walt left, it never did. There were only two rooms – the living room/kitchen in which they were standing and a bedroom with a small attached bathroom. The walls in the living room were paneled in a light oak that matched the kitchen cabinets. The sofa was beige and saggy with a small oak coffee table and side table that had a western-style lamp sitting on it. The bedroom was painted white with a small desk and chair in a corner, and another chair under the window. The desk proved to be empty. There was nothing stuck up under the drawers. There were no false backs or bottoms. The cabinets in the kitchen were full of inexpensive dishes, glassware, and cooking pots. The refrigerator was cold, but empty. The sofa cushions proved to be just cushions. They moved the sofa, sliding it away from the wall and carefully tipping it forward; there was no secret panel under the sofa or any tell-tale sign of another clue hidden under the springs and stuffing. Pictures on the walls held no secrets. The bathroom was tiny and empty. There was nothing under or behind the double bed. The chest of drawers and the night stand were just as empty as the desk had proved to be. The closet in the bedroom had only a few wire hangers; the bare bulb light fixture was activated by a long string with a lead washer tied to the end of it.

They were almost out of options when Adam glanced up at the light fixture. Next to it was the access panel to the attic above them. He shone the flashlight on the panel itself and saw nothing. But, on one side of the molding around the panel was something scratched into the old wood. He went out to get the ladder and carefully carried it through the little house. Lance, who had still been searching the living room, followed him into the bedroom. Adam only needed to climb two steps to see that the scratching read '**WED**'.

Reaching higher, he pushed up on the access panel and slid it over out of the way. Up two more steps, his head was inside the hot, musty attic. The flashlight shone on cobwebs long abandoned. He made a slow circle of the tiny space. It, too, seemed to be completely empty.

Then, as he turned to look around the other way, leaning sideways to shine the flashlight on the area behind him, there it was. He found it directly opposite from his position on the ladder, nailed onto one of the ceiling joists. A dust-covered capsule. This one was larger than what they found in the McConahy building. It was closer to the size they had found buried in Marceline, Missouri. It was about fourteen inches long and six inches in diameter. Other than the dust coating it, the plastic was in perfect condition.

"We have about fifteen minutes before Mario comes back. Do you want to open it here?" Lance seemed inclined to opening the capsule, but he left the decision up to Adam.

Adam shook it gently. There was no clinking noise. It must hold paperwork. "Let me get the ladder down and outside again." He closed the access panel and folded up the ladder, careful again as he carried it out through the rooms. Other than some dust falling from the open attic, nothing looked changed or moved.

Lance finally released the seals on the end cap. His hands were cleaner than Adam's, so he pulled out the rolled-up papers inside; he found a sealed envelope and two pieces of paper. The smaller paper looked identical to the one that held their last clue. The larger paper was heavier, not exactly parchment, but good stock in an off-white color. There were Disney characters banked around the top edges of the form. The words in bold, flowery script said 'Grant Deed' and was dated 1965.

There was an embossed Seal of California in the middle of the bottom section, banked by signatures. He quickly read through the legalese and handed it over to Adam. At Adam's curious look, he explained with meticulous wording, "Walt left us something."

Adam looked at the form. Still being a renter, he wasn't familiar with documents such as this. "Is it shares in something like the railroad stock?"

Lance suddenly grinned. "Something like that. He left us this little house. And the pool, I assume," he added off-handedly.

Adam was stunned. "No fooling? I thought this ranch was all privately owned now."

Taking back the deed, Lance looked it over again. "Everything except this little piece of dirt. It grants us full access whenever we want, providing we don't interrupt any filming or make nuisances of ourselves."

"Wow. That's probably why this place doesn't feel like anyone had been here in a while."

Lance nodded. "It can be assumed nobody knew exactly who owned it since this deed was hidden all these years."

Still dazed, Adam wandered out the front door and perched on the edge of the ladder. He looked around at the ridge they were on and the trees off to the west. He could tell by their curving line there was a river cutting through them. He could hear nothing. Absolute silence. Oh, he knew it would be different if a crew was filming something. The Western Town was just below the ridge there. But, unless there was a chance airplane flying overhead, it was perfectly silent. It felt odd to him after living in bustling Orange County all his life.

Lance had come out to join him. Both men stood in silence while they thought about the gift Walt had given them. In the stillness of the ranch, they could hear the pickup long before it got to them. "Do we tell Mario about this?" was Adam's question.

Lance thought about it, listening to the truck getting closer. "Well, he welcomed us with almost open arms. He knew this was 'something' that Walt set up. He is devoted to the ranch and preserving it. He was entrusted with this secret almost forty years ago and kept it. I would vote 'yes'."

Nodding slowly, Adam tended to agree with him. Before they could discuss it any further, Mario pulled into sight and parked. There was a look of curiosity in his eyes, but he wasn't going to question them. Adam picked up the ladder and carried it to the back of the truck. By the time he came back for the hammer and flashlight and pulled the door of the guest house shut, Lance was showing the deed to their host.

Silent, Mario looked it over carefully. He handed it back to Lance and held out his hand. "Welcome to the Ranch. We will be very glad to have you. I only ask that you give us a little advance notice when you would like to come."

"Just like that?" Adam asked, stopping at the tailgate of Mario's truck holding the hammer and the flashlight, still somewhat astonished by both the treasure and the reception of it.

"Yes," Mario said simply. "Just like that." He paused a few moments while he thought about how to explain it. "Mr. Walt did a wonderful thing in setting up this ranch. At the time, there were many ranches like this. Many of the big studios had their own. But, Mr. Walt knew his would last. The others, they folded. Now they come here. We have done much towards keeping the land just so. If you have been entrusted with this little house, then we know you will take the same good care of it that we would. I think you know the film crews have the right of way out here. But, if you would like to ride, there are horses in the Bottom Region."

"Who would we need to let know about this?" Adam asked, pointing at the deed in Lance's hands.

"It is done now. I will tell only the ones who need to know. You have only to call."

They piled back into the cab of the truck and Mario drove them back to Lance's car. At the clearing, they shook hands with Mario and promised to see him again soon. As the entry gates clanged shut behind them, they gave him a final wave. In the excitement of the day, Adam had forgotten all about something: He would have liked the thick coat of dust that covered the entire Mercedes.

As they drove back towards the freeway, Adam remembered something else. "The next clue! I forgot all about it with the Deed and all. Do you have it?"

He knew the sealed envelope was with the Grant Deed on the back seat behind them. Lance pulled the clue out of his shirt pocket before entering the onramp for the Antelope Valley Freeway. Handing it over to Adam, he asked, "What does it say? I didn't read it either."

Adam looked over the familiar handwriting with a growing sense of excitement, not only just from the treasures they were finding, either; they were visiting the places important to Walt. They were learning more about his history. And now, they talked to someone who had actually known him. This was fascinating to Adam. He knew Lance was excited too, but Lance wasn't as much of an enthusiast as himself. Had Lance looked over, he would have noticed a melancholy shadow sweep across Adam's face. *Oh, wouldn't Be...*No, he wasn't going to think of 'her'. Yes, she would have loved all this. But, he blew it. Maybe some day he would run across her and tell…

"Are you going to read it or just stare dreamily out the window?" Lance's amused voice came through Adam's reflection. *I cannot believe he is thinking about her again! Wonder if he'll ever figure it out. Probably not*, Lance thought while grinning at his friend.

Adam snapped back to the present. *Good thing*

Lance isn't a mind reader. I'd never hear the end of this.
"Yeah, sorry," Adam mumbled, focusing his eyes on the clue.

"This is the house the little princess built. Check out my desk. Hand the envelope to Manny, Mo, or Jack if you can't find it."

CHAPTER 6

THE HOUSE THE
LITTLE PRINCESS BUILT

TUESDAY, MAY 7TH, 2002
5:15P.M.

"We have to go to Pep Boys??" Adam had to read it again.

"Well, unless Walt was secretly into auto repair, I doubt it. Who is the little princess?" Lance asked as he slowed for the rush hour traffic as they neared the turnoff for the I-5 Freeway. The freeway was becoming filled as people headed home from work. Lance looked over and smiled at a blonde in a red Mustang convertible. Catching his gaze, she moved her sunglasses down off her eyes to get a better look at him. She looked sorry when the traffic started moving again and Lance pulled ahead out of sight.

Adam shrugged. "I'm not sure. Is he talking about animation or a nickname for someone? A house for a princess would be a castle, right?"

"Does he mean Sleeping Beauty's castle in Disneyland?"

"Well, how would a desk figure in there? Walt didn't have an office inside the castle...At least none that I know of," Adam amended. "Why would he need one if he had his apartment over the Fire House?"

Getting no answer, he glanced over at Lance. Lance was looking at his side mirror. The blonde was getting closer as his lane of traffic had slowed again. "You're going to miss the I-5 turnoff if you don't get in the far right lane," Adam reminded him.

Lance gave a sigh and one last look in his side mirror. Signaling, he managed to swerve over two lanes without even a horn blasting him. "Happy now?" he grumbled.

Not knowing what was going on, Adam was confused. "Did I miss something?"

Lance watched the red Mustang continue south on the Antelope Freeway as he slowly inched towards the I-5. "No. I did," as a manicured hand gave him a final wave before disappearing.

"Care to explain? I have no idea what you are talking about."

"Nope. Just wistful yearnings."

Adam gave a sudden laugh. "Oh, now I get it! Blonde, brunette or redhead?"

"Blonde of course. Brunettes are your thing," he answered with a sly smile over to Adam.

"I refuse to be baited," Adam declared smugly. "Shall we get back to the little princess or do you want to keep sparring?"

"'I refuse to engage in a battle of wits with an un armed opponent' ", he quoted.

Adam just smiled and let Lance think he had the moment. They had been friends too long to take words like that seriously. "To pass the time, name all the princesses up until the 1960's."

"Well, there's Princess Margaret of Great Britain…."

"Smart ass. How about Disney princesses," Adam cut in.

"Well, you weren't specific. How about Sleeping Beauty and Cinderella? Are they more to your liking?"

"They are both blondes, so no," Adam had to throw in. "There's Snow White. Alice wasn't considered a princess, was she?"

"I don't think so. What is the name of that princess in *Peter Pan* they rescue?"

"You mean Tiger Lily? Ok, she would fit. Ariel, Belle, and Jasmine were later in time, so they wouldn't be included. There might have been a cartoon with Minnie as a princess. I'd have to look it up. Any others?" Adam finished.

"Gosh, I don't know. Animated princess movies weren't my favorites. So what do we have so far in regards to princesses and their houses?"

"Cinderella has the castle in Walt Disney World. There is a restaurant on the second level, I think. Don't know about any offices. You already mentioned Sleeping Beauty and Disneyland." Adam didn't think this was the right track. "What about the houses they had in the movies?"

"Well, they all had their castles. And usually another house when they were in trouble, right?"

Adam ticked off on his fingers: "Snow White had the dwarfs' house in the woods. Sleeping Beauty had the woodcutter's cottage. Cinderella had…wasn't it just her step-mother's house? Tiger Lily had a teepee, I guess, but no castle."

Lance shook his head. "I don't see what this has to do with the clue, though. Or Walt's desk. Did he refer to his daughters as little princesses, maybe?"

"Don't all doting fathers?" Adam asked with a smile.

Still thinking it through, Lance amended, "But he would have built the house for his daughter, not the other way around."

They were almost at the turnoff for Adam's apartment. "Think we should open the envelope?" Adam asked, looking back at it.

"I don't think so. To me it sounds like a last resort if

we need help. This Mary, Mike or Jill…"

"Manny, Mo or Jack," Adam corrected.

"Whatever. I think it should stay sealed," as he pulled to a stop at the curb.

After the quiet solitude of the Golden Oak Ranch, Adam and Lance became aware of all the noise around them as they walked up to Adam's apartment: a leaf blower, wheels screeching, police siren, doors slamming, someone arguing in a different language, laughter from the pool, heels clicking on the sidewalk, a baby crying somewhere in the complex. They were just the normal sounds of life. What a sharp contrast to the peace and quiet they experienced out at the ranch. What a gift Walt had granted them – the gift of tranquil solitude.

Adam laid the Grant Deed on top of the railroad shares and the Alice script. He had wanted to add Walt's nametag to his collection box, but, out of deference to Lance, he waited. He heard his computer ping and groaned out loud. "Will you please fix that for me? I don't even have to look and I know its 7 o'clock."

"Then you don't need a clock," Lance kidded. "But, it is too early for my reminder. It's not even 5:30 yet. It's probably an email." He read the clue one last time. "I'm going home. I'll give you a call tomorrow or Thursday if I come up with anything." He knew Adam would do the same.

"You want some pizza? I was going to have one delivered."

"Tempting as that sounds, no, thanks. I have other plans tonight." He glanced at the clock in the kitchen. "And if I don't leave now, I'll be late."

"Big date?" Adam was curious. He should be thinking about one of those for himself…someday.

Lance paused at the door. He didn't want to lie to Adam, but he also didn't want to explain himself. "Something like that. Later."

No wiser, Adam just grinned. If Lance didn't want you to know something, you did not find out. He was still grinning when he picked up the phone and ordered a ham and pineapple pizza.

Since *Sleeping Beauty* came out the same year as the purchase of the Golden Oak Ranch, Adam focused his search on her. But he was getting frustrated as he found nothing in his books indicating Walt referred to her as 'the little princess'. The movie was not a financial success when it came out, either. It would be a couple of decades before it saw a positive monetary return. He looked over at his computer and wondered how in the world Lance had gotten so much out of it. He glanced at the clock. It was getting close to 8:00. If Lance was on a date, they should be done with dinner by now. He probably wouldn't mind a quick call. And if he did mind, well, that would just be a bonus for Adam.

Lance's cell phone rang about ten times before he picked it up. He gave a hushed, hurried, "Hello?"

Adam was amused. Usually Lance was always friendly, almost glib on the phone. "Hey, it's Adam. Am I interrupting anything important?" was asked with the double entendre only guys could give it.

Before Lance could answer, Adam heard two blasts of a steam whistle in the background. A very familiar steam whistle. "Hey! Was that the Mark Twain? Where are you? Disneyland? And you talk about me needing a life!" he kidded, with a laugh.

Lance didn't share the amusement. "I'm a little busy right now. What do you want?"

"Sorry," Adam smiled, not sorry at all. He figured Lance had a pouty blonde on his arm who didn't like sharing. "I am coming up empty on my princess search. How do you find stuff on my computer? What do I do?"

He could hear Lance's muffled, "Sorry, sir, I'm getting

off right now." Lance must have had his hand over the receiver. Louder, he said, "Listen, Adam, I have to go. Just pull up any search engine and type in whatever words you want to look for. Bye."

"'Sir'?" Adam repeated into the dead phone. He was amazed Lance was so brief and, well, not himself at all. He would have to grill him next time Lance came over.

Adam stared at his blank computer screen for a minute, trying to remember what Lance had done. He didn't know much about the tool bar or the history tab or how to find what Lance had already searched. He saw an unfamiliar space at the top right of his screen. When he ran his mouse over it, it read 'type here to search the Web'. "Ok, that was easy enough." He typed in 'little princess Walt Disney'. He got over one million results. Just like that. "Oh, this is going to take a while," he groaned as he looked through listing after listing of little princess party supplies and little princess clothing and little princess posters. He looked over at the relative haven of his nice, organized research books all stacked in a neat pile. He just wished they had told him what he had wanted to find.

Knowing he didn't have to click on each link to know it wasn't what he wanted, he quickly went page after page through his search result. He saw that the princesses listed were usually Snow White, Cinderella, Aurora, Jasmine and Belle. In his mind, he had already dismissed Aurora, Belle and Jasmine. That left Snow White and Cinderella. Scrolling faster now, he concentrated on those two ladies. There wasn't much on just those two alone other than copies of their movies. He finally found, around page twenty-five, an article out of a book he didn't currently have. The article talked about the studio on Hyperion Avenue in Los Angeles, California and all they had to do to make *Snow White and the Seven Dwarfs* an outstanding piece of animation history. It was the first animated movie to use a multi-plane camera that would give the scenes depth and a three-dimensional feel. In December 1937, it premiered at the ornate Carthay Circle Theater in Los Angeles with searchlights streaking through the sky as Hollywood's most luminous stars crowded inside. It went on to win an Academy Award and seven small ones. It was a financial success from the first day it was shown.

Adam stopped here. He felt he had his answer. The 'house' for the 'little princess' Snow White would have to be the Hyperion Studio. He found the address to be 2719 Hyperion Avenue in Los Angeles. He leaned back in his chair, smiling. He and Lance could take a quick run out to L.A. tomorrow, check out the old buildings, and take it from there. The envelope was probably for some security guard who would be keeping watch over the site. There were probably displays of offices as they had been, including possibly Walt's. It would be a fascinating tour. He glanced at his phone, but hesitated to call Lance again. Some of Lance's girls could be 'difficult'. He would wait until tomorrow.

FRIDAY, MAY 10TH, 2002
11:47A.M.

It wasn't until late Friday morning that they could make the short trip. With a flashlight, screwdriver and a hammer stowed in the trunk, and the envelope hidden inside a jacket pocket, Lance and Adam made their way forty miles northwest on the I-5 Freeway towards Los Angeles. The moderate traffic was moving along at a good speed. They were looking for the Los Feliz Boulevard exit where they would take a left on Griffith Park Boulevard. Lance loved driving, so he was at the wheel again. Adam didn't mind. He felt rather proud of himself for solving the clue single-handedly. Yes, that Internet was an amazing thing. He would have to spend some time learning how to use it more efficiently.

Lance took the off-ramp and they found Griffith Park Boulevard with no problem. Adam told him to make a sharp left onto Hyperion Avenue and they would be at the studio. Whistling softly to himself along with the '50's music playing on the radio, Lance did as he was instructed. The whistling stopped, however, as Lance pulled into the parking lot at 2719 Hyperion Avenue.

They were sitting in front of a huge grocery store.

The entry of the store was painted dark red, and the sides were a dark gold color with five high arched windows facing the street. There were a few trees planted in front of the store on the Hyperion side of the building.

The two men got out of the car and just stood there. "You sure this is right?" Lance asked the stunned Adam.

The address on the front of the store proclaimed '2719' and they knew they were on Hyperion. Adam could see the hillside off to the side from where they were standing. It had been empty in the black and white pictures he had seen of the studio. Now it was covered with what might be either apartments or condos and private homes. But the huge sprawling white studio was gone. Behind the store – where the bulk of the studio should have been – were a few more businesses before they gave way to apartment complexes and houses.

They spotted a purple colored marker and wandered over to it, stepping around shoppers and carts. The marker declared:

> *"Point of Historical Interest.*
> *Site of Walt Disney's original animation studio in*
> *Los Angeles.*
> *2719 Hyperion Ave. 1926 – 1940.*
> *Cultural Heritage Board Monument #163."*

That was it. That was all there was to commemorate the legendary studio that put Disney's name even more securely 'on the map'.   Adam was deflated.

Lance could tell his friend was both disappointed and embarrassed. He gave him a light, "Well, back to the old drawing board."

Adam just nodded glumly and got in the car and fastened his seat belt. It was a quiet ride back to the city of Orange.

SATURDAY, MAY 11TH, 2002
5:15 P.M.

Since Adam hadn't felt like tackling the research again, Lance just dropped him off at his apartment but came back late Saturday afternoon. As he had looked the week before, Lance appeared to have been out all day. He still refused to answer any direct question from Adam as to where he had been or what he had been doing. He did accept some leftover pizza and a beer.

"At least you are heeding the reminders," he managed to joke as Adam's computer chimed.

Adam just shook his head and deleted the box. At least that was getting easier for him to do. Now all he had to do was figure out how to delete the entire reminder process…

"So, what did you come up with today?" Lance asked him from the kitchen as he washed the pizza remains off his fingers.

Glad his friend wasn't dwelling on his embarrassment the day before, Adam went over some notes he had written. "I thought the word 'house' in the clue might be literal, so I looked into where Walt was living at the time period of *Snow White* in 1937. I was thinking maybe they moved into a bigger house or something after the movie became a success. But they were still living in the nice home on Woking Way which Walt built on the hill overlooking the studio in 1932. They wouldn't move to the big house on Carrolwood until 1950. I find all of this amazing since he came to California in 1923 with only $40 in his pocket."

Lance nodded as he retook his usual seat on the sofa. He had been thinking of a literal house, as well. Now he knew it was time to shift gears. Perhaps Adam's idea of a studio wasn't wrong. What if it was just the wrong studio? "Okay, we know *Snow White* was a resounding success and he made a lot of money of it. What did they work on next?"

Adam flipped through some of his older notes. "They were working on *Bambi*, *Pinocchio* and *Fantasia* all around the same time. But, they were having trouble with all of them. With *Bambi* and *Pinocchio*, it was story trouble. Also with *Bambi*, they were having problems trying to draw the animals more realistically than cartoonlike. There were a lot of creative problems with *Fantasia*. *Bambi* was shelved and didn't come out until 1942. *Pinocchio* was released in 1940, then *Fantasia* and *Dumbo* in 1941. But, neither *Pinocchio* nor *Fantasia* did well at the box office."

Lance was still thinking along the lines of a studio. "If Walt didn't use that money to build himself a better home, what did he build next? It was way too early for Disneyland. When was the studio in Burbank built?"

"I didn't even think to read about that studio. I thought it was too 'new', but I could be wrong," Adam thought out loud. "What dates did that historical marker say yesterday?"

"1926 to 1940", Lance was able to instantly quote from his almost photographic memory – an ability he didn't like sharing with too many people who tended to expect it to work every time on every subject and have him perform like a trick pony. He knew Adam was distracted enough not to notice. "So, the Burbank studio opened in 1940. That corresponds with the new movies we are talking about."

Adam leaned back in his chair. "So, do you want to get into this tonight or tomorrow? You look pretty tired. Another big date at Disneyland?" It was worth a shot if Lance decided to tell him anything…

But it didn't work. "Tomorrow sounds better to me. If I feel like it tonight, I'll try to find a Manny, Mo or Jack who may have been at the studio in the 1960's. See if you can find where Walt's office was, if you do anything tonight."

"So, you really think the Burbank Studio is the answer?" asked Adam as Lance went towards the door.

Lance nodded seriously. "Yeah, I'm pretty sure. Even though going to the Hyperion Studio yesterday wasn't right, it felt right. A movie as successful as *Snow White* would give Walt the resources he needed to do a lot of things he had in mind. We just need to find out what his next big goals were. We're close, I do know that. See you tomorrow." He lightly slapped the doorframe twice as a good-bye and shut the door behind him.

SUNDAY, MAY 12TH, 2002
9:18 A.M.

"Did you find any of the three men," Adam asked when Lance showed up at his door the next morning.

"Good morning to you too," was Lance's comeback as he walked over to the sofa. He added some pages of his own notes to the ever-growing piles in Adam's living room. "I found one of them. Jack could have referred to Jack Webb who worked with them to build Sound Stage 2 in 1949. Jack then was able to film his own show *Dragnet* there. But, Jack passed away in 1982. If the note refers to him, I'm afraid he won't be of much help."

Adam watched Lance walk into his kitchen and begin to rummage through the refrigerator. *Good luck there, buddy,* he thought to himself with a chuckle. *I can't remember the last time I went to the store.*

Coming into the living room empty-handed, Lance wanted to know what Adam had found in his research.

"Not much," Adam admitted. "I found an animator who has been with the Studio since 1953, but his name doesn't fit. Well," he amended, "unless we get really creative with his last name and switch the two 't's' for 'n's' and get rid of the last three letters altogether...." He broke off at the confused look on Lance's face. "Here." He held out his notes to show Lance what he meant.

"So, instead of 'Manny', you have 'Matty'. Well, it's closer than anything else we have. And you know for sure he is still there?"

Adam nodded. "Yes, I read an interview he had done not too long ago. He sounds like a really nice guy. We could start there and maybe he could help."

Lance was skeptical. "You think we should give him the envelope?"

"I don't know how else we are going to get into the Studio. It isn't open to the public. Well, one building has a sort of reception area and some current movie memorabilia on display. But that is about it. Too bad. It would be a fascinating tour."

Lance thought about it for a minute. He didn't like giving up the envelope to just anyone. He didn't know what was written in it, but he felt it was their only link to finding the next clue. "Well, I don't think we would do much good going there on a Sunday. We might have more luck on Monday. Want me to try and get an appointment with him?"

Adam gave him a grin. "Going to sing him the campfire song?"

"Only if I have to," Lance sighed. "Only if I have to."

WEDNESDAY, MAY 15TH, 2002
10:30 A.M.

Wednesday morning at 10:30, the two friends were at the guard house at the W. Alameda Avenue entrance of the Burbank studio. They had just passed under the huge entry arch that proclaimed "The Walt Disney Co." in big red letters in the distinct cursive Disney lettering. The two sides of the white metal arch were held up by green-topped palm trees. Off to the right they could see the Team Disney Burbank Building that held the offices of their president and board-members. It was a huge glass and brick building completed in 1990. Its most distinctive feature were the 160-foot tall six dwarfs that were holding up the roof of the building. Dopey had the place of honor above the other six at the apex of the roof. The Disney Legends plaques were on the orange columns leading up to this building. They weren't directed to this building, however. They were sent around the parking lot to the left and told to park there. This was the original Animation building with its eight wings. Here, on the third floor in Wing H, had been Walt's offices. The building was surrounded by mature trees on inviting grassy patches. The innovative louvered screens designed by Walt were still in place over the many windows. The animators inside those offices would be able to adjust the amount of light coming into their work area. They could see the tall silver water tower with its picture of Mickey off to the left.

They were met at the simple entrance by a friendly face. He first asked Lance for some identification. Stepping between Adam and the animator, Lance showed him something pulled out of his wallet – just as he had done at the Golden Oak Ranch. "I guess you can call me 'Manny',' he said with a laugh. "Glad to have you. While I know you would love to have a tour of the studio, I'm afraid that is impossible today. Too much going on in the sound stages and too much back and forth with the back-lot." He was leading them through the busy building towards an elevator. They had glimpses of animators through open doors, busy at their desks. There were friendly smiles and 'hellos' from everyone they passed in the long hallway. "You probably saw the big Sorcerer hat across the street there on Riverside?" Manny was telling them, "that was done in 1995. That's our Feature Animation Building. The Chairman of Feature Animation has his office in the hat."

"Roy? Walt's nephew?" Adam asked.

"That's right. He might like meeting you since you have something from Walt. Maybe we can give him a call later."

Lance and Adam exchanged a look. That was the last thing they wanted. Lance distracted him from following that line of thought. "So, tell me, who do you think of when you hear 'The Little Princess'?"

"Oh, Snow White, of course," he told them immediately. "Walt always referred to her as the little princess. You probably know the money he made from that picture financed this studio, right?" 'Manny' led them down a quiet hallway. He threw open a door and led them into an empty room. "Well, here it is. Walt's office. There's another room through that door."

Adam and Lance just stared, open-mouthed, at the empty room.

'Manny' looked around with a smile, misunderstanding their silence. "Yeah, I know what you mean. Kinda leaves you speechless. He was a great man."

Lance laid a hand on the letter tucked in his jacket pocket out of sight. "We were hoping to see his office as it looked when he was here."

"Oh, that was all packed up years ago. Some of it went on display at Disneyland and some of it went to Florida."

"Do you happen to know where his desk ended up?

We were told his desk was of special interest." Lance knew he sounded odd. He looked at Adam. Adam gave him a slight shrug. He didn't know what to say either.

'Manny' thought about it for a minute. "You know, I think the original desk went to Disneyland for that Disney exhibit in Mr. Lincoln's show. Some of the awards were there too. The other stuff went to Florida with a replicated desk. I don't remember the desk being anything too special."

Lance knew they were going to find nothing here. Their only hope now was at Disneyland – and he thought he knew how to find the desk. He motioned to Adam that they needed to go. "Thank you so much for meeting with us." Lance led the way to the elevator. The animator was surprised. Most visitors were reluctant to leave. "So, what is out on the backlot?" Lance asked as they headed for the ground floor.

"Oh, a lot of the individual departments like Paint, Molding, Sign Graphics, the mill, and Costuming. Now, Costuming is interesting. There is 32,000 square feet, in three tiers, of costumes going back to the 1930's. Fascinating...." He broke off when Lance extended his hand.

"We sure appreciate your time. Thanks for meeting with us and showing us the office."

'Manny' held up a hand for them to wait a minute. "You know, I could call Roy for you. I'm sure he would love to hear about your Walt research and what it is you found." He turned aside into an animator's office. "Just give me a minute and...." But when he turned back, Lance and Adam had already gone. He shrugged. "Odd guys," and headed back to his own office to resume his day. He never did see the envelope and the unmistakable handwriting on the cover. He didn't give Lance or Adam another thought.

Lance and Adam held themselves back from actually sprinting to their car. They didn't want to meet up with anybody who might ask about their interest or what they found. It was better to get out while they could with only one person thinking they were very strange. Lance drove sedately through the lot and waved thanks to the guard. They relaxed when they turned onto the 134 Freeway and headed back to Orange County.

"That was close," Adam groaned. "I would have loved to meet Roy under different circumstances. But, how in the world would we have gotten around explaining to him about the envelope or the diary? Damn, I thought we were going to have to run for it. What do we do now? How do we get to a desk on display at Disneyland? He had to mean The Walt Disney Story in the Opera House."

The Ventura Freeway wasn't too busy. Lance knew where he needed to hit the I-5 Freeway, and then they had about a fifty-minute drive home. Lance also knew he had to be careful what he told Adam. There was something going on that he didn't want Adam to know about. "I was thinking about that, too. We need to see what is still on exhibit. It's possible the desk isn't there any longer. If that is the case, we need to find out where it is, and possibly, use the envelope. Do you agree?"

Adam was frustrated. He was discouraged. All the clues and searches had been easier than what they were running into now. Sure, they had flown across country a couple of times and had to dig and search a condemned building. But the actual tree and the actual building and the actual ranch were all still where they were supposed to be. Now they had to find a missing desk. "Do I agree with what you just said? Yes, but what do we do if the desk is gone?"

"Well, let's just go to the Park and see what's what. Do you have time now?"

Adam glanced at the clock on the dash of the car. "Sure. I'm not expected back on the job today. I don't have any bids to deal with today. Want to get some lunch first? "

"Let's check out the Opera House first, then my treat at the Blue Bayou."

Staring out the window of the car, Adam mumbled, "Fine."

Lance ignored Adam's mood. "You have your annual passport?"

"In my wallet."

Lance knew Adam always got the premium passport. It allowed full access to Disneyland every day of the year and gave free parking in the structure. "Get it out and we'll use it for parking. It's easier to get to than mine."

Adam looked at him oddly. "You will need yours to get into the Park."

"I know, but I don't want to dig it out of my wallet while I am driving."

Considering Adam had seen Lance eating lunch and driving with his knees, he thought that was weird for Lance to say. But, he had too many other important things on his mind. They drove the rest of the way in silence. There was no use making plans until they knew what they were up against. After parking and riding the tram to the entrance of the Park, they made their way the short distance on Main Street to the white Opera House – the first building actually completed when Disneyland was built.

A cast member, dressed in the formal tuxedo and tails befitting the Opera House, greeted them at the entrance and told them the next Mr. Lincoln show was in ten minutes. They wandered around the plush red carpeted waiting room to look at the displays behind glass walls. There was a lot of Disney memorabilia to see. One case full of awards – ranging from the Oscar for Snow White and the seven miniature Oscars to honorary awards from universities to recognition from foreign countries. Included were plaques, medals, statues, cut glass, parchment and plates. Another display held photos from the early days of Disneyland. The Opera House in which they were standing was shown in framework. The Matterhorn Mountain was a mass of girders. Adam's favorite display was sped-up movie footage of the Park being built. It was a year of construction shown in about two minutes. He wished he could get some of his construction guys to move that fast. Other pictures showed a former president getting into a Monorail. Movie stars and heads of state were photographed, all posing with their famous, smiling host.

In the last display in the room they found the contents of Walt's studio office. The dark wood desk was shown with an assortment of drawings and cels covering the surface. A storyboard was set up in the background showing the last animated picture Walt had worked on – *The Jungle Book*. The scene depicted was Baloo and Mowgli and their confrontation with King Louie. There were fake windows in the background, showing the same louvered shades that were installed at the actual studio.

However, the two men were only interested in the desk. It was turned sideways in the display. They could see drawers on either side of the swivel chair. Were the drawers untouched? Were they empty? Was this the original desk or a copy?

Adam was about to ask Lance those questions. But, when he turned, Lance was gone. He wasn't even in the waiting room any longer. Adam doubted Lance went in to see the Lincoln show. Since Adam didn't feel like standing on Main Street and shouting for him, he pulled out his cell phone and punched in Lance's number. "Where the hell are you?" he demanded without any preamble.

"Be right back. Just wait there a second." And Lance hung up.

Adam stared at the silent phone. He knew calling back would be a waste of time. So, he wandered through the rest of the exhibit and waited.

Lance strolled in fifteen minutes later, smiling and whistling to himself. "Let's go eat." He held up a hand to stop Adam's probable tirade. "I'll explain while we eat."

Lance stuck his hands in his pants pockets and resumed whistling 'When You Wish Upon a Star' as they walked down Main Street and headed through Adventureland to New Orleans Square and the Blue Bayou restaurant. Adam just bided his time.

As soon as they had ordered from a most helpful waitress who tripped over herself getting Lance exactly what he wanted right away – Lance had to tell her what Adam wanted as she didn't seem to notice Adam was sitting there – Lance told Adam what he had found. "The desk we saw is the original desk from the studio, so that is good. I didn't feel like taking a trip to Florida right now. Anyway, as far as they know, nothing was touched inside the desk. Pens, paper, whatever is still all there. They hope," he broke off, taking a drink of water.

"What do you mean 'they hope'?"

"Well," Lance told him, "they hadn't examined the desk themselves. It is all hearsay. But, they think it is intact."

"Who did you ask? Did you give them the letter?" Adam was getting a little neurotic right now. In his mind, Lance was being too secretive as to 'who' and 'what'. "And who are you talking about?"

Lance was nonplussed by Adam's questions. "I still have some friends here. One of them works at City Hall. She was very helpful," he ended with a half smile. He knew that would end Adam's suspicions for now.

"Oh, I see. 'She' was very helpful," Adam grinned, instantly appeased. "I should have known. How do we get in the display…"

He broke off when the server came back, refilling Lance's water glass and ignoring his own. She told Lance his dinner would be out in just a minute or two. Would he like another roll? When Lance said he would not, but his friend would, she looked confused and looked around. She seemed startled to see someone else at the table with Lance. Adam waved at her. Blushing, she left them to go check on the dinners.

"Do you think she wondered why you ordered two entrees?" Adam asked with a grin. He was distracted by a sudden flash of light. Someone riding the Pirates of the Caribbean just took a flash picture of the restaurant as they floated by. Adam took a minute to look at the peaceful surroundings of the floating houseboats and listen to the croaking of bullfrogs. The restaurant was lit by colorful flickering Chinese lanterns and each table had a little oil candle in the center. He hadn't been here in a while. He had forgotten how nice it was.

Lance chuckled. "I don't know. Should we ask her?"

Adam turned back to his friend. "No, better not. She was probably hoping one of them was for her."

"Then I hope she likes Jambalaya because she isn't getting my Filet Mignon."

Adam picked up the interrupted thread. "So, how do we get to the desk?"

Lance smiled up at the server as she set his filet in front of him. She seemed to be waiting for him to eat it as she just stood there. Adam coughed into his hand, and she remembered to drop his steaming bowl of Cajun Jambalaya in front of him. She turned back to Lance. She wasn't going to leave until he took his first bite and it was to his liking. Lance obliged her and told her it was perfect. Smiling, she left, leaving Adam with an empty water glass.

"Nice girl," Lance muttered between bites.

Adam finished off Lance's water. "Yeah. Super. Now, about that desk…"

"Oh, it's all arranged. Security is going to close the show for about an hour. That should give us enough time to do our search."

Adam stared at him, a forkful of hot sausage stopped halfway to his mouth. "What? How did you manage that? What did you tell them?"

Lance waved him off. *Adam and his damn questions.* "I just told them what I needed to say to get what we wanted. Trust me on this, Adam. One of the security guards has been here a long time. I might have to use the letter if we find anything. I think it will be okay. Finish eating. We have to be there right at five o'clock. The show isn't very busy around then."

Adam ate the rest of his meal in silence. Lance used a credit card to pay and tucked the girl's phone number into his shirt pocket. They walked back towards the Opera House and crossed over in front of the Main Street Trolley pulled by a huge black Belgium horse named Pat. The conductor clanged his bell. Lance waved hello.

The security guard, Kenneth, was in his mid-sixties. He had been working at the Park for over forty years. He had started as a ticket-taker in Fantasyland, worked Autopia through three eras of car style changes, had been a conductor on the Railroad, and finally, ended in Security, his knowledge of the Park coming in handy. He greeted Lance familiarly and motioned for the two cast members on duty to shut the ornate front doors to the Opera House. They would wait outside, asking guests to come back later. Kenneth led them through a small, unmarked door hidden in the white and gold trimmed wall. They were backstage now and could hear the last of the Lincoln speech going on next to them. The audience would stream out the doors on the other side of the building at the conclusion of the performance. Kenneth pulled a set of keys out of his uniform and after searching for one, wound it off his key-ring and handed it to Lance. He indicated the door in front of them. "This is the display you want. You have fifty-six minutes now. That's all I could give you, Lance."

Lance shook hands with him. "Appreciate it, Kenneth. Thanks."

Lance fit the key handed him into the lock and opened the door. Part of the storyboard covered the door, hiding it from the audience. They walked through the middle of the panel and entered the glass-enclosed case, closing the door behind them. They felt odd for a minute, looking out through the glass at the empty waiting room – as if they were part of a display now.

They shook off the feeling and got to work. When the time was up, they would have to leave. There was no question about that.

They didn't talk. They just each took a side of the desk and started opening the drawers. They pulled each one completely out from the desk and set it carefully on the carpet. They figured they were looking for another gray capsule, but weren't sure. They were careful that they didn't take anything completely out of the drawers. It had to look like no one had gotten into them when they were finished.

There were all kinds of correspondence, memos, pens, drawing pencils, all the usual paraphernalia in a usual desk. Only all of this was written to or from Walt Disney. Adam resisted the urge to read any of it or even sneak out a personal item of Walt's that had been left behind all these years. He just didn't have enough time and he had some semblance of integrity.

They looked under each drawer and they looked in the back of desk before sliding the drawer back in place. When Lance got to the middle drawer in the top of the desk, he found it to be very shallow. It held pens and a gold letter opener and some clips and a stamp pad. He noticed the facing of the desk was deeper than the drawer actually was. He called Adam's attention to it as Adam was sliding his last drawer back into place.

"Help me pull the drawer out without messing up the contents. I don't want to tip it a lot."

Adam held the supplies in place with his hands as Lance lifted out the drawer. They could see the bottom of the wood under the runner for the drawer. He pulled out the chair and looked underneath. "Put your hand on the runner and then under here. What do you notice?"

Adam tried it and said, "There is a good three inches difference. Do you see any openings under there?"

"No. I think we need to remove the runner."

"That's not possible. The opening is too narrow. It had to have been done from below. Let me look."

Lance moved aside and Adam slid under the desk. He used his carpenter skills to figure out how it could have been done. "There has to be a place to loosen the bottom panel without weakening the whole surface. It is probably held in place by friction. The drawer runner wouldn't put any stress on it. There isn't that much weight in the drawer. Let me see that key."

Adam ran the edge of the key around the base of the desk below the drawer. He found the inlet towards the back. He inserted the key sideways and gave it a little pressure. He could feel the panel move. He gave another turn of the key and the back of the panel dropped into his hands. It was hinged on the inside, nearest the front of the desk. A flat, gray plastic container slid out of the opening. Adam set it on his stomach as he felt the rest of the panel to make sure nothing else was there. He fit the panel back into place and used the palm of his hand to gently hit it back in place. It settled back and he felt all around the edges to make sure it was tight. Lance, meanwhile, had put the unneeded drawer back in place.

This plastic case was about twelve inches long, ten inches wide and only three inches deep. There was excitement in their eyes now where there had been defeat before. Before they could celebrate the find, Adam happened to look outside their glass cabinet. He then remembered they were in a very public place – and soon to be more public once their limited time was up. And that time was approaching very quickly.

"Lance, we have to hide this somehow. Do you want to fold it up in your jacket?"

Lance didn't think that was a good idea. "It is too stiff to hide. I guess down the front of your pants won't work this time," he smiled, remembering the diary.

"Well, if the front of my pants won't work, how about across my back? How about if I tuck in my shirt and stick it down my back. I could wear your jacket. If I don't try to bend over, it might work."

Lance took off his jacket. "It doesn't go with your pants."

Adam didn't know if he was kidding or not. "Who cares!!?? Here, put it down my back. Make sure it is centered as much as possible. Ouch, that's cold!" Adam exclaimed as Lance slid the plastic into place. Adam had broader shoulders and was shorter than Lance. The jacket wouldn't be a very good fit. He would have to remember to stand up straight. He put on Lance's jacket and turned around. "How does it look?"

"A navy jacket does not go with black pants."

"Before I kill you, does the capsule show?"

"Walk a little. Try to bend over. Okay, don't do that again. Now walk over that way. Now walk over there. Now turn. Now look up. Look over to the side. Jiggle a little."

It sunk in that Lance was playing with him. Adam rolled his eyes. "Let's get out of here. I feel like a monkey in a cage."

Lance sobered. "I know. I do too. Kenneth should be back any time now." He pushed on the panel, stepping backstage once again and gratefully closed the door behind them.

"Think we should just leave?" Adam suggested.

"That would be rude *and* suspicious," Lance pointed out. "No, we will thank him and tell him it was interesting but fruitless."

"Well, you'd better handle it. I'm not good with lying."

Lance shot him a quick glance, but he could see Adam was just making a statement, not aiming an accusation at him. "Fine. Just try not to look guilty," he asked as Kenneth came back in the room. Kenneth shot an odd look at Adam who was now wearing a jacket obviously too long for him. Lance took over and warmly thanked him for his help, but, sorry to say, it wasn't what they thought.

"Aw, sorry to hear that, boys. You come up with anything else, just let us know!" Kenneth waved them off and Adam wondered why he added, "See you later, Lance."

But before he could ask, Lance quietly told him to stand up straight. It looked like he had a giant book across his back.

They sat in an empty tram car on the way back to the parking structure. Adam groaned and bit his lip at every bounce of the tram because it scraped the edge of the capsule across his back. He hoped he would not have cuts and be bleeding from the capsule's jostling. They waited until they were inside the Mercedes with its tinted windows before Lance pulled it out of Adam's shirt.

There were twelve hand-painted animation cels hidden inside the plastic case. Ten of the sheets were eight inches square and two sheets were eleven inches by eight inches. Each of the clear sheets had a layer of wax paper to protect it. The smaller cels, as the two friends carefully and reverentially went through them, were Snow White and each of the seven dwarfs, Pinocchio looking at Jiminy Cricket, and the Blue Fairy as she appeared in Geppetto's house. The larger paintings were background scenes. The first was the dwarf's cottage in the dark woods and the second was Geppetto's toy-filled work area. There was a small number in the bottom corner of each celluloid that indicated where it was used in the filming sequence.

Snow White was holding a little bluebird on her extended finger. Each picture of the dwarfs was a close-up head shot. It was easy to identify them as Doc, Grumpy,

Sleepy, Sneezy, Bashful, Happy, and Dopey. Dopey was holding up two large diamonds to his eyes.

It was an amazing find for Adam and Lance. The cels were in pristine condition. These probably had been stored as soon as they had been filmed. Possibly, they had been part of Walt's own private collection.

As with the other treasures they had found, there was no explanation, no conditions. The diary had explained the significance of where they went and what they would find. These had meant a lot to Walt. And, now, they would mean a lot to Adam and Lance. Adam was thinking ahead about making his own frames to display the wonderful artwork. Yes, that wall over there, in the dining room, would be good, he decided as he looked around his apartment. No direct light from the sun; far enough away from the kitchen to be safe from heat or smoke. Maybe teak for the frames... He broke out of his daydream when his glance fell on Lance who was carefully examining the brushstrokes on the picture of the Blue Fairy. The cels would be shared with Lance. Of course they would be shared. But how could you break up the Snow White set? It wouldn't be right.

Too soon, Adam told himself. *Don't get excited*. They weren't through with their search. There was another clue; another page ripped out of the diary. It had been at the bottom of the cels, another sheet of wax paper protecting the painted back of the first celluloid.

"**I met Little Red Riding Hood there. Then the four musicians of Bremen. Look up from Mickey. Something doesn't fit.**"

CHAPTER 7

LITTLE RED AND
THE MUSICIANS

THURSDAY, MAY 16TH, 2002
11:45 P.M.

Dressed all in black, Adam and Lance blended into the darkness. They hugged the side of the old building, keeping out of the sliver of light coming from the crescent moon. A dog barked in the distance, but that was the only sound they heard. So far. The hair on the back of Adam's neck tingled. He knew someone was looking for them.

They spoke only in whispers. Sound would travel far in the silence that surrounded them.

"Are you sure this is the spot?" Lance spoke quietly in Adam's ear. He held the shovel in one hand, ready to dig.

Crouching, Adam lit a match and shaded it with his other hand. He shone the dull light on the map at their feet. He glanced over the maze of lines and boxes. The seemingly random grid made sense to him. "Yes, two paces more to your left. That's it. Start digging. I'll stand guard."

Adam blew out the match as it started to burn his fingers. He could hear the shovel as it bit into the earth. He went to the edge of the building and peered around the corner. He could see two shadowy figures move in the opposite direction from where they were. Their searchers hadn't heard the shovel as it continued to dig deeper and deeper. He and Lance were safe for now.

"You find anything yet?" he went to the edge of the hole and looked at Lance. Another shovelful of dirt went past his face. "You need to hurry. They're getting closer."

There was no reply from Lance. He heard a clink of metal against metal as Lance found their target.

A dog barked again, only this time it was closer. The searchers brought their own dog. It wouldn't be long now. They had to go.

"Lance!"

"I got it," came the muffled answer. "Help me out of here."

Adam got down on his stomach and reached into the dark hole. Something cold and metallic was put into his hand. It was their capsule. He set it next to him on the ground and reached into the hole again. He couldn't feel anything. Lance wasn't reaching for him. He began to panic as he leaned in further and further. "Lance!" he whispered frantically. "Grab my hand."

He could see the beam of a flashlight searching the ground. They were coming closer. He could hear the dog sniffing the trail. The flashlight beam waved back and forth in a search pattern. They would find their footprints soon.

"Lance!" he whispered again. "We have to go."

He finally felt Lance grip his hand and he pulled, helping Lance get out of the deep hole he had dug. Lance's head finally emerged and he was able to hoist himself up. He was covered with dirt. "So, what's in the capsule?" he asked, wiping the dirt off his face, only to smear it worse.

"Shhh! They'll hear you. We have to go," Adam tugged on his friend's arm as Lance bent down to retrieve their find.

The dog must have heard them because he started barking furiously. The two men holding the leash gave a shout and started running across the yard.

Hearing the footsteps pounding towards them, Adam pulled on Lance to get him to move. Lance seemed transfixed by the gold capsule he was holding. "Run!" Adam hissed at him, pushing him in the opposite direction of the nearing footsteps. He could hear the dog snarling.

Lance finally started running. They rounded the building and broke out into the silvery moonlight. They could hear the dog barking near the hole they had just left.

They ran past the dark farmhouse and cut across the yard. The yelling and footsteps behind them began again as their pursuers resumed the chase after they had found the hole empty.

Lance had parked their car a block away and they pounded down the middle of the sidewalk. There were no streetlights, no porch lights, nothing for illumination except the moonlight. Adam, now panting heavily as they continued to run, concentrated on the broken sidewalk in front of them. Lance was keeping pace without a word as the dog's barking was getting closer on their heels. They must have let him loose, he thought. Neither of them looked back. They kept their eyes on their car.

Lance broke away from Adam as his longer legs got him to the car faster. He flung open the driver door, threw himself in and slammed the door shut behind him. As the engine started, Adam flung himself into the passenger seat. The dog reached the car and jumped at the driver's window, barking and snarling. He kept jumping at the window, trying to get at Lance, his claws scratching at the glass and down the side of the car door, leaving dozens of scratch marks, Lance was certain, on the rental Pontiac.

"Put it into gear! We have to go!" Adam kept his eyes on the dog, but caught sight of headlights coming up from a half a block behind them. There was a sharp whistle and the dog turned and ran back to a black car. He could hear a door slam shut behind the dog. The glaring headlights moved away from the curb and Adam could hear tires screeching as the car hurtled towards them.

Lance slammed the car into first gear and they finally lurched forward. "Headlights!" Adam called to him as they wove down the unknown, dark street.

Lance fumbled with the gear shift and then found the headlight switch. He swerved down another street as the black car gained on them. Ignoring the stop signs, Lance plowed through empty intersections and finally got the car into fourth gear.

Adam's eyes were glued to the back window as the black car continued to gain on them again.

"So, what's in the box, goose?" Lance lightly asked Adam as if they were sitting in Adam's living room and not hurtling down some unknown quiet residential street trying to find the freeway. He shifted again and barreled up the onramp, swerving to get in front of a tanker truck in the slow lane. The black car found itself stuck behind the tanker.

"You watch the road. I'll worry about the box," Adam snapped at him, his breathing still coming hard, his heart pounding in his chest.

"Want to go swimming over at Rose's tomorrow?" Lance asked, reaching over to turn on the radio. He couldn't find a station as there was only static. He gave a shrug and leaned his left arm out of the open window.

Adam could see the black car swerve around the tanker. They were gaining on them. "Lance! Speed up."

Lance glanced in his side mirror and began whistling softly to himself. He veered over two lanes in the freeway and pressed the gas pedal to the floor. The rental slowly picked up speed. He ran a hand through his hair. "You have a comb?"

"No, I don't have a comb!" Adam clutched the gold capsule to his chest, his heart still pounding. They would never get the capsule from him. It was his!

Without warning, the back glass of their rental car shattered as a bullet tore through the car, embedding itself in the dash. Fragments of glass blew around them like pale green confetti and finally settled throughout the car.

"That was close," Lance observed, checking his teeth in the rear view mirror before swerving into the middle lane next to the tanker truck that was keeping pace with them.

"Damn! They're shooting at us!" Adam was getting frantic. "Can't you drive faster? Get away from the tanker truck! They could hit it!"

"You could give them the capsule," Lance suggested as he veered back into the fast lane of the empty dark highway.

"No! It's ours! Walt left it for us!"

"Walt left it. He might not have left it for us." Lance had his arm resting out on the window frame of the car again. Another bullet shattered Adam's side mirror. He didn't know how many bullets had flown past them.

"What do you mean?" Adam clutched the gold tighter.

"It might belong to them," a nod of his head indicated the fast approaching car. Lance held out his hand. "Let me have the gold. I'll toss it over to them."

Adam looked back through the glassless window. The black car barreled down on them. There were less than two car lengths between them. Adam could hear the dog barking. As his head jerked back, Adam could see Lance was still holding his hand out for the capsule.

The faceless passenger in the black car shot at them again and blew out one of the back tires of the rental. The car swerved onto the shoulder of the road causing a cloud of dust to billow up and blow back towards the black car. Lance had to fight the steering wheel to keep the car going straight. Still, he held out his hand for the capsule, waiting for Adam to give it to him to end this chase.

"I can't keep this up for long," Lance calmly told him.

"Give me the gold."

Adam looked from Lance's hand to the car behind them. It was getting closer and he could see the car was going to pull up next to them. As Lance still fought with the steering wheel, Adam could see the silver barrel of the gun as it pointed at him. The dog was snarling, barking in the back seat. As he looked, the back window of the black car was slowly lowered. Excited, the dog hurtled itself at the growing opening. The gun turned away from Adam and blew out the back passenger window of their rental. The dog was going to jump! Adam watched in growing horror as the gun barrel now slowly turned towards him. The black car swerved closer, but Lance managed to pull away.

In a burst of speed the black car slammed into the side of their car, causing Adam's window to shatter over him in a cascade of glass. He threw his arms up to protect his face. The black car pulled away to ram them again, to force them into the freeway divider. One more slam would do it. Smoke was starting to pour out of the exhaust. The black car was coming at them again. But it didn't ram them yet. It pulled up next to them, keeping pace with the weakening rental. The dog had its paws on the window frame. Powerful muscles bunched, he gathered his legs under him and leapt.

Lance stood on the brakes, screeching tires protesting as the car immediately jerked and squealed to a stop. Adam watched the dog fly through the air to where their car had been seconds earlier. Lance jerked the wheel to the right and gunned it, heading for an off-ramp. The car wasn't going to last much longer.

The driver of the black car slammed on his brakes and did a smoking 180 degree turn in the middle of the freeway.

The onramp was getting closer, but they weren't going to make it. Lance had to fight the rental into each gear as they surged forward. The black car approached them at an angle, its powerful Hemi undamaged. Not taking his eyes off the ramp, Lance concentrated on his driving. Adam watched as the black car got nearer and nearer. He thought they were going to ram the front of their car.

As Adam watched, he saw the passenger window begin to lower. The silver gun barrel emerged out of the darkness of the car. It pointed at Lance now. Lance didn't see the gun. He was trying to make the final distance to the offramp. Adam saw the lower portion of the gunman's face for the first time as he leaned towards the open window. There was a thin mustache above the smiling lips. It was a smug smile. The finger tightened on the trigger. Adam watched as a plume of smoke emerged from the gun barrel.

FRIDAY, MAY 17TH, 2002
4:47 A.M.

Adam heard a loud noise and jerked. Drenched in sweat, his heart pounding, he bolted upright. Looking wildly around, his eyes focused on nothing. There was only darkness around him.

Breathing hard, his eyes finally settled on a soft green glow that read 4:47a.m. He didn't hear that noise again. His hand went up to his bare chest and settled on his pounding heart.

He felt for the shattered glass and felt only cool cotton sheets. The vision dimmed and slowly he realized the sound he had heard was himself. Did he yell in his sleep?

A dream. It was only a dream.

He looked at the clock next to his bed again. 4:48. He ran a hand through his hair and swung his legs over the side of the bed. *Damn that was real.* He sat there for a minute while his mind calmed down and his breathing returned to normal. As he pushed himself to his feet, he vaguely wondered what happened to the dog....

Not bothering to put on any clothes, he padded into the living room and dropped onto the sofa. He knew he wouldn't get back to sleep any time soon. Clicking on the table lamp, he leaned forward and looked over the animation cels on his coffee table. Snow White was smiling sweetly at the little bluebird. Doc looked kindly. Happy looked, well, happy.

Adam took a deep calming breath. He shook his head. He hadn't had a dream like that in a long time. *Must have been from concentrating so much on the clues.*

At least he hoped that's what it was...

He would hate to think that's what awaited them at their next destination.

"**W**ell, you look like crap," was Lance's greeting later that morning.

"Thank you. Thank you very much. Just what I wanted to hear," Adam grumbled, black smudges under his eyes and his face unshaven.

"Rough night?"

Adam sighed. He didn't know if he wanted to tell Lance about the dream and be subjected to his probable ridicule. Ah, why not? "I had a bad dream last night. Couldn't get back to sleep."

Lance grinned and held his arms out. "Aww. Need a hug?"

"Get away from me," Adam growled.

"What was it, then? Rose coming after you in a bikini?"

Giving a grimace, and taking another swallow of coffee, Adam replied, "Thanks for the mental image I could do without. And, no, it wasn't that. I would think that would be your dream, not mine."

Lance helped himself to a cup of coffee and

munched on some crackers he found in the cabinet. "Hardly," he gave a laugh. "So, what was your dream, then?" he asked again.

Again Adam hesitated. Dreams are just dreams. They don't really mean anything. He shook his head, fingers surrounding the coffee cup, feeling the warmth. "Oh, it was just something stupid about finding a clue in a gold capsule and being chased and shot at...and a flying dog," he mumbled into his coffee cup as he took a sip.

"Ok, now it's getting interesting. Tell me about the flying dog."

"Would you like me to lie down, Dr. Freud?" Adam scoffed, wondering where Lance had found the crackers. His stomach growled.

"Well, if you do, you will probably be asleep within minutes, so no. So, did the dog have wings?" He seemed to find this very amusing.

Adam rubbed a hand over his tired face. "No, he didn't have wings! He was just a dog who was leaping into our car on the freeway. You slammed on the brakes and the dog went flying past the car. That was all."

"What happened to the dog?"

"I don't know. I wondered that myself when the dream awakened me. I think I yelled myself awake."

Lance offered Adam one of his own crackers. "Did this dream take place in one of the locations we have already searched?"

"Lance, it was just a dream!"

Lance just calmly stared at him, dunking the crackers in the coffee.

"Fine," Adam conceded. "No, it wasn't. It was someplace different. A farmhouse. Middle of the night sort of thing. You wanted me to give the capsule to the men chasing us."

That perked Lance's interest. "Did I now? How interesting. Why?"

Adam poured himself the last of the coffee. "I don't

know. We were arguing. I didn't want to give it up, but you said something like it might belong to them, not us."

"Sounds like a little guilt coming through," Lance observed, eyes on his coffee mug.

"Guilt? I don't..." Adam stopped for a minute. He had to think about it. Did he feel guilty about finding all these wonderful things Walt left behind? What did he plan on doing with them? Sharing? Giving them back? Keeping them all to himself and enjoying them? He didn't know. He hadn't thought that far into the future. He was more intent on their next destination than what would happen afterwards. Perhaps he should be thinking about it.

Lance just let him puzzle it out. He had had the same thoughts that must be going through Adam's mind now. What were they going to do after they found the last clue? Lance didn't know how the search would end, but he thought it would be big. How could it not be when it involved the man who started with $40 in his pocket and ended with a beloved multi-national empire? He, Lance, had taken one important step that he felt would help them in the end. Hell, it had already helped them. But, that was his secret for now. Yes, he definitely felt the final treasure would be something to behold.

He just wondered if Adam realized that yet.

Later that morning Lance was sitting in Adam's office chair, typing something into Adam's computer. Adam, book in his lap, had his head back on the sofa. He was sound asleep. Lance let him be. He was busy canceling the 'Feed Lance' reminder that Adam hadn't yet figured out how to delete. Just so Adam wouldn't feel completely left out, he programmed in "Do Lance's Laundry" to chime at 6 a.m. every morning. Password protected, of course.

Next, he pulled up his travel site and booked a flight for two leaving next Monday. He had been a little surprised at having to do this again. They both thought the searches had finally settled in California. Apparently Mr. Disney didn't want them to get complacent or lazy. Walt never got that way himself. It made sense he would keep his searchers busy. Lance figured by now he should expect the unexpected.

Lance knew Adam was going to have a hernia when he learned they had to fly out again. The treasure hunt had taken up a lot of Adam's work time. Lance knew it bothered Adam to be gone so much from the job. Adam prided himself on his work – and he did excellent work to earn that pride. Good work didn't come from being absent all the time. Well, that was one of the benefits from having excellent people work under you. Another lesson Walt knew was valuable. What did he say in the diary? 'You might need some help…Choose well. I always tried to.'

At least Lance gave Adam some time before they left. They weren't leaving until Monday morning. Lance gave a slow smile. That would also give Adam some time to figure out the clue himself. He wasn't going to tell him.

Lance printed out a copy of the itinerary and spent a little while erasing the final destination. He made a copy of the altered page and added a note on the bottom: "This time BE READY when I come at 5:30 a.m. to pick you up. You are out of coffee. Love, Lance." He found some duct tape in a drawer, tore off a small piece and carefully stuck the note to the sleeping Adam's chest and let himself out the door, taking the original with him.

He had an important phone call to make…If he could find a listed number, that is.

Adam awakened with a jolt. The book in his lap fell to the floor, reminding him of where he was and what he was doing….What *they* were doing…Lance was supposed to be working at his computer. But Lance was gone, a circumstance that didn't overly surprise him. In reaching for the fallen book, he felt and heard the paper crinkling on his chest. Pulling the gray tape from his shirt, he saw immediately it was an itinerary and it was for three days later. He gave a mild curse as he saw the destination was removed. He figured that Lance was going to make him find the solution himself.

Or, he could just wait and hop on the plane and see where it took him.

No, that wasn't right. He knew as soon as he thought of it that he wouldn't do it. He never did like things just handed to him. He preferred working for them, earning them somehow. It should be no different for this search. Even though he had found some of the answers and Lance had found some of the answers, they both had been active in looking. Lance knew he would find it himself, too. But, it didn't hurt to yell at Lance a little. Lance probably expected it.

He went over to the phone on his desk and punched in Lance's cell number. There was no answer. Not surprising. He then called the home number. Again, no answer. He left a message on Lance's machine knowing full well it would not be returned. He also knew he would not see Lance again until… he checked the handwritten message…5:30, Monday morning. Adam also knew he would be ready and packed this time.

Stifling another curse, he gave a last glance at the research books. He already had taken them back to the library and checked them out again. As he went into the bedroom to change for work, he wondered how many more times he would have to keep checking them out.

Putting Lance and the books out of his mind, he concentrated on work. The replacement beam had come in early and would go up either this afternoon or tomorrow. It wouldn't be cut to size unless he was standing over it watching. Once the beam was in place, they could finish the ceiling, place the Jacuzzi, set the windows, and get the wallboard up and ready for texture. They also need to get the flooring installed; the French doors leading out to the patio and pool installed, paint, lighting fixtures, faucets and hardware. Then install mirrors, window treatments, towel bars before the final payment and final inspection.

Well….that was how it was *supposed* to go. It was Mrs. Anderson, after all. He mentally added another two to three weeks to the job. Even that might not be enough.

1963

Walt walked up the familiar walkway to the familiar porch and knocked on the familiar door. He smiled to himself. *At least I didn't just walk right in!* Still, it gave him an odd jolt when a stranger answered the door. There were so many other faces that should have opened the door to greet him. But, most of them lived in other places now.

He was greeted warmly, if nervously, and asked in. They glanced at the black valise he carried in his hand. They didn't know Walt was prepared this time. He had the capsule ready to be put in place. He already had the location in mind. He had a little speech made out for the new owners of the house. And he had something already made to guarantee the capsule would be safe for however long it took before somebody came looking for it.

How he wished he could watch the whole search process! It would be keen to be a fly on the wall and watch that person or persons figure it all out. He would love to see the look on their faces when they opened each capsule. He always liked seeing the end result of his work. It felt strange knowing he wouldn't see this.

Walt accepted the offer of a cold lemonade. The day was muggy. He was looking around the familiar living room and remembering the original furniture and pictures. His glance fell on the expectant faces around him, silent faces, a mixture of excitement and wariness in their eyes. He had asked if he could visit his old place and had only told them he had something for them.

He stood, and they became alarmed. No, he wasn't leaving just yet. He just had something to show them. Walt pulled open the valise and pulled out a wooden plaque he had specially made in his shop back at Disneyland. It was solid golden oak carved in the shape of Mickey's head. The ears were plain, except for two of the three holes for hanging. The face of the plaque was engraved and there was a bright brass nameplate towards the bottom, below the darkened lettering. The plaque read: 'My 1st studio. Thank you for preserving my memory for future generations'. Etched on the brass was Walt's own signature. The third hole was under the brass. The oak was about eight inches wide and about eight inches tall and about an inch thick. It was a striking piece.

Walt gave them his speech on how much his family had loved this house and what had been accomplished out back where the plaque would go. He told them he appreciated the care they had taken of the place and hoped it would continue for years to come. And, if it wouldn't be too much trouble, would it be alright with them if he picked out the place and hung the plaque in his old studio himself?

Stunned, the family accepted the plaque and looked it over, handing it to each member. After it made the rounds, it was handed back to Walt. He again thanked them and asked if he could have some time alone in his studio – who knew? Maybe he would get inspired again for something new!

When they stood to take him out back, he chuckled and had them stay. He knew the way. They laughed with him, finally at their ease. When the back screen door slammed shut, they tiptoed out to the kitchen window to watch him walk slowly across the backyard. When he stopped to look around, they ducked down, then laughed at themselves and went back to the living room to wait.

Walt entered the old garage. He thought about the old mahogany camera he had borrowed from the president of the Kansas City Slide Company, a Mr. Cauger. They had hung incandescent lights overhead. He had also enrolled in night classes at the Kansas City Art Institute. A lot going on at that time. *1919? Is that right? Was I really only eighteen years old?* he asked himself.

He looked around at all the usual stuff in a usual garage. He picked out a clear wall on the west side of the building. The garage, like the house, faced east. For the most part, on the other side of the back alley, there were vacant lots behind the garage. Just one house faced the other street. He set down the black bag and took out a plain piece of wood. It was a two by six, twelve inches long. The size matched what he had remembered had been above his head in the garage. It was an artificially aged piece of wood, matching quite well except for the staining which wasn't quite right. But, that was the effect he had wanted. He turned the wood over and smiled looking at the back, the side that would be hidden from view. Walt's little two by six had been hollowed out back in California. The opening was one and a half inches deep and four inches wide by eight inches long. Out of the bag he now drew the gray capsule and fit it inside its new home. Pulling out some screws, he pocketed them as he found a ladder leaning against the side wall. Whistling softly to himself, he set up the ladder, got out a screwdriver and set the new two by six in place on the side of an old beam. It wouldn't be seen from the doorway. Climbing down, he took another three screws – bright brass ones – and set the new oak plaque onto the bare wall.

He stepped back and surveyed his handiwork. It looked good. Glancing up, he knew where the capsule was hidden, but nobody else would see it that easily. Good.

Good luck! He saluted his unknown followers in the future. Turning, he gave the garage a last once-over and went to say good-bye to his hosts.

He knew the plaque would not be touched.

MONDAY, MAY 20TH, 2002
9:27 A.M.

"**S**o, how long did it take you?"

Adam had settled into his seat on the airplane and leaned his head back, his eyes closed. It was too much to expect Lance to allow him to sleep. "Take me for what?" He knew what Lance meant.

Lance gave him a half smile. "To finish setting the beam."

Adam's eyes came open. "The beam? Oh…" he broke off when Lance grinned at him. He would never get one past Lance. He sighed and closed his eyes again as the plane hurtled down the runway for takeoff. "Half of Saturday and most of Sunday. I was still looking in California."

Lance was amused. "Even though you had the itinerary showing we had to fly somewhere?"

Adam grunted. "I thought it was a joke. I never figured Walt would send us back to Missouri again. How long did it take you to figure out the clue?"

"Less," was all Lance answered. *Much less.*

Now that he realized Lance wouldn't let him sleep, Adam was inclined to be chatty as the plane leveled off and headed for Denver. "I guess I didn't think of *Little Red Riding Hood* and the *Four Musicians of Bremen* as 'Disney'. Well, I guess they weren't, as we know 'Disney' to mean," he amended. "I finally found a reference to them and saw some of the drawings. Pretty different than what we're used to."

"Yeah, they were," Lance agreed. "Pretty rough.

But, considering how new animation was and how young Walt was, it is amazing."

"He drew them all himself, too. *The Four Musicians* got a little more attention with the watercolor wash he used in the backgrounds."

"My, you did do your homework."

"You aren't the only one who knows how to read, Lance."

Lance laughed at him as he got the flight attendant's attention. He got each of them a drink and an extra bag of peanuts.

"Lance, it isn't even 10 a.m. yet and you're ordering us cocktails?"

He shrugged. "We have a long day ahead of us. We might need them." He thanked the attendant and handed Adam his cup. "Ah, nothing beats a gimlet served in plastic," as he took a tentative sip. Lance picked up the thread of Adam's conversation. "So you knew which studio the clue meant?"

Adam ignored the gimlet. He didn't care for gin. He popped a few peanuts in his mouth before answering. "Actually, I first thought we were going back to the Mc-Conahy building. Wasn't sure why, but I thought that was his main studio around that time period. Wrong. Took me a while to figure out how far back and how primitive we had to get. Are you sure the place is still there?"

Lance sipped his drink. "Oh, yes, it is still there. We get in too late to do anything today, so we have an appointment tomorrow morning."

Adam finished his peanuts. "An appointment with a garage?"

"The garage is still standing, as is the family house," Lance told him, starting on Adam's gimlet. He eyed Adam's empty peanut bag. He had meant to grab that… "I had a nice chat with the owners. They assure me the plaque is still there in the garage."

Adam hadn't read anything about a plaque. "What plaque?"

Lance settled back further in his seat, head resting against the back as he sipped Adam's drink. "Well, that was the interesting part. I hadn't found anything about it either. They told me the story of how Walt himself had come to that house thirty-nine years ago and presented the owners with a lovely award of some sorts thanking them for preserving his first studio."

"And you find this so humorous because...."

"Don't you see? Walt did this to make sure the garage was there for all posterity. Which includes us. It is just an old garage. Sure it has special history, but it is just a jumble of wood. My word, look what happened to the Hyperion Studio! But, with the special blessing of Walt and the plaque, no one would dare tear it down. It is brilliant, actually," he concluded with an appreciative chuckle. "Brilliant!"

Once in Denver, they again had to run to catch their connecting flight. After they were in the air, Lance managed to get them some extra snacks from their new flight attendant. There had been no time to stop for lunch.

With the Rocky Mountains behind them and the open plains below, Adam asked Lance what story he used to get an appointment. He doubted they could just go out in the garage and look around for the capsule.

Lance yawned. The cocktails were taking effect. "Oh, the usual. I am making a documentary about Walt and you are the cameraman."

"Of course I am. What else would I be?" Adam snorted. "How will you explain the lack of camera or sound equipment that usually accompanies a documentary?"

Lance was almost asleep. "I brought them."

Adam shook his head and looked out of the little window over the open prairie. "Of course you did," he mumbled. He stared at the huge dark green circles 32,000 feet below them. He had seen them on every trip over and back, but never had asked what they were. *Great.*

Crop circles. And maybe the little aliens are going to come back for Lance some time soon.

Hands on his hips, Adam looked at the camera and microphone laid out on the bed in Lance's room of their suite at the President Hilton. "You really brought a camera and sound equipment."

Lance was checking something on the camera. "I told you I did. You never believe me."

Adam rolled his eyes. "Silly me."

"So, you know how these things work?"

Adam just stared at him. "Yes, I use them all the time on the job. How the hell would I know how to operate a camera like that!!??"

"Now don't get testy. You know your blood pressure."

"My blood pressure would be just fine if I kept away from you!"

Lance ignored him. "Here is how it works." He hefted the huge camera to his shoulder, setting the harness firmly in place. "You hold it like this with your left hand, and push this button with your right. See the light come on? That shows it is filming."

Adam frowned. "You don't actually expect me to work this thing, do you?"

Lance lifted it from his shoulder and set it back on the bed. "Well, you are the cameraman, Adam. Of course I do." Before Adam could begin with his next string of objections, Lance held up his hand. "No, you don't actually have to frame anything or even have the sound on. The light just has to come on so it *looks* like we are filming. You could be shooting a hole in the wall for all I care. Just point it in my general direction. I will be doing what I do best – talking – and working our way out to the garage."

Adam was starting to get the picture. God, he felt like an idiot around Lance most of the time. He figured

Lance had a lot to do with orchestrating his feeling… "Ok, I get it. How do we keep them from following us out to the garage?"

"Oh, this is a sensitive microphone and picks up the least little noise. Well, it would if it actually worked. I think Sandy said it was already broken, so I don't have to take too much care with it. Just make sure you don't bang the camera into any walls or anything. I don't want to have to replace it."

Lance had Adam lift the camera into place a couple of times to get used to the feel and to make it look as if he knew what he was doing. It wouldn't look very convincing to have the camera pointing backwards.

"What time are we supposed to be there tomorrow?"

"Around 10 a.m. That gives us plenty of time to search for the clue. It ought to be pretty easy to find the Mickey mentioned in the clue. I have a feeling Mickey is the plaque even though I never saw a picture of it."

Adam hefted the camera again and nodded. He could do this. "Is there any film in here?"

"Of course not. You might actually figure out how to use that thing and waste it!"

As they were leaving to go out for dinner, Adam casually wondered if strangling Lance with the microphone cord would be considered aggravated assault or justifiable homicide.

TUESDAY, MAY 21ST, 2002
9:40 A.M.

Parking the rented Jaguar down one house from their objective, Lance emerged from the driver's seat like the Phoenix arising from the ashes. It was a sight to behold. He gave a beaming smile to whoever might be looking out the windows and, tilting his head back, shook his brown hair to achieve that special windblown look. He ran a hand through his hair just to make sure it was perfect and fiddled with the lapels of his shirt for no apparent reason to Adam. Taking up the microphone, he 'tested' it and ran a 'sound check'. Adam had to keep from grinning as he hoisted the camera into place. Lance started talking into the microphone and walking backwards towards the red house at 3028 Bellefontaine Avenue. Adam remembered where the switch was and started the camera, red light prominent as he followed Lance at a good distance, keeping him in the viewfinder. He had no idea what Lance was saying – probably Lance didn't either – as they worked their way up the front walk, Lance gesturing around with his free hand. Adam wasn't sure if he was supposed to 'film' what Lance was pointing out or not. He kept the camera on Lance.

The front door of the house opened and the owner was surprised to find a camera in her face. She blushed and stammered and told them to go around to the back. They would find the garage with no problem. She touched her hair and smiled at the camera as Lance thanked her and gave his devastating smile. Adam continued to look through the eye piece at his left eye. He had found it worked better if he kept both eyes open and navigated with his free right eye.

Lance walked down the narrow side yard and into the expanse of the back yard. Several neighbors had come out to see the excitement and were peering from the front sidewalk. Lance figured it would be just a matter of time before they started coming through the alley to get a better look. He motioned to Adam to 'cut', and went out to talk to them.

Being Lance, he charmed them all. Smiling and shaking their hands, he was pleasant and asked their help to make this something special. He told them about the sensitivity of the microphone and asked that they give the two men about an hour to work; then they would be available for questions if anyone had any.

He came back to where Adam was waiting and took the microphone from him again. He started talking about the history of the garage and grandly gesturing around the yard. Adam panned the garage and brought the camera back to Lance's face. Lance seemed so natural at this Adam wondered if he had any training.

Lance opened the door to the garage, but talked a while before going inside. He finally finished whatever he was saying and went inside, Adam following, red light obediently glowing. When he slid the door shut, Adam lowered the camera carefully to a bare spot on a work bench. They found the plaque with no problem. Lance had already gotten permission to use a ladder, saying Adam might need to shoot higher 'for atmosphere'.

"Okay, the clue said 'look up from Mickey. Something doesn't fit'. Do you see anything out of place, Adam?"

Adam was up on the ladder; Lance was below looking at everything piled up on the rafters. "No, this is all a bunch of usual attic stuff. I don't think it is anything piled up here. I don't see anything right above Mickey either…That's a nice plaque. Did you look at it?"

Lance nodded. "Yes, I did. I still think it's brilliant. Possibly forty years later and it is still here."

Adam was about to get down and move the ladder. He put his hand on a beam to steady himself so he could lean over further to check out the wall above Mickey. "Wait a minute. Hey, Lance, look here. Notice anything?"

Coming over to the ladder, Lance looked up at where Adam was standing. "Other than you needing to tuck in your shirt, no. What am I looking at?"

Adam patted the beam next to him. "Notice anything about this rafter?"

"Does it have his initials carved into it?"

Adam shook his head. "Nope. But notice how wide this section is compared to all the other rafters? It is double width. You can't see it, but there are screws in each end of this rafter. I think this is it. Find me a screwdriver. Flathead, not Phillips."

"Of course," Lance mumbled, looking at some tools strewn on the work table. "Here, finally," handing it up to Adam.

Adam anchored his legs on each side of the ladder and sat on the top rung as he worked on the screws. Having been set for so long, they didn't want to give. He wished he had his Makita cordless screw gun. They would have been home by now.

He handed the screwdriver back down to Lance, and pulled the rafter the rest of the way off. He watched as the gray capsule fell out of the hollowed-out wood. "Grab it!"

Lance missed, but the capsule was undamaged after bouncing on the floor.

Adam brought down the rafter to show it to Lance. "Walt really had this one figured out! Look at the color of the wood. The outside doesn't match the back that was nestled against the original rafter. He had it stained to match. You are right. It was brilliant!"

Lance pocketed the capsule. "We need to go out and finish our documentary. Our audience awaits."

"What should we do with this rafter? Should I put it back?"

Lance looked around. "How about tossing it in with that other wood in that pile? It will probably be a while before anyone finds it."

Adam buried it in the bottom of the pile, and then he put both the screwdriver and the ladder back where they had been found. He put the camera back on his shoulder and turned on the switch.

Lance slid open the garage door and started talking into the microphone. "So that concludes our special visit to Walt's original studio. We hope you enjoyed our stay here in Kansas City. We sure did. Just remember: Great things can come from humble beginnings. That's a wrap."

He had to motion for Adam to quit 'filming'. There were more people standing around now. Lance waved to them and went over to chat. He thanked them all for their hospitality. But he was vague when asked when the movie would come out. "Oh, you know these Hollywood things," he laughed. "Who knows? But we got what we came for and thank all of you for your help!"

"That's the first honest thing you said," Adam muttered as they walked back to the Jag. They carefully stowed the camera and mike in the backseat.

"What do you mean?" asked Lance, waving at the people as he started to pull out from the curb.

"That we got what we came for."

Lance smiled. "Well, we did, didn't we?"

It wasn't until they were driving away that Adam recognized the house as the farmhouse in his dream.

A group of neighbors stood on the sidewalk and watched the Jag drive off. Some waved back at the departing two men.

"Now that was a real gentleman. Don't you think so, honey?"

He gave a snort. "He was as much a filmmaker as I am. Must think we're a bunch of hicks."

"Why do you say that? That camera was huge."

"Yeah, it was big alright. Did you notice that blonde fella never once adjusted the lens or zoomed in or out or checked the film? The idiot was shooting into the sun half the time they were out there. All he did was hold it up on his shoulder. Filmmaker, my ass."

"Now why would they lie about a thing like that and go to all that work?"

He gave another snort. "Probably just wanted to poke around Walt's old stomping grounds. We've heard bigger whoppers than that since we lived here. Hmmph, all they have to do is just ask." He turned to go to the backyard.

"Where are you going now?"

"I'm going to check the garage. If that plaque is gone, I'm getting my double-barrel down. And I ain't loading it with birdshot."

"Now, honey. I think that tall one was just lovely."

'Honey' didn't answer. He was already heading towards the garage. "Filmmaker, my ass."

It was just a ten minute drive back to their hotel. On the way, Adam had cautiously shaken the capsule and heard nothing inside. They figured it was another paper trail.

The content of the plastic container turned out to be one page that had been torn out of the diary. It read:

**"Go to the only place outside of Disneyland to fly the official Disneyland flag.
60 07 17 19 55"**

CHAPTER 8

BACK TO SCHOOL

TUESDAY, MAY 21ST, 2002
12:30 P.M.

"**W**ell," Adam sighed in relief, "It looks like we can finally go home."

Surprised, Lance looked up from the clue. "You know where the flag is? That's great."

"Uh, no, but it has to be at the Burbank studio."

Lance didn't agree with him, so he asked, "Why do you think that? Did you see it when we went there?"

"Well, where do you think it is?" Adam retorted.

"I'm not sure, but Walt had to have brought us all the way back to Missouri for a reason. He didn't leave anything else in the container. I don't think we're through here."

Adam was looking out the window at the interesting architecture of Kansas City's downtown. He was tired of flying half way across the country. Yes, he found all this fascinating and he was intrigued by what Walt had done. But, he had work to do at home. He had things he had to take care of. And, he was just plain tired. "Maybe we aren't supposed to get something each time. I don't know," he shrugged. "Why don't you fire up your computer and see what you can find. There are also those numbers to consider."

"Good idea." Lance brought his computer out of his travel bag. After their mistake the first time they flew to Missouri, they weren't going to travel without it again. "While I'm doing this, why don't you look at those numbers again. See if you notice something familiar about them."

"I already looked them over. It looks like a combination code, but there are too many numbers." Adam walked back to the clue and looked it over. A smile slowly came over his face. "Ah, I see it now. Surprised I missed that. I don't know what the '60' means, but the rest of it is the date Disneyland opened – July 17, 1955. Maybe the '60' is for the flag reference?"

It took a few minutes for Lance's laptop to boot up. "Have you seen the flag the clue is talking about?"

"I think so," Adam said slowly, thinking back. "I didn't notice when we were running the race, but it did fly over the Fire House and Walt's apartment. Be…someone pointed it out to me once. I remember it was kinda plain with a big Mickey face on it."

Lance caught his slip of the tongue and hid his smile. "'Be..someone' huh?"

Adam shot him a warning look. "Don't go there. I didn't mean to mention her. Are you finding anything yet?" Adam asked, hoping to turn the conversation away from his personal life. It looked like Lance was engrossed with the computer screen.

"Oh, sorry, I was checking e-mails."

Adam rolled his eyes. "Do you think you can concentrate on the clue for a minute? I'd like to get back home and back to work while I still have any customers left, if you don't mind."

Lance didn't respond. He could tell Adam still wasn't seeing the possible 'Big Picture' here. But, he wasn't going to get into that discussion yet. The way Lance figured, they were still in the 'Enjoyable Search' phase at this point. But he felt the 'Final Big Search' was coming.

Just not yet. "Sorry," he said affably. "I'm sure that will be more enjoyable than reading messages from my father as to why there are so many flights to Missouri charged to the business account."

Adam forgot his grumpiness and became all ears. Lance didn't mention his family much. *Okay,* he amended, *never.* "Problems? I told you I would pay for my share of the flight tickets."

Lance waved him off. "No problem. What's the point in having a Gold Card if you can't use it?"

"You could tell him you are on a research project. That might appease him."

"I could. But, I won't," Lance muttered, more to himself than Adam. Adam had his 'uncomfortable zones'. Lance had his own. "Okay, I am searching 'Disneyland Flag'. Okay," he suddenly laughed. "There are only 700,000 references. How many do you want to take?"

Adam looked over Lance's shoulder at the screen. "Well, that's less than I found searching 'Disney Little Princess'."

"It looks like most of them are about the flag retreat ceremony every evening at the Park...Flags at the Hotel...Some flag at Pirates of the Caribbean...flag pins for sale...Ah, here we are. Marceline, Missouri. Bingo."

"What does it say?" Adam leaned in closer to read the computer screen.

"If you would like to sit in my lap, I'll have to push the chair farther back," Lance said dryly.

Adam backed off. "Sorry. Just wanted to see what it said."

Lance read quietly for a couple of minutes. He could hear Adam's impatient pacing behind him. Smiling to himself, he pretended to read a couple of minutes longer than he actually needed. Finally he told Adam, "Well, it looks like we are going back to school."

That surprised Adam. "School? What for? What school?"

"In 1960," Lance explained, "Walt came back to Marceline to dedicate the new elementary school. The town named it after him, and he arrived by train for the dedication ceremony."

Adam waited for him to say more, but Lance didn't. "Do you think the '60' in the clue stands for 1960? How does a flag figure into this?"

"I thought you would never ask. Walt presented the school with a flag identical to the one you saw at Disneyland. Here's a picture of it."

Adam saw a huge orange flag with a vintage-looking black and white Mickey in the middle. A group of girls, who were either cheerleaders or dressed in some kind of school uniform, were sending it up a flagpole. He studied the picture a moment longer. "Well, I guess that's our destination. But, what do we do when we get there?"

"Try to learn something, I guess." Lance clicked off the picture and looked for the address to the school. It was pretty easy to find. He also found that visitors were welcome anytime and any questions were answered. "Tomorrow is Wednesday, a school day. We fly out Thursday. Hopefully we will figure it out once we get there."

Adam was thoughtful. A regular school day meant a lot of kids around. A lot of curious on-lookers would be around if they had to do something obvious like before, whether it was digging or climbing or pulling up boards. He just hoped Walt knew what he was doing there.

Adam should have known by now that Walt almost always knew what he was doing.

WEDNESDAY, MAY 22ND, 2002
10:30 A.M.

The rented Jaguar made the two-hour drive from Kansas City to Marceline very comfortable. The men played around with the radio trying to find a station they both agreed on. They settled on a '50's oldies station and drove in silence, enjoying the clear spring day.

Lance broke the silence first. "I forgot to tell you something: Your folks said hi."

Adam gave a short laugh. "When did you see my parents?" Lance never ceased to amaze him.

"At dinner last week. It must have slipped my mind."

"Oh really? You all end up at the same restaurant?" Adam was interested now. If Lance had been out on a date, maybe he could find out from his mom the identity of this mystery woman Lance had been seeing so much of lately. Lance sure wasn't telling him anything.

"Restaurant?" Lance looked momentarily confused. "No. It was at their house. You missed out. Great pot roast. I like their new house, by the way. Great view."

"And I wasn't invited because…"

Lance shrugged as the Jag purred down the I-35. The US 36 highway was coming up soon where they had to head east towards Marceline. "I don't know. It never came up. We were discussing Rose's remodeling job. Your dad likes the design you came up with."

"Thanks," he mumbled dryly. He hadn't been to his parent's house in ages. And he loved his mom's pot roast. *Okay*, he argued with himself, *you haven't exactly checked in with them lately yourself.* "I need to give them a call."

Lance didn't comment on that. John and Margaret Michaels always made him feel welcome. They tended to treat him more as a long-lost son than a visitor. And they didn't pry into his personal life. They were curious, of course, but never nosy. A trait he wished their son had inherited. He knew Adam wanted to know about that time the phone caught him at Disneyland. Well, let him be curious. Keep him on his toes. Lance certainly wasn't going to explain himself yet.

Adam saw Lance suddenly smile to himself. When

there was no explanation forthcoming, he turned his attention to the soft green of the landscape as it flew past the window. Adam took it for granted that Lance's amusement had to do with some embarrassing tidbit of information his parents had passed along to Lance. He also took it for granted that the information would come out in the open at the most inopportune time.

Such was friendship with Lance Percy Brentwood.

Now it was Adam's turn to smile. Adam knew Lance hated his middle name.

It was just before eleven in the morning when the two friends pulled into the parking lot of the Walt Disney Elementary School in Marceline. The school consisted of grades kindergarten through fifth. They had arrived before the lunch hour, so there weren't many children walking around. Within half an hour, the kindergarteners would be dismissed and there would be the daily mad scramble as their parents would arrive to pick them up.

They found the flag pole to be in front of the school as all flag poles should be. The plaque mounted near the base read that it was a gift from Walt Disney in late 1960, and that the pole had flown a flag which had flown in the 1960 Squaw Valley Olympics where Walt had been the Chairman of Pageantry. However, there was no bright orange flag blowing in the soft breeze today.

Hesitating, they stood on the walkway leading up to the main entrance and looked over the neat and clean single story building. "Do we just walk right in?" Lance wondered out loud. Even with his vast social experiences, elementary school was one area in which even he was unfamiliar. They had brought the 'documentary' camera and mike with them again, but these props didn't feel right for this situation. He wasn't sure how to proceed.

Adam shrugged. "Not sure. You read that visitors are welcome. I guess we just go in and see what happens."

They entered through the double doors into the quiet hallway. They immediately saw one of the two murals that Walt's animators from California had created special for the school. There were pictures, awards, and more Disney memorabilia behind glass in cases lining the hallway. As they looked over the artifacts, a woman came out of one of the offices. She had been heading away from them, but spotted them and came back. "Are you here to see the Disney collection?" she asked with a friendly smile.

"Yes, we are," Lance brightened and extended his hand to her. "We are visiting the area and just had to see the murals. I didn't know there were so many other things here."

"Oh, yes, we have quite a collection." She indicated the glass cases. "We have these items, and more in that office over there. And, since you are interested in the murals, there is another one in the gymnasium."

Lance kept eye contact with her. "Do we need to make an appointment?"

She laughed. "Oh, no. We are too informal for that. Please, just look around. And, if you dare to go to the gym, watch out for the dodgeballs. There's quite a tournament going on."

She resumed her previous journey and left them to their own devices.

"That was easy," Adam muttered. "You'd think they would wonder about two men wandering around a grade school"

"Oh, I'm sure we'll be watched to some extent. Well, we still need to figure out what the numbers stand for – if they are anything besides just numbers. Want to go to the gym?"

"Sure. Where is it?"

Lance just smiled and stuck his hands in his pockets. "No clue. Let's just wander around, then come back to see that other display room. I didn't see the Disneyland flag in these cases."

The gymnasium was pretty easy to spot. It was off to the side and the doors were open. They could hear the happy shrieks coming from inside as the tournament was in full swing. They stood in the doorway and could see the Disney mural stretching down the side of the basketball court, all the familiar characters as they had been drawn in 1960. The walls were a soft yellow around the mural, with a darker paneling on the end walls. The two men were largely ignored. Apparently visitors came more often than Adam and Lance had thought.

They walked back to the offices as the bell rang. Kids of all ages poured around them as some headed to lunch, some headed to recess, and the happiest of them headed home. A small flock of girls spotted Lance. After a lengthy discussion amongst themselves, they all apparently agreed and started following the two men, giggling behind their hands. In their awe-struck eyes, Prince Charming had just come down off the mural and appeared in their midst.

"You can really attract them, buddy," Adam kidded.

"Can I help it if they have extremely good taste at such an early age?" he sniffed, pushing through the doors and walking towards the office that had been pointed out to them. He actually thought the girls would go off to whatever they were doing once they saw he was heading for the offices. But, he underestimated the tenacity of a ten-year old girl. They continued to follow him. He decided to make the best of it and do what he did best – talk and charm. The woman who had helped them earlier came in to see what all the noise was about. She had planned on trying to herd the fifth-graders back outside. But, Lance started asking them all kinds of questions about their school and about the legacy Walt left them. Soon, they were all talking as if they were old friends, and the girls continued to giggle with each other. Each of them tried to capture Prince Charming's attention by pointing out their favorite item and trying to out-talk her friends.

Adam took the time to wander alone around the other side of the room. Looking in the glassed-in and protective cases, there were identification markers with each item to tell its particular history. He easily spotted the orange Disneyland flag. The same picture Lance had found on the Internet was framed next to the stretched-out flag.

He stopped walking when he found Walt's original desk from his school days. On the dark top of the desk was engraved WED. His heart sped up a little as he looked at the picture attached to the desk. It showed an adult Walt sitting there, pointing at his earlier handiwork. Adam wondered if this was what they were supposed to find. He studied the desk from different angles. It was just a solid desktop built into the seat back of the next desk. The top was held up by black filigree scrollwork. From what he could see, there was no place that opened; no place to hide a capsule.

Disappointed, but not dismissing the desk entirely, he looked over the rest of the display. He finally settled his attention on a gray metal book locker like the ones typical in high schools. This was the size of a regular locker, about three and a half feet tall by ten inches wide...perhaps a foot deep. It looked just like the locker Adam had had in high school. Only this one had a nameplate on it – 'Walt's Locker'. The numbered rotating dial was sitting right below the slide latch. It wasn't behind glass like most of the collection. The locker was sitting on top of a specially built box. Testing it with one finger, Adam found it was solidly fixed, probably bolted to the box. It put the rotating dial at just the right height to spin. In Los Angeles, the locker would have been littered with graffiti, scratched out with gang letters and initials, and possibly have a few bullet holes in it. In this still-small town of Marceline, kids for the most part respected other people's property. And, on top of that, the school and its staff still inspire in its students a sense of enduring love and respect for the man for whom the school was named.

"You don't talk much, do you?"

Adam startled to hear a girl's voice right next to him. His head spun around and his vision had to drop about a foot to see who was talking. "Who, me?"

She must have been one of Lance's admirers who had abdicated. She looked to be around 10 or 11, soft brown eyes half covered by brown bangs. She was leaning against the wall, watching Adam. "Yeah, you. I was watching your friend," with a tilt of her chin indicating Lance. "He kinda takes over, doesn't he?"

Adam smiled at that. *Observant little thing.* "Yeah. I guess he does." Lance was still holding court, deep in a discussion with the girls and a couple of teachers who came in looking for them. "I'm Adam. What's your name?"

"Mandy." She looked back over at Lance, frowning a little. "My best friend is just like that. She's pretty, too. Most popular girl in the school." She didn't sound envious or jealous - just making a statement.

"Never get a word in edgewise, do you?"

Mandy grinned and pushed her bangs away from her eyes. "Nope."

"Then why do you hang around with her?" Adam asked, amused. He had wondered that about Lance from time to time.

She shrugged. "She's my best friend."

Adam nodded as he thought about it. "I guess that's what it comes down to, doesn't it? Just friendship."

"Yeah." They leaned against the wall together in companionable silence, watching Lance. She didn't seem interested in rejoining her friends.

"So, what's the story with this locker?" Adam might as well see if he could learn something. Adam glanced across the room at Lance who looked like he was about to let them braid his hair or polish his fingernails.

Mandy looked at the locker. "That's been here a long time. Nobody has been able to open it. We don't know what's inside…if anything," she replied with a shrug of her shoulders.

Adam's interest perked. "People actually try to open it? Isn't there a rule or something against it?"

Mandy gave him a 'duh' look. "That's what it's for." He could see her form the word 'dummy' in her mind.

"Really?" Adam went back to study the locker. "Anybody can try to open it. What's inside?" His breathing got shallow as his heart beat faster. This could be it, couldn't it?

He received another shrug. "Dunno. Nobody ever got it opened."

Adam's hand went to his shirt pocket where the clue was hidden. A locker combination? Was that what the numbers were? But there were too many numbers. Were they supposed to leave off one? Which number?

Mandy stared intently at Adam, her brown eyes slightly closed. She almost whispered to Adam, "You know the combination, don't you?"

His eyes were wide as he turned to his new little friend. "I think I do," he answered in a low voice.

Mandy looked back at the noisy group. "You could open it now. Nobody would notice with him around." She didn't sound very pleased with Lance.

"You think?"

She looked Adam over again. He felt she had to be older than ten or eleven. She had to be an adult hiding in a child's body. "Is what's inside very important?" she finally asked him.

Adam nodded slowly. "Probably."

She scrutinized him again with serious eyes. "I can help."

"Why would you want to do that?"

"Curious," was all she answered.

Adam nodded. "Me too."

Before he could say anything else, she glanced quickly over at the group. The bell was going to ring soon and they would have to go. She licked her lips before looking back at Adam. She knew she probably shouldn't do this. It could be what her mom had warned her about. But it didn't feel wrong inside. "Can you guys come back late tonight?"

He nodded again.

"Meet me at that side door around 9:30. Okay?"

Adam could see she was serious. "You're not trying to set me up, are you?" he asked with a half grin.

The bell rang for the next class. Mandy just rolled her eyes and walked off, shaking her head. Adults. Who can figure them out?

Adam went over to rejoin Lance and his diminishing crowd of admirers. Lance was turning down an offer for dinner from one of the teachers. He still accepted her phone number 'just in case they get back to Missouri'.

"What a nice group of girls," Lance smiled as the last of them filed out.

"What did you find out?" Adam asked him.

"Find out about what?"

Adam just stared at him.

"Oh, that. Nothing really. We were just chatting. Though, Mary, the tall blonde? She said we need to go check out the new museum by the train tracks. Remember that big red brick building we saw? It used to be the train depot, but they are turning it into a Disney and Santa Fe Railroad museum. It isn't open just yet, but she thought we could get in."

Adam smiled at him. "I'll bet we can. Come over here and look at this." Adam led him over to the displays which Lance hadn't yet seen. Adam was about to explain the locker when the doors opened again and some more students came in. This was a popular room. "Let's go have lunch and I'll explain then."

They found a cute diner not too far from the Uptown

Theatre where they had stayed last time. Over hamburgers and fries, Adam explained what Mandy had told him.

"So," Lance asked after a sip of his strawberry milkshake, "you think the numbers we have are the combination to the locker?"

"I think so. Considering that almost every combination lock is a set of four numbers, it's no wonder nobody has been able to open the locker. People would try their four numbers and quit. If this is the answer, it is pretty brilliant."

"How come you didn't try it while you were there?"

Adam shrugged. "I thought about it, but there were too many people around. It would probably be a big deal if someone got it open. I doubt we could just take the clue and leave."

"You're probably right. This Mandy girl is going to help us? What did you tell her?"

Adam ate a couple of fries. "Nothing, really. I think she figured out it was something important to me. She seemed pretty bright. She wasn't drawn in by your good looks and charm," he added with a wide smile.

"Hmmph. She can't be all that intelligent, then," Lance kidded back. "Then we will see what happens at 9:30. If we end up in jail or on the 11 o'clock news, it will be your fault."

Sobered, Adam pushed the rest of the fries around. "Thanks for your vote of confidence."

Lance leaned partway across the table, his voice noticeably lowered. "Excited or not about possibly finding the next clue, we are going into a closed building at night with a young girl. I doubt anyone would look highly on that. And if we try to get into the school on our own it would be 'breaking and entering'."

Adam knew he was right. "Well, I did ask her if she was setting us up."

"What did the little darling say?" Lance seemed

amused by this.

Adam smiled at the memory of her response. They all learn that trait so early. "She gave me the eleven-year old version of 'The Look', rolled her eyes, and left."

"So, what do you want to do?" Lance finished off Adam's fries.

Adam looked out the window of the diner at the quaint Main Street. Life was quieter here. He could see people coming and going, doing their business. They all knew each other by name. They welcomed the strangers who came to see some of Walt's life. And, he knew they protected their own. It wouldn't go well if someone thought something was amiss with Mandy. Was it something they wanted to risk? Was it worth it? He thought about her eyes. He felt he could trust her, and thought she trusted him. He gave a quiet sigh. They had to fly out tomorrow. This was all the time they had. "I guess we take the chance and meet her at 9:30."

Lance agreed with him. "Maybe we can talk her into staying outside while we try to open the locker. So, what do you want to do for the rest of the day? We didn't do much sightseeing last time we were here."

Adam smiled. "Yeah, we were too busy getting out of here as fast as possible! Wonder if that kid ever went back to the tree?"

"We could go look for him."

"No thanks. I was worried he might recognize us at the school. Let's let well enough alone."

Adam paid for lunch and they went out into the bright sunlight.

They didn't get in to see the museum. The foreman wasn't as enamored of Lance's rapier wit as most people were. They were politely told to come back sometime in June for the grand opening. With the way they were traveling, they might be back again in June in time for the big opening anyway. For now, they had to be content walking around outside the two-story red brick building. All the windows, doors and the roof were trimmed in bright white. It was a huge building. The nametag, high above the five thin windows on the second floor, proudly proclaimed 'Marceline' to all onlookers.

They found the Walt Disney Municipal Park that in 1966 had held the Midget Autopia ride that was donated by Walt and Roy. The ride was removed from Fantasyland to make room for the Its a Small World ride walkway expansion and shipped to the children of Marceline. There had been ten Autopia cars which ran along 603 feet of winding roadway. The children had a few years to enjoy the first ride ever to be taken from the Park and operated outside of Disneyland. But, just like at Disneyland, the cars were too troublesome and expensive to run. The metal guide track had been long removed, but the roadway was still there and even the tunnel the drivers passed through. Lance and Adam learned that one of the cars was scheduled to be included in the museum.

The two men puttered around E. P. Ripley Park and examined the steam engine and car, and admired the beautiful white gazebo. They were wandering down Main Street when Lance's complaints about the lack of food picked up momentum. They headed back to the same diner where they had lunch and enjoyed a leisurely dinner. Adam had pot roast on his mind, thanks to Lance bringing up his dinner with Adam's parents, so he ordered that. Lance felt adventuresome and tried the catfish. Both men were not disappointed.

By 9:30 that evening, they had left the Jag parked under some trees a distance down the street from the school. They walked slowly down the dark street towards the side entry that Mandy had pointed out to Adam. The school was predictably dark and quiet.

They heard an occasional car driving by and other typical noises of a quiet neighborhood. They waited next to the door for a couple of minutes. A rustling in the bushes announced their guide before her face peeked around the corner. Her smile faded a little when she spotted Lance. "You brought him?" she complained to Adam in a quiet voice.

"I had to," he explained, trying to keep as serious as she seemed to be, "because he is driving."

She looked Adam up and down again, dubious. "You don't drive?"

He rolled his eyes, as she had done to him. "Of course I know how to drive. It's just his turn."

That seemed to appease her. Lance watched on in amused silence. "Come on in. I have the key," she told them.

"How did you get that?" Adam asked, surprised. "You didn't steal it, did you?"

"No, Dad," she replied, sarcastic as only eleven-year olds can be. "My mom is a teacher here. I, uh, borrowed it. But we have to hurry. I have to be home soon." She expertly opened the lock with a minimum of sound. It was obvious she had done this before. "You bring the combination?"

"Yes, Boss," kidded Adam.

She tried to keep a straight face, but couldn't. She pulled a small flashlight out of her jacket pocket.

"Isn't Barbie going to want this back?" Lance remarked as he took it from her and shone the tiny beam of light into his hand.

"I don't see that you brought one," Mandy glared up at him, resisting the urge to snatch it back.

Adam took the light from Lance with a look for him to knock it off. He had to try this even though he knew it wasn't going to work, "Maybe you should stand guard out here, Mandy. In case someone comes."

She wasn't buying it. "Nobody ever comes here at night."

"It might be a good idea anyway."

She thought she knew what he was talking about. "You won't get in trouble."

"Somebody could come looking for you."

"Not as long as I am home by 10."

Adam could see he was getting nowhere. He crouched down to her eye-level. "I know you mean well. And you know we do, too. Right?"

She nodded, wary.

"Well, somebody else might not know that. It would really be better if you stayed out here. Please?"

Her face fell when she realized Adam meant it. "'Kay," she agreed in a tiny voice.

Adam stood back up. "Thank you, Mandy. If we find anything, we'll show you," he promised.

Mandy gave an 'I-don't-really-care' shrug and sat with her back against the wall, staring across the street.

Adam didn't know what else to say, so he motioned for Lance to follow him inside. They walked through the dark hallway and entered the office. Going over to the locker, Adam whispered, "Okay, I'll hold the light, Lance. You do the honors." He handed Lance the combination out of his pocket.

Lance accepted the paper without feeling the need to tell Adam he already had the number combination memorized. He gave the lock a couple of twists to clear it. As the fifth number was hit, they could hear the old tumbler fall into place. Lance grasped the handles and slid the lock up, pulling the door open. Adam felt a brush of a movement as Mandy sneaked in beside him. He knew her agreement to stay outside was too good to last. Adam shone the weak beam of light inside the locker that had been closed since 1960.

Mandy crowded in closer, obviously overcoming her objections to Lance in her curiosity to see what was inside. There was one shelf inside the locker, towards the top. It was on that shelf, rolled in the back, that Lance could see their next capsule. There were a few items on the bottom of the locker. They could see a hat sitting on some orange material that proved to be another flag like the one across the room. As Adam and Mandy looked over the floppy hat, Lance reached back, grabbed the capsule and pocketed it. "What kind of hat is that?" he asked, shining the light over the blue and white striped, billed cap.

"It's kind of hard to tell in the dark. We'll have to examine it later."

They heard a soft gasp from Mandy. "Look back there!"

Lance shone the light inside the locker again. Standing upright in the back, protected by a sheet of clear plastic, was a tall porcelain doll. "Go ahead and grab her, Mandy."

She looked up surprised at Lance. "I can touch her?"

He smiled kindly back. "See who she is."

The old Mandy returned, "Gosh, anyone can tell it's Snow White." But that didn't keep her from reaching in and carefully bringing out the doll. The Little Princess had eyes that closed when she was tilted and rosy cheeks and lips painted on a fragile porcelain face. On her head was a tiny crown that sparkled like diamonds even in the insignificant light. She was wearing her blue and yellow princess dress, and there were crystals sewn over the blue bodice of the dress. The blue cape was wrapped tightly in the back, but they could see the shining red lining where a corner bent back. "She's beautiful," Mandy whispered, unable to see the look exchanged over her head by the two men.

"She looks like part of the mural in the other room," Adam observed.

Mandy still hadn't looked up from the doll. She had worked a finger under the plastic to feel the silky black hair under the crown. She just nodded to whatever Adam had said.

Lance smiled at her reaction and turned the light back inside the locker. He found some papers that turned out to be twelve passes to Disneyland signed by Walt. He showed them to Adam. "Think we should leave these?"

"What for!?" The collector Adam momentarily warred with the fair-play Adam. Original passes to Disneyland would be worth a fortune. He finally nodded. But as Lance was putting them back on the shelf, he said, "How about if I take one?"

"Adam, it would look weird to have eleven passes. That number doesn't make sense. Besides, you don't need it."

Adam knew he was being selfish. "Put them all back," he sighed.

"That's a good boy," Lance crooned. "That's everything. This way, if somebody does figure out the combination later, there will be something inside to reward them."

"I know. I know. Come on. Mandy, we need to get out of here. And you need to get home."

Her head snapped up from Snow White. She looked crushed, but tried to cover it. "Oh, right." She gave a last, lingering look at the delicate face and handed the doll to Adam.

"My hands are full with the flag. Why don't you hold her for now?"

She nodded and led the way to the side door. Adam had removed his jacket and covered up the bright orange flag and the hat. That orange material would stand out like a beacon. If anybody spotted them walking back to their car, he didn't want anyone thinking he was stealing the school flag. At the door Mandy was torn between having to release the doll and locking up the school. After a careful look around to see if anyone was around, Lance held out his hand for the key. She misunderstood what he wanted and glumly handed him Snow White. He shook his head and asked for the key. Confused, she did as he asked. When he returned the key to her, she tried to give him the doll. He just told her it was nice meeting her, and walked off in the direction of their car. She turned to Adam who was smiling at her.

"Thanks for all your help, Mandy. I hope you're good at keeping secrets."

Still thinking about her precious doll, she didn't know what he meant. Then it sank in. "Oh, don't worry. I won't tell. Besides, I wanted to know what was in the locker. Here." She held out the doll to him with a deep sigh.

Adam looked at the proffered Snow White and the miserable face of Mandy behind it holding it out to him. "Hey, I still have my hands full. Why don't you hang on to her and give her a good home. Okay?"

"But she's yours."

"Oh, I'm too old to play with dolls. We would rather you have her. You be good now and get on home. Okay?"

With a happy shriek and a 'Thank you!,' Mandy jumped up and down and raced off towards home. She looked back once and waved before Adam got to their car.

"You did a nice thing," Lance told him as he started the car and headed out of town. It would be midnight before they got to their suite in Kansas City.

"The passes or the doll?"

"Yes."

Adam smiled in the darkness of the car. "Yeah, I know. It felt good, too."

"I wonder."

Adam glanced over at Lance, his face softly lit by the instrument panel. "You wonder what?"

"I wonder if that's how Walt felt setting all this up. Donating the Autopia ride to the kids in the town. Helping the school. All of it."

"I'll bet he did," Adam agreed, thinking about their

benefactor.

"Yeah, me too."

"**W**ow. This flag is in pristine condition," remarked Adam, going over the orange material very carefully.

Lance was pulling the end cap off their latest capsule. "It's probably been in that locker since Walt put it there. What did we figure? 1960? There!" He finally got the seals to release. Four small shiny chrome screws fell out onto the table and scattered. Three stayed on the table and he had to dig one of them out of the carpet. "That's odd." He looked inside the container and pulled out another diary sheet. It had only two words written on it: **Lilly Belle**.

CHAPTER 9

LILLY BELLE

THURSDAY, MAY 23RD, 2002
12:47 A.M.

Adam brought over the hat that had been found in the locker when he saw the container was open. He looked over one of the screws and proclaimed it a 'machine screw'. He put on the pale blue and white striped hat to show Lance. It had a small, stiff bill in front, and a stiff band going around the head. The top of the hat was full, standing up a little, with pintuck pleats shaping it into the bill. The pintucks caused the sides of the hat to stand up from the bill instead of falling over the side. "What do you think?" he asked Lance.

"You look very cute."

"That's not what I mean. Do you know what kind of hat this is?"

"Well, I didn't see one like it last time I went to Barney's, so no."

Adam took the hat off his head and mentally counted to ten. When he got to fifteen, he told Lance, "I think this is an engineer's cap. Do you think it could be Walt's personal hat?"

Lance looked at the hat with more interest now. "That might explain the clue then." He handed the ripped page to Adam to read.

Adam looked up from the note. "*Lilly Belle*? That's one of the trains, isn't it?"

Lance nodded, "Yeah, that or his wife." He tried the cap on. It was too small for his head. He handed it back to Adam. "Here. This fits your pinhead. Obviously I have too big of a brain."

"Uh huh." Adam accepted the hat back gladly. He could make a special display case…Maybe mount it next to the brass nametag…He missed what Lance just said. "Sorry. What did you say?"

"I noticed you were too busy drooling over the hat to hear me. I asked: if the clue was referring to a train, do you know where it would be?"

Adam set the cap on top of the flag and glanced at the clock. It was close to 1 a.m. Good thing their flight didn't leave until right after lunch at 12:45 tomorrow. He could sleep later than usual. "Not sure about the location. I don't know the names of all the engines at Disneyland. And, there are some trains at Disney World in Florida, too. Not sure if those fit our timeframe, though."

Lance grunted. "I'd rather concentrate on California. I don't relish a trip to Florida right now. Fresh start tomorrow?" he asked, rubbing a hand over his eyes.

Adam agreed. He was tired and ready to go to bed now and looking forward to returning home tomorrow. Well, it was already 'tomorrow', Adam realized, looking at the clock, stifling a yawn in the process. Later today, he amended his thought. "Yeah. See you in the morning. Late morning," he added as he shut the door to his bedroom.

Lance sat alone in the front room of their suite. He was too wound up to sleep right now. The situation with his father was bothering him – as it always did. He didn't know why he should have to account for every dime he spent. It was his money. Theoretically. Just because he didn't want to sit behind a desk like his father did doesn't mean grandfather's trust was invalid. Theoretically.

He decided he would just have to live quietly for a while until his father calmed down. No more trips! That should placate his father if the Gold Card showed no unusual activity for a *reasonable* amount of time.

However, 'reasonable' to Lance and 'reasonable' to his father were two vastly different things.

No more trips. He would have to remember that. No more trips.

Unless, of course, it was absolutely necessary.

The two men had a quiet breakfast late in the morning. Neither had slept well or long enough. The drive to the airport took only twenty minutes. Lance ran a lingering hand over the burlwood dash of the Jaguar as they got out of it for the last time before returning it to the rental office. Lance always appreciated a thing of beauty. And this was indeed a beautiful car.

They had an uneventful flight to Denver; their hour layover there allowed Lance to have some lunch in the airport's food court. Returning to LAX at 3:50 that afternoon put them in bumper-to-bumper traffic on the 405 Freeway all the way back to Orange County and Adam's apartment. What should have been a forty-five minute drive took two hours. Both of them were tired; Adam just grabbed his bag out of the trunk and waved his good-bye to Lance as the Mercedes pulled away. They would meet up some time on Saturday to see what they were going to do next.

SUNDAY, MAY 26TH, 2002
1:15 P.M.

It wasn't until early Sunday afternoon that the two friends were able to get together again. Adam had been busy with the Anderson job, and Adam figured Lance was off being Lance. He knew better than to question Lance.

As they discovered that afternoon in Adam's apartment, both men came up with information on *Lilly Belle.*

Adam went first. He shuffled through some of the mounds of sheets of notes on his coffee table and handed a stack of them to Lance. Lance glanced at the papers and pushed them back. "Can't read your writing. Just tell me," Lance leaned back, putting his feet up on the table.

With a frown, Adam looked at his carefully written notes. "There's nothing wrong with my handwriting." Lance was giving him the same look Mandy had used right after she had said 'duh'. "Fine," he sighed. "I'll read them to you, Your Highness. I'm sure you know that the first *Lilly Belle* was the name of the engine Walt built for his backyard railroad on Coralwood Drive. He had commissioned Roger Broggie to build the engine back in 1949. It made its first run sometime in 1950. It was quite a layout. He had over 2600 feet of track, a 46-foot trestle, and a 90-foot tunnel under Lillian's garden. As he did later at Disneyland, he built a berm around the property so his neighbors wouldn't be bothered by the train. I found some pictures of the backyard, the train barn, and the train itself, if you want to see them."

Lance nodded when Adam was finished. "Yeah, that matches what I found. The house was on two and a half acres, so he had lots of room for the train – which is one of the reasons he picked that lot in the first place."

"Then you probably also found that the house no longer exists."

"I did read that the new owners tore down the whole thing right after buying it. Something about asbestos, I think." When Adam agreed, he continued, "Too bad, though. I would have liked to have seen the house. Did you find out what happened to the train?"

Adam shuffled to another yellow tablet of paper. He flipped a couple pages to find what he was looking for. "Well, there was also the train barn in the backyard, built along the lines of the barn we saw in Marceline. After Lilly died in 1997 and the house was sold, the barn was dismantled piece by piece, I believe, starting in 1998. Griffith Park made an agreement with the Los Angeles Live Steamers – train enthusiasts and friends of Walt – who donated some land to reconstruct the barn in Griffith Park. That was finished in 1999. Quite a ceremony, too. They have a tremendous amount of Disney railroad memorabilia. I had hoped the *Lilly Belle* ended up there on display. That was my first thought when I read about it."

"No such luck, though."

"Nope," Adam replied, with a hint of dejection. "They do have some of the original track from the backyard on Carolwood, but that doesn't help with what we need. Did you find out anything about the actual train?"

Lance took up the gray capsule as Adam was talking. "I did some asking at the Park yesterday." He could see Adam's eyes open a little wider in surprise. "Yes, I was back at the Park yesterday. Don't ask. The train on display inside the Disneyland Train Station on Main Street used to be the real deal. But, sometime before the year 2000, it was taken down and a duplicate train was made by Broggie's son."

"That's too bad," Adam cut in. "We would have had a chance to look it over."

"I thought that, too, at first. But, on thinking about it some more, it would have been a lot more difficult to get at than Walt's desk had been. The train station is the focal point of Main Street and pretty busy all the time. I don't think we could have gotten to it."

Adam couldn't resist. "Not even with the help of one of your girls?"

Lance refused to be baited. He just answered along the same lines he had been pursuing. "Well, shutting the doors of a relatively quiet show is a lot different than shutting down a popular train station that is full of windows and has trains coming and going every ten minutes or so. There is a limit to what even I can do."

"Your humility is touching."

Lance ignored that comment. "What about these screws?" Lance had dumped them into his hand and was looking at them.

"Not sure on that either. Obviously, from the size of them they would fit something small. They look like #6 or #8 screws. Maybe that's a hint on what to look for. We might need them to replace some screws we have to remove. The fact that they are machine screws and not carpentry screws might indicate something *on* the train as opposed to a building surrounding it." He stopped and shrugged. "I don't know. But I suggest that wherever we end up going, we bring a screwdriver that fits those screws."

Lance just nodded his agreement and dropped the screws back into the capsule. They had been safe in there for forty-two years; they should be fine for a few more days. "So," Lance summed it up, "we have about two years that the train has been 'missing'."

Adam smiled. "Well, 'missing' from our perspective, yes. I'm sure whoever has it knows exactly where it has been each step of the way."

"And now we need to know who that is and see if we can get in for a look."

"Too bad about Griffith Park. I wouldn't have minded a trip out there."

Lance put down the capsule. "We could take a run out there and ask around."

Adam glanced at his clock. "That's a good idea, but I'm meeting my folks for dinner...Don't look so smug. It was time to get together with them anyway. Why don't you go out to Griffith Park and then let me know what you find."

"I could do that. Where are you going for dinner?"

"I was going to take them to Granville's Steakhouse at the Disneyland Hotel. Why?" he asked, suddenly wary and wondering if he should have asked the 'why' first.

You never knew what Lance was up to.

Lance looked all innocence. "No reason. Sounds nice. Tell Allison I said hi. I'll go ahead and take off then and see what I can find out."

"Who is Allison?"

"The server."

"Of course she is."

Adam didn't know why he was surprised when Lance, dressed in an expensive, tailored dark brown suit, showed up at Granville's and pulled a chair up to their table. Adam's mom, Margaret, gave a cry of delight at seeing Lance, and John, his dad, thumped him on the shoulder a few times. Then they gave Adam the "what a delightful surprise, you sly dog" look as if he had arranged the whole thing. Adam also noticed Lance didn't meet his eyes for the first half hour. Lance felt Adam needed to get used to the idea that he, Lance, had invited himself along.

After a bubbly greeting from Allison, the attractive blonde server who Adam figured was still in college, Lance ordered a drink and dinner and caught up on the salad portion of dinner that had just been served. Chatting animatedly with John and Margaret, Lance covered everything from John's golf game, to the new tennis instructor Margaret had started working with at their racquet club, to the new carpet in their living room. At one break in the conversation, when the plates were being removed and his parents were distracted, Lance leaned over to Adam and said in a low voice, "San Francisco."

"Damn!" Adam exclaimed loudly, much to the chagrin of his mother.

"You know, Lance, I did train him better than that," Margaret said as a way of apology for her son.

Lance nodded seriously. "I know, Margaret," he said in a low, conspiring voice. "You do your best and hope they turn out well." Lance looked over to Adam and gave him a stern, fatherly glare. Adam just rolled his eyes, shaking his head in disbelief.

John just looked on, amused. He knew Lance liked to get Adam's goat whenever he could. He figured Adam would get his shot in at some point during the evening. Things were always more interesting when these two got together.

Adam didn't have any chance to question Lance during the rest of dinner. He knew what Lance had meant. That had to be where the *Lilly Belle* was now residing. *Crap! Why couldn't the train be here in Southern California*, he groused to himself.

While Margaret and John were busy choosing dessert, Lance leaned over again and added, "Invitation only."

"You get an invitation?" Adam whispered back.

"Couldn't."

"Crap!" he burst out.

"Adam!" Margaret cried, looking around, embarrassed. "We are in a lovely, public place, son. Mind your manners!"

"Yes'm," Adam mumbled, swallowing the next expletive that was on the tip of his tongue. She would have liked that choice phrase even less.

Now John was curious. He knew the two boys were spending a lot of time together lately. Scott had mentioned it during their golf game earlier that day. But the 'why' and the 'where' hadn't come up. It was obvious Adam didn't like some bit of news Lance had just given him. And it was equally obvious Adam was trying to master his 'nothing-is-wrong' face. He wasn't doing a very good job as yet, but he was getting closer. Well, he and Margaret were available if either of the boys needed to talk. Adam was pretty good about confiding in them if he needed to. But, judging from Adam's reaction just now, he figured it would be Lance who would be more apt to come to them than Adam. Yes, Adam was a chip off the old blockhead, as his mother was fond of saying.

After getting good-bye hugs from Margaret and John and a promise to come out to the house again soon, Lance walked happily to Adam's truck. "What a nice dinner!" he exclaimed as if he had been invited all along. Then he added seriously, "You know, you really should control your language around your mother. She really doesn't appreciate that kind of talk."

Adam muttered something under his breath as he unlocked the Silverado.

"Ooh, she wouldn't have liked that one at all," Lance grinned as Adam slid into the driver's seat. "So, when do you want to take our road trip?"

Adam leaned back, resting his head tiredly against the headrest. "I knew you were going to say something like that," he groaned. "I don't suppose there's any way around it."

"Only if you don't want to find the next clue."

"Yeah. I also suppose you have it mapped out already."

"Of course. It will take us about six and a half to seven hours to drive to San Francisco. I have the location of the warehouse where all the memorabilia is stored."

Adam's head came up, frowning. "Warehouse? Aren't we going through the relatives?"

Lance leaned against the side of the truck. "Think about it for a minute, Adam. We ask permission. We are escorted into the building. We are watched while we look at the train. We are escorted out of the building. When exactly do you see us getting anywhere close to *Lilly Belle* with a screwdriver?"

"Yeah, okay, I see your point. And I don't suppose even you could distract them long enough for me to accomplish whatever it is we need to do with a screwdriver." He expelled a breath. "So, it sounds like we have to go into the building ourselves."

Lance just nodded slowly.

"Any ideas on how?"

Lance continued to nod. He looked like one of those little dogs in the back window of a car. "I have an idea, yes, but I need to work on it some more. I'll do that while you are at work Monday. Hopefully we can leave Tuesday or Wednesday."

Adam gave a laugh. "Seems like we always leave on Wednesday."

"Well," Lance stated, standing away from the truck as Adam started the engine, "it's worked well for us so far. Let's hope our luck holds out."

Adam's window rolled down after he slammed his door shut. His face was very serious as he looked at Lance. "You do realize you are talking about 'breaking and entering', right?"

Lance looked over towards Disneyland. The firework show was just starting. "Let's just hope we don't break anything and it is just 'entering'."

Adam gave a small smile. "I'm sure the judge who throws us into jail will consider that."

"Good thing I know a bunch of lawyers," Lance called back as he headed for his car. *Too bad they were all related to him – and on less-than-friendly terms,* he thought grimly.

MONDAY, MAY 27TH, 2002
7:15 P.M.

Monday evening found Adam in an empty furniture store that had been turned into an extreme sports training facility. He and Lance were strapped into harnesses that went around their legs and waist with hooks in the middle of their back and in the middle of their stomach. Attached to those hooks were ropes dangling from the three-story-high ceiling. At that moment, they were dangling about twenty feet up in the air, suspended over huge cushioned mats in case the novices slipped.

Lance was bobbing comfortably about ten feet away from Adam. Adam wasn't faring so well. He had played out the rope through the figure 8-ring, but apparently had done something wrong. Again.

"Why are you upside down?" Lance asked him, not bothering to hide his smile, since, from Adam's current position, he couldn't see it. "You're leaning back too far."

Adam saved his energy by not answering. He pushed against the loops holding his feet and moved the metal ascender up a little. Struggling, he got back into the correct sitting position. Breathing hard from the effort, he glared at Lance. "Why is everything so easy for you?"

"Superior breeding?"

Adam let that go and played out some of the line, lowering another foot.

"Now go back up to the top and start over," the instructor Hans ordered.

Adam watched Lance alternate pushing with his feet, sliding his ascender higher with each step. It was called a 'Frog Rig' because of its resemblance to a frog's kicking motion. When Lance got to the top, he leaned back and used his descender friction device to drop steadily to the ground. He stopped within a foot of the cushioned mat and looked expectantly at Adam, waiting.

"Very good, Lance. Adam, you want to get started. Tonight?" Hans prompted. Both Hans and Lance had failed to mention to Adam that Lance had been there most of the morning learning and practicing.

Adam struggled to get the rhythm right for a smooth ascent. It was getting easier, but it was tiring.

"That's better," Hans called as Adam neared the top of the rope. "Now, lean back some and relax your legs. Not so far. That's right. Play the rope through. A little faster would be good…"

Adam finally got to the same level as Lance. Lance was swinging a bit side to side a little. "You know, Adam, we could get personal lifters to attach to the harnesses. Clip it on the rope, push the button, and you're there."

"Really? Those sound good. Why are we doing this then?"

"Because they are about $8,000 each," was Lance's reply. "Besides, you should know how to do it correctly anyway. If the batteries gave out you would have to do it manually."

Adam sighed. "I knew you would come up with a reason. Are we done here tonight? My arms and legs are killing me."

Hans walked across the cushion to where they were dangling. "Yes, you are done for tonight. Now I want you to correctly remove yourselves from the ropes. Tomorrow you will feel more confident."

"Tomorrow?" Adam groaned. "Thought we were done."

Hans shrugged. He had already been paid for two lessons. "You don't have to practice. But there is less risk if you learn how to drop and climb properly and safely. One lesson usually isn't enough. It's up to you."

"See you tomorrow, Hans," Lance called as they were leaving. "Why are you limping, Adam? Gees, I thought you construction guys were tough."

Adam sank gratefully into the soft gray leather seat of the Mercedes. "If I could lift my arm, I would hit you and show you how tough I am."

Lance just laughed as they pulled out of the parking lot.

WEDNESDAY, MAY 29TH, 2002
10:00 A.M.

By ten o'clock Wednesday morning, the twosome were heading north on I-5 freeway. The final destination had been programmed into Lance's navigation system. The helpful female voice that had been telling them unneeded turn-by-turn advice on getting out of the Los Angeles area was now quiet as they headed through the mountains and dropped down the Grapevine into the long, fertile San Joaquin Valley. The land was flat and dry as they continued to head north, passing towns like Bakersfield and Los Banos. They were glad they were too late in the season for Tule fog that could cause a problem with vision. The Sierra Nevada Mountains off to the right became more obscure the farther north they traveled. They could constantly see the Coast Range off to their left and would cut through those hills once they reached the 580 freeway that would take them towards the ocean.

When Adam tired of playing 'Guess the Crop' with himself, he asked Lance if he had brought everything they would need.

Lance had been humming along with the radio, occasionally checking his mirrors for traffic. "Hmm? Oh, yeah. I think so. I know you have the proper screwdriver and those little screws." Adam nodded. "I have the climbing equipment, flashlights, face masks, gloves, grappling hook, fake license plates, layout and design of the warehouse, security system layout – which is pretty minor considering the value of the artifacts –, motel reservations, and a dinner reservation in Ghirardelli Square for tonight at 7:00. I think that covers everything."

"Back up a minute…Grappling hook and fake license plates? What are those for?"

Lance sighed. "Really, Adam, you can be so dense sometimes…"

He broke off when the nav system told him the next turnoff for the west I-580 was coming up in two miles. After that, they had only about two hours to go before they were in San Francisco.

Adam's eye narrowed. "Humor me. Since what we are planning is basically illegal, I would like to know the particulars, if that is all right with you."

"Well, we did go over the warehouse design last

night after our rappelling lesson. I thought you understood what we had to do." Lance checked his side mirror and swept into the right lane.

"I do understand that aspect of it. The grappling hook and fake license plates are new."

"Oh. I thought they would be self-explanatory. The license plates are for this car that has to sit somewhere outside the warehouse until we emerge again. If it is seen, it would be better if the plates couldn't be traced back to me. Even though this fine machine is just leased, and I am quite fond of it, I would rather somebody tracing it would end up with a car that is at the bottom of a heap in a junkyard rather than in my garage. And, as for the grappling hook, how did you propose we get on the top of a two-story warehouse?"

"Stairs?" Adam replied meekly. He hadn't realized Lance put so much forethought into this venture. And, now, thinking about it, he was glad he did. It might keep them out of jail. He hoped.

When Lance didn't reply to his sheepish answer, Adam knew he had better say something. He looked out the window at the dry yellow fields stretching into the distance. Adam wasn't good at apologies. "You've, uhm, you've done a lot of work on this. Thanks. I appreciate your efforts."

Lance just nodded and pulled into the first gas station they came to. "You want to drive for a while? I'd like to take a nap before we get there."

Adam was surprised. Lance never let anyone drive his car. "Sure. No problem."

As they resumed their route, Adam was impressed. "This handles nice!"

Lance, leaning his seat back, snorted. "You mean it doesn't drive like a truck?"

"Hey, my Silverado doesn't drive like a truck, either. This just handles…better."

Lance adjusted the air conditioner vent to blow over

him and closed his eyes. He was asleep before he could reply.

The navigation system directed Adam to the motel where they would be staying. He looked over the squat, one-story building with its flashing neon sign. He nudged the still-sleeping Lance. "Wake up, Sleeping Beauty, we're here. Well, we're somewhere. Is this the right place?" The motel wasn't Lance's usual style.

Lance reached for one of the buttons on the door panel and his passenger seat returned to its upright position. He looked at the motel and grimaced. "Yes, this is it. It looked a little…uh, bigger on the Internet." A jumbo jet screamed overhead on its approach to the San Francisco International Airport. "But, it is only $60 a night. We'll be paying in untraceable cash."

Adam handed Lance his keys. "Isn't that price missing a zero for you?"

"For what we came to do, this is fine." He sounded less confident than his words implied. "Maybe it looks better inside."

It didn't.

They changed into some fresh clothes for dinner and gladly left the small, stale-smelling room. "I thought we would drive by the warehouse while it was still light, and then go to dinner. See if there is anything obvious about it we should know."

Again, the navigation system took them to their destination, winding them accurately through the city streets. The warehouse was in an older, industrial section of the city near the piers, not too far from the building where the museum would eventually be housed. They already knew their target was on the corner of the street, with an entry door and a roll-up delivery door on each street. The skylights they would be using for their entry couldn't be seen from their car at street level. It was nearing 6:00 p.m. and the surrounding buildings looked closed for the night.

A delivery truck took off from two buildings down and a few cars pulled away as Adam and Lance sat across the street and watched. Other than the address, their building was unmarked. No lights shown through the windows. Lance pulled out from where they had stopped and drove slowly down the alley behind the warehouse. Trash bins, empty crates, litter occupied the sides of the alley. After a short discussion, they decided to leave the car in the alley halfway down between the next two buildings. There was a delivery truck inlet there where the car could be left and the alley would not be blocked. Lance drove down the rest of the alley to the next side street. A left turn would take them to the piers and the ocean. A right turn would take them through the industrial section and back into the city.

"Look okay to you?"

Adam's mouth was dry. He was starting to get more nervous about this whole idea. "I guess. Wish we had a different plan."

"Me, too," Lance admitted quietly. "I don't look forward to facing five to ten if we get caught. But, I couldn't come up with anything else."

"I know."

They were quiet with their own thoughts throughout dinner. Neither had much of an appetite, but knew they would need their strength. The glowing view of the city from the restaurant was lost on them as they pushed their food around and managed to get most of it down. Under different circumstances, the view and the city itself would have afforded them a lot of enjoyment. The fog was beginning to roll in and slowly envelope the city. It should have been stunning from where they sat.

Both knew the seriousness of what they intended to do. Both felt they had to take the chance.

WEDNESDAY, MAY 29TH, 2002
11:18 P.M.

The grappling hook made a huge clatter as it again fell to the blacktop of the alley. Adam had tried twice to hurl it up to the roof. He almost had it – one more swing. Leaning back, he got the momentum going and made another grunting heave.

The curved hooks caught on the parapet of the building. Adam tested it with his weight. It held. They pulled their ski masks into place. In addition to black masks the two wore black climbing gloves, black jackets, black pants and black shoes. They blended into the side of the building as they slowly walked their way up the rope.

"You remember the old Batman TV show?" Lance suddenly asked, his soft voice sounding overloud to Adam.

"Shh! Yes. What about it?" Adam grunted as he struggled. They were almost to the top.

Lance chuckled. "This was how the Dynamic Duo always got to the top of buildings. I keep expecting a window to pop open next to us."

Adam reached the top and hauled himself over the edge. "Well, I, for one, am glad that didn't happen. So, who am I? Batman or Robin?"

"Well, I drove and you went up first. That makes you Robin."

"Figures," Adam muttered and sat back on his heels. Lance crouched down next to him.

They stayed still for a minute and just listened. There was no activity around them. The streets were silent and empty. The fog might obscure their vision, but it would do the same to anyone who might come by.

"Damn, it's cold up here!" Adam exclaimed rubbing his arms in spite of the jacket he was wearing.

"Well, you know what Mark Twain said, don't you?"

"'Go West, young man'?" Adam quoted.

"No, that was Horace Greeley. Mark Twain said: 'The coldest winter I ever knew was the summer I spent in San Francisco'."

Adam just chuckled as he bent down to fit a socket wrench over the exposed bolts surrounding the skylight they had chosen. The humor helped relieve some of his nervousness. Just some, though. He still had plenty to spare.

Lance was attaching their drop ropes to vent pipes on each side of the skylight. They each had their own rope to expedite their drop into the warehouse. Adam was able to undo the four half-inch bolts on each corner of the skylight. The painted plexi-glass covering was convex, curving out towards him, and about three feet square. Lance helped Adam lift the front corners off and then slide the panel back to give them room to enter. Lance leaned into the ropes, testing the strength of the pipes. He was stepping into his harness as Adam started getting into his. There was no need to talk. They knew what they had to do. Now was the time to do it.

Lance walked his rope to the opening into the warehouse and dropped it into the darkness below. He looked over to see if Adam was ready and doing the same. Through his full-face mask, Adam's eyes were wide as he backed to the edge of the dark hole and lowered himself through. Lance could hear the mechanics of the decender as it caught and released. Adam was slow, but doing fine. Lance pulled a larger device out of his backpack and snapped it into place on his thin rope. Checking the resistance one more time, he backed over the edge and pushed the lever. He slowly descended with a soft whirl of the motor. He was on the ground before Adam made it.

Lance could see Adam's eyes frowning as he slid past. "Hey!" Adam whispered when he finally got to the floor, "I thought we weren't going to use the automatic ones!"

Lance casually shrugged as he unhooked himself from the rope. "It's not my fault you're too cheap to buy one."

Adam growled as he freed himself from the ropes and pulled out a flashlight, and, wisely, stayed silent.

They both knew without being told to keep the lights away from the windows as they played the beams over the jumble of boxes and cabinets and covered items in the dark warehouse. The larger boxes were marked with their contents: Disneyland Memorabilia, Walt's Office, Animation. There were tarps over some items that proved to be a bright yellow Autopia car, a blue Peoplemover car, a red and white Bobsled, and an orange Skyway Cab.

Adam's gloved fingers slowly went over pieces of remembrances of his Disneyland past – rides that were either no longer there or had been changed. He itched to get into some of those boxes to see what was in them.

No time. No time to explore. No time to remember. They had to get out as fast as possible. As far as they knew, only the doors and windows were alarmed. They didn't want to delay inside in case they were wrong about any other alarms that might be in place.

They walked slowly through the irregular aisles between boxes, looking for something that indicated the *Lilly Belle*.

Adam found it near one of the doors. The train was in parts, each car in its own open crate. A tarp had been thrown loosely over the crates, but the packing was incomplete.

"What do you make of that?" Adam asked when Lance joined him.

Lance shrugged, his face hot inside the mask he didn't dare remove in case of hidden night-vision security cameras. "Maybe they are getting ready to ship it somewhere for display."

"That could be. You look over the car Walt sat on to drive the train. There should be some open space up under the padded seat. I'll focus on the engine."

Their flashlights did a slow scan back and forth across the pieces. Adam wished he could take the train out of the box and sit on it like Walt had done. *Concentrate, Michaels, look for four screws.*

Lance had his head inside the box so he could see under the little red seat. He saw no screws and no little gray capsule. He went to the next box which was the 'cattle car' Walt's friends used to sit on. He began his sweeping search.

Adam was about to unwisely remove the train from the box. He hadn't found any matching screws on the body. The smokestack was empty. The whistle would not be used for a hiding place. The wheels would not have been used because they would have to be replaced periodically. He went so far as to put his fingers under the little roof of the section where a conductor would stand if it had been a full-sized train. He was about to lift the roof when he noticed there was a discrepancy in the depth of the roof. "Lance! I think I found something."

The second flashlight joined his. In each corner of the roof, was a point of unevenness that Adam had missed when he first looked it over. Each slight indentation was covered over with some kind of colored putty. Scraping the putty off with the edge of the screwdriver, Adam found his matching screws.

"I'm going to have to take my gloves off," he told Lance, "or else I'll never to able to handle the screws."

"I brought a cloth to wipe off the fingerprints, so go ahead."

Adam used the least pressure he could on the delicate roof of the train. He was sweating profusely under all his dark clothes and the stress. He dropped the first screw as it came out.

"Let it go," Lance told him when he stopped to look for it. "We don't have time."

Adam didn't bother replying, but got the remaining three screws up and into Lance's waiting hand. He was just about to lift the lid when they both heard the first police siren faintly in the distance.

"Oh, crap! You think that's for us!?"

"I don't know. Hurry up!"

Adam lifted the roof and immediately saw a diary paper and some kind of button inside the inch and a half deep tray. Handing them to Lance, he heard the siren was getting noticeably closer. Trying to hurry, Adam put the roof back on the train and started putting in the new screws.

They heard a second siren now. They couldn't tell how far away it was, but the first one was definitely louder now.

Adam willed himself to slow down and concentrate on the screws. If he moved the screwdriver incorrectly he could scratch the delicate lid of the train. Lance's flashlight had gone out and he was getting out the cloth to wipe off any fingerprints.

Two screws.

Three screws.

Four screws in. With a sigh of relief, Lance wiped off the train lid as Adam put his gloves back on.

The sirens could only be a couple of blocks away.

"Go up your rope, Adam! Get started! I'm almost finished here. Do you have the rope connected right?"

Adam was fumbling with the hooks that connected the rope to the harness. "Almost there."

Lance ran over to him and shone the light on Adam's harness to make sure he was properly fastened. "Go. Go. Go!" Lance urged him.

Adam pushed with his feet and was sliding up the ascender in a smooth, rhythmic pattern.

"Don't look back!" Lance called up to him. "Just get up there!"

The sirens were almost there. Was that a third police car that joined them? There was so much noise!

Adam continued to struggle upwards. When he was

within ten feet of the opening, in a whirl of movement, Lance shot up past him. Stopping at the edge of the skylight, Lance pulled himself over the edge, hauled up his rope, and disappeared. Cursing to himself with aching arms, Adam grunted with effort and shoved the final feet upwards. He pulled himself over the edge and pulled up his rope. He dropped the skylight back into place. As he unhooked his harness, he looked around. Lance was nowhere to be seen. Running to the edge of the warehouse, Adam didn't bother with the figure-8 rings that would make the descent smooth and safe. He just grabbed the rope attached to the grappling hook and speedily rappelled backwards down the side of the old building.

The sirens were deafening. They must be on the front side of the building. Adam raced down the alley and jumped into the open door of the running car where Lance was waiting. With no headlights on, Lance pulled out of their hiding place and headed down the alley. At the end of the alley, he just let the car slow instead of using his brakes. The red brake lights would have been like a beacon even in this fog. Fortunately there was no oncoming traffic. Instead of taking the first street, he continued bouncing through the next alley, letting the fog envelope the black car. At the second street, he turned right towards the city and turned on the headlights.

The sound of the sirens faded as they headed away from the industrial part of the city. Adam was going to say something to Lance, but when he turned to do so, he realized they both still had their ski masks on. He reached over and pulled Lance's off while they were at a stop sign. Adam took off his own and tossed it on the floor of the car.

Lance was startled but then figured out what Adam had done. He pulled off his thin climbing gloves and ran a hand through his damp hair. Lance pulled into an empty lot and went out to switch the license plates back to the real ones. After wiping the untraceable plates carefully with the cloth, he dropped them into a dumpster among the trash and debris.

He got back in the car and dropped his head onto the steering wheel. He took a deep breath before sitting upright again. They could hear the sirens again, far away. Were the police searching for them now?

Lance started the engine again and followed the pleasant female voice of the navigation system back to their motel. Another jet screamed overhead preparing to land while Adam unlocked their door. Lance was behind him, holding the bags with all their gear.

Inside the two men threw themselves onto their respective beds.

"Damn."

"I agree," was all Adam replied.

They both fell asleep without another word.

Thursday, May 30th, 2002
10:12 a.m.

The fog still hadn't burned off by the time the two men awakened late in the morning. Lance got up first and pulled off his clothes to take a much-needed shower. The tiny bar of soap was almost gone when he finally emerged, dripping and refreshed.

There was no one pounding on their door, so he figured it was a good day so far. After getting dressed, he threw his wet towel over Adam's face, awakening him. He was still shaving when Adam emerged from the bathroom.

"Thanks for leaving me no hot water and barely enough soap for my face."

"Any time. Not my fault you didn't get up first."

There was no clock in the room. "Do you know what time it is?" Adam's watch was on the other side of his bed. It seemed too far for him to walk over there and get it.

"I would guess around 10, 10:30. You hungry? I'm starved."

"You're always starved," Adam reminded him. "Do you want to eat here in San Francisco, or put some distance between us and the city?" he asked as he got dressed.

Lance thought about that. "You do have a point. I guess I can hold off my starvation a couple of hours. Should we grab a newspaper?"

"What for? You want to catch up on the comics?"

"My, aren't we grumpy this morning. Just wanted to see if our exploits made the paper yet."

"Ah. Isn't that like returning to the scene of the crime?"

Lance laughed as he put his shaver away. "No. Going back to the warehouse would fit that description. And I have no intention of doing that. I even erased the entry from my nav system. In fact, I erased all mention of San Francisco from it. I guess we can figure out how to get home from here."

"I certainly hope so. I didn't think I would ever be so anxious to see Orange County again." He paused and was deep in thought a couple of minutes. "Lance?"

Lance looked up from packing up what few dirty clothes he had worn. He could see Adam was in his serious mode. "What?"

Adam sat back on the bed, his clothes packed, ready to go. "I know why we did what we did last night. But, it bothers me a lot." He held up a hand when Lance was going to interrupt him. "No, wait a minute. What we did was illegal, whether or not we damaged anything or stole anything. I don't believe Walt, for one minute, would have sanctioned our action. Even though his hiding place made it necessary, I don't think he would have liked us breaking and entering." He broke off a minute and took a breath. "I just don't want us to be in that position again. I conduct my business legit. I try to treat people fairly and give them what they pay for. I feel I am an honest man. I don't want to have to break the law again. I don't think you do either."

That was a long speech for Adam; Lance agreed with it. The adrenaline rush was a great high, but, Adam was right, it was legally wrong. Their luck couldn't hold out forever, no matter what precautions they took. They needed to play it by-the-book from here on out. "You're right, much as I hate to ever say that out loud. You know what a big head you get. We'll keep it legal. Now, let's get out of here before we get all mushy and have to hug or something."

Adam gave a hearty laugh at that. "Say, where is the clue and that button? I can look them over on the drive."

He saw Lance's face go slack. Lance patted his shirt pocket, then frantically unzipped his bag and flung out the clothes in it.

"You lost the clue!" Adam yelled at him. "Did you leave it at the warehouse?"

Lance was going through each one the pockets of the jacket he had worn. "Didn't you take it from me? Don't you have them?"

"Crap, Lance! I handed them to you right before I set the lid back on the train. What did you do with them?" Adam started going through Lance's clothes. He pulled out every pocket. Then he noticed Lance was just standing there, smiling.

Lance reached into his shirt pocket and slowly pulled out the clue and the button. "Just kidding."

The color started coming back into Adam's face. Then more color came and he looked very angry. "That's not funny!"

Lance proved him wrong by breaking out in a hearty laugh. He looked at Adam's red face and laughed even harder. Then it seemed he couldn't stop.

Nobody has ever been able to keep a straight face in the presence of someone else's hilarity. Adam tried to hang on to his anger, but it didn't stand a chance at the sight of Lance laughing, holding his sides, tears running out of his eyes. Lance's humor erased all the stress and strain. He was purged and it felt good.

When he finally could stop, he sat on the bed, wiping his eyes. "Should have seen the look on your face!" He was threatening to start laughing again, and his stomach hurt too much for that. "Oh, gee! Ouch. Man, that was funny."

He could tell Adam was going to get angry again if it continued. "Let's get out of here, Adam."

Adam knew he was maneuvered out of being mad again. But that was all right. What good would anger accomplish? They loaded their bags in the car, shoving the climbing gear in the back. There was more room without the grappling hook and ropes they had to leave behind. The motel room had been paid in cash when they arrived, so they simply got on the freeway and headed south. The city of Alameda was just half an hour to the south of where they were and would be a good place to look for a restaurant.

"So, what does the clue say?"

Adam looked up from the gold and black button stamped with the letters **SFDR** he was studying. He read the clue to Lance: "**This canyon isn't so grand, but you are on the right track. Bring a rope. You probably have about 5 minutes.**"

CHAPTER 10

Moving Trains

MONDAY, JUNE 3RD, 2002
2:55 P.M.

Back home, the men met up at Adam's apartment. As they talked, Adam fingered the gold button with the raised black lettering. SFDR. Santa Fe and Disneyland Railroad. It could be nothing else. This button was no longer used since Santa Fe had pulled out of their Disneyland sponsorship in 1974. Amtrak moved in on their passenger train business in 1971, and Santa Fe could no longer justify the expense. The little button was now a much-sought after collector's item.

"You agree, Lance?"

"With what?" Lance was stretched out on Adam's beige sofa, the papers once carefully piled on the cushions now littering the floor. They had been discussing the possibilities of the clue for a couple of hours.

"Button. Train. Remember?"

"You have any beer? Never mind… Yes, but I was thinking about the 'canyon' and 'rope' part. It sounds like spelunking, as opposed to rappelling like we did in San Francisco."

Adam hoped not. "I don't know of any caves deep enough at Disneyland for that," Adam thought out loud.

He pictured the topography of Disneyland for a moment. "We could rappel down the Matterhorn," he added with a light laugh. "That would be fun since we now have so much experience at climbing."

From the look on Lance's face, Adam could tell he was actually considering climbing the Matterhorn. He was relieved when Lance finally said, "No, it all points to the train, the big train. And considering we found the clue inside Walt's little train, it follows a certain logic. My guess is that part of the clue hints that the trains come along every five minutes at certain times of the year - depending on how many are running, of course."

Looking back at the clue's "this canyon isn't so grand", Adam felt it couldn't mean the Grand Canyon Diorama that had been there since 1958. It was secure behind glass anyway. They couldn't get to it from the front. An obscure bit of trivia popped into Adam's mind: "Did you know the Diorama was painted on one huge sheet of canvas? There aren't any seams in it."

"And all the trains were blessed by a Hopi chief when it opened. That's common knowledge," Lance stated without skipping a beat.

"Oh, I forgot about the chief. You remember his name?" hoping to stump him.

"Yes," was all Lance replied, smiling.

"Too bad that didn't come up on the Mouse Adventure race. That would have been worth some points."

Lance gave him a mocking chuckle. "Maybe next time we can actually finish the race. Are we doing it again this fall?"

Distracted by the clue, Adam answered, "Don't know. Probably. Why do you think we need a rope for this?"

"Maybe we need to go up on the roof of the Diorama building and drop down inside the display. We both know what we need to be able to do it. Do you think the roof is alarmed?"

"How in the world would we be able to get down there and back up in less than five minutes? Plus search for a clue? The area is too huge. It can't be that."

Lance sat up and stretched. "The only way to know is to go to the Park and ride the train. Check out all the tunnels on the ride and be prepared for anything. Including jumping off if need be. You have any rope? I took all the equipment we used back to Hans."

"Wait a minute…You *rented* that automatic ascender? You didn't put out $8000 like you lead me to believe?"

Lance laughed. "Now why would I pay that much money for something we would use only once? You didn't say for sure you wanted one…" he broke off. "So, do you have any rope or not?"

Adam nodded and bit back the remarks on the tip of his tongue. He knew it would make no difference now. "In my truck. I have some pretty strong line left over from a job. It's a thin nylon. A different type than we used before, but it would work. It could hold either of us."

"Not both of us?"

"I ain't hanging on to you and jumping off a cliff," Adam replied flatly.

Chuckling, Lance asked when he wanted to start.

Adam checked his clock. It was a little after 3 p.m. "What do you think? If we go now, rather than in the morning, the employees might be a little drowsier after being at work all day. Might help if I do have to jump or dive or whatever."

"There are shift changes to consider, but you are probably right. Are you going to jump or do you want me to?"

Adam knew his friend. "You are better at distractions than I am. When you're around, people tend to ignore me. I'll do the jump."

Lance shrugged his indifference. "What are you going to wear?"

"What do you mean 'wear'? A prom dress?"

Lance grimaced at the image. "No, smart ass. I was just thinking that if you don't want to be noticed when you are doing whatever you are going to be doing, you should probably be wearing something darker and less obvious that your bright yellow Michaels Construction shirt."

"Oh." Adam looked down at his clothes. Yes, the yellow shirt did stand out in a crowd – which is why he had them printed for all his construction crews. "Fine. You go ahead to the Park and check out the trains while I get changed," Adam suggested. He looked at his watch. "Let's meet in one hour, at four o'clock, at the Main Street train station." He paused. "We might as well start at the beginning."

Before he went out the door, Lance had one more piece of advice. "Wear a dark hat. Your blonde hair stands out. Oh, and a black jacket you can take off in a hurry might be a good idea. Empty the pockets. I'll get the rope out of your truck on my way out."

MONDAY, JUNE 3RD, 2002
6:35 P.M.

Adam, dressed all in black, pulled his baseball cap a little lower on his forehead. He resisted the urge to tug at his collar. It was too warm to be wearing three layers of clothes and to be dressed in black.

"Quit fidgeting," Lance told him when they met as planned in front of the Main Street Train Station. "This has to be it."

Adam looked enviously at Lance's khaki-colored shorts and white short sleeve polo shirt as they walked up the brick steps and through the station. They gave a quick glance at the replica of the *Lilly Belle* encased in glass on display at the top of the waiting platform. "I'm not 'fidgeting' about the clue. It's too hot today for black jeans and a jacket. Where is the rope? They didn't see it at the

Security check, did they?"

"Not to worry. It's in my backpack. The girl hardly looked through it."

Adam snorted. "Yeah, go figure."

Lance missed his point. "Do you still want to sit in the back car?"

Adam nodded, thinking ahead. "Have you been here long enough to see how many trains are running?"

"I've seen two trains," as they sat on one of the benches. "There is one of the regular passenger cars and one Excursion car. The Excursion might be the best. The seats face forward."

The regular passenger car had seats facing the right side of the train. It made it easier to load and unload passengers, but also made it more difficult for what he had planned. If he had to jump off the slow-moving train, he would rather everyone be facing another direction.

"You're right. Let's…." Adam broke off when he saw a group of five girls taking their picture. Well, he figured, they were taking Lance's picture. Adam was just in the way.

"Let's what?" Lance asked, oblivious to the attention he was drawing.

When Adam indicated with his head what was going on, Lance looked over at the girls. He flashed them his smile. Four of the teens started giggling and looked embarrassed. The fifth one smiled back and snapped another picture with her digital camera. She didn't share her friends' laughter…only looked at Lance with a smile that spoke her intentions. *She's going to be trouble,* Adam thought.

They heard one long and one short whistle – the signal that a train was approaching the station. The *Fred Gurley* steamed past them and squealed to a stop. The crowd waiting in the station surged towards the entry gates as some of the passengers got off and headed toward the exit. The five girls held back, obviously waiting to see where Lance went.

"Get rid of the girls," Adam whispered to him. "Pretend you're getting on this train."

Lance stood up and walked towards the open gate. He looked back at the girls, and indicated the gate with a sweep of his hand. "Ladies? After you."

The giggling started again as they trooped through the gate and went into the first car which had quite a few open seats. They scooted down far enough to leave one open space for Lance. The giggling stopped when Lance went back to the bench and sat down next to Adam. The two men could hear the girl's disappointed "Aww" as the train started with a jerk and slowly pulled out of the station. Lance waved good-bye to them as the bold one snapped another picture.

"How do you stand it?" Adam asked him.

"Stand what?"

"Never mind," he sighed. He glanced at his watch. "Let's see how long it takes the next train to arrive. The clue said five minutes, but we aren't sure how many trains were running when he wrote it. In peak times, they have had four trains going at the same time. That would be rough if I have to jump."

Lance leaned back, stretching his long legs out in front of him. "Well," he yawned, "there are only two trains today. If," he stressed, "we figure out what it is you are supposed to do."

Adam checked his watch again, getting up to pace the platform. Lance watched him through half-closed lids. "Will you sit, Adam!? You're making me nervous now."

Adam looked over Lance's 6' 2" frame. There wasn't one inch of nerves showing. If anything, Lance looked more ready for a nice long nap. Still, Adam sat down and checked his watch again. Five minutes had passed and no train yet.

"I'll do it if you want, Adam. I offered before, you know."

"You draw too much attention. We already talked about that. I need you for the diversion."

Lance shrugged. He didn't see what the fuss was about. "Okay. How much time so far?"

"It's been five minutes. This is good. More time to figure it out."

"You have the train signals memorized?"

Adam nodded, but still drew out a little notepad out of his shirt pocket. "Yeah. But the only one we have to worry about is one long whistle – which is 'train in distress'."

They were silent with their own thoughts as the station filled up with more people waiting for the next train. Adam couldn't believe it had been only four days since they were in San Francisco. It seemed a life-time ago. And here they were preparing to possibly do the same thing again. To keep from dwelling on what was ahead, Adam turned his mind to his surroundings. It was late-afternoon, a sunny, beautiful day. A light breeze caused the flags overhead to flutter nicely for people taking pictures. From where they sat, they could see more people coming in through the entry turnstiles. Many of them took a moment to pose by the huge floral Mickey face centered on the hill beneath the train station. The mood around them, among the many guests – families and couples - was light and happy. Even the youngest of children had had their lunch and a nap and were excited to ride the Big Train.

Presently they heard the approaching whistle as the P.A. system announced the train's arrival and called with a long, drawn-out, "Board!"

Adam glanced at his watch. It had been ten minutes. Good. That helped. The men stood as they saw the *E P Ripley* pull past. It had the Excursion cars. Some of the people waiting around them groaned when they saw those forward-facing seats. Not liking to have to turn their heads to watch the scenery, they forestalled cricks in their necks by deciding to wait for the next train. The guys took the rearmost seat in the last car, putting the backpack between them to take up more room and discourage anyone from sitting next to them.

A female conductor named Louise walked the length of the last two cars, checking to see if everyone was properly seated. She waved her arm to signal to the next conductor that all was fine. The signal was carried up to the engineer who gave two short blasts on the whistle as they began to get underway. Louise settled on her outside perch at the front of their car, her arm around the standard for stability. Adam noticed her glancing a second time in their direction. He waved to her. She didn't seem to see him. Her eyes were focused on Lance. He smiled to himself. *Good. That will help.*

The recorded announcement started as they chugged around the Park. The guys carefully examined all the tunnels on the circuit. The tunnel leading to the Frontierland station was corrugated metal. The tunnel leading into Critter Country opened into Splash Mountain, but the ride section was behind glass. The tunnel before Fantasyland was way too short. In about eighteen minutes, they were at the entrance to the Grand Canyon Diorama and Primeval World. They knew this wasn't what the clue meant, but they examined it anyway. As they already knew, the whole display was behind glass. The other side of the long, dark tunnel was broken up by exit doors. There had to be something in the other tunnels they missed.

Lance looked over at Adam. "Once more around?"

Adam just nodded. He fingered the conductor's button in his pants pocket that Walt had left with the last clue. None of the cast members working the other trains in the Park had that type of button. Even the cast members on this train no longer had that particular button on their uniforms since Santa Fe had withdrawn their participation in the Park. The clue had to mean this train. It had to be here. He just knew it.

More people climbed off and less got back on. It was nearing dinnertime, as Adam's stomach reminded him. Louise was still with them as she waved her signal and climbed back on her perch.

The first tunnel had been added in the mid-60s and went over the Pirates of the Caribbean ride. The second tunnel was built at the same time and went through the berm behind the Haunted Mansion façade. Adam knew that if the clue was pointing to something hidden on the big train, it would have to be in one of those two tunnels. But there was nothing in the first tunnel. It was short, bright, and had no breaks in the metal. In the second tunnel he noticed the two small lit caverns on the Park side. Twenty-five seconds later they rode over the trestle through Critter Country.

"Lance, did you notice those two holes off on the side? One was blue and one was yellow? They looked like caves with little stalagmites."

"Yeah, I saw them the first time through."

"You think that could be it?"

"I didn't see anything in them."

Adam shrugged. "Wouldn't that be the point? We wouldn't necessarily see anything. We would have to go after it."

"You willing to give it a try?"

Mouth dry, he nodded. "Yeah, I have to."

"I'll go if you want," Lance offered again.

"No, you're too tall. Those openings didn't look very big."

"You're claustrophobic."

"Not any more." Adam reached for the backpack. He pulled it close to him, found the hidden rope and stuffed it in his jacket. His hands were a little shaky as he zipped it up. "I'll be fine", he said, more for himself than for Lance. "When we ride around again, you go to the front of this car with the backpack. Make sure the conductor sees you. Transfer at the Frontierland station."

"You'll have to come out the far end of the tunnel into Critter Country."

Adam looked up. He hadn't thought that far ahead yet. "That's right. I'd be in sight of the whole train station if I came out at the entrance."

"And you know to go out on the *left* side of the tunnel, don't you?"

"Umm, no. Why? Because of the window into Splash Mountain?"

"Not just that," Lance explained, "there is a sheer drop on the right side that ends up in the ride flume."

Adam winced. "That could hurt. What's on the left side?"

"A wooden gate and stairway that goes down to the ground level. It goes either into a cast member-only door or into the ride line."

"When did you see all that?" Adam wanted to know.

"Last time around. I think you were timing the tunnel or something."

Adam was thoughtful. "Cast member-only area. Great. Well, I'll have to worry about that when the time comes. You just cause a diversion as soon as we're in the tunnel."

Lance smiled. "I think I can do that."

"Too bad we got rid of all those girls."

"Too young," was Lance's comment.

They were silent as they rode around the Park again. They saw the canoes paddling around Tom Sawyer's Island. Fantasyland Theater was still showing *Mickey's Detective School - A Musical Toondunit*. Autopia cars in Tomorrowland were crashing in to each other in spite of the warnings to 'not bump the car ahead of you'. Ferde Grofe's "On the Trail" was still playing on the sound system as they rode the train past the Grand Canyon diorama again. More people got on and off at the various stations. The conductor Louise stayed with them and eyed Lance as he swung down from the train at the Frontierland station. Adam saw her little smile when Lance got in the second seat facing forward in their car, about three people in. Yes, there would be enough of a diversion. Louise was perched about four feet in front of Lance.

Adam found he was breathing harder and his pulse rate accelerated as the train pulled away from Frontierland. *I don't think I'll ever get used to stuff like this,* he admitted to himself. He slowly edged towards the far side of the car until he was next to the railing. It seemed like it took hours before the train came into the tunnel. It was getting darker when he heard Lance's loud "excuse me, coming over, excuse me," as he tried climbing over the people seated next to him. "Can I have the edge seat? Excuse me."

"Sir, you will have to remain seated while the train is in motion… Sir… ok, Lance," she amended. Adam could hear the soft change in Louise's voice as Lance gave his name to her and sat down on the end seat.

However, Adam didn't have time to listen to Lance's pick-up scenario. Adam gave a quick glance at the few riders in the rows right in front of him. They all seemed to be turned towards the commotion in the front of their car. Grasping the metal railing, he quickly threw himself over the side, dropping with a grunt to the graveled ground. He immediately crouched into a dark ball, motionless. If anyone looked back, they would be hard pressed to see his dark clothes in the darkness of the tunnel. He waited, resisting the urge to cough in the smoke-filled tunnel. The noise of the train faded as it continued its journey. Adam listened to hear if someone may have seen him – or heard him – and told the conductor to stop the train. He finally risked peeking out of his crouched position. When the back lights of the train disappeared from his view, he unzipped his jacket and ran towards the first little opening.

He first reached in, hopefully, feeling around for a capsule like the ones they had already found. Doing the same at the next cavern, he came up with nothing. Sticking his head in the opening, he found it was big enough to drop into. He checked his watch and set the timer for eight minutes, giving him a two minute extra notice. Going to the opposite side of the tunnel, he felt around for something to tie the rope to. He found an exit door, but knew it would probably be alarmed. He found a wooden beam pulled away from the wall. Testing it with his weight, he hoped it would hold.

Adam quickly tied the rope around the beam and tugged. Both the beam and his knot held. So far, so good. He went over to the first cavern. Tossing the rope in, he was somewhat surprised it played out. It was deeper than he thought. He checked his watch again. He had five minutes now to get in and out and get the rope off the track before the next train arrived.

With a silent prayer and a curse, he took hold of the rope and backed over the rim of the blue-lit cavern. With his back against the far wall, he walked himself down the rope, using the blue light to see. Every few inches he felt around. No cracks. No edges. No inset. No capsule. He reached the end of the twenty-foot rope and could see the bottom of the cavern. He reversed the process. Hand over hand, he worked his way up. He saw nothing different. When he heard the two short blasts of the train whistle, his alarm went off. He had to get out of the tunnel. Now!

Working faster, he popped out of the cavern and coiled the rope into a tight circle. He left it behind the beam and sprinted through the tunnel, keeping away from the glass opening of Splash Mountain. With a quick look around, he vaulted over the wooden gate and ran down the stairs to the Cast Members-Only door. Leaning against it, he tried to look casual for the guests waiting in the Splash Mountain line in front of him, ignoring their questioning looks and stares. Within a minute, the *Fred Gurley* steamed past; its passengers all looking off the right side of the train, away from his hiding place.

Knowing he was in plain sight now and in a prohibited area, he tensed when he heard the train give one long and two short whistles. That either meant a general greeting, like someone waving from the Hungry Bear Restaurant, or there was a crew member on the track. There was no way for him to know which. But since the train was on a trestle and he heard no alarm, he hoped it was a greeting for the crowd below.

Drawing in a calming breath that did nothing for his pounding heart, Adam hurried back up the stairs and opened the gate as if he knew what he was doing. Once in the tunnel, he sprinted back to his rope and dragged it over to the second cavern, the yellow one. He repeated the process from the first time and began lowering himself into the bright hole. *I'm too old for this*, he groaned. This cavern proved to be deeper than the blue one. He got to the end of his rope and saw there was still a few more feet below him. He found if he stretched out his legs, his feet would be on one side of the cavern and his back tight against the other. He hoped he could get back up to the rope as he muttered a curse and let go, edging lower.

It wasn't until he had gone down another three feet down that he felt the indention on his back. He worked his body to the side a little and reached inside. Heart still pounding, his fingers closed over a wide capsule. It felt like the same smooth plastic as the other capsules they had found. He held it up to his face and was about to congratulate himself when his alarm went off.

"Crap!" He had forgotten the time. Jamming the capsule in his pants pocket, he pushed back with his aching leg muscles and inched upwards. His fingertips grabbed at the rope, which swung away from him.

"Crap!" He pushed himself higher and grasped the rope, pulling himself up faster. Just as he reached the edge of the cavern, the headlight from the *E P Ripley* began to illuminate the tunnel. Not bothering to coil the rope, he hurled it at the opposite side of the tunnel, taking only enough time to make sure it was completely off the track. He didn't want the engineers to see the rope, something that would surely stand out in the darkness against the strong beam of the engine's front headlight.

As the train neared, Adam realized he didn't have time for subterfuge. He broke into a full run down the middle of the track. He heard the whistle shrill one short blast – Attention! "Crap!" He ran past the Splash Mountain window. The headlight was getting brighter against his back. Grabbing the edge of the tunnel, he swung himself around the corner. He dropped like a brick over the short gate and half fell down the wooden stairs, rolling through the line of people waiting. Not taking time to apologize to the startled people, he climbed to his feet, pulling off his jacket and his cap as he went under the trestle. The train emerged from the tunnel just as he rounded the corner out of sight from the trestle. He heard another short whistle and could tell from the sounds that the train had slowed down even more. Not daring to look back, wiping the sweat from his face Adam headed for the Golden Horseshoe where he knew Lance would be anxiously waiting for him. Looking like any other visitor in his white T-shirt, he hoped he blended in. If only his heart wasn't pounding loud enough for everyone to hear...

When he got to the curve around Splash Mountain's entrance, he did, finally, glance backwards. The train hadn't stopped, as he feared. It was now out of sight.

Inside the tunnel, holding flashlights, two crew members were examining his rope, wondering what they should do next.

Billy Hill and the Hillbillies were into their lively rendition of "The Orangeblossom Special" as Adam tried to locate Lance in the cool darkness of the Golden Horseshoe Saloon. When his eyes finally adjusted to the change of light, he found Lance sitting at one of the side tables on the left side of the room under the curving staircase. Totally relaxed, and keeping time to the music, Lance seemed to be enjoying the show. There was a tray on his table filled with the remains of Lance's dinner. He seemed surprised when Adam grabbed his soda and finished it off in one gulp.

Adam dropped into the chair opposite Lance, leaning his head back against the rail of the chair, still trying to get his heart rate back to normal. He became disgusted when Lance adjusted his chair to see the stage. Apparently Adam was blocking Lance's view.

"Enjoying the show?" Adam asked, sarcastically. He used one of the napkins to wipe his forehead.

The room exploded in hoots and applause as the song finished. Lance heartily joined them. "These guys are hilarious! You would have liked the sing-a-long."

Adam just glared at him.

"The Orangeblossom Special" turned out to be the last song of the show. Billy and his troop said their good-byes to a thunderous applause. The main lights of the room came back on, wooden chairs squeaked as they were pushed back and the audience started surging towards the exit doors. Lance offered Adam the four French fries that were left in the paper basket. Adam just sat there.

Lance sat in silence as the room cleared out. There were a few tables still occupied around the room. Some guests were still up in the balcony. When the majority of people were gone, Lance asked, "Where's your jacket?"

"With my hat."

"And that would be....."

"Probably either taken to Lost and Found by now, or being trampled on in Critter Country."

"Or Security," Lance suggested with a half grin.

Adam closed his eyes and groaned at that thought.

They were almost alone now as the room had emptied out. A few of the Golden Horseshoe hostesses were busy wiping tables and picking up some of the litter left behind. Lance eyed one in particular; a short blonde whose scooped fringed neckline of her 'can-can' costume punctuated her cleavage as she bent down to wipe the table next to him. "Sue," according to her nametag, smiled at Lance after he gave a subtle wave with his hand before leaning forward and grabbing his tray of spent food to hand her.

"Thank you," Sue said; her large brown eyes sparkled at Lance before turning and sashaying the short flared hem of her candy-apple red outfit across the back of fishnet stockings.

"Now that the place is empty…did you find anything?" Lance said, speaking low enough so he would not be heard by the working hostesses around the floor.

Adam now realized that was what Lance had been waiting for. "Sorry. I guess I'd make a terrible spy. My heart is still pounding. But, yes, I did. It's in my pants pocket. It's a little bigger than the other capsules."

Lance gave a half grin. "I thought you were just happy to see me."

Adam made a rude noise. "I don't want to open it here. Let's go back to my place. I need a shower….and a stiff drink."

MONDAY, JUNE 3RD, 2002
9:15 P.M.

Lance opened the gray capsule while Adam showered. A heavy piece of gold fell out first. It looked like some kind of coin that had been inexpertly cut in half.

The cut line was jagged, obscuring what was left of the embossing. The back of the coin was mostly smooth with some almost illegible writing in what could have been Spanish or Latin. After admiring the weighty coin, he dug out the paper wedged inside the capsule. It was the same kind of paper again as all the other clues – pages torn out of the old diary. The handwriting matched.

The clue read: **"Ride the cab to see the cup and walk 20 paces N. Sometimes my heart is like an island. Look for Jeremy B. He has the other half."**

Lance was pondering the message when Adam came out, a pair of shorts pulled carelessly on. Adam headed for the kitchen and his bottle of 15-year Glenlivet Scotch. Not finding a clean tumbler, he used a water glass and dropped some ice in before returning to his living room. His offer to Lance met with a negative shake of his head. Lance held out the clue as he looked over the half-coin again. Adam took the clue and dropped onto his sofa.

After taking a healthy swallow of the smooth scotch, Adam read the clue a couple of times. He dropped the paper in his lap, his mind still on his narrow escape from the tunnel. He took another swallow and felt some of the edge wear away as the scotch warmed its way down his throat. "What's that?" he asked of the coin Lance was still studying.

"It's fascinating, actually." Lance felt along the ragged edge and around the small hole pierced in the top. "Somebody was in a hurry when this was cut up," he decided. "What do you think about the hole in the top?" Knowing it was probably solid gold and wouldn't shatter, Lance tossed it to Adam. Lance was excited about this find, very excited. It fit with what he had been figuring all along – that there is more to the picture than some stock certificates and souvenir buttons. His face was a blank mask, though, had Adam cared to observe it. But his eyes…his eyes were bright and alert as he watched

Adam with the gold.

Adam silently examined the coin, as Lance had. He felt the hole in the top. "Yeah, that wasn't there originally, I'll bet. The way it is sharper in the back shows it was done with some kind of an awl. I have one in the shop that would do about the same job. This seems pretty old to me. You know anything about gold coins? Any idea what these markings are?"

"Most of the markings seem to be on the other half of the coin that apparently 'Jeremy B.' has. The writing on the back might be Latin. I think the first words curving upwards are 'His Majesty'. But, the way the hole is punched, do you agree we are supposed to concentrate on the front of the coin?"

Adam slowly nodded. "What about the clue? Riding in a 'cab' and seeing a 'cup' suggests Disneyland to me. The old Skyway ride and the Mad Party Tea Cups. I don't think Walt would have us grab a taxi and go somewhere."

Lance walked over to the big Disneyland souvenir map Adam had thumb-tacked to the wall when they realized they would be going back to Disneyland. "Twenty paces north from the Tea Cups would be the Storybook Land Canal Boats. Even though the Skyway ride is gone, all three rides were there in Walt's time. But, what do these have to do with the old coin? It looks more like pirate loot – authentic pirate loot - to me rather than something from Fantasyland."

"That would be interesting, wouldn't it? Some pirate loot buried under the Storybook Land Canals Boats!" Adam gave a hearty chuckle at the thought. "No, I think we should concentrate on the island clue and finding somebody named Jeremy who worked for Walt. The coin will probably be explained after we find him and match the two halves together."

Lance's head had jerked up when Adam jokingly mentioned some kind of loot. *You don't know anything yet, Brentwood*, he told himself; *pure speculation*. "Do you want me to work on the person or the island?"

"Let's start with the person. You work on the computer and the Disney records. I'll go through the books I still have and see what I can find. We might have to go to the Disney Archives."

With a new purpose now, the men once again got to work. Lance pulled up countless databases from different times in Walt's history. Adam searched through the indexes of his reference books. Neither could find anyone with that name. "Should we go to the library?" Lance wanted to know. Hours had passed and the room had gotten dark.

Frustrated at their so-far fruitless search, Adam rubbed his eyes. "Too late today. How about getting something to eat? I'm starved."

"I ate at the Golden Horseshoe."

"Yes you did, didn't you."

Lance grabbed up the coin. "I'm going to head home then. I'll see if I can reference this in some way," he mentioned, holding the coin up in his fingertips. "What time tomorrow? You want to go back to the Park?"

Adam just nodded, still thinking about the clue. "Maybe we need to ride the Canal Boats." At Lance's groan, Adam added, "Hey, it's not my idea. Seems Walt wants us to."

"Well, we'd better do what Walt wanted. He didn't like to be told 'no'!" With a grin, Lance closed the front door behind him.

"No, he didn't," Adam said quietly to himself. "And that's how he got to be as great as he was. He got an idea in his head and didn't allow anyone to turn him from it with a 'no'." He finished his now-watered down scotch and tried to find something in his barren refrigerator. "Need to go shopping one of these months," he muttered, wondering what that brown thing in the back was.

TUESDAY, JUNE 4TH, 2002
11:25 A.M.

"Want to go to Lost and Found and see if they have your jacket?" Lance asked him the next day as they rode in from the parking structure to the main gate.

"You're kidding, right?" Adam wasn't sure if Lance was joking or not. "I don't even know if I can get in the front gate."

Lance chuckled. "As long as the pockets were empty, you'll be fine. You weren't wearing one of your Michaels Construction hats, were you?"

"No, it was a Disneyland cap. Cost me $8."

"I'll buy you a new one," Lance crooned to him and received a glare back. "You remember the route of the Skyway, don't you? How it left the Chalet near the Casey Jr. Train, went up through the Matterhorn, and then dropped down to the terminal near the Tomorrowland Autopia?"

"Right. Maybe we should check out the Chalet before riding the Canal Boats. Even though I know how anxious you are for that." It was Adam's turn for a dig.

They looked around as they entered the Main Gate turnstiles. "A lot more people here for a Tuesday. Might take a while in line for the Boats. For some reason they are really popular."

"Come on, admit it," Adam teased. "You want to ride them."

Lance ignored him as they rode the Omnibus down Main Street. Adam noticed there seemed to be a lot of girls riding on top of the bus with them. The girls weren't looking at the scenery.

What Lance did notice were the names stenciled on the windows above Main Street. Each window was a tribute for some person singled out in the Disney industry. The ornate lettering would have their full name or just their first initial and last name. Then it would give their department or specialty as if that window advertised their place of business. "Adam, had you checked out these windows and who they represent? There could be a 'J' and then a last name starting with a 'B'."

Getting out his notepad, Adam wrote down the suggestion. "Worth looking into. Might be a performer, for that matter. Good idea."

When the Omnibus deposited them between the entrance of Tomorrowland and the Castle, the men headed up the drawbridge and through the Castle. Lance gladly turned left away from the dreaded Storybook Land Canal Boats and went towards the far edge of Fantasyland. The Casey Jr. Circus Train was loading up passengers in its "Monkeys" and "Wild Animal" cages, getting ready for its trip through the miniature world of Storybook Land. The train covered the same scenes as the Canal Boats, but from a different elevation and was a lot faster than the slower moving boats.

Above the busy walkway that led to a short-cut between Frontierland and Fantasyland a profusion of pine trees and flowering vines hid what once was the Swiss Chalet that was the starting point of the popular Skyway to Tomorrowland ride. The brown railings with the multi-colored carved tulip cut-outs were still visible to anyone who thought to look up. The cement steps were still in place up the curved path through the green vegetation and flowers, blocked off only by a drooping rope. There was a Bavarian-themed souvenir stand and ice cream cart in front of the walkway. One cast member was busy helping guests with their postcard choices. Edging behind the check-out stand, the men waited a moment to see if there was any opposition. Hearing the sale go on and on, they stepped over the rope and walked slowly up the path. "Always act like you know what you are doing," Lance had wisely suggested earlier. "More people will tend to believe you have a right to be there." Once out of sight, they relaxed a bit and walked to the front of the Chalet.

The area that had been the point where the Buckets finally took to the air had been enclosed. All the ride mechanisms were gone. The huge wheel that had held the cable and allowed passengers on and off before swinging the cab around to the drop-off was gone. The inside was now dirty and filled with dead leaves and a creeping vine that had found a crack in the wall. They stood back a ways from the edge, out of sight of anyone who might look up. The pine trees that used to be severely pruned to allow the Skyway Cabs clear sailing had been neglected and now encroached on the view. However, they could still see where the wire run would have been all the way to the Matterhorn. They could tell where it would have crossed over the Tea Cups before heading up higher into the Matterhorn.

Their trip down the wide steps was not so uneventful. The cast member, Roger, was now unoccupied with any customers. He spotted them as they stepped over the rope. He was reaching for his walkie-talkie when he stopped them. "Hey! You aren't supposed to be up there! What do you think you're doing?"

Adam's heart started pounding again. It had been too easy. Lance, though, was all innocence. "Oh? Us? I'm sorry, Roger," after checking the nametag. "I thought the men's room was up there. Didn't it used to be there?"

The walkie-talkie lowered. "Uh, no, it's over there," Roger pointed across to the other side of the walkway they were on.

Lance looked so surprised. "Oh, gosh, do I feel stupid! Well, what was up there? I wondered what that rope was for." He looked so sincere, Roger felt obligated to tell him the history of the Skyway Ride. "Aww, that sounded fun. Can I get an ice cream from you while we're here? You want anything, Gary?"

It took Adam a moment to realize Lance wasn't using their real names. "Sure, Percy. That sounds good."

Lance hated his middle name. He tossed Adam the

frozen-solid fudge bar he had just bought. It hit him in the chest like a rock. "There you go, Gary. Thanks, Roger, you were really helpful."

Roger turned his attention to other customers as the guys walked off, dropping the unwanted ice cream in the first trash can they found. Adam resisted rubbing the sore spot on his chest. He knew there would be a bruise. They stood at the northern edge of the Tea Cup Ride and looked in each direction. To the east was the Matterhorn Mountain with its Bobsled ride. To the south was Alice in Wonderland's ride. West was the Mad Hatter Hat Shop. After checking the distance from the Tea Cups to the Canal Boats, they got in the long line. "Seems like it was longer than twenty paces," Adam observed.

"Maybe it depends on which part of the ride was being referred to," pointed out Lance. "The canal runs past the walkway for a good ways. The entrance is farther away, yes, but was it referring to the entry or just the ride itself?"

Adam just shrugged as they worked their way slowly around the chain maze. This attraction was the only ride just north of the Tea Cups. In thirty minutes, they were ushered onto the "Ariel" boat along with twelve other passengers. The cast member guide sat at the back of the little boat – designed with Dutch, English and French influences – perched on top of the engine housing. Her name was "Tally" and she spieled with enthusiasm, adding a true "storybook" accent to her descriptions of the small objects along each side of the boat. The six minute trip included complete descriptions of all the miniature houses and villages they passed, but nothing stood out for the two men. They could see no tie-in to the clue or the coin, but had no place else to look.

With a sigh, they got in line again. Their next boat was the "Snow White" and a "Lisa" motored their boat through Monstro's gaping mouth. After passing through the twenty-foot tall black whale's jaws, the boat went through a tunnel and back into daylight, finally entering the narrow canals once more. The Casey Jr. Circus Train tooted by overhead and they were all encouraged to wave to the "Wild Animals" (guests!) in their cages. The miniature trees and closely pruned shrubs enhanced the manicured lawns. On the back hill, plants of various colors were contained inside square boxes jointed by giant cross-stitches. It looked like a gigantic quilt made of alternating squares of colored flowers. They saw the miniature pumpkin coach on its way up the steep hill to Cinderella's Castle. People on board their boat pointed and commented on the details within the castle turrets and windows, the moat and the perfectly manicured plants miniaturized to match the same ratio of size to the castle. They looked through the waterfall at the end of the ride to see Ariel's Grotto, but the miniature set like all the other sights along the ride seemed to hold no secret.

After lunch at the Redd Rocket Pizza Port in Tomorrowland, the guys rode Space Mountain just to placate Lance so he wouldn't do anything drastic. Smoothing his wind-blown brown hair back into place after the high-speed roller coaster, Lance led the way back to the Canal Boats himself and silently got in line.

There were thirteen different Canal Boats all named after Disney heroines. Lance swore they had ridden all of them at least twice. Adam started taking pictures as the afternoon wore on. Cast members Tally, Lisa, Julia and Suzi were starting to look at them strangely as the men kept coming back over and over. Even Lance's good looks and charm didn't hold up to two grown men without kids riding the Canal Boats for over two hours. They were secretly relieved when the men exited the ride the last time and never came back. You never know…

Adam ordered a Cherry Coke at the Refreshment Corner on Main Street. Lance got a warm Mickey-shaped pretzel and seemed delighted to bite its head off. They

sat in the white wire-backed chairs and listened to the
Honky Tonk piano player who was entertaining the diners.
The perky music helped lift them out of their ride-induced
stupor.

"I think we need to go home and download these
pictures," Adam suggested when the caffeine and sugar
finally hit his system.

Lance groaned. "*You* go home and download those
pictures. I can't take another minute of it. You do that,
and I'll work on the names in the windows on Main
Street," he offered, finishing off his pretzel. "How about
we meet again at your place on Thursday?"

Adam let out a sigh. "Yeah, I'm tired." Adam thought
for a moment. "I have to get caught up on some work,
check on Mrs. Anderson's remodel, and…" Adam
paused, "I need to get some sleep."

Frustrated, they were silent all the way to Adam's
apartment. Lance kept the coin and promised to research
it as well. There was nothing more to say.

They felt like they had run into a brick wall.

CHAPTER 11

HELPING HANDS

THURSDAY, JUNE 6TH, 2002
11:35 A.M.

When he came back on Thursday, Lance looked over the clutter littering Adam's living room and spilling over into the dining room. Most of it, he already knew, was notes in Adam's handwriting. Adam had even added some kind of a model of Fantasyland since Lance had been here last. The model took up most of the kitchen table. "You know, Adam, you are going to need help with this."

Adam didn't even look up from the pictures of the Storybook Land Canal Boats he had taken and was using for reference. He was trying to put them in order of occurrence on the ride. "You could start helping me."

"I've *been* helping you all along. We rode those blasted Canal Boats a millions times. I think pursuing that idea is a waste of time. It is not there!" Lance exclaimed in his typical, blunt manner. "But, if you insist on pursuing it, you will need help."

"I know."

Lance's seemingly careless shrug went unnoticed. "Help from someone who knows the Park even better than you do."

Adam flipped back a snapshot and wrote something

down, his reply coming out a little strained, "I know."

A smile came and went from his friend's mouth. "The only person I can think of outside of a Disney Suit is......"

"I know!" Adam bit out between clenched teeth.

Lance had walked over to Adam's desk - if it was still actually there under the mountain of paper - and leaned his hip into it. "And you got her fired."

Adam lowered the photograph of Pinocchio's miniature Bavarian village he was examining. Adam's eyes looking over that photo lost their focus. "I know," he said, his thoughts now somewhere in the past.

"Fired from the only job she ever wanted."

"I KNOW." Adam's head snapped back to the present and he looked up into Lance's face, meeting his eyes for the first time; a glare of resentment and frustration issued forth from them.

Lance relented a little when he saw the anger and the hurt that was in them. "How long as it been?"

Adam regained control over his features and the emotion clamped shut. "Let's just call it two years."

Lance gave a snort. "More like five," he muttered. "Do you think she'll work with you?"

Adam gave a ghost of a smile. "Now, that I don't know."

"Any idea where she is now?"

Adam slowly shook his head and put down all the photos. It was no use. He had looked over those same pictures for hours now and couldn't find anything that helped. "Nope. But I know who might. She keeps track of everyone." *Everyone I ever had as a friend, dated, or loved,* he told himself.

Lance flashed a big grin. "Mom."

"Yeah. Mom."

There was a low whistle. "That's not going to be pretty. Margaret liked her. I mean really, really liked her. I really liked her. Hell, everyone..."

"I know!" Adam cut him off exasperated. "Sheesh." He paused and looked away, back five years to be exact. "I ....liked her, too." *Loved, adored, worshiped. Fill in the blank*, his brain reminded him.

Lance ignored Adam's use of the verb 'liked'. "But," he emphasized, examining a torn fingernail and wondering when that happened, "you still got her fired."

Adam glared up at him. He knew that. It had been eating at him for five long years now. "Let's hope that's all water under the bridge by this time."

"Lot of water," mumbled Lance, still examining his fingernail.

Ignoring him, Adam gave a sigh he didn't realize was audible. "I need to call Mom," and reached for the phone.

Lance's infectious grin was back. "Can I stay and listen in?"

An hour later, Adam found that staring at a telephone does not: 1) make it easier to pick up the handset; 2) make it ring by itself; 3) make his heart stop its erratic pounding; and 4) help him come up with the right words to say.

"**W**hy don't you meet me in the Park."

"It's raining."

"Yes, Captain, I am aware of that," Adam added with a chuckle. "There won't be as many people around while we check some things out."

She didn't have to ask where he wanted to meet. There was only one place. "I didn't realize you took up smoking," Beth bantered, smiling in spite of her mixed feelings at the familiar use of her old nickname, Captain Obvious. Lance had dubbed her Captain Obvious years before. He found her habit of stating the obvious amusing and the nickname had stuck. The guys working the Keel Boat ride with her had even started using it right before…Crap. It still hurt. She closed her eyes and held the phone so tightly her knuckles turned white.

"I didn't, but the old Keel Boat dock should be deserted with the rain coming down like it is," Adam was saying.

It took her a moment to remember what she had asked. Her voice was quiet, not quite masking her feelings, when she responded, "Gosh, what a waste. One of the best rides in the Park, and now my old dock is a smoking area."

"How soon can you get there?"

Ah, he doesn't know where I live, she realized. "Give me an hour or so, depending on the freeway traffic." *Or fifteen minutes, depending on red lights.* After a brief pause, Beth added, "Adam?"

"Yeah?"

"This had better be good."

"It is," he promised and hung up, checking the time.

Two hours later, damp from the unexpected spring rain that was still lightly falling, Adam poked Lance in the ribs and motioned with his chin. Lance grinned as he saw the 1980's Mickey Mouse umbrella bounce up and down as Beth approached them along the Frontierland Rivers of America. Waiting a moment, Lance realized Adam wasn't going to go out and meet her halfway. In fact, Adam didn't move at all from the spot on the dock where he apparently had taken root. Rolling his eyes, muttering, "Stubborn," Lance went to meet her himself, arms out.

Adam could hear her happy little shriek. "Oh my god! Stinky!"

"Shrew!" Lance called back, his grin threatening to take over his entire face.

"Are you still hanging around with him? Gosh, no accounting for taste!" Beth threw herself into his open arms, umbrella forgotten as her arms went around his narrow waist.

Adam watched as they hugged as old friends always do, then watched as the hug lasted longer than a hug between old friends should last. Inexplicably he started getting irritated with Lance. His face darkening, Adam was just about to march over there and do....something. His brain took over his emotions as he realized he had no idea what he would do. He had no right now, no claim. He lost that right years ago. Adam forced himself to remain in his rooted spot as he observed that Beth was subtly trying to extract herself from the bear hug. "Okay, you big oaf, let me go!"

They both laughed at that and turned back to the Dock. When her gaze reluctantly settled on Adam, her happiness visibly dimmed. It was like watching a bright light bulb begin to fade. "Buck up, old girl," Lance told her, taking her arm through his.

"I'm fine," she managed to mutter, her voice unconvincing even to her own ears.

"'If you cain't smile, then grit yer teeth. It all looks the same from here'," Lance quoted part of her old Keel Boat spiel.

"'Guaranteed to make the next few minutes fly by like hours'," she automatically added, smiling again. "Gosh, it's good to see you," with some of her old animation coming back. She looked up at him with her big brown eyes. "I missed you, Slick. You could have kept in touch, you know. It's not like I died."

He touched the side of Beth's face with his fingertips. Adam tensed again. "I know. It just felt like you did."

She gave his arm a grateful squeeze. "Why don't we just go ride Space Mountain and forget this."

Lance tugged her towards the landing. He could feel her holding back, resisting. "Come on," he encouraged. "I think you're going to like this."

"That good, huh?" Beth asked, leaning back to look up at his 6 foot 2 inch height.

Lance just nodded and came to a stop next to

Adam. Lance looked from one to the other. They just stood there unsmiling, looking at everything but each other. He rolled his eyes and did the best thing he could for them: "I think I hear a churro calling me." With that, he abruptly turned and left.

They both stared in disbelief as Lance sauntered off towards New Orleans Square, still mindless of the drizzling rain. Adam turned back to face Beth, but she still stared after Lance, not believing that Lance had actually left her there standing with Adam all alone. She was still unable to look Adam in the eye. Neither of them said anything. The moments stretched on. The silence between them started to get a little embarrassing now that their buffer was gone. One of them had to say something. Adam cleared his throat. "Nice umbrella," he ventured. *Are you kidding*?

"Thanks," was her mumbled reply. Beth couldn't say any more at that moment. It had been so different when she talked to him over the phone. True, it had been a complete shock when she realized who was calling her. But, on the phone, she didn't have to look at him. She didn't have to see the way his wavy blonde hair was dripping rain into his soft blue eyes…Hair that needed to be brushed off his forehead. Scenes of past rendezvous' with Adam on this same dock tumbled over in her mind. She had known this moment was coming since his mysterious phone call. She had known she was going to have to talk to him, look at him, be near him…remember him. She just didn't realize the memories would still hurt so much. She was trying to make the tightness in her throat go away.

When she said nothing else, Adam tried again. "I, uh, I like some of the stuff they came out with in the '80's." *God you sound lame,* he told himself.

"Thought…," she had to clear her throat before she could continue. "Thought you might like it. I figured you wanted us to look like tourists, from what little you said on the phone."

"I do," not bothering to clarify which he meant. He couldn't take his eyes off her. She hadn't changed since he last saw her. Her brown hair was still shoulder length, cut to frame her oval face, the ends flipping under. Same lovely brown eyes. Same pert nose. She had on a short bronze-colored raincoat over her preferred stretch jeans and tennis shoes. *Well*, he amended to himself, *at least she wasn't soaking wet now. No! Bad memory!*

She could see he was scrutinizing her face. Did he remember? Beth cleared her throat, which was very dry at the moment. "I think we need to clear up something first if we might possibly work together." She looked over at Tom Sawyer's Island, not meeting his intense look. "It's been a long time..."

"Five years," he mumbled as if to himself. He probably didn't realize he had spoken out loud.

She felt something thaw a little inside. He knew? "It's been a long time," she repeated quietly, "and I want to know something about that day."

He didn't have to ask what day she meant. He shifted uneasily to lean into the imitation log railing, some ducks apparently capturing his attention. "I was hoping we could get past that. You know, water under the bridge." He knew that tactic wouldn't work.

"Lot of water," Beth mumbled. "You got me fired." Then she waited for him to say something, something he didn't say on that fateful day. Something he hadn't said at any time since that awful day. *Adam, say 'I'm sorry'. Tell me you were wrong.*

When he didn't say anything, and shifted his attention the Mark Twain chugging by, she continued, hurt by his on-going silence. "Do you realize how much that position meant to me? I was the first, heck, I was the only female Keel Boat pilot in any of the Parks. And I was good, Adam, I was damned good!" She gave a little ironic laugh. "You should know. You helped me improve the spiel." Beth paused to get her voice back to normal, marshalling her emotions. She refused to cry. She had done enough of that in the months that had followed that awful day. "I still don't realize exactly what happened, why I fell into the River. Everything was normal. I was pushing the Boat into the river with the shove stick. Bertha Mae's nose was far enough out to start the trip. And then I...I was in the River. You jumped in – why, I don't know – to save me? I got fouled up with the stick and the tie rope and you." She paused, her cheeks flushing red with her still-vivid memory. "My shirt came half off. People were snapping pictures, laughing. You were, like, wrestling with me. Then, a Suit showed up probably because some Raft guy radioed that a worker was in the water. You disappeared under the Dock. I got pulled out of the River by Peter and the Suit. Got hauled to the area office. Dressed down for nearly stripping in view of the guests! Fired on the spot. And," she finished, struggling with it all, "banned from the Park for three years."

"I didn't know you were banned," was his comment seemingly addressed to the ducks bobbing in the wake of the steamship.

Her hands came down on the railing with a loud smack. "That's all you can say?! That I was banned? Not that I was fired? Not that I was in line for promotion? Not that you didn't stick up for me? What happened to you?!"

Adam was silent for a long time. *Because everything got out of hand so quickly. Because I didn't think about the consequences. Because I was going to propose to you before I helped you out of the water. Because you were so angry and hurt beyond anything I had ever seen. Because I didn't know how to fix it.* He finally managed to tell her, "I don't know what I can say. They would have thrown me out of the Park too."

"Isn't it *possible* that I wouldn't have gotten fired if you had helped explain it was an accident?" *Say it,*

Adam, tell me you're sorry. When Beth realized he wasn't going to say anything else, she sighed. It seemed nothing on his side had changed. There was no point beating a dead horse. He apparently wasn't going to tell her what she desperately needed and wanted to hear from him. She asked instead, "How did you get out of it? You were in the River too."

"They didn't see me. They were too focused on your, uhm, chest."

Beth blushed, then shook her head at Adam. "You know how many photo albums I am probably in around the world?"

He managed a little laugh at that. He glanced sideways at her. "Three year ban, huh?"

She nodded. "Usually for the charge of 'indecent exposure' as they termed it, means a ban for life."

"And yet here you are, Captain."

"Obviously," Beth added dryly. "They relented a little after I asked them to review my past employment history and flawless record." She didn't add the uncontrolled sobbing she had broken into when they told her she was fired and banned for life.

She turned with a frustrated groan and punched him in the arm. Hard. He realized she still had the strength she had had when she needed to push the nose of the Keel Boat out towards the center of the river so it could make it past the docking cove of Fowler's Harbor.

"Feel better?" he asked, restraining from rubbing his aching arm.

She laughed. It was the first honest laugh he had heard since Lance deserted them. He could tell she was relenting a little. "Actually, a couple more punches would make me feel a lot better." She sighed and shook her head at the conflicting emotions churning inside her. "You know, you could at least have had the decency to go fat and bald since the last time I saw you."

He just chuckled softly.

She was quiet for a few minutes. "Do you know they had me followed the first time I came back to the Park?"

"Really? Was it a Suit, or Security?"

Beth smiled at the memory. "Al."

"Al? Was he still working then? Gosh, he had to be 100 years old. How did you know he was following you?"

She gave him a sarcastic look. "It was Al. He never was very subtle. I doubt he would have had a career with the CIA."

"How long did it take you to notice you were being followed?"

"All of five minutes. He was there before I got to the end of Main Street. I guess they wanted to make sure I wasn't going to expose myself to the kiddies again. But, I took it easy on him. Had lunch at the Golden Horseshoe because I knew he liked the show and would want to get off his feet for an hour."

Adam nodded and smiled. That would be just like Beth, to think of the comfort of an old man rather than the indignity of being followed.

"So, have you said 'yes' yet?" The intrusion of Lance's voice startled them both. They took a step farther away from each other.

"We haven't gotten that far," Adam snapped, for some reason irritated that his friend was back.

Lance ignored him. "Well, you've talked so long the rain has finally stopped. Come on, Captain, let's go ride the Bobsleds," he pulled on her arm.

She pulled free with a laugh. "You've got to be kidding! I ain't sitting in your lap again!"

He wiggled his eyebrows. "Could be fun."

"No, thanks. I tried that once, remember? I still don't know how you got your hands up..." She broke off when she saw the wicked grin on Lance's face and the frown on Adam's. "Never mind," she mumbled, red-faced.

"Hey, Adam, did you get to the part about your costume collection?" Lance asked him, noticing the sour expression which had been on Adam's face since he came back to join them.

Adam silently winced and cursed Lance in the same breath. That had been Beth's goal – to collect a costume from every ride. She would have been able to do it if she hadn't gotten fired. He could feel her eyes burning into him as he looked at Lance, willing him to shut up. Lance smiled calmly back at him, rocking back and forth on his heels.

"Yeah, well, I kept in touch with some of your old friends from here…" Adam stammered, breaking off at the accusing look on her face. She hadn't been allowed to keep in touch with her old friends. "Listen, I think we need to get to the point of all of this."

"Yes, Adam, I think you're right," Lance agreed, taking her arm again. "We're going to go ride Mansion. There isn't any line right now."

"The sun is out," Beth stated unnecessarily, glad for the break in the tension. She folded up the red and black umbrella, stashing it in her purse and walked off with Lance. Adam wondered what Lance was up to when he saw their heads go together as they neared the entrance. She suddenly roared with laughter. Adam sighed as he followed them up the walkway to the ornate front porch of the Haunted Mansion. He had a long way to go.

There were only about twenty-five people in the Stretching Room, the expanding room within the foyer of the Haunted Mansion; Beth standing between Lance and Adam in the middle as everyone looked up at the comical elongating portraits that adorned each wall. After the point where the lights went out and the blood-curdling scream followed the announcer's "Of course, there's always my way," referring to the "way out" of a room with no windows and no doors by revealing a hanging body in the rafters, way up above the startled guests, the lights came back on and the hidden doors opened onto the Portrait Gallery outside the room. As Beth waited to exit, she looked to her right and noticed Lance wasn't with them. Unknown to them, Lance had ducked out a hidden cast member's door with one of the female "Ghostess" cast members and headed to the French Market for lunch. After waiting a couple of minutes in the Gallery to see if he would rejoin them, the remaining twosome got into a Doom Buggy that would take them through the Haunted Mansion.

It was then that Adam started his explanation as to why he needed her help.

FRIDAY, JUNE 7TH, 2002
1:35 P.M.

The next day, Beth hesitated outside of Adam's apartment – the same apartment she had practically lived in when they were dating. She tried to still her pounding heart, wiping her sweaty palms down the leg of her jeans. *Come on, girl, you can do this. You've already seen him. The worst is over… yeah right*, her mind argued.

She shook away the images of the past and rang the bell. She heard two male voices say "I'll get it," then a scuffling, a muttered oath, and Lance flung open the door, with Adam scowling at him a few paces back.

"Hey, Captain, come on in," he extended his hand to her, gallantly taking her arm as she entered the apartment.

She couldn't help but notice Adam's sour expression, so she asked, "Did I miss something?"

Lance was all innocence. "No, no, you're right on time."

Adam just grunted something about "his apartment" and went back to his paper-covered desk.

"You want to see it?" Lance asked, taking Beth over to the far side of the apartment, her arm still tucked in his.

She didn't need to ask what 'it' was. The dread of being back in Adam's apartment and being in his vicinity again was being pushed back by excitement: Excitement over a new discovery. Excitement over a possibly priceless piece of history. She wanted to see for herself all that Adam had explained to her the day before at Disneyland.

Adam could see that excitement in Beth's eyes as she looked at the small black book in his hands. She pulled away from Lance's grasp and reached out to touch the cover with a finger. "That's it, huh?"

He couldn't resist. "Obviously, Captain," as he handed it to her.

She didn't seem to hear him. She was turning it over in her hands, examining the front and back. Adam noticed she didn't even look up as she went from the desk to the sofa, walking around the armchair without even seeing it. She almost mistakenly sat in Lance's lap. They were both silent, giving Beth her moment with the diary. She carefully opened the cover, found the first page with writing on it and started reading. The men watched her lips moving as she silently read the words they had already memorized. When she paled, they looked at each other with a grin. She was hooked. They now knew they had her help.

She read it again, more quickly this time. She found the glued pages in the back and the secret compartment. Then she tried to count the number of missing pages in the front. Murmuring, "can't tell," she sat there staring into space.

"What are you thinking?" Adam's voice was like a foghorn to her.

"What?" Beth snapped back to the present, looking at him.

"I wondered what you thought of it," he asked, studying her wide eyes and heightened color.

"This is amazing. Have you had it authenticated?"

Lance and Adam looked at each other. Lance answered, "We thought it best to keep it to ourselves at this point. We've followed the clues as far as we could. When we got stuck, we called you."

She was pacing around the room now, unable to sit still. "You said you found it in Walt's apartment?"

"Yeah, during the Mouse Adventure race."

"And no one saw you?"

Adam looked at Lance with a smirk. "Seems the cast member on duty couldn't keep her eyes off Pretty Boy Floyd here. For once that came in handy."

Lance just smiled and explained, "Wendy." At Beth's blank look, he added, "She was the cast member. We had dinner a couple of weeks ago."

"I'll bet you did," she laughed. "You're too much!"

"What?" Lance asked with a shrug. "You know I still love you the best."

"Focus, people," Adam cut in. "Considering *where* I found it, and *how* I found it, we decided it was better to keep quiet. There was an article in the paper that they've closed Walt's apartment to the public now that there is an investigation is going on."

Beth's mouth fell open. "That was you two!!?? Oh my god. I saw that article. You did that? You destroyed the ancient shrine!"

"It was four lousy stitches in the back of a stinking cushion, for crying out loud!" Adam protested. "Well, maybe eight....But, they made it sound like we tore up the carpet and threw the sofa out the window. Hell, they aren't even sure it happened during the Race."

"Doesn't matter. They'll tar and feather you if they find out." She looked at Lance. "And this Wendy didn't suspect you guys?"

He looked a little embarrassed. "Uhm, no. She didn't even remember Adam being there. She just remembers meeting me."

She knew enough about Adam and his pride not to

laugh right at that moment. "Well, that's good then. Wow, this is amazing." She started pacing through the room again, stopping abruptly at the kitchen table which held Adam's home-made model of Fantasyland. She pointed at the Matterhorn. "How old are these mashed potatoes?"

Adam looked up from the paperwork and clues he was organizing to show her what they had accomplished so far. "What? I don't know. You hungry?"

Beth just shook her head and moved away. She went back to the wall next to the front door. There was something she wanted to examine. She took an eight by ten inch picture off of the wall, staring at it. Lance watched her study the picture, turning it this way and that to watch the light play over the face. Adam was engrossed in what he was doing and didn't notice. "So, how do you know the diary is authentic?" she asked. Lance waited for Adam to answer as she was looking at Adam, not him.

Adam looked up, distracted. He saw Beth was studying his autographed photo of Walt on the wall. It was taken at the Burbank studio, an informal black and white shot, signed 'To Georgie, thanks for all your help! Walt". She wouldn't have seen it before in any shop or online. It was one-of-a-kind. There was a hint of smugness as he shuffled through some of their notes, making a cross-reference in the margin. "Oh, I just know. I, uh, consider myself something of an expert."

"Ah." Putting the picture carefully back on the nail in the wall, she moved over to the trophy case filled with his cast member nametag collection from around the Disney world. She had gotten him started on that collection. They had had plans to travel to all the Disney Parks and fill in the missing tags. It didn't take her long to notice her nametag was gone from the box. Batting down a sharp wave of hurt and remembrance, she went over to the huge '40 Years of Adventure' Park map he had tacked up next to the trophy case. This was safer territory. Beth cleared her throat and then asked, "Adam, do you still keep all your receipts?"

Adam looked up from the diary, frowning. "My what? Receipts?" He shrugged. His attention was only half there. "Yeah, I guess. Why?"

Lance had been unnaturally silent through all this, watching them as if he were at a tennis match. He took a swig of his beer, feet propped up on what he assumed was a coffee table, and waited. Knowing Beth, he figured this would be good.

She walked over to Adam's desk and took the diary from his hands. "Just wondered… You are right, you know."

Adam waited.

Beth waved the diary at him, then placed it reverently back on the desk. "This," indicating the black book, "is real." She walked back to the signed photo of Walt. "This… well, this is worth about $9.00."

Lance choked on his next swallow and started coughing. He knew Adam was proud of the fact that he won that picture at an auction for just under $3000. Adam's mouth dropped open and then abruptly closed. He opened it again, but couldn't say anything. He knew she meant it. And, more importantly…deep down, he knew she was right.

She moved over to Lance, helpfully pounding him on his back as he tried to stop choking and laughing. When he asked her to move her hand "lower, lower, a little more," Beth suddenly realized she was almost patting his behind. She gave him 'The Look' and stopped. He just grinned and shrugged. "Worth a try."

"Pampered Poodle," she shot at him.

"Prima Donna."

"Playboy."

Adam, still staring at her in shock, automatically mumbled, "Will you two knock it off?"

She went back to Adam's desk and reached for the pile of clues they had deciphered so far. She looked over the various bits of treasure and memorabilia they had collected. She gazed longingly at the Conductor's button. She had been trying to win one through an online auction. At her request Adam walked her through the steps he and Lance had taken to solve the clues so far and the places they had gone. She nodded through his explanation, trying to picture it in her mind. "Very good. Wow, you've been to a lot of places I would like to see. Like Marceline."

"Yeah, they were interesting trips. But then we get to this clue and we are stymied."

Beth looked at the ancient coin that had been cut in half. She held it up by the chain Lance had attached to it and let it slowly twist in front of her. "Any idea what the other half looks like? Have you found anything similar during your research?" At their negative reply, she took the folded clue and carefully opened it. She went through the same process they had gone through ever since their first paper clue in Kansas City. Yes, the paper matched the diary paper. One edge was rough, showing it has been ripped from the book. Yes, the ink and the handwriting matched. '**Ride the cab to see the cup and walk 20 paces N. Sometimes my heart is like an island. Look for Jeremy B. He has the other half.**'

"Sounds like Walt was getting a little poetic here," she smiled softly, still unable to believe she was holding in her hands something actually written by Walt Disney himself. She started pacing the room again, and then went back to the desk to look at all the other clues. She shook her head. "You know what? I need some time away from all of this to mentally process everything you've shown me. I'm a little overwhelmed right now. There is so much for me to think about."

Adam looked surprised. He somehow expected her to snap her fingers and lead them to the right destination.

"You want to leave?" He sounded a little desperate. Now that she was here, he didn't want her to leave. Ever.

"I guess I'm hungry." With a grimace, she looked over at the kitchen table and the mashed potato Matterhorn. "Why don't we go out for lunch?"

Lance bounded off the sofa and shoved Beth's purse into her hands. "I'll drive." He took her arm and herded her towards the door.

"You still have your Benz?" Beth asked Lance.

"The black one?"

"Yeah."

"No, I traded it in."

She looked disappointed. "Aww, I liked that car. What'd you get?"

He smiled at her. "A Benz."

"What color?"

"Black."

She started laughing as the three of them headed for the street. Adam got in the plush back seat without a word.

"So, where do you want to eat?" Lance asked as the car silently pulled away from the curb.

"I don't care," Beth shrugged.

"No, really. Where do you want to eat?"

"I... don't.... care," she answered again, very slowly.

"And just where is 'I Don't Care'?"

"Right across the street from 'I Don't Give a Crap'. Of course, 'I Don't Care' is a lot more popular than 'I Don't Give a Crap'."

"I suppose it would be," Lance grinned as he pulled into an expensive French bistro. When he saw her hesitation, he added quietly, "My treat."

"No, we can't. It's too expensive, Lance. Adam, back me up here."

Adam slammed his door shut with more force than was necessary. "He said it's his treat, Beth," as he opened her door to hand her out, beating Lance by seconds.

She smiled her thanks to Lance. "Trust Fund Brat."

He held the bistro door open for them. "You're welcome."

All through lunch they again discussed the clues and how the men had arrived at their solutions. When they told her what they had done in San Francisco, Beth got really quiet. "That's pretty serious, guys."

Lance and Adam exchanged a look. "We know," Adam said, expelling a long breath. "We also agreed never to do anything like that again."

"Adam doesn't know this yet," Lance brought out, "but we made the San Francisco Chronicle." He noticed Adam's face went pale. "Well, 'we' didn't make the paper," he amended. "The article said 'two bungling burglars' broke into a warehouse but didn't manage to steal anything. It reported there were ropes left behind – which you still owe me $100 for, by the way – and a grappling hook, but nothing was taken. The owners couldn't believe it, considering how valuable everything is. All they could find misplaced inside was one little screw. They are getting a new security system, by the way, in case you want to go back."

"'Bungling burglars'!" was all Adam could say. "We didn't bungle anything!"

"I think you are missing the point, Adam," Lance said as if he were talking to a slow child, "we are not in trouble and we are not suspected. And nothing was harmed."

It took a moment for the news to sink in. Adam was finally appeased and they could now focus on the last clue, which had the men stumped.

"To me, there's no doubt it refers to Disneyland and riding the Skyway to see the Mad Tea Party. But, you didn't have to ride the Skyway to see that," Beth pointed out.

"True," Adam agreed. He paused to organize his thoughts. "But it seems to me like we are going on a journey with Walt. We've gone to all these places in his history. I think he wants us to really appreciate his life and his work, like Disneyland. That is just as important to him as us getting to the final destination – wherever that is."

She nodded, taking a final sip of the Chardonnay Lance had ordered with lunch. It was from Fess Parker's Vineyard, Marcella's Reserve, 1999. "Seems appropriate," he had said when it arrived.

"And you went twenty paces north, which was….."

"Storybook Land Canal Boats," Lance groaned. "We've ridden that damned ride about a dozen times now. I can't take it another time!" as he paid the bill and they headed for his car.

"Did you take into account that some of the houses are in different places now? Like Toad Hall used to be where Aladdin's Palace is."

"Yeah, I tried that too, but nothing. I just don't see what he apparently wants us to see."

"You made a model of Fantasyland," Beth grimaced again, thinking about Adam's Matterhorn. "Do you also have the locations of everything in the Canal Boats?"

"Well, I started taking pictures of all the houses when Lance started griping."

"Hey, man, I rode it twelve times. There is a limit."

Beth thought it all over. "Well, I'd like to see those pictures, in order. Something doesn't add up."

"We even snuck up to the old Skyway Chalet in Fantasyland to get a bird's eye view of the run as it would have been all the way to the Matterhorn."

She looked envious. "Aww, I would have loved to have seen that again! I miss that ride."

"We almost got caught," Lance told her.

"You charm your way out of it again?" Beth asked, smiling fondly at Lance.

Adam choked out a laugh. "It was a guy cast member this time. But, yes, he did. I told you, Brentwood, you're just too pretty."

This time Lance was embarrassed. "Never mind

that. We didn't get thrown out and that's what's important," he muttered, keeping his eyes on the road as he drove.

When they got back to Adam's apartment, Beth went straight to the Fantasyland display he had built. She shook her head at the Matterhorn. Adam's model made with mashed potatoes was just plain disgusting. "Never heard of Styrofoam?"

"Didn't have any."

She looked at the coffee mug and knew that would be the Tea Cup Ride. The rubber ducky (an old joke present from herself) proved to be the Storybook Land Canal Boats. A silver foil horse-like shape was the Carrousel. Beth picked up a small picture of Lance. "What's this? Prince Charming from Sleeping Beauty's Castle?"

"That would be Prince Phillip from Sleeping Beauty's Castle, but no. It represents Dumbo," Adam explained with a smug grin.

"Boys, boys, boys," she muttered. She looked over at the map on the wall. "I don't see why you built the model when you have the map."

"I needed to get the feel of it better."

Beth nodded. "Makes sense." *For Adam*, she added silently. She went over to the map and looked from it to his model. "What year is this map?"

"It says it's the 40th anniversary right on it. You should know that would be 1995, Captain. That much i͏ obvious."

She didn't reply. She was deep in thought. Yes, t͏ ͏ was obvious. But something about it wasn't right. Yes, the map was right. For 1995. But it wasn't right for today, 2002, as some attractions had changed. His model was right. For 1995 and for now. But *something* just wasn't right. She was missing something. The key.

But, what was the key?

Sighing in frustration, she went back to the diary and just looked at it. It was old, cracked with age. More age than the map showed. The age of the two items didn't match. The map was wrong for the diary. The diary had to have been written around 1964 or 1965. It had to be…the map. The map needed to be older.

"What are you thinking?" Adam tried to break into her concentration. He watched her move from the desk to the kitchen table, hands on hips, ignoring them. She picked up the foil horse and moved it to the left. "Hey!" he objected, "I have that just right." Then she moved the picture of Lance up near where Adam had placed the horse. He stopped when he saw she wasn't listening. She picked up the coffee mug and looked at it. A smile slowly appeared on her face. She put the mug over to the left of where the picture of Lance had been.

Beth stood back then, her confident smile fading. No, that's not right either. "Adam, can I use your computer a minute?" She walked around Lance who had come to stand behind her to watch.

Adam was staring at what she had done to his model. "Sure. You know where it is… Why did you mess up my model? I don't see…" He stopped complaining as he stared at his display. He arrived at the same conclusion Beth had a moment earlier. "Oh, crap, that's it.…The rides moved," he muttered. "I never even thought of that." He looked up at Lance and said louder, "The rides moved! Brilliant!"

She nodded, but didn't answer. She was accessing a favorite website that had pictures of the old Fantasyland. "Here!" she exclaimed, excited. "Look," she pointed as the men gathered around her. She pointed at the Tea Cups. They were close to the current location of the Carrousel. Dumbo was pushed back further to the side. There was a large pirate ship in the spot where Dumbo now sits next to the Canal Boats.

Adam had the Tea Cups on the wrong side of Fantasyland.

She went back to the table and rearranged Adam's items one final time. "There," when she was satisfied. "Now *that* is the way Walt would have seen it."

Adam stared at it. "And twenty paces north of the Tea Cups would be the...."

"Chicken of the Sea Pirate Ship," Lance finished for him. "We didn't have to ride the Canal boats at all. Damn!"

Adam beamed at her. "That's why we hired you, Captain!"

Beth was pleased with herself, too. They were one step closer. Closer to what, they didn't know. But they were closer.

"So, what does Captain Hook's ship have to do with all of this? Do we need to ride Peter Pan now?" Lance groaned.

"Aw, I love that ride," she said. "Do you think we need another trip to the Park?"

Lance threw himself on the sofa. "Well, I ain't riding the Canal boats ever again."

"I don't think we need to, Lance. Can I see the clue again?"

Adam got it from his desk and handed it over to Beth. "What do you think? Do we need to concentrate on the 'island' part now, or finding a Jeremy B.?"

"Not sure," she answered slowly. "What islands are involved with Peter Pan?"

"Just Neverland, which is the island of the Lost Boys and Captain Hook," Lance answered, stretching out on the sofa, head back on the pillows.

"And the Mermaid Lagoon and Tinker Bell," she counted off. "The story was set in England."

Adam shook his head. "I don't see any of that as a logical setting for a next clue. We already searched for an Imagineer named Jeremy something-with-a-B, but couldn't find any."

"Maybe it is the pirate ship," Lance offered with a

yawn. He was almost asleep.

She looked at Adam. "We need to go to the Park. I think we should ride both Peter Pan and Pirates of the Caribbean."

"Pirates?" Adam was surprised. He hadn't even considered that ride. "But Pirates wasn't finished when all this took place," he pointed out with a wide gesture that took in all the clues and the treasures they had found already.

"I know, but Walt was really into the planning stages. It was the next 'Big Thing' for the Park." Beth shrugged. "I don't know. But I think we should at least check it out."

"Do you want to go now? How late is the Park open today?" Adam asked, glancing down at his watch, seeing it was only 2:45 p.m.

Her former cast member training kicked in. "The Park is open until 11 tonight. California Adventure closes at 10:00. Fantasmic starts at 9:00. The fireworks will begin at 9:45." She broke off at the amused look they were giving her and turned red. "Sorry. It all came back to me."

FRIDAY, JUNE 7TH, 2002
5:30 P.M.

Using their Annual Passes, they once again entered Disneyland. Adam and Lance kept their faces averted as they passed by the Fire House and Walt's Apartment.

"Jumpy, guys?" Beth teased. "Want to go say hi to Wendy?"

Adam walked a little faster down Main Street. "The only Wendy I want to see right now is waiting inside Peter Pan."

They went straight down Main Street and walked through Sleeping Beauty's Castle. Turning right in the Fantasyland Courtyard, they got in line for Peter Pan.

This ride was the most popular of the "dark rides", the group of Fantasyland rides that employed the use of black lights to brightly illuminate painted scenes in each of the rides. Because of the phosphorescent lights, the non-painted areas of the rides remained very dark, hence the name "dark rides". The three friends had to wait twenty minutes before climbing into their Peter Pan Pirate Ship with an orange and black sail. It was a tight fit for the three adults in a single padded seat as the lap bar was pulled down over their legs. The ride whisked them up into the air and through an open window to see the Darlings' nursery below them. Nana the dog, well, an 'audio-animatronic version of Nana, stood guard; Wendy was reading a story to John and Michael and the shadow of Peter Pan greeted them with the familiar voice: "Come on, everybody! Here we go!" They sailed out of the nursery and were now flying with a bird's-eye view of the busy streets of London as they circled Big Ben. The words of the song "You Can Fly" played softly in the background. The sky around them moon-lit, filled with stars.

Their pirate ship banked around a corner for their first glimpse of Neverland. The whole island was laid out below them. They could see Capt. Hook's pirate ship floating in the lagoon; the Indian Village had smoke coming up from the teepees. Even the volcanoes were steaming as they rounded the side of the island to see a rainbow over Mermaid Lagoon.

Next, they were flying into the sword fight between Capt. Hook and Peter Pan. The Darling children were tied to the mast of the ship, guarded over by Mr. Smee while Wendy bravely walked the plank.

The ship now went into a dive straight towards Tiger Lily who was tied up in the water below. Just in time, their pirate ship veered left to go past her father's village. They found Capt. Hook's ship had turned to gold with help from Tinker Bell's pixie dust. Peter Pan was steering them towards home. "Second star to the right and straight on till morning." The trio swung past Captain Hook trying desperately not to fall in the Crocodile's open mouth while Mr. Smee ineffectively tried to row his boat closer. Going around to the left took them past the Mermaid Lagoon, Peter's ship leaving a trail of golden pixie dust behind in the sky overhead. And the ride was over.

The group now stood outside the exit gate. King Arthur's Carrousel was making its rounds. Merlin the Wizard was surrounded by a large crowd as he chose a youngster to pull the sword from the stone. Adam put a restraining hand on Lance's arm before he could head over there.

"So, what do you think? Any ideas?" Adam asked.

"I love that ride," Beth sighed.

"Not what I meant…."

Lance interrupted him, "Say Beth, did you know there is a Lead Horse on the Carrousel?"

"You mean Jingles?"

His face fell. "Oh, that's right. You worked here. I forgot."

"Back to today, people," Adam tried again. "This is like herding mercury."

The other two looked at him blankly.

"Never mind. Did either of you see anything that could actually help?" he asked slowly.

A large cheer went up from the Sword. Lance starting edging over.

"Brentwood! We're getting in line again. Come on."

With a barely stifled groan, Lance joined them in the queue. Beth suggested they look at the building blocks on the floor of the nursery. Adam was going to look for any patterns in the traffic on the London streets. Lance was assigned to study Neverland for any discrepancies. Adam would examine the pirate ship fight and Lance said he would be more than happy to study the mermaids more closely.

When they finished riding a second time, Beth had

seen the word 'Disney' spelled out in the blocks. Adam and Lance had seen nothing of any importance that would help.

Adam was determined. "One more time around. Beth, you take Neverland. Lance gets the nursery and the Indian Village. I'll take the rest."

Beth cheerfully got back in line. Lance walked like he had twenty-pound weights on his shoes.

"Spoiled brat," she teased him.

"Perky Penny."

"Whiner."

"Slave Driver," Lance fired back, warming up to the challenge.

"Loafer."

"Task Master."

Adam thought seriously about buying a gun as the two of them kept up their favorite game through the entire line. The same cast member who had loaded them two times before looked at them oddly as she lowered their safety bar again.

Using a falsetto voice, Lance explained, "She just loves this ride."

The odd look on the cast member's face didn't change as the pirate ship lifted them from her view once more.

Once more they looked in vain for some clue to help them out. Once again, they found themselves standing outside the exit.

Lance was the first to say it. "I really don't think there is anything here to find. And I AM NOT going to ride it nine more times to come to the same conclusion!"

"I agree with Lance," Beth said, looking around Fantasyland. "From what you have shown me, none of the clues were situated in one spot very long. My opinion is that Fantasyland is done. I think we need to go to Pirates."

"Ok, I'll go along with that. Lance, you agree with Pirates?"

He gave a fake deep sigh. "I love that ride," came out in the same falsetto he had used five minutes ago.

Beth punched him in the arm. "Can we ride Storybook Land? I haven't been on that in years!"

"No, no! I apologize! You know I love you, Beth dear, but if I have to go on that ride one more time I swear I will kill Adam."

Adam was halfway hoping she would rush to his defense; to state that she couldn't live without him. Instead, she looked as if she was thinking it over. "Thank you very much," he snorted to her as he strode off through the castle and headed towards New Orleans Square.

Behind Adam's back, Beth winked at Lance. With a shared silent laugh, they followed their intrepid leader.

It was nearing dinner time at the Park. The lines were getting shorter as the guests started thinking about the restaurants or the snack stands. They had to wait only about ten minutes before they were ushered into the five-row flat-bottom boat that would take them through the world of the Pirates of the Caribbean. They didn't have any preset ideas on what to look for yet. Adam was on the outside left end, Lance in the middle, and Beth on the other end of their seat. She ducked her face into Lance's side as they splashed down the first waterfall to keep from getting wet. His arm went around her shoulder and stayed there even after the second, shorter fall. For the most part, they were silent on this first time through the ride. They studied the skeletons at the Bar Scene. Lance did ask Beth if she had an outfit like the girl in the painting that hung over the bar. The girl was a stunning red-head wearing only a pirate hat, eye patch, short skirt, sword, and tall boots. Her long hair hung down and covered her bare chest. Beth didn't answer. Adam silently answered to himself *yes she does… well, except for the sword*, and then wished he hadn't remembered that.

They went slowly past the Captain's Quarters, invisible ghostly fingers playing "A Pirate's Life for Me" on the white harpsichord. They viewed the Treasure Room and Lance thought how much fun it would be to get off there and play in all the gold and riches...even though Beth had told him most of the "money" was sheets of imprinted plastic made to look like a large scattering of coins. A dark, misty tunnel warned them that "Dead men tell no tales" and deposited the riders in the middle of a gun battle between a full-size pirate ship and a fort. Hidden air cannons made it feel like real cannon fire was whizzing by overhead. Geysers of water shot up all around the floating boatload of people. Further past the cannon fire, their boat floated into a town scene filled with audio-animatronic people and pirates. They studied the scene where the mayor of the town was getting a dunking in the well while several more prisoners shakily awaited their turn. A group of village women were being auctioned off in the next scene, with a stunning red-head attracting all the attention of the drunken pirates doing the bidding. The ransacked town was next, with the happy, singing pirates doing their rendition of "A Pirate's Life for Me". The Jail Scene followed, leading into the Burning Building and the drunken pirates shooting at each other amid piles of ammunition, dynamite and boxes stenciled with "TNT". A steep ninety-foot waterfall was in front of them and their boat carried them upwards against the current, the pull chain clanking beneath the boat. They bumped quietly around the entrance island with its squawking parrot and treasure map.

Knowing what Adam would want next, Beth and Lance headed back to the entrance to get in line again. There were even fewer people in line than when they had first ridden. Beth had indicated the treasure map at the entrance when they walked past it. "That's a new addition, isn't it?"

Adam nodded. "Yes. It wouldn't have been there at the time we are interested in." They were almost at their boat already. "Any thoughts, you two?"

Lance just shook his head. Beth sighed. "There is so much to consider. I'll concentrate on the 'island' portion."

Adam nodded. While Lance was saying a prolonged hello to the female pirate-dressed cast member, Adam got in their boat next to Beth. Lance climbed in last and leaned back towards the edge of the boat. He considered resting his legs across Adam's knees, but figured that wouldn't go over very well. Their boat started off with the familiar head-snapping jerk followed by their deployment into the ride flume off the conveyor belts that had pulled them out of the loading dock area. Their boat settled down into the dark, murky water surrounded by simulated willow trees and realistic looking fireflies darting about above the tranquil waters.

Even though the riders were warned to "Keep hands and arms inside the boat at all times", Lance trailed a finger in the water as they slid past the houseboats. The Blue Bayou Restaurant was still setting up for dinner, the clink of silverware mixing with the sounds of frogs croaking and banjo music. A full moon peeked through wispy clouds and soon the boat left all the sights and sounds behind them and entered the mysterious waterway that led to the first waterfall that the boat would plunge down.

"I'm sure it can't be in the bayous of Louisiana. I don't think there is any indication that Walt ever went there," Beth reasoned.

"The mayor of New Orleans did come for the dedication and opening of New Orleans Square," Adam replied.

"True, but I don't see how that would relate to the clue," Beth figured.

"But what about the front of the building, the façade?" Lance asked with a yawn.

"What about it?"

"Oh, I thought you knew. It was partly inspired by

the Cabildo Building in New Orleans. Jackson Square."

"Ok," Adam prompted when he fell silent. "What else? Anything we need to know about that building?"

Lance shrugged. "I don't know. The Louisiana Purchase transfer ceremonies were held there in 1803."

Beth gave a mock dramatic intake of breath. "You mean Walt left us Louisiana!!??"

"Well, that and Arkansas, Missouri, Iowa, Oklahoma, Kansas, Nebraska, most of North Dakota, and part of Minnesota, New Mexico, Texas, Montana, Wyoming, and Colorado," Lance counted off.

"Nice treasure."

"You left out South Dakota," Adam added dryly.

"I did?" Lance started over, counting back on his fingers. "Wow, you're right. Hmmph."

She gave a little laugh. "I keep forgetting you two actually went to college."

"I did minor in History," Lance sniffed.

"Same college. Same fraternity," Adam reminded Beth.

"Oh, yes, how could I forget? Frat House Dumba Dumba Guys."

Adam let that pass. *God, I've missed her.*

The slow journey again took them past the grotto, the bar scene, the Captain's quarters, the treasure cave. Nothing gave them any inspiration. As they sailed through the fight scene between the pirate ship and the fort, the guys debated the actual words heard in the dark passage they had just gone through. Beth's voice came through the on-going discussion – the discussion that was beginning to irritate the other passengers around them. "You do know the fort is patterned after Puerto Rico, right?" Beth looked over at them fully expecting to hear the now-familiar, "Of course, Captain." But it never came.

"What did you say?" Adam asked, cutting off Lance's spirited rendition of the ghostly voice: "*Perhaps he knows too much. He's seen the cursed treasure. He knows....*"

"I said the fort is like the one I saw in Puerto Rico."

His eyes narrowed. "When were you ever in Puerto Rico?" Even in the darkness he could see the blush mount her cheeks. She turned to face the bidders of the auction scene and coughed. He thought he heard the word "moon" somewhere in that cough. "Pardon?"

Beth rolled her eyes and faced forward. "I said I saw it on a honeymoon cruise."

"'A' honeymoon cruise, or 'your' honeymoon cruise?" he demanded, his glance falling down onto her left hand, but she had tucked it into her pocket.

"My honeymoon cruise," she mumbled.

Before Adam could react, Lance leaned over the top of him, pushing him back, trying to give her a hug. "Hey! Wow, congrats, Captain! I didn't know."

If possible, she looked even more embarrassed. "Yeah, well, that was years ago."

"You're married," came out as a statement, strangely calm considering the sudden pounding of Adam's heart.

"Was married," Beth slapped away Lance's hands as a disembodied, but very human, voice came over the hidden speakers for everyone to 'remain seated, please'. "Can we get back to Puerto Rico, please?"

"What happened, Captain?" Lance asked, looking concerned, not just nosey.

She looked at the burning town around them. Apropos. *He wasn't Adam.* Resigned, she told them, "He decided he didn't like being married to me and told me – with some regularly – to get out."

"And you did."

Beth nodded. "After about six months of trying to make it work." She tried to change the focus. "But, hey, I got to keep my car."

"Oh, cool," Lance leaned over Adam again. "What did you get?"

"Lance, who cares about a car!" Adam's snap came

over the top of Beth's, "Thunderbird."

Ignoring him, Lance asked, "The big one?"

"No way. The two-door."

"Nice!"

Adam leaned his head against the back rail and groaned. Lance was practically in his lap again. "'55?"

"'57."

"What color is she?"

"Thunderbird Bronze."

"Porthole?"

"Of course."

"Rag top?"

"Duh."

"Stick?"

"Automatic."

"Lazy," Lance snorted. "Can I drive her?"

"No!"

"Please exit to your right," came from the pirate cast member as their boat rose up on the unload conveyor belts and stopped between the waiting guests and the exit on their right. Lance climbed over the still-seated Adam to grab Beth's arm. "Sorry about the jerk, Captain," he said quietly as they walked towards the ride's exit.

"Which one?" Beth smiled sadly as they emerged from the Pirate's exit corridor into the late afternoon sunlight.

"Where are you going!?" Adam had finally caught up to them as they headed over the bridge into Adventureland, bypassing the entrance to Pirates.

Lance looked at her and gave his grin. "I thought that was obvious."

She never could resist that smile of his. She laughed for the first time in hours and gave his arm a squeeze. Beth looked back over her shoulder at Adam, her eyes shining, and answered:

"Puerto Rico."

"Puerto Rico?" Adam echoed. "That's not right…"

He trailed off as Lance and Beth kept walking. He had to hurry down the slope of the Adventureland bridge to get in front of them. He finally got them to stop in the shade near a little waterfall. "That's not right," he repeated, his eyes dropping to her arm still tucked into Lance's.

"What's not right?" Beth's eyes followed his, and she leaned a little closer to Lance, daring him to say something else.

He shook his head, frustrated. "No, Puerto Rico isn't right."

"But the fort..." Lance started, only to be cut off.

"No, it may be true the fort was patterned after Puerto Rico, but the rest doesn't fit."

"But it fits the clue, too, 'My heart is sometimes like an island'. Puerto Rico is, after all, an island. I thought that was obvious," she said with a little smile at her own joke.

Adam paced, still frustrated. It just didn't feel right. But how? He went over the tie-ins they had found so far and Puerto Rico just didn't fit. Nothing happened there of any importance in Walt's life that he could find. He leaned against the railing facing away from Beth and Lance and the hundreds of guests moving to and from Adventureland. He stared unseeingly at the baby elephant squirting water into the tropical stream that wound down from Tarzan's Treehouse and emptied into the Jungle Cruise river. Lance leaned back against the rail next to Adam facing the other way and watched the crowd go by. Beth stood apart and stared at Adam's back, mentally going over the clue and where their mistake might be.

The scream of a leopard could be heard overhead and the excited laughter of the children who caused it. It was followed by the noisy din of pots and pans being used as musical instruments. Tarzan's Treehouse. Beth looked over at the exit gate that was right next to them and saw the Kitchen Area of the attraction. There must have been fifteen kids in there, two of them pulling on the rope that activated the leopard scream overhead. As she stood there, a few tired parents managed to herd their children out of the exit with a grateful sigh at the relative quiet outside. Smiling at the parents' expression of relief, Beth opened the little exit gate and went up the stone steps past the stream and the little elephant. A few more kids left, dragging their parents over to the Indiana Jones Adventure. She wandered around the Kitchen Area thinking about the scene from the movie *Tarzan* that inspired it. She remembered that the movie's version of the noisy racket had been a lot more enjoyable, almost melodic, than the clamor of what she was hearing right now.

Beth looked up at the higher elevation and thought about the view of the Jungle Cruise she always liked from up there. As the guys still seemed to be working on the problem at hand, and she was lost in her memories, she thought about taking a stroll through the Treehouse. Figuring she needed to go back to the entrance and do it the right way rather than fighting against traffic all the way up, Beth turned back the way she had come. There was a lull in the noise as she walked towards the exit. In that moment of peace, she heard the scratchy organ music used as subtle background noise.

She froze. That subtle background noise – and something else. How could she have forgotten? She laughed as she stood there and looked up again at the treehouse. It wasn't Tarzan's Treehouse she saw, but what came before. The music was a tribute to the first family that occupied the Treehouse before Tarzan and Jane moved in. The music was the *SwisskaPolka*. The Swiss Family Robinson had been in the Treehouse when it opened in 1962. The Treehouse had been built after the tremendous success of the movie… She had loved that movie, had a crush on Ernst, and always visited the Treehouse whenever she came to the Park.

The clue made sense now. It wasn't 'my heart is sometimes like an island'. It was "My Heart was an Is-

land". Mother sang that song in the movie while putter-
ing around her new kitchen.

"Adam!" Beth yelled, laughing again. "Lance! Get in
here!" She ignored the angry looks of those into whose
ears she just hollered.

The guys came in frowning at their rude summons.
The look on their faces became puzzled when they saw
her laughing, arms outstretched. They watched, silent,
as she turned a full circle pirouette.

She laughed at their looks. "Can't you hear it?"

Adam looked over at the table of pots and pans and
the kids joyfully beating on them. "All I can hear is that
awful racket. Is that what you find so amusing?"

Beth ignored the sarcasm. "Wait for it," was all she
told them.

When there was a lull, she pointed at the gramo-
phone in the laboratory scene and the delightful music
coming out of it. Lance still didn't understand. Adam listened for a moment. "It's a polka."

"It's not just a polka. It's the *SwisskaPolka*," she
elaborated, still smiling.

It took Adam a full minute. He was still frowning at
her. The frown faded as he thought it through. Suddenly
his face lit up. That was it! She had figured it out! "*SwisskaPolka* from *Swiss Family Robinson*." With a whoop,
he grabbed her by the waist and led her into a wild two-
step polka around the stone-covered floor. She effort-
lessly fell into step with him.

Still puzzled, Lance watched as the impromptu
dance continued and saw how they were now laughing
together. "So? I don't get it. This isn't very obvious to
me, Captain!" He didn't like being left out of the loop.

She was a little breathless as she broke from Adam
and two-stepped over to him, still exhilarated. Lance's
attitude couldn't take the happy look on her face.
"And….," he prodded in a more decent tone of voice.

Beth got her breathing back to normal. "And one of

the songs in the movie was "My Heart was an Island". And," she paused for some dramatic impact. Lance looked like he would strangle her. "And the movie was filmed on… an… island."

"Which island?"

Her giddy expression faded a bit. She looked over at Adam. Same puzzled look on his face. "I… hmm… I'm not sure. It shouldn't be too hard to find out, should it? Adam?"

Adam walked over to them. "I don't know either. How could we not know that? Do you have the movie?"

She tilted her head to the side, and gave him a "Duh" expression. Did every female on earth feel the necessity to give him that same look? "Of course you do. Let's go check it out." He made a move to grab Beth's hand, but she took a step back toward the relative safety of Lance.

Her reaction had been immediate and involuntary. Too many years of hurt. Embarrassed at herself, and not knowing how to fix it, she looked down at her feet, her expression guarded again. "How about if I bring it over to your place?" He just stared at her, silent. "Well, all the re-search you've done is already there," she mumbled lamely.

Hurt, he glared at her a moment longer. "Fine. Lance, you coming?"

But Beth wasn't finished. "Look, guys, it's been a long exciting day. Why don't we start fresh tomorrow af-ternoon."

"Afternoon? Beth, this is important. We have a lot to do yet."

"I know, but I have something to do in the morning. I should be back around 3:00." She looked up at Lance for help and support. He could see a little desperation in her eyes. "You'll be there, right?"

Lance looked back and forth between them and rolled his eyes. "Wouldn't miss it. I'll bring the popcorn."

She managed a smile for him. "Thanks, Sparky."

"No problem, Grouch."

"Slacker."

"Tyrant."

"Slave."

Lance got in "Dragon," before Adam let out a loud groan as their favorite game resumed and led the way out of the Park. Adam knew he had to let Beth's rebuff roll off him right now. He would somehow fix it later – somehow. For now, they had work to do.

They had to find Walt's island.

CHAPTER 12

ISLE OF WALT

SATURDAY, JUNE 8TH, 2002
8:35 A.M.

With her T-Bird warming up in the garage, Beth hurried around her condo, gathering what she needed for the day. Check-in for the car show at Pearson Park in Anaheim was 9:00 a.m. She was putting a couple of sodas and water in her little cooler when there was a knock on the door. She glanced at the clock and considered ignoring it.

Then the bell rang three times in a row and she heard a familiar voice call through the door, "I know you're in there, Guppy! Open the door!"

Surprised, Beth flung the door open. "Lance! How did you know where I lived?" Ignoring her question, Lance ambled past her into the living room. "Well, why don't you come on in," she said dryly.

"Thanks. I came to see your car. I saw smoke pouring out of a garage and figured I was at the right place."

"Yeah, well, it takes a while to warm up."

"Don't we all?" he mumbled, opening her fridge.

"Can I get you anything, or do you just want to graze?"

"Where are you going?" as he grabbed an apple.

She watched his perfectly formed mouth bite into the

apple and wondered, for the thousandth time, why she had never been attracted to him that way. *Something has to be wrong with me*, she sighed to herself, thinking instead about another man's mouth.

"You're staring at my mouth."

"What?"

That perfectly formed mouth with its straight white teeth smiled and carefully enunciated every word: "You…are… staring… at… my… mouth."

Beth reddened and turned to fumble with her purse. "No I'm not. I was just thinking."

"About…" he prompted, taking another bite.

"Human idiosyncrasies," she mumbled.

Lance just chuckled at her. "Where are you going?" he repeated when her high color faded.

"I have a car show at Pearson Park. I really have to go," glancing at her watch. "Did you want something? I thought I was going to see you later at Adam's."

"Can I go with you?"

"To the car show or Adam's?" Beth asked with a smile.

"Yes."

"Fine," as she tried to herd him out the door. "But I have to leave right now. Do you want to meet me there?"

"I'll ride with you. Can I drive?"

"Fine. Yes, you can ride with me and no, you can't drive." She came to a sudden halt halfway out the door. "Oh, wait! I forgot. I'm supposed to pick Anne up."

Lance perked up. "Anne with the curly black hair?"

That surprised her. It had been five years since Lance had seen herself or Anne…as far as she knew, she reminded herself. It was typical Lance, after all. "You remember my friend Anne?"

Lance grinned at her and then looked around to throw away the remaining apple core in his hand. "Of course I remember her. She never struck me as a 'car person', though. You usually met her at the mall. Does she really want to go?" Lance asked, and then spotted her open trash can to the side of the garage. With a perfect basketball-like shot, it landed squarely inside. With a self-satisfied smirk, he looked back for Beth's approval only to find she had missed his excellent shot.

"Of course she does." At his skeptical look, she admitted, "Ok, fine. She was coming along as a favor so I didn't have to go alone." She tapped her finger on her lip, debating. "She would probably rather go shopping. Let me call her," Beth finally said, walking back past Lance into her kitchen.

Lance listened to her side of the conversation, leaning against the door jamb. "Hey, Anne…..yes, I know I'm late…. Listen, something's come up… you remember Lance?...." She held the phone away from her ear and grimaced at the shrill, happy noise at the other end. "Yeah, that Lance… He showed up and wants to go with me to the show… No, I don't know why… " She looked over at Lance, "Anne says hi… Anne, would you mind terribly if I took him instead… I'm sure you will be… See you then. Thanks, bye." She hung up the phone and handed him the cooler. "She said she will see us there later. We really have to go."

As she locked her door he asked for the second time, "Can I drive?"

She mentally envisioned him getting his 6' 2" frame behind the steering wheel. It would be like watching a giraffe come in through a doggie door… "Nope. Trust me. You wouldn't fit. It will be tight enough for you in the passenger seat."

He shrugged indifferently. He folded himself into the T-Bird's bench seat and gave her the 'see, I told you I would fit' look. Waiting, Beth let him get settled. Then she flashed him a smug smile as she moved the seat all the way forward so she could reach the pedals. She heard a muffled curse as his knees connected with the chrome dash, but he gamely rearranged his legs. She almost expected him to hang them out the window.

"Ready?" she asked sweetly.

"For anything, darling," as he draped his left arm across the seat back, his fingertips brushing against the back of her neck. "Turn on the radio."

"Doesn't work."

"Air conditioning?"

"Roll down your window."

"Piece of crap…"

"Hey!" she cried, backing out of the driveway. "This is a classic!"

"Oh, I'm sorry. Classic piece of crap."

Concentrating on driving the forty-five-year old classic, Beth didn't see Adam pulling up to her curb. As they rolled smoothly down the street, Lance turned back to see Adam standing next to his truck watching them drive away. Lance did the only sensible thing he could do for his friend: He gave Adam the one-finger salute over the roof of her car.

As they neared the park, they followed a '41 Willys, painted candy-apple red with yellow flames near the side exhaust pipes. A '56 black and white Chevy BelAir fell in behind them at the check-in for the car show.

Lance perked up. "Wow. I thought you were just going to see a car show, not be in one."

"Shoulda asked," Beth mumbled, as she took her entry number and goodie bag from one of the event volunteers, and received directions on where to park.

After rooting through her goodie bag and pocketing the free pen, Lance sat in an awed silence. As Beth drove to her place to park, he was looking down each row at all the classic cars and hot rods that were already there. He spotted a roped-off silver '54 Mercedes 300SL Gullwing Coupe. It was parked between a British Racing Green '61 Jag E-Type with a sweet carbureted V-12, and a super sleek black '94 Jag XJS V-12. He let out a low appreciative whistle. "You keep some nice company, Squirt."

She was concentrating on backing into her assigned spot. She hated backing up. It was slightly better than having to parallel park, but not much…"Thanks, Colossus. Great, I'm in some shade. You want to help set up the chairs or wipe the dust off?" Beth asked as she took out some of her special dusting clothes from the trunk. However, Lance was striding off towards that little Mercedes pretending he hadn't heard her question. "Or not. I'll do it myself. Thanks," she called after his retreating back.

She was parked next to a Thunderbird Green '56 T-Bird. *Shoot, I never win against him*, she thought to herself as she admired the immaculate Ford next to her. She pulled out her polishing spray and unfolded the micropore towels and got to work wiping off the street dust. Several of the show car owners walking past said hello to her. A bright Goldenrod yellow '55 T-Bird pulled into the spot on her other side. It's black and yellow interior was flawless. They had the hardtop off. She smiled her greeting and set up her camp chairs behind her car where she could sit later. She always brought two because somebody always came over to chat, and an empty chair was always a neighborly invitation to her fellow car show participants, many of whom she had come to know by name.

Knowing Lance would find her when he wanted something, Beth headed over to registration to finish signing in and get her lunch voucher and raffle tickets. She bought an extra lunch voucher for Lance, the bottomless pit.

She wandered around the cars. This early in the morning the temperature in the park was cool. But the day promised to be bright and sunny. Even though they were inland by a good twenty miles, an ocean breeze would hopefully come in around noon and cool the afternoon. It was nice right now before the crowds started filling the park. Some of the owners were still wiping off their cars. Some were taking the time to look at the competition before they sat in their chairs to answer questions or keep youngster's hands off their $20,000 paint jobs. The cars were as colorful as an English garden in the spring. Good turnout, she noted. Close to three hundred cars and more pulling in every minute.

A '23 T-Bucket with blown Offenhauser Flathead roared into the park, its orange metal flake paint sparkling in the sunlight. A large stuffed Mickey Mouse was strapped in the passenger's seat. The owner, George, had on his trademark brown aviator hat with black Mickey Mouse ears sticking out of the sides. Beth knew he would change to a black Stetson once he got parked. She made a mental note to go by and say hi later. She loved the theme painted onto the Bucket. The silhouette of the Southwestern desert stretched across the pickup bed that covered the gas tank; a Native American on one side, and a flying eagle on the other, all airbrushed. The purple and green flames stretched from the engine frame rails to the body and were edged in 24-karat gold. "I know now who will get the Best Paint award," she thought to herself, admiring the artwork.

All across the park everyone's head turned when a bright yellow '31 Model A Pro-Street entered. The 18" back tires left wide grooves in the grass, his engine thumping a deep baritone candescence. The five-inch dual exhaust pipes were smoking when he goosed it one last time before shutting down. "Rusty's here," Beth heard around her. The car never won many awards, but the guys loved the sound of that Big Block. Beth had looked out of the front window of that '31 once. It was chopped with the classic eyebrow. Without the little mirror mounted on the dash, it was impossible to see stop lights. Rusty left on his sound system, built in overhead in that small cockpit. The sound system was as loud as the exhaust. She not only heard the Beach Boys from where she stood, she could feel the compression in her chest from the eighteen-inch JBL speakers mounted in the back. At least his music was in style with the event. Some of the car owners weren't that considerate. Later, a band would take over the grandstand, but for now, it was good.

Beth smiled when an arm slipped through hers. She asked, "Where have you been? Out breaking a few hearts?"

She was startled when she recognized that it was Adam's voice that answered her, not Lance's as she was expecting. "No, not today. But, the day is young," he kidded.

Realizing she had hurt his feelings the day before, Beth resisted the instinctive urge to pull her arm free and allowed him walk along side of her. "I thought you were Lance."

"I get that a lot!" Adam smiled at her.

"How did you know where we were?"

"Followed the trail of smoke you left," he answered with a chuckle.

"Needs a tune-up. No, really, how?"

"The same way I got your phone number the first time." At Beth's puzzled look, he explained with a one-word answer that would placate Beth: "Mom."

She brightened up. "How is Margaret? I haven't had lunch with her in months."

"'Months'?" he repeated. "You have lunch with my mother?" First Lance and now Beth. This was news to him and he stopped walking in the middle of the pathway. The crowds, used to observers at a car show, just parted around them.

She pulled gently to see if he would relinquish her arm. He would not. "We've kept in touch over the years. She is a delightful woman. We enjoy each others company," she answered defensively.

"That would explain how she had your number and address."

"But it would *not* explain why she gave them to you," was her pointed reply.

Adam smiled at her. "I'm her favorite son."

They resumed walking. "You're her only son…"

Adam felt he had better explain. He didn't want Beth on the defense. He already had too much to make up for. "Well, she knows Lance and I are working on some mysterious project about Disneyland. I told her we were stuck on something and she agreed you were the best person to help us."

Beth stopped to admire the row of Corvettes. Her favorite '58 was there with its flawless red and white paint job. She nodded to Art, the owner. He was busy answering questions – something Beth knew she would be doing if she was sitting behind her car.

"So Margaret doesn't know what the project is. Does anyone else?"

Adam answered right away, "Nope, no one…well, unless Lance has blabbed to some of his girls. But, I don't think he would do that. Where is he, by the way?" he asked, looking around.

She shrugged. "I don't know. He left as soon as I got out the polishing cloths. Just look for the biggest group of girls."

He playfully tugged on Beth's arm. "Jealous?"

She laughed at that. "No. That's just Lance. Always has been. I would have thought he would have settled down by now."

"I think he's waiting for you."

Now it was her turn. "Jealous?"

"Completely." He paused in front of the Volkswagen section.

"Now, *that* is green," she commented on one of the cars that stood out from the others.

He couldn't resist. "Obviously, Captain. It's kinda

cute." 'It' was a 1962 V.W. painted Neon Green with green metal flake in the paint. There was a huge toy wind-up key perched in the middle of the roof. Green fuzzy dice dangled from the rearview mirror. Kermit the Frog sat behind the steering wheel. "Think there is a theme going on?" Adam rhetorically asked with a chuckle at the sight.

They finished walking around the circuit and were back at her car. There were six T-Birds now of various years and colors. Hers was the only one that was authenticated as Thunderbird Bronze. It was about as rare as the Seaspray Green that came out the same year. "Is this yours?" he asked, the surprise sounding in his voice.

"A little different than my Wrangler, huh?"

Adam just nodded and walked around the car. Beth had the trunk lid up to show the original checkered liner, and the driver door was open to better see the polished chrome dash and embossed Thunderbird leather door panels. The hood was propped open with bronze-colored poles about a foot long to show off the clean original engine. Adam noticed a couple who had stopped to ask her about the car. As she chatted amicably with them, he sat down to wait in one of her camp chairs. He watched her as she talked. She was still as animated and bubbly as she had been when she was doing her spiel as a Keel Boat pilot.

The couple Beth had been talking to wandered over to the yellow T-Bird and asked that owner some of the same questions they had just asked Beth. "It's like working in the Park," she explained to Adam as she sat down next to him. "You answer the same questions over and over and try to make the answers sound like it was the first time you said it."

She opened a soda for him and took a bottled water out for herself. "Thanks. How did you get into all this?" His gesture took in the park and all the cars. "You never seemed too interested in cars before."

Beth paused before answering, all her conflicts with Adam racing through her mind. Did she owe him anything? Explanations? Reasons? Anything? Did she want to open up to Adam – the man who broke her heart? He did trust her enough to bring her in on the treasure hunt – if there really turned out to be a treasure. Was five years long enough? Was any length of time long enough? Maybe it was time to bury the hatchet. His mom seemed to think so or she never would have given Adam her address. Beth always admired and trusted Margaret and her judgment...even though she had questioned Margaret's son's judgment five years earlier.

Adam guessed the reason for her hesitation and asked no more questions. She hadn't kicked him out of the car show. That was something. He had a deep suspicion that he was being watched by her male car friends – that, if she just snapped her fingers, a dozen of them would be more than happy to escort him to his truck and beat the crap out of him. He sensed the camaraderie in the large group. It probably made Beth feel better, too, about hanging out with them. While he was glad they watched out for each other.... Well, some of these guys looked like they probably had a crescent wrench and a pair of jumper cables handy...something he didn't want to find out.

Settling back in the camp chair, he watched people taking pictures of the cars, smiling when they aimed their cameras at the T-Bird. One cocky looking man in a dark blue blazer, tan chinos and Alligator loafers – with no socks on – walked up to Adam and motioned at Beth's car with his chin. "Is that the original engine?" he asked without the usual chitchat.

Adam shrugged. "I have no idea. You'll have to ask the owner." He looked over at Beth, expecting her to answer. He wondered why she just sat there, a fake smile plastered on her face.

"When is the owner coming back?" the man asked

her, managing to look bored by his own question.

"Probably in about half an hour," was her curt reply.

The man just moved off to the next car without another word. Adam looked at her. "What was that about?" He thought he heard her mumble something nasty under her breath.

She looked disgusted. Adam hoped the look was for the man who just left. "Oh, nothing really," she said with a wave of dismissal. "I get that all the time. He wouldn't have listened to a woman's answer if I told him. So I don't bother."

"Will he be back?"

"Nope. Just likes the sound of his own important voice. I was supposed to be flattered that he deigned to notice my little car." She gave a wicked smile. "Hope he goes over to that white '32 five-window coupe – the one with the 327? That guy will eat him up and spit him out."

"So, how did you get into this? Or have you decided to answer me yet?"

She glanced over at him out of the corner of her eyes. No animosity, just curious. "Long version or short version?"

"Surprise me."

Beth took a deep breath and looked around before answering. *You don't have to do this, girl.* "Once upon a time, there was a brown-haired princess who married her blonde Prince Charming. He gave her lots of pretty things, including a bronze-colored chariot to show to the other princesses. He owned a Silver Shadow that he liked to show off, too."

"So, Prince Charming was into car shows. A Rolls? Nice."

She nodded. "It was. He had had it completely restored, a frame-off restoration. It was beautiful. He showed her at car shows, so I got interested in them, too. An interest to share, I guess. Then, one day not too long after Puerto Rico, he started treating me differently."

"Your honeymoon Puerto Rico?"

She nodded, staring straight ahead. "Yeah, that Puerto Rico. I soon found out there was someone named Katherine, and Katherine was pregnant. Katherine who had dumped him for someone named Phillip. But Phillip galloped off into the sunset alone when he found out she was already pregnant. Now she wanted Prince Charming back. Keeping up with me?"

Adam just nodded. "Does Prince Charming have a name?"

A little bitterness came through. "Prince Charming has lots of names. None of them fit for the kiddies walking past us right now." Beth paused. "So, was this the long version or the short version? I can't remember."

"I don't think I specified…you are doing fine, though, Beth," Adam said with a sincere look of care on his face.

"Anyway, I wasn't high on the priority list. I got some consolation prizes; he filed for divorce and they now live on the beach in Malibu. End of story."

Adam indicated her car. "Consolation prize?"

"One of them, yes. He bought me my condo, paid the taxes for the first two years, gave me a decent settlement. All so I would agree for 'Irreconcilable Differences' on the divorce papers." Beth shrugged. "I guess coming to the car shows stuck. I find them enjoyable. Get to meet a lot of people. Occasionally I win a trophy. That's nice too." She didn't want to talk any more about Brent or how foolish she had felt when it was over within a matter of months. She had to face friends who had warned her about this guy. His square-jawed, blue eyed, blonde hair features reminded her of Adam – a fact she hadn't wanted to acknowledge. His cool, cruel dismissal of her. No, she didn't want to think or talk about him any more.

"Yeah, I can see you know quite a few of the owners." Adam's voice was welcome as it dragged her back to the current from her painful, embarrassing memories.

Beth smiled and looked around. "Yeah, most of them are pretty decent. We all love our cars. Some of them I see at every show."

Adam hedged a little, trying to sound casual, asked, "Anyone in particular?"

She looked him directly in the face. "Are you asking if I am seeing anyone?"

He blinked. "Well, yes."

"Adam, we have known each other for a long time. You don't need to beat around the bush. Just ask."

He was a little surprised by her candor. "All right. Are you seeing anyone?"

With a half-smile she turned back, tilting her face to the sun. "None of your business."

"Touché."

After a couple of minutes of good-natured silence between them, Beth looked around for Lance. "I think I've been stood up by my date. Are you hungry? They always have a terrific barbecue for lunch."

"I could go for that," he replied happy to stay with Beth longer.

They walked silently over the expanse of green grass that made up most of the park. The lunch tent was off in the rear, smoke pouring from the ever-burning fire pit. Lunch was tri-tip sandwiches, chips, baked beans, salad, and a drink. She had a rolled-up flannel blanket that she had pulled out of the trunk earlier and opened it under a huge oak tree. Now that the cars were silent, the birds were venturing out with song again. The breeze picked up a little, making the day perfect. Beth sat with her back against the tree digging into the beans. Adam watched her eating with gusto and laughed softly. Her head shot up, suspicious. "What?"

"You always were a good eater."

"You sound like my mom," she managed to say around a mouthful of beans.

He opened his mouth to say something, but closed it and shook his head. He took a bite of his sandwich instead. The tri-tip was pink in the middle. Fresh salsa gave it some zing. Perfect.

She still watched him, eyes narrowed. "What were you going to say?" When he hesitated, she added, "Hey, I told you my big story. I've never told anyone those nasty particulars." *And never will again*, she noted to herself.

He looked down and poked at his salad. He didn't like Italian dressing. "I… I was just remembering a picnic we had."

Careful here, she warned herself. "Which one?" *Damn it*, she couldn't stop herself.

"The one on Tom Sawyer's Island. That one."

Beth choked on her soda. "Oh, god. You would remember that."

"Come on! That was a classic! I'll bet they're still talking about it."

She didn't have to ask who "they" were. All the canoe guides and all her Keel Boat friends. "I don't know how I let you talk me into that," she muttered.

"If I remember right, it didn't take much persuasion," he pointed out. "You did manage to steal the canoe for us."

She sniffed. "I didn't 'steal' it. I just borrowed it while no one was looking… There is a difference."

"Uh huh."

What a picnic that was. Adam had brought the dinner in his backpack on a day when the Mark Twain and the Columbia were not in service. The Raft guys were too far back towards New Orleans Square to see them. Beth had bribed one of the Canoe guides to leave out two paddles in the barrels. During the excitement before the Fantasmic show, when literally thousands of guests poured into Frontierland and all the cast members were busy handling them, they had sneaked down to the Canoe dock and untied the one canoe that had been 'forgotten'. They paddled around the island to Uncle Jed's cabin and tied up at that little dock. She had covered the spotlights so they wouldn't be seen by the passing Steam Train. They had a leisurely dinner sprawled out on a blanket, watched over by the eagle perched on top of the neglected chimney of the cabin. Then, ah, then he had started kissing her. It was as if they were in a wilderness all their own. Two hours later they debated paddling all the way around the Island, but that was too risky. The Canoes had closed at dusk and it had already been dark for quite some time. The next day at work all the guys had teased her, but it was a good teasing. Her rating with them really went up. Not everyone stole a canoe.

"What are you looking all dreamy about?" Lance asked, suddenly plopping down beside her and finishing off her chips.

"Am I?" Beth reddened.

"Yes, you are. Thinking about me?'" he asked hopefully. He knew his presence had not been noticed by either of them.

Adam was instantly irritated at his friend again and puzzled by his annoyed reaction. Adam suddenly felt he had to one-up Lance. "No, we were discussing our picnic on Tom Sawyer's Island."

Lance started laughing, ignoring the jibe. "Oh, that was a classic! I don't know why you didn't invite me."

"I do," Adam grumbled to himself.

Beth needed to change the direction of the conversation. "Did Anne find you?"

"Me?" Lance sounded surprised. "She's your friend. No, I didn't see her anywhere."

They finished up their lunches. Or rather, Lance finished up what they hadn't yet eaten. Adam folded up the blanket while Beth gathered up the Styrofoam containers, soda cans and plastic forks. Together, the three walked back to the T-Bird.

Once they returned to Beth's Thunderbird, Beth noticed her car was starting to get a lot more attention now that Lance was in its vicinity. Some of the women who canvassed the area even pointed their cameras at the T-Bird once in a while. Lance didn't seem to notice. "So, how long are we going to stay?" he asked, leaning over the back of her chair, his chin resting on the top of Beth's head.

Beth ignored the looks Adam was shooting at Lance. "Judging is probably already over and the awards are at 3 o'clock. All the drivers usually stick around and leave together. It makes quite a parade for the spectators."

"Oh. Well, we could leave early and go watch that movie of yours," Lance said referring to *Swiss Family Robinson*, the movie that they hoped might hold some information regarding the last clue they had been working on.

"I always wait until after the awards. You never know," she tried to look nonchalant about receiving a trophy, but failed.

Standing, Lance finished off what had been her soda. "You might as well go. You aren't winning anything today."

She sniffed. "Thank you, Mister Car Expert."

"I was talking with the judges. They showed me the list of winners."

She just shook her head. "Is there any place you can't get into?"

He looked pointedly at Adam. "Apparently just Tom Sawyer's Island at night when others plan a unique picnic. Can we leave?"

Disappointed by her up-coming and yet-to-be announced loss, Beth shrugged. "I guess. Adam? You ready to go?"

"Sure. Can I drive the car to your place?"

"Hey!" Lance protested. "You wouldn't let me."

She rolled her eyes. Men. "I don't care, Adam. Lance, you are too tall. You barely fit riding over here."

With a victorious chuckle, Adam tossed Lance his set of keys and told him where his Silverado was parked. Lance stalked off, grumbling about where something else could be parked. Looking back at the classic car, Adam was more excited than he tried to let on.

She gave him a few instructions as they packed up the chairs and stowed away the hood props. "Put her in neutral to start the engine. Pump it twice, then turn the key. Let her warm until the choke drops."

At car shows whenever a hot rod or classic car starts their engine, all the people in the immediate vicinity usually stop to watch. Beth slid easily into the passenger seat. Adam had a large audience as he got behind the wheel...or tried to get behind the wheel. The seat was moved up for Beth's shorter legs. He banged his head on the door frame and hit his knee on the wheel. She was all innocence. "Gosh, sorry, Adam! I should have moved the seat back."

Pushing together, the bench seat was rolled back to a comfortable position for Adam. Holding the ignition key in his right hand, Adam was unable to find the place to insert the key. After a few embarrassing moments, Adam found the ignition was on the opposite side of the steering wheel. "Anything else you want to tell me?" he said in a low voice as the windows were still open and everyone was watching.

"No, no. You're doing great. Give it a little gas after you start it."

The motor purred to life and he pressed the gas pedal. The V8 responded with a huge roar and a cloud of black smoke blew out the exhaust. Cursing under his breath, he tapped it a little easier and the idle dropped. He looked at Beth, who was trying to hide a grin, and got a nod to proceed. He put the car into drive and lightly turned the steering wheel. Nothing moved. "Lot of play in the wheel," she explained.

He slowly pulled out onto the walkway and headed

towards the flags marking the exit. A man talking on a cell phone crossed the path in front of them. Adam hit the brakes and they came to a screeching, smoking stop. "Oh, yeah, the brakes are a little touchy." He could see some snickering from the Cobra owners. "Anything else?" he asked through clenched teeth.

She waved to the owner of the '29 Hi Boy Roadster. "Think I should get ghost flames when I get my car re-painted?"

He growled and aimed the car through the exit banners. He tested the brakes twice at the stop sign. There were no more mishaps on the short drive to her place. Lance was already waiting for them. She halfway expected him to be inside the condo eating dinner.

Adam came to a jerking stop inside the garage. He seemed relieved to hand her the keys. "Thanks, that was… fun."

"Sheesh, Adam, you drive like a girl! No, wait, I take that back. Even Beth drove better than that!" Lance tossed Adam his Silverado keys and snickered all the way to Beth's door.

"Boys, play nice!" Beth warned, looking way too pleased with herself as she unlocked the door and went in. She found her *Swiss Family Robinson* video. "Here or at your place, Adam?"

"Well, we're already here. It's time to find Walt's island….Lance, what are you doing?"

Lance was going through all her cabinets in the kitchen. "Popcorn… Found it. Give me two minutes."

"Okay, kiddies," Adam started when they were all settled. "Movie or extras?"

"Extras," they all decided.

Lance stretched out on the sofa, his head in Beth's lap while she fed him popcorn and played with his hair. He was asleep within 5 minutes. However, by that time they already had their answer.

CHAPTER 13

JEREMY B.

Tobago. The movie was filmed on Tobago in 1960. And...most importantly, Walt had been there early on in the filming. Adam made some more notes while the extras continued.

"Gosh, that was easy," she commented slowly when they turned it off. "Too easy? Think we are on the right track?"

Adam watched as Beth continued stroking the sleeping Lance's hair. Irritation with Lance started to surface again. "Yeah, it has to be right. It all fits: the time period of the film, Walt was there on the island, the song in the movie. It has to be right." He reached over and gave Lance's feet a rough shove. "Lance! Wake up, lover boy. We found it."

Lance just grunted and turned on his side, burrowing a hand under her thigh. Now she wasn't too sure he was actually asleep. She leaned down next to his ear. "Lance?" she crooned softly, "wakey wakey."

He turned to his back again, and opened his eyes. His deep brown eyes with their gold flecks were still blurry from sleep. Their faces were just inches apart. Still not completely awake, he gazed up into her face. "Run away with me," he whispered.

Why, why, why have I never been drawn to you???

"And leave all this?" she lightly laughed out loud.

"Yeah, all of it. I can give you anything you want."

She didn't even realize her eyes barely shifted towards Adam. "Oh, I don't think you could," she answered softly.

He hadn't missed her glance. Now wide-awake, he flashed Beth his infectious smile and quickly kissed her before she could move out of the way. "You wound me deeply," dramatically clutching his heart.

She smiled fondly back at his handsome face and wondered – again – what was wrong with her. "Oh, you'll get over it. And probably a lot sooner than you should," Beth said to Lance as he continued with his theatrics.

He flung his hand across his eyes. "Heartbreaker."

"Drama Queen."

"Spinster."

"Spoiled Brat." She could hardly keep from laughing.

"Vulture."

"Trophy Boy."

"Hag," Lance managed to get in the last one before Adam threw a Scotty dog-shaped pillow at them and told them to knock it off.

"So, what about Tobago?" Adam ground out.

Lance sat up and brushed his hair back from his forehead. "When do we leave?"

Not having worked with them on the first clues, Beth was surprised. "Just like that? You just hop on a plane and take off?"

"Well, there is some planning involved, but, basically, yes. You don't walk away from the crap table when the dice are hot," Adam explained.

Beth suddenly looked embarrassed. "It's, uhm, not a good time for me to leave," she stammered, not wanting to have to explain her money troubles. "There's work and the condo. And, uhm, taxes are coming due and all," she floundered.

Adam looked confused. "I thought you said he....."

"That ended two years ago."

Lance looked at her for an explanation. "I'll tell you later," was all she said as she went over and sat down at her desk.

"Is two days from now good for you both?" Lance held up a hand to stop Beth's protest. "No argument. You are coming with us. We're all partners now. You can pay me back later."

And, considering the messages from his father, she would probably have to, Lance thought to himself.

Adam pulled out his pocket organizer. He didn't want to have to leave so soon, but he could shuffle some of his bids around. Scott could handle Mrs. Anderson one more time. "I need to call my foreman, but Monday is good for me. Are you going to arrange the tickets, Lance? Do you even know where we are going?"

"Sure. Toboggan."

Adam groaned. "Maybe if you hadn't fallen asleep…"

Deciding to go with the flow, and still not believing she was actually going back to the Caribbean – in two days, Beth started pulling up information on her computer. "Tobago is an island off the coast of Trinidad, Lance." She switched over to a travel website. "We can fly from LAX to Miami. From Miami it looks like we have to fly into Port of Spain, Trinidad. Then we can take a ferry over to Tobago. Looks like there is regular service every day. Gosh! The ferry's $70 each for round trip to the island! Lance!"

Looking over her shoulder he told her, "Don't worry about it, Captain. Really. I'll take care of it. Just write down what I need to know."

"How much paper do you have?" Adam mumbled, automatically reaching for the phone on her desk that was ringing. "Hello?" Adam answered. "Yes, this is Beth's residence… Who is this?....Hey, Anne, this is Adam…….Yes, 'that' Adam," he turned red, and handed the phone to Beth who was glaring at him. "What? I was right there when it rang….never mind, here you go."

She grabbed the phone from his outstretched hand and sat down at her desk. "Hey, Anne, I was just going to call you…..How come you didn't show up at the car show?...Yeah, Lance is here too…. Don't ask…..Say listen, I need a couple of days off…..Monday….yes, this Monday……Can I call you back later when these guys are gone? They are leaving now," she said pointedly to Adam, who was listening intently to her side of the conversation. "I'll call you back."

"You work for Anne?" Adam asked as soon as she had hung up the phone. "I thought she worked in a dress shop."

Beth hesitated for a moment. Lance walked over to her and pulled her out of the desk chair in front of the computer. "Tell Adam about it while I look at flight availability." Beth didn't argue, standing next to Lance and began filling in some of the missing years. "She did work in the boutique. Now she owns it. As a favor, she let me work there after I left Disneyland. Then, after my divorce she let me come back. I've been there ever since."

After watching her run the Keel Boats, he couldn't picture her working in a fashion boutique. But, it wasn't his business. And, by the look on her face she didn't want it to be his business. "I should tell my mom. You know how she loves to shop."

Now Beth smiled. "Oh, Margaret knows. We call her when something she might like comes in."

Lance looked up from the computer screen. "I have the flights booked."

"What?" This surprised Beth. She still expected to spend a couple of hours discussing plans and making arrangements. She didn't realize the guys were used to this by now.

Lance printed their itinerary and handed her a copy. "We leave LAX at 8:45 a.m., get to Miami five hours later.

Two hour layover, then an almost four hour flight to Trinidad. We arrive there at 10:45 p.m. I made a reservation for overnight near the airport. Next day, we'll catch the 10 a.m. *T&T Spirit* ferry to Scarborough, Tobago. We have a suite at the Blue Haven Hotel. I figured four days should be plenty. Sound good?"

Adam looked over the itinerary, nodding. Beth was still stunned. She didn't know what to say. "You just did all that?"

"Obviously, Captain. I'm not completely useless," he claimed, sounding hurt.

She felt instant remorse. "I didn't mean it that way, Lance. Really. This is just so much for me. I mean, poof, you two show up after five years. There's Walt's diary. Now I am going to have to pack for a trip to the Caribbean to search for a treasure."

Lance gave her a hug. "I know. We felt that way too at first. I guess we're used to it. So, are you okay with this? You know we wouldn't go without you."

She looked skeptical at that. "Oh really?"

"Well, we would go, but we wouldn't have nearly as much fun!"

"Okay, fine. I'm going. Now get out of here so I can take care of a few things."

Adam folded up the paper. He found he had been holding his breath when he thought she might not be able to go. He kept his face averted on the itinerary he seemed to be intent on folding just so. "Then we will pick you up Monday morning around 5:30 a.m…."

"5:30! In the morning?? I thought the plane leaves at 8:45!" Beth was not known to be an early riser.

Adam smiled at the incredulous look on her face. He remembered the early morning hours when she had to train for the annual cast member canoe races at Disneyland. That month just about killed her! "It takes about one and a half hours to drive to the airport at that time of the morning." Adam then realized that Beth might not have traveled much in the last few years since her divorce. He then explained, "Since 9/11, the extra security at the airports can take up to two hours. We almost missed our first flight to Missouri because we hadn't planned on that. Anyway, we can take my truck. The bags will fit in the bed. Pack light."

"It's going to feel weird to fly," she said softly, suddenly somber.

Adam just nodded. "We'll see you then. Lance, you coming?" as he opened her front door.

"I have my own car," as he plopped back down on the sofa. At Beth's stern look, he got right back up, lightly kissed her cheek, and followed Adam out the door.

MONDAY, JUNE 10TH, 2002
8:40 A.M.

The second flight from Miami to Trinidad left right on time. Adam had boarded first, and was seated in the middle of the plane before he realized Lance and Beth weren't behind him. He stowed his carry-on beneath the seat in front of him and waited. He finally saw Lance's head, tall above the other passengers, come onboard. But Lance didn't come back to the seats next to him. He turned to his right and apparently sat. Standing now, Adam could see Beth follow. They were in First Class. That dirty son of a….. Adam was forced to retake his seat when a couple climbed over him to claim the window seats. From their animated chatter, Adam could tell that the man and woman next to him were on their honeymoon. The seats around him were also filling up, mostly couples he noted dryly. When the seat belt light came on and the flight attendant started his safety drill, Adam stifled his cursing and grabbed the magazine from the pouch in the seatback in front of him. The couple next to him were kissing and murmuring sweet nothings to each other.

It was going to be a long flight.

Beth felt guilty about the 'surprise' Lance had sprung on her right before they boarded. Guilty, that is, until she sat in the wide, plush leather seats and was handed a warm towel and a glass of champagne. She noticed their flight attendant, Heather, was giving Lance more attention than the other First Class passengers, seemingly indifferent to the fact that Lance was obviously there with Beth. Eventually Beth was offered a choice of current magazines from which to choose, and settled in with that as Lance chatted with Heather from his aisle seat. If there had been an empty seat between Beth and Lance, she was sure Heather would have been sitting in it.

Heather reluctantly left Lance's side when another passenger rang the call button – three times. Lance turned back to Beth. "Enjoying your surprise?"

Beth chose a slice of thin sliced Edam cheese off the platter in front of them. "This is wonderful! I never flew First Class before. You think Adam is all right back there?"

"Who?"

She lightly punched his arm. "You think he is mad?"

"Undoubtedly." Lance motioned for Heather with his empty champagne flute. He tucked her phone number into his shirt pocket after she walked off. "This is a lot better service than yesterday."

Beth was confused. "Yesterday? What happened yesterday?"

"Oh." *Crap.* Lance thought quickly. "I had to fly to Boston."

She could tell it hadn't been a pleasure trip. "Kinda sudden, wasn't it? Is your family all right?"

Beth knew Lance came from 'old money' in Boston. 'Boston Proper' as they liked to refer to it. He didn't talk about it much. And he rarely went to visit. His parents weren't too pleased he preferred his California lifestyle to his 'rightful place' in the company of the aristocratic Boston Society. He gave an uncharacteristic angry sigh. He hadn't meant to mention it. "Just more of the same," he mumbled bitterly. He noticed a brunette a row over giving him a look. With his mind on the demands his father had ordered, he just automatically smiled back without flashing his typical 'come on over to my place' look.

Beth saw only his smile, not really knowing what was going on with Lance. She gave him a good-natured dig in the ribs. "You'll make Heather jealous. I might want another hot towel later. So, how many girls do you have now?"

Glad she wasn't pursuing the topic of his trip to Boston, he answered, "Oh, I don't know. Can I count you?" At the negative shake of her head, he continued, "Let's see…..Only eight. Oh, wait. Nine."

She could see whatever cloud covered him since he mentioned his family had retreated some. "Nine? That's awful!"

"Why?"

"'Why'?" she echoed. "What if someone gets hurt?"

Inexplicably, his eyes hardened. "I'm not your ex-husband, Beth. There isn't going to be any 'Mr. and Mrs. Rebound' in my future."

She looked down, hurt. "That wasn't nice. These women have feelings too, you know."

"As do I. Sometimes women can be just as shallow as you seem to think I am." With that, Lance bound up from his seat and stormed back to the Coach section.

Beth, stunned at the sudden turn of events, just sat there, her mouth open. Heather, who had watched the whole thing, glared at Beth as she grabbed up their two empty champagne flutes and took away the gourmet snack tray.

Within a couple of minutes Adam slid into the seat

besides her. "What did you say to Lance!?... Wow, this is nice up here," Adam marveled, running his hands over the leather arm rests, wiggling his rear in the expanse of room in the first-class seat.

On the verge of tears, Beth shrugged. "I guess I hurt his feelings. I didn't mean to. I thought we were just talking. Then he said something nasty…. Hey, did you refer to me as 'Mrs. Rebound'?" she demanded with an accusing stare.

Stammering, Adam swallowed. "I might have mentioned what you told me about your marriage. Where are you going?" as she stood and made to leave.

"I need to fix it with Lance."

He grabbed her hand. "He'll be okay. Really. Just let me enjoy these seats a little while longer. We still have at least two hours in the air. Come on. Please. I can't take those googly-eyed newlyweds sitting next to me back there any longer!"

Beth allowed him to tug her back into her seat. She knew Lance didn't hold a grudge. And, it had been a dirty trick on Adam to seat him back in coach. "Okay," she signed, relenting. "I'll fix it later." She rang the call button for a glass of champagne for Adam. Heather ignored her.

Adam, taking advantage of the time alone with Beth, settled into the plush leather seat and told her about his construction company. He had taken over when his dad wanted an early retirement. Their specialty was teardowns and remodels. Beth let him talk. She knew all this from her lunches with Margaret, but it felt good just to talk with him like they used to. She had been alone now for almost three years. It was nice having anyone talk to her. While it had been overwhelming to suddenly have both men back in her life, she felt at ease with them. She knew them so well. And, now she realized how much she had missed them. She didn't know she had been staring into Adam's blue eyes while he talked. She always loved the way his eyes crinkled at the corners when he laughed.

Adam saw her expression change from distress over Lance to interest in what he was telling her to a relaxation of her whole being – something she hadn't done around him up to this point. He remembered she had welcomed Lance back literally with open arms and had immediately fallen into that easy, joking camaraderie they had always shared. But, it wasn't Lance who had hurt her. He had. Big time. Maybe now was the time to fix that. It was worth a shot. It was not like she could walk out on him, they were 40,000 feet over the ocean. He had to try.

"You know, you're going to have to forgive me some-time," Adam said suddenly changing the conversation.

"I am? And when did you become such an expert on human nature?" Smiling, Beth hid her surprise at the turn in their conversation.

"About two minutes after I let you walk out of my life."

Beth frowned at the memory. "If I remember cor-rectly, I was half dragged, half carried out of your life."

"Can I tell you a secret?"

"Will I like this secret?"

"Probably not."

"Then by all means, tell me," she smiled.

Adam took a deep breath. "It was my fault."

Beth was confused. "What was your fault?"

"You ending up in the River."

Beth thought back to the day she was fired from Dis-neyland. "I don't understand. You were nowhere near me when I actually fell in."

"When you were shoving the nose of the Keel Boat and leaning past the point of no return, I told Randy to turn the rudder the opposite way and goose the throttle a little."

"That would have pulled the nose of the Bertha Mae away from the dock too fast," she muttered, picturing her-self leaning out with the shove pole over the green water. "No wonder I couldn't figure it out."

Adam nodded. "You were already off-balance when he pulled away. You had no chance to push yourself upright as you always did. You had to fall in."

Her eyes suddenly turned hurt and angry. "But why? Why would you do that to me?"

He wanted to take her hand, but didn't. "I can't tell you that part yet. But I wanted you to know. Will you trust me to make it all right later?"

Her earlier warm, fuzzy feeling had evaporated. "What are you going to do? Get me my job back? Reopen the Keel Boats? Buy back the Bertha Mae?"

That was news to him. "They sold the Bertha Mae?"

"You're changing the subject, but, yes. It was sold in an online auction." A side of her mouth turned up in a wry grin. "I even bid on it."

"Where would you put a Keel Boat??"

"I wasn't planning on winning the bid. I stopped at $200."

"What did it go for? Do you know?"

Beth sighed. "Of course I know. It was my boat. It went for $15,000."

Adam gave a low appreciative whistle. "Do you know who won it?"

She shook her head, down again. "No, that wasn't disclosed. I just hope they are taking good care of her." She had really loved her job. The remaining Keel Boat, the Gullywhumper, was now being used as a prop around Tom Sawyer's Island. It drew a nostalgic memory in Beth every time she went past it on the Mark Twain Steamboat.

Adam broke into her thoughts. "So, will you ever forgive me?"

Those blue eyes of his looked sincere. *Will you ever say you're sorry, Adam?* "Probably. But not right now," she replied, with a sad tone in her voice. She thought then, for a moment, that this might be Adam's way of saying he was sorry…but, she didn't want it glossed over.

She wanted a sincere, heartfelt "sorry" from Adam.

He would wait. He had waited five years so far. "Fair enough. Why don't you go talk to Lance? I noticed a couple of empty seats back by the lavatory. Maybe you could talk there."

When Beth walked back to coach, Adam rang the call button. Heather didn't even look his way.

TUESDAY, JUNE 11TH, 2002
10:12 A.M.

The *T&T Spirit* flew over the blue-green water of the Atlantic. The black and white 900-passenger ferry boat made the trip in two and a half hours. Her slower cousin, the *Panorama*, took over four hours. After trying to stand at the rail to watch the flying spray, Beth laughingly gave up fighting the wind and occasional mist that blew around her. Seated in the more comfortable observation deck, the three friends watched as they neared Tobago.

It was a long, narrow island measuring only 26 miles long and 6 miles wide. The island was mostly hills of volcanic origin. The southwest portion of the island was flat and consisted of coralline limestone. The hilly spine of the island, called the Main Ridge, holds claim to the oldest protected forests in the Western world. The Tobago Forest Reserve located there is relatively small, but has government-appointed guides for the birds, mammals, snakes, and butterflies who inhabit the area. The ferry was fast approaching the capital city of Scarborough. Situated in Rockly Bay on the Atlantic Ocean side of the island, the capital was home to about a third of the population of Tobago. The history of the island dates back to 1498 when Christopher Columbus arrived and claimed the lush property for Spain. Because Tobago has naturally calm and deep harbors, it became an important way-station for the exploration and conquest of both

South America and the rest of the Caribbean. Because of that importance, the island had a very bloody, violent history. The 17th century saw Tobago as a haven for marauders and pirates. Henry Morgan, Captain Finn and even Black Beard used the island as a hideaway and supply station. The situation became so bad that the British Government located in Barbados had to send a squadron of ships to drive out the pirates, only one of the many bloody battles fought on the island. For two hundred years, Tobago changed hands frequently among the Dutch, the French, and the English. America even tried to get into the mix, when, in 1778, an American squadron tried to take the island from England, but was repulsed by the British warship Yarmouth. When slavery was abolished, the sugar trade collapsed. Once Wards of Trinidad, both Trinidad and Tobago became independent Commonwealth countries in 1962, and together became a Republic in 1976.

With the half-medallion safely secure around his neck, Adam was thinking more of the pirates in Tobago's past than the rest of its colorful history. So far they had been unable to identify the old coin left by Walt. There was no other coin like it in the research books he poured through. Since he and Lance had plans to scuba dive Barcolet Bay, he would send Beth into town and up to the remains of Fort King George where the Tobago Museum was located.

As they slowed to enter Rockly Bay and the harbor, they could see the remains of the fort situated on a rocky point. Several aging cannons stood guard as they once did to repel the marauding pirates. But, exploration of the Fort would come later. They first needed to get situated at the Blue Haven Hotel.

The crowded wharf and the dry, dusty town were left behind as their taxi wound through the famous 100-year old Palm Alley that led up to the front of the brilliant pink walled, white roofed resort. Nestled on five acres of plush tropical vegetation, the hotel boasted fifty-five rooms – all ocean views as they were surrounded by azure blue water on three sides. Robinson Crusoe was claimed to have been stranded on this exact location. More importantly to the three treasure seekers, the adjoining white sand beach of Barcolet Bay was where *Swiss Family Robinson* was filmed in 1960. During the 1940's the hotel had been haven to many celebrities from Hollywood's Golden Years. However, these three seekers were interested in only one celebrity and his association and activities within the surrounding area.

Their deluxe suite had two bedrooms, a sitting room and a small kitchen. Dark paddled ceiling fans kept breezes moving throughout the rooms. The suite had hardwood floors, deep white cushioned chairs facing the large patio sliders, four-poster queen-sized beds covered with lacy white cotton, white wicker furniture on their private balcony, and even vases of hibiscus and Birds of Paradise in each room. A welcome basket of island fruits with a resplendent gold bow sat in the middle of the kitchen table.

Beth walked in a happy daze through the rooms looking at everything, trying to believe she was actually here. The fatigue of the long journey yesterday, and the slight seasickness on the ferry ride over were all forgotten. Standing at the edge of the balcony off her bedroom, she stared out over the swaying palm trees and rolling white caps of the ocean. The breeze was cooler now. Inside, the two men had pushed aside the fruit basket and laid out their research papers. Adam's mind was divided between the work at hand and wanting to share some of Beth's first impressions. He recalled the tropical honeymoon he had planned for her – plans that immediately evaporated when his little joke backfired on the Keel Boat dock and he never saw her again. Lance thumped Adam's arm and brought him back to the present. Lance seemed unusually tense and focused on their mission. Adam would have to talk to

Beth about him later whenever they might be alone.

Beth was called from her reverie and with great reluctance she left the balcony. Her retort to Lance's abrupt summons was stilled by the look on his face. She could tell he didn't want to joke around right now. Whatever happened in Boston with his family must have been worse than he let on. This wasn't really Lance.

Lance reminded them of the time element they were working around.

"We have three days," Beth broke in.

A little smile flitted across Lance's face. "Thank you, Captain Obvious," he told her not unkindly. "Yes, we have three days. After lunch Adam and I have reservations at a dive shop. We're going to go scuba diving in Barcolet Bay. We would like you, Beth, to go through the museum in the Fort. See if you can find any links to treasure discoveries or anything that might be of use. You know it can be obscure. Look for any references to the filming of the movie, too, if there are any. We still need to identify our 'Jeremy B.' Anything else, Adam?"

Adam could tell Beth was disappointed she didn't get to go to the beach with them. "You'll get plenty of beach time, don't worry," Adam reassured her. "We just need to get the obvious searching done first."

She just nodded. "What about the medallion? Should I take it with me? Or will you wear it diving?"

The guys looked at each other. They hadn't thought of that. "Maybe you had better wear it under your blouse. I wouldn't want to lose it out in the ocean somewhere," Adam conceded.

She watched them leave the suite, white T-shirts over their swim trunks. The 80-degree water was so warm they wouldn't need a wetsuit for their dive. She waited until they were out of sight on the little path winding through the palm trees and ferns. Disappointed to be alone again, she went out to the meet the taxi Lance had arranged to take her to the Fort.

The turquoise-blue dive boat swung around in a tight arc. The skipper, standing spread-legged at the wheel, looked over the side into the clear water. He checked his position relative to the distance from the beach and cut the motor. The gentle lapping waves gave a rocking motion to the boat as he dropped anchor to the sandy bottom. The only two divers he brought were busy fastening on their fins. Air tanks were strapped on and face masks spat into to rid the mask of respiration fog; regulators placed in their mouths and tested; watches set for air time. Uncharacteristically taking the lead, Lance backed to the edge of the boat. Sitting, he held his face mask in along with his regulator and fell backwards, disappearing into the crystal blue water. Adam followed a moment later after Lance had begun his descent towards the bottom of the Bay.

The friends leveled out a few feet above the coral reef, mindful not to damage the frail organisms with a careless brush of their swim fins. They knew these waters were home to giant manta rays, sting rays, and even nurse sharks. But they weren't there to view the colorful inhabitants of the region. Their eyes scanned the seabed, the coral, and the many varieties of sponge below them. Lance motioned for Adam to go further west. They crisscrossed, looking for anything that might be an indicator of hidden loot. As popular as they knew this location was, they weren't surprised there was nothing obvious. They were looking for possible remains of a ship, something that might indicate the gold medallion now around Beth's neck could have come from this region.

Adam froze when a dark shadow passed his peripheral vision to the left. Lance was swimming steadily towards the beach, head down. Adam released some air from his buoyancy compensator and sunk deeper in the water. The shadow, looking to be about ten feet long, banked right and snaked closer. The diving knife strapped to his leg wasn't much, but it did make him feel better to place a hand on it as he watched. He glanced at his watch. There was plenty of air if he had to wait it out. He did wonder if Lance had noticed that he had fallen back. He could always signal by banging the knife against his air tank. The sound would reach Lance underwater.

He was a little surprised, but relieved, when the shadow revealed itself to be a nurse shark. He was surprised, because this kind of shark usually traveled and hunted only at night, preferring to sleep during the day on the sandy bottom or in a secluded nook somewhere. He was relieved as this shark ate mostly crustaceans, mollusks, and other fish. Nurse sharks aren't known to attack humans, but he didn't want to test the theory.

The shark circled lazily a few times and swam slowly back into the distance away from the two divers. Whatever had disturbed its sleep was probably gone. Adam made sure the shark didn't decide to return before he added air to his BC and rose in the water. With his heart pounding, Adam took a couple of deep breaths through his regulator to calm himself and resumed his search of the seabed floor.

Lance swam back to him and gave him the two palms up gesture, asking if he was all right. Adam returned with the gesture for 'shark' and pointed off to the west. Lance pointed to the surface, asking if they should go back to the boat. Adam shook his head no and pointed to his watch. They had about another twenty minutes of air. Satisfied, Lance returned the way he had come, making slow strokes with his long legs.

Beth wandered over the grounds of the old Fort King George. She noticed the lighthouse next to the fort was the reverse colors of their hotel. It had brilliant white walls with a pink roof. However she doubted this was the kind of information she was supposed to looking for.

Unlike the freshly painted lighthouse, the Fort was dark brown and had dingy Cathedral windows facing the ocean. Cannons and remains of cannons still stood on their battlements. A flame tree, or a Royal Poinciana, was in bloom behind the cannons. Enjoying the view of the harbor of Scarborough a little longer, Beth let the island breeze blow over her, tugging at the hem of her short broomstick skirt. The medallion lay warm against her chest, a reminder of why she was here.

The Tobago Museum closed at 1 p.m., so she had an hour to snoop around. The Fort had been built in the 1770's and well used during the frequent times the island changed hands. Now the museum stood in the Barrack Guard House. She found many documents from the Colonial period of the island, military relics, and items used in earlier times. She read a few of the yellowed papers. Many dealt with the cruelty of slavery. Some were farm reports. No mention was made of pirates or any findings of significance in the waters surrounding them. Beth didn't know enough about treasure finds to know if this was common or not. She wandered around the grounds. She spotted a gift shop but wasn't interested in the shell animals or the colorful native wraps.

Instead of asking for a taxi, she decided to walk down the steep hill back to town. She had gotten directions for a café that was known for its Italian coffee and ice cream parlor. She found the Ciao Café down Carrington Street at the Burnett Street turn. Opting for her usual strawberry ice cream, she sat in one of the café chairs outside under the awning. The café was popular, so she had a lot of people to watch while she rested her sore calf muscles. *Boy, I'm out of shape!* she thought as she ate the quickly melting ice cream.

In another couple of minutes of walking, Beth arrived in the main part of Scarborough. The main market day was Saturday, but there was still plenty of traffic on the narrow streets and congested sidewalks. Posters on walls told of the just-finished annual goat races. Not sure what they were exactly, Beth thought it looked like a lot of fun. She did some window shopping as she walked slowly along the main street. It was hot and dusty in town, but the air was getting cooler the closer she got to the harbor. There was a book store on the other side of the street, next to a small jewelry store. About to cross over, a honking stopped her. Expecting to have to wave an apology to some driver, she was surprised to see Adam hanging out of a taxi window, waving at her. Noticing the street was clear, she ran over to the car and got in the front seat with the driver. As Adam and Beth compared notes on what they did – or more specifically what they did not – find, the driver merged into traffic with some good-natured yelling and cursing.

In the jewelry store across the street from where Beth had gotten into the cab, unseen by the three friends, the sun caught the gleaming shine of a gold half-coin pendant hanging on a display bust.

The driver pulled up in front of the Blue Haven. Beth was handing the medallion back to Adam. The driver chuckled as he accepted their payment for the ride. "I see you like local legends. Dat is good," he told them.

"Sorry?" Adam looked confused as he slipped the chain over his head.

"Dat pretty gold you wear. You got it from da jewelry store, huh, miss?"

Beth shook her head. "I, uh, no, I didn't." Beth hesitated, thinking about the jewelry store next to the bookstore she had been before getting in the cab. "No, I was heading for the bookstore when you honked."

"Ah, my mistake," the driver told them. "Many visitors like dat coin as, how you say, souvenir. But, now that I think, it is set wrong. The engraving on wrong side. My mistake," he repeated good-naturedly.

Adam felt the hair on the back of his neck tingle. He looked at Lance, who had edged closer. "Do you think you could take us back to the jewelry store? I'd like to get another one for my friend here," indicating Lance.

The driver chuckled again. "Ah, he be long eye, huh?" At their blank looks, he explained, "He likes what other people have, no?"

"Yes, that's me," Lance shrugged. "I always want something else. Ha ha."

Beth looked at him strangely as they got back in the car. He indicated to her not to say anything.

The three stood on the sidewalk staring through the shop window at the mirror-opposite of their coin. There it was, sitting in the open in a little shop on the main street of town, and nobody seemed to care. Adam had tried the door, but the shop was closed for the day. Adam felt his coin through the material of his shirt. He could feel the jagged edge and the raised figures on the face. He mentally put the pieces together. "That's it," he said quietly. "That's the other side. We'll have to come back tomorrow."

"But how can that be?" Lance wanted to know. "Who would display an old coin like that out in the open? Don't they know its value?"

"Do we?" Beth asked, thinking. "You didn't have it valued, did you?"

Adam shook his head, disappointed the store was closed. "Let's go back to the hotel. There's nothing we can do tonight." He opened the door of the cab waiting by the curb, while Lance and Beth climbed in.

They were quiet in the taxi on the ride back to the Blue Haven. Lance paid the driver again who cheerfully waved good-bye as he pulled away from the hotel cabbie drop-off zone. Later, as they sat down to dinner, they forgot their perplexing dilemma to enjoy their first Caribbean sunset. All the windows in the hotel dining room were thrown open to catch the trade winds. The sun dropped slowly in pools of pink and yellow and orange. The few clouds that remained from the daily afternoon shower turned dark red when the sun finally slipped into ocean's blue horizon. "Wow," Beth uttered. It seemed a sufficient exclamation for all of them as the last of the daylight faded and the room became illuminated only by candlelight, pale by comparison to the panorama of nature outside.

They turned their attention to the menu. Adam tried the local favorite, crab 'n dumplings – crab stewed with curry and coconut milk and served with flat flour dumplings. Lance muttered something like "to hell with him," and ordered the steak and lobster. Beth opted for a kibbie, a mixture of meat and corn wrapped in pastry and deep-fried. The guys had a locally brewed Carib beer; Beth asking for bottled water. As friends often do, they sampled off of each other's plates. They found the curry dish spicy, but not over-bearing. The lobster was perfect with the drawn butter. All agreed none of them would order a kibbie again.

After a second beer Lance seemed to relax a bit. They strolled around the hotel grounds after finishing dinner and finally ended up back in their suite. As Adam made notes on their find in town, Beth discovered she forgot her toothpaste. She accepted Lance's offer to walk her to the gift shop. As the door clicked shut, Adam grumbled over another missed opportunity.

The gift shop in the lobby of the hotel held the usual postcards and souvenir shot glasses depicting scenes of the famous hotel. There were plush white Egyptian cotton robes for sale like the ones hanging in the closets in their rooms. Also for sale were racks of candy, a small liquor supply, and refrigerated drinks not found in their suites cooler, sunglasses, sunscreen, and a jewelry display.

Lance looked up as Beth pulled away from his arm. He had been asking her what brand of toothpaste she used when she paled at the sight of the display of jewelry. He watched her hands go through what had to have been fifty of the half coins. Gold ones. Silver ones. Bronze ones. There was even a cheaper pink plastic one tied with a ribbon. "Lance! Do you see this?" She just kept letting them fall through her fingers. She turned back to Lance. "Call Adam."

Lance went to use the hotel phone. Beth couldn't move. In just a couple of minutes Adam rushed in, his hand clutching the medallion still beneath his shirt. The gift shop clerk had seen Beth's interest in the necklace and pulled out another tray full of them. "You liking other colors, miss?"

Adam pulled out his coin and fitted it next to one of the gift shop versions. It fit perfectly. The raised pattern now made a completed set of crossed bones forming a perfect X. Over the X now showed a grinning skull, un-recognizable before with the jagged cutting.

The clerk, interested in what they were doing, looked over the counter at the pieces put together. "Ah, how pretty! I never seen another side but dis."

Adam tried to control his features and voice. "You wouldn't happen to know the history of this necklace, would you?"

She laughed and waved them away, "Ah, what history? We be selling dis necklace many year now. Many a saga boy likes them. Usually wears more 'n one. You know, fancy boy." She looked over Lance with a grin.

"We saw one like it in a jewelry store in town. The taxi driver mentioned some local legend," Adam prompted.

"Well, I know nothing of dat. If you want to know anyt'ing about this island, go to Mooma. She runs book store. If it be known, Mooma knows it. Fuh true."

Lance gave her a couple of dollars for a gold version of the necklace. They would have to wait until to-morrow to find out what Mooma really knows.

WEDNESDAY, JUNE 12TH, 2002
4:10 P.M.

Mooma was dressed in a bright orange cotton shirt and pink shorts. Sitting behind her counter, she slowly fanned herself with a woven palm leaf fan. She watched the three visitors enter her little book store. Only a superficial look at the books, she noticed, as the three perused the selections with no apparent interest. They would ask her soon enough what they want.

Adam smiled politely and wondered how best to come to the point. "Are you Mooma?"

Unsmiling, she nodded sagely, her eyes half closed. "And you be interested in tales from the past," she muttered in a low, creaky voice. Adam's eyebrows shot up and his hand went to the medallion. Not being able to keep a straight face, she chuckled. "My cousin, Missy, she works at da hotel. Said you would be coming. You thought maybe I was a jumbie?" At his blank expression, she added, "You know, spirit!" She chuckled again.

Adam realized he was in for a long haul. "Well, Missy says you know everything about Tobago."

"Is true, is true."

He pulled the cheap necklace out of his pocket and laid it on the counter in front of her. "We were wondering if you could tell us about this."

"If'n you pay more'n fifty cents, you pay too much!"

He did get a laugh out of that. "I think Lance gave her two dollars for it."

"Ah, then, your boy there probably went to school in August and his best subject was recess."

Beth was the only one who laughed at that. "I'll explain it to them later," she told Mooma.

"If'n you have to explain, then it must be true! Okay, I quit kidding round. You like soda or a Carib?" she offered, showing the hospitality of the island.

The friends thanked her and said no. Adam asked

her about the island legend the taxi driver had mentioned.

"Yes, yes, I know all about dat. It took place long time ago. Way before you came along on dis earth." On another question from Lance, she added, "Probably thirty, forty years I know about it. Long time. Long time. Lots of good people gone now…Was I around den? Oh yes. I been here all my life. Lots of changes to my island. Lots of good changes. Lots of bad…Remember what?... oh yes, I remember da Mister. He was very big man. Brings lotsa folks with him for his movie." She chuckled to herself again at a memory. "We t'ink it strange, some of the t'ings he did. He brought lots of animals here dat didna belong. Oh, dat tiger! Now he was a Ba-John! Very bad. Nobody wanted to work when da tiger was around. We liked da zebras. Now dey were fancy t'ings. Many of us work for da Mister. Da roads, they weren't so good like dey are now. Der were only coupla trucks to tote da big t'ings. When da rains came, like dey come everyday, all dem workers stop. Animals stop too. Mister he got real upset. Oh, but one day very bad wind come. The Mister's fancy set got all torn up. Nobody could get out dee to da Bay. My friend, now, he could. He best driver on dis island. He was special driver for Mister. One day real early before sun wakes up, he drives da Mister to da ruined set. He tell me later big tree was torn out of ground. At first, Mister real upset. Den my friend say it was okay. Mister got all happy and dey drive back to the fancy hotel. Two days later da Mister left. He not come back, but movie people stay. My friend, he keep driving back and forth." She paused and sat back in her chair, her fan never missing a slow beat, her eyes distant.

"Did something happen?" Beth wanted to know, breaking Mooma's reflection.

Mooma nodded slowly, frowning. "It was my friend. After da last of da movie people left, he started playin' social." At their blank looks, she shook her head, "How you say? He t'inks he better dan us now. He talk like da Mister is best friend and will come back for him. Peoples say, 'No, mon, you just goin'ort', you know? Crazy. Poor mon. He take it real bad nobody believe him, you know? Pretty soon he is a Nowherian. His home is gone. Even his little mutt dog who go wid him everywhere, he go away too. Da Mister loved that little mutt dog. He was dirty white and had des ugly black patches all over. He ride in da truck with 'em every day. Anyways, now we get to legend. My friend showing everyone who will look this broken up gold piece he say da Mister gave him. He say it special and da Mister gave it just to him. Everybody just laugh. 'You goin'ort, mon, you goin'ort.' And final, you know? He does. He goes crazy in da head because nobody believe him." She trailed off, saddened by the memories. Her voice was low when she continued, "We find him. We find him face down in Barcolet Bay, not too far from remains of da movie set. There not much left. We had big hurricane come here. Never seen da likes of it since. My friend, he couldn't take people not believe him. It kill him." She picked up the cheap necklace off her counter and looked at it. "We felt like bad people. Dis was around his neck when we find him. We could do no more for da man hisself, so we do dis for his memory. To say we sorry. It still not enough." Her voice trailed off to a whisper.

Beth had tears in her eyes. Adam, his heart pounding again, knew he had to ask. "What was your friend's name, if we might ask?"

Mooma stared at the necklace a while longer. She put it back softly on the counter and smoothed the chain with her fingertips. "He was good mon. I shoulda believe him. All dos years and it still hurts so. His name? Yes, I be proud to say his name. His name was Jemybie."

Adam and Lance exchanged an incredulous look. "Jemybie?" Adam repeated, confused.

"I can show you where we bury him. I know little Missy here," indicating the solemn Beth, "would like dat.

We put up nice headstone for him. We might not under-stand, but we carve nice and deep what he try to tell us. Poor mon. We jest call him Jemybie. His Christian name we put on da stone. Mr. Jeremy Bey."

Adam, Beth and Lance felt the hair on their skin shoot straight up. Beth cleared her throat and swiped at her eyes. "We'd love to see his grave," Beth sniffed. "Could you tell us where to find it?"

"Yes, yes, you go see it. We pick most beautiful spot on da island. Just above Barcolet Bay. You see a little trail leading t'rou cotton trees. It go to clearing. We be keepin' it beautiful for seem like forty years now. It still not enough," her voice dropping off again. "You go say hello to my Jemybie. Tell him Mooma sends regards."

They thanked her for her hospitality. Mooma usu-ally would have shown them other items in her shop, but she was lost in her memories of her departed friend. The shop door closed quietly behind them.

Lance looked up at the waning sun. It was going to be another beautiful sunset. But, did they have enough time to find the grave site before darkness fell? He asked them what they thought.

"That was the saddest thing I ever heard," sniffed Beth. Adam took the opportunity to put his arm around her and draw her close. She wiped her eyes with the sleeve of his shirt.

"Not what I meant," Lance clarified. "Do we look for the grave today, or wait until tomorrow?"

"Well, we have another full day here tomorrow and we leave Friday. Let's find it tomorrow. We feel this is it," Adam decided. "Beth, you agree?"

"Poor little dog."

"What?" Adam was confused until he remembered what Mooma had said. "Oh, the dog. Too bad Walt couldn't take him back to the States with him. Would have been a better ending to that part of the story, at least."

Lance suggested they go back to the hotel and discuss it there, rather than on a busy city street. He waved down the passing taxi. It was the same driver they had yesterday. "You finding what you want from Mooma?" he asked. "Everybody gets what they want from Mooma. If there is maco around, she know it and tell it!"

Back in their rooms, they changed into their swimwear. There was a hotel-sponsored swim and barbecue on the beach tonight.

Not feeling up to any rambunctious swimming, they paddled around on life rafts, drifting with the current. Facing the horizon, they watched another glowing, vibrant sunset, more pink tonight, fading to red. The smell of the barbecue drifted over them with the breeze, making their stomachs growl in hunger. It had been a long time since lunch.

Beth wrapped a rainbow-hued sarong around her damp bikini. The men pulled on T-shirts when it was time to eat. A blazing bonfire lit the night, sending sparks up towards the palm fronds swaying over their heads. The meat was shark steaks served with pelau – pigeon peas and rice cooked with meat flavored with coconut milk. Dessert was called Black Cake which was a rich cake made with dried fruit, cherries, brandy and rum, iced and decorated like a traditional wedding cake. "Whew!" Adam exclaimed after trying a bite. "That cake will get your motor running! That's a lot of proof in there."

After stuffing themselves, the three friends sat on low wooden chairs at the water's edge. Their feet played tag with the waves coming and going. The warmth of the bonfire at their back kept them warm enough in the cooler night air. Beth sat in the middle. Both guys had taken her hand closest to them. It just seemed right for the moment, she thought. Lance held hers loosely. Adam's thumb kept rubbing back and forth over the back of her hand. Without any preamble Lance got to his feet and said he needed to make a call and that he would see them in their rooms. "You all right, Lance?" Beth asked before relinquishing his hand. The high cheekbones in his face and his firm nose were highlighted in the firelight. He looked like the bronzed statue of a Roman god. "I think I will be now," was all he said quietly as he bent to kiss her cheek and then left.

Beth turned to Adam with questioning eyes. He just shrugged. "I don't know, Beth. Something happened in Boston. Until he tells us, we won't know. He won't talk about it. You know that."

She had to agree whether she liked it or not. If Lance didn't want to talk, he wouldn't talk. She sighed and listened to the lapping of the water. There were sounds coming from the jungle behind them. Night sounds they couldn't identify. She felt like they were alone on this island, even with the muted sounds of other people talking somewhere behind them. It was a pleasant feeling. She looked over at Adam. He was content. That was the best word to describe him at that moment in time.

He felt her gaze and turned to look at her. Her hair had dried straight after the swim and now it blew softly in the ocean breeze. Her face had the beginnings of a tan and looked clean and freckled across her nose. She looked lovely. That was his perfect word for her at that moment in time.

They continued to look into each other's eyes. He gave a slight tug on her hand, inviting her to come over closer. She studied his familiar face a moment longer. Getting up, she came over and sat sideways in his lap, her legs dangling over the side of his chair. She snuggled her head onto his shoulder, looking out over the moonlit water. He hid his surprise and put his arms around her, holding her close. He had just wanted her to bring her chair closer. This was much better. She gave a deep sigh of contentment. Adam turned his face to plant a soft kiss on her forehead.

Quietly they sat together on the white sand beach. The bonfire was burning down. Other couples headed arm-in-arm back to the hotel. The staff quietly cleaned up the remains of the dinner. And still they sat, content in each other's arms.

They were alone now on the dark, secluded beach. He turned his head and lifted her chin with his fingers. The moon was reflected in her eyes. She never looked more lovely to him. "Can I tell you something?" he whispered. Any sound louder than a whisper would have been wrong. He felt her nod against his fingers. "I'm really sorry for what I did to you that day." He heard her breathe in. "I don't think I ever told you that before. But I am. Will you forgive me?" She reached up with her hand and gently drew his face lower. Her kiss was his answer.

Lance came down the path, one of the heavy cotton robes in his arms. He figured Beth would be plenty cold by now if Adam kept her out so long. He stopped when he got close enough to see her chair was empty and her legs dangling over the edge of Adam's chair. Lance watched her bare legs slowly swing out and back. His face motionless, he looked out over the moonlit ocean. Coming to a decision, he softly laid the robe over the back of the empty chair and made his way back to the hotel. He went to the bar and ordered a drink. Finding a quiet table in the corner he sat back and listened to the band. He wasn't sure how he felt right then. He just knew he would wait a long time before going back to their suite tonight.

THURSDAY, JUNE 13TH, 2002
9:10 A.M.

The morning broke cloudy and damp. The daily rain shower would be early. Dressed in shorts and light shirts, the threesome headed back to the beach to look for the little trail Mooma told them to find. The beach was less than five hundred feet long and very narrow. It stretched out in a long slowly curving crescent shape ringed by tall palms and cotton trees. Native orchids bloomed profusely.

They found the trail more than halfway down the beach. It was well-trodden and easy to follow as it led them up the side of a fern-covered hill. In a few minutes they reached the top. Mooma was right. The view was superb. They could see the pink of their hotel peeking through the dense vegetation. The whole ocean spread out below them. The grave was sitting in the middle of a large clearing. A Bird-of-Paradise was planted behind the marker, its orange and red flowers leaning over the top. A flame tree stood alone off to the side, its crown a mass of red blooms. River rocks had been placed evenly all around the marker in a perfect circle. The marker was clean of moss and mold. His name was carved deep. 'Mr. Jeremy Bey'. It gave his date of birth and the day he died. He had been twenty-eight – the same age I am, Beth thought to herself, sad. Carved below was the apology from all the people – 'we believe you'. And below that was what made their mouths go dry. Hands shaking, Adam got out a little notebook from his pocket and copied it down exactly as the people of Tobago had carved it long ago: **X. Marc the Spot**

CHAPTER 14

X. MARC THE SPOT

1960

The tropical storm raged on all night. Filming had stopped. The set, so carefully constructed, was being blown to bits piece by piece. There was nothing anyone could do. The actors were safely ensconced in their hotel suites. They soon adopted a party attitude and took over the dining room, swapping stories and comparing notes on their varied lives and careers. The animals, bitterly complaining about the screaming wind, were safe in their shelters. Their handlers griped about 'working conditions' and forgot the early days of balmy tropical breezes and warm hospitality.

Very early in the morning, just before the sun rose, a beat-up dirty brown truck that looked old in 1940 slowly made its way over swollen streams that hadn't been there the day before. Within the spattering of raindrops, the dim headlights of the truck illuminated destruction. Palm fronds littered what little there was of a road; an occasional uprooted tree blocked parts of the road and had to be driven around; water and sand still blowing across the dirt road which consisted of leaves, dirt, and mud. There was no beauty to be seen in that early hour as the truck bumped and bounced towards what was left of the movie set, the truck's worn-out springs screaming in protest. The driver concentrated only on the road. Even though he was being thrown around the small cab like a rag doll, the one passenger was thoughtful as he contemplated what he might find on his wonderful set. A wet white and black dog lay shivering on the floorboard at the passenger's feet. Now and then, the man would reach down to comfort the dog that gratefully licked his fingers.

The driver aimed his truck's headlights at the middle part of the beach and pulled to a squeaking stop, the one working windshield wiper finally able to keep up with the waning rain. He turned his worried eyes on his passenger now that they were safely stopped. He didn't like what little he could see outside the truck from the narrow beam of light. "You sure you want to get out, Mister? It be nasty out dere."

The rain was finally abating. As their eyes adjusted more to the darkness, Mister wasn't sure at all he wanted to get out. The ground floor of the treehouse was in tatters. What remained of the furnishings was strewn about everywhere they looked. He only hoped the remains of the ship were still out in the Bay. They weren't done filming out there yet. *Too dark to tell*, he told himself.

Never one to shirk from what had to be done, he forced open the passenger door which was stuck and jumped down onto the wet, sandy beach. The dog elected to stay put, hopping up on the deserted, warm seat. Holding his fedora firmly in place against the wind, the man made a slow inspection of the set as the sun peeped timidly over the horizon behind the mass of retreating storm clouds that blended with the grey, churning ocean. Face grim, he mentally calculated how long it would take to rebuild and reset. Not the cost of the repairs; the cost never entered into his mind, just the time. Time was always the enemy. He had to leave in two days. They would have to have the repairs done by then.

He knew they would.

Now that that issue was settled in his mind, he changed the direction of his thoughts and wondered if they should film the destruction of the set first, in case he wanted to add something later…Yeah, that was good. Maybe there could be a hurricane that would hit the island…He wandered around the ruined set and thought about angles and lighting…Father could be holding the ropes while Ernst and Fritz tried to tie down the furniture. Mother could be huddled under the banyan tree with Frances. The dogs Turk and Duke would be running everywhere barking…

While he turned the scene over and over in his mind, he continued walking around the set. He wasn't seeing what was actually in front of him; he was seeing the finished movie playing in the theater. He turned as a camera would turn to pan the set, walking backwards. He didn't hear his driver calling to him to watch out. Suddenly finding himself flat on his back in the mud, the movie in his head faded to black. He looked around with a chuckle as the driver rushed over to help him to his feet.

"You okay, Mister? You no hurt?"

"No, no, I'm fine. A man needs to be knocked on his ass once in a while," he chuckled, allowing the driver to seat him on an uprooted palm trunk that had smashed their wooden walkway. "Some storm, huh, Jeremy?"

"Yes, Mister. Bad winds. Dis not look too good here."

Walt looked around, nodding his head. His glance took in the overturned props, the dangling floors of the treehouse, and, finally the uprooted tree on which he was seated. Its roots were massive, creating a huge hole that would have to be filled in. He would get them to use the elephants to pull the tree off the beach. Both men looked towards the truck as the dog began barking furiously at something on the beach. Jeremy went off to check on the barking dog that quickly jumped from the cab of the truck as soon as Jeremy opened the passenger door. As the dog dashed out chasing some birds that were down the beach, Jeremy went running off after the animal. Walt looked back at the hole he had stumbled across. He could tell that the hole was formed by the heavy runoff of the rain being funneled off by the fallen trees and debris that littered the beach. The morning was a little lighter now and Walt could see the dull glint of something metallic that was reflecting the early light. From his vantage point, the protruding object was obviously something buried. Walt stood back up, unconsciously brushing his legs of wet sand, and walked back towards the hole. Now curious, he knelt down and started brushing away the sand and vegetation around the object.

It was a small, ugly chest made of flat-sided, unadorned silver metal slightly corroded. It was about eighteen inches wide and ten inches deep and with its lid, it was also about ten inches tall. An ancient lock dangled from the holes, broken open either by time or the elements; sturdy metal handles were still firmly attached to each side. The chest was heavy, but not so much so that he couldn't lift it. Walt, however, dragged the box across the sand, leaving deep tracks in the sand as he went. He sat on the ground, his back against the fallen tree and rested a moment with the chest straddled between his outstretched legs. Curious, he wiggled the old lock off the metal hinged latch, looking it over for a moment before setting the lock on the sand beside himself. With the sun casting new rays of sunlight through broken clouds and across the ocean, the beams illuminated the man as he slowly opened the lid. It creaked on the rusty hinges and stuck half-way up. Walt pushed harder to get the lid to open all the way, breaking off one rusty hinge. The other hinge held as the lid fell back against the back side of the box.

The small chest seemed to be filled with just sand and shell fragments. Scooping out some the wet sand and the remains of some poor sea creature, his fingers brushed against some hard, smooth objects. Clearing out more of the sand, he picked up one of the rounded pieces, holding it up to the sunlight for inspection. His eyes widened.

"Holy crap."

He quickly glanced around to see where the driver was. Spotting Jeremy halfway down the beach yelling for the dog, Walt hurriedly cleared the rest of the sand out of the chest.

Jeremy came back to the dismembered set and ruined treehouse with the now-happy dog bounding at his feet. He found Mister Walt carrying a couple pieces from the set back to the truck. "Can I help you wid dat, Mister?" Walt had found an intact wooden box that he had placed the old chest in, and piled some other miscellaneous objects in with the chest. "Yes, Jeremy. Help me lift these props back into the truck," Walt instructed. Walt, with Jeremy's help, lifted the box and set in on the floor of the cab on the passenger side.

"Are dees props broken too? Can I help you fix?" Jeremy asked as he moved around the truck and got in behind the wheel. The dog bounded up over Walt's lap, leaving sandy paw prints on his wet trousers. "No, no, Jeremy. I need to take these back to the hotel to be fixed."

"Right away, Mister. You wanting me to put little mutt in da back?"

In a very good mood, Walt rubbed the dog between the ears. "No, he's fine. Aren't ya, boy?"

Two days later Jeremy loaded a small, newly-made wooden crate marked "Props" onto Walt's private plane alongside his luggage. Giving the dog a final pat good-bye, Walt turned to Jeremy. Shaking hands with him, Walt thanked him for his excellent driving and pressed something into his hand. As the plane engines roared to life, Walt told Jeremy to look him up if he ever got to California. With a final wave, Walt disappeared into the plane, already thinking about his next move.

2002

The threesome walked slowly back to the hotel. They were silent. Each was thinking over the carving on the headstone. It had to be the clue. It just had to, didn't it?

A light rain started falling as they entered the lobby. There were a few couples out in the pool overlooking the ocean. A group that had been playing croquet came running, laughing, into the lobby from the open French doors. Someone was complaining at the front desk.

Going to their suite for privacy, Adam and Beth sat close together on the sofa. Lance pulled up an overstuffed chair. "What do you think about the clue?" Lance asked them, pensive. Adam slowly shook his head. "I don't know. Why would his friends spell it that way? It should be 'X marks the spot', not 'm a r c'," he spelled.

"Maybe it refers to the coin," Beth shrugged. "Now that we have both sides we know the design in the middle is an 'X' made out of crossed bones."

"Mooma indicated they didn't understand it either. She said it was 'what he tried to tell us'."

"I still don't get it," Adam frowned, taking up Beth's hand without even realizing it, his thumb rubbing the back of her fingers.

Lance stared at the caressed hands, then abruptly went to the window to look out unseeing towards the ocean. "Rain stopped," he muttered. "Should we try talking to Mooma again? See if there is anything else she can tell us?"

In agreement, they walked back to the lobby to wait for the taxi to come. "Sun's out!" Beth declared, eyes closed, face up to the warming rays.

"Yes, thank you, Captain, we hadn't noticed," Adam kidded her. Lance said nothing.

"You be back," Mooma smiled. Today she was even more colorful. A lime green scarf wound around her head, and she wore a golden yellow billowy blouse and a royal blue full skirt. "What you t'ink of my Jemybie grave?"

"You were right," Beth told her, feeling plain in her white cotton tank top and tan shorts. "It was a wonderful spot. Thank you for sharing it with us. It…it meant a lot to me." She was starting to tear up again.

Lance got right to the point. "We were wondering about the inscription – why it was spelled that way. It is very unusual."

"You like cool drink? No? Okay den." She settled back in her chair. "Yea, we t'ink so, too. But after he be wavin' dat paper 'round our faces so long…" she trailed off with a shrug.

"What paper?" Lance prodded, leaning forward on her counter. He seemed intent on getting the whole story, more focused than his usual laid-back attitude.

"You not turnin' quenk, are you," she asked him with a sly grin. She gave a chuckle at the blank look on his handsome face. "Oh, I sorry, you not know our talk. I mean bol'face, yes?"

Still not sure what she meant, not knowing she was calling him rude and pushy, Lance felt he had better apologize. He tried his charming smile, but Mooma still just grinned at him. "Could you please tell us about the paper and the markings?"

"That better! That show you broughtupsy! You too pretty not to ha' manners."

Adam got a big kick out of Mooma putting Lance in his place. He thought Lance was acting strangely also, but 'broughtupsy' was a descriptive word that he would have to remember.

"Is there anything else you could tell us?" Adam asked in a much more pleasant manner than Lance.

Mooma thought back. They could see the memories still bothered her. Would anyone care so deeply about them forty years from now, Adam wondered to himself.

"I t'ink it was dat awful day we find Jemybie. It seem proper 'n all it take place on dat beach. Too much happen to him der. Dat paper? I never seen what written on it. It was clutch tight in his hand, no good no more 'cause of dey ocean water. It was what he did to beach dat scare us."

"The beach? What did he do?" Beth whispered, caught up in the story again.

"You know all dem rocks 'round his grave? We no dig dem up. We found dem all on de beach. My friend had put dem der. Musta taken him long time. We figure it be important to Jemybie. Musta be'n or he not do it like that. We copy it just so for his grave."

Adam's mouth dropped open. "You mean he spelled out 'X. Marc the spot' in rocks on the beach? That was his message?"

Mooma nodded sadly. "It musta been from The Mister somehow. Dat was all he talk 'bout. Musta been on dat paper. De fancy hotel, they get all upset. Can't be havin' da guests see my poor friend on der pretty beach. Dey woulda wrecked it for sure. So we took de rocks and made it pretty 'round his grave. Nobody spoil it now."

That was the end of the story for Mooma. She had nothing left to tell him about Jeremy B. or the mysterious paper that could have been torn out of the diary. It was gone. The other half of the medallion had been buried with Jeremy B. It was beyond their reach now as well.

Before they left Mooma's shop, Beth bought a book all about Tobago and its history. She asked Mooma to sign it for her. Mooma just chuckled at the silly things some people ask for as she signed it with a flourish.

When they were at the door, Mooma had one more thing to say to them: "Remember not put fowl to watch de corn," directing it to Lance as he stopped at the door with a confused look on his face. "You will figure it out," Mooma called out and watched as Lance turned and exited her shop. She watched the three through the front window as they crossed the street to hail a cab. "Only hope it not too late when you do," she muttered to herself as they disappeared from her view.

On Saturday, the friends had agreed to meet at Adam's apartment. They had each agreed to some alone time to think over their trip and sort it out in their minds.

Beth walked slowly through Adam's apartment complex when she arrived on Saturday, looking at the white birch trees and the purple-blossomed agapanthus. They were poor substitutes for the beauty in which they had been immersed while on Tobago. Even back in her own condo, she had found herself going to her living room window to gaze out over the brilliant blue/green ocean. Only it wasn't there. The carefully mowed green grass that met her eyes was a disappointment.

Adam opened his door to find her sighing. "What's wrong?"

"I miss paradise."

Lance was sitting at Adam's computer, busy researching the coin, now that they knew what it looked like. At her greeting of, "Hey, Heartthrob," he just gave her a distracted smile. His playful retorts and spontaneous hugs seemed to be a thing of the past. She silently wondered if it had to do with Adam or with Lance's visit to his family in Boston. She missed the old Lance too.

Glancing around the room, Beth was glad to see Adam had gotten rid of his disgusting model of Fantasyland. She would never look at mashed potatoes the same way again. Most of the clutter had been cleared away as well. The notes pertaining to Walt and his life had been filed and replaced by books on pirates, legends, lost treasures, and sunken ships. She picked up an *E-Ticket Magazine* that featured Walt's Pirates of the Caribbean ride. Indicating the magazine, she asked, "You find any connections with the coin?"

Adam blew out a frustrated breath. "Well, the skull and crossbones design is so widely used in regards to pirates it's hard to separate fact from fiction. Lance has found some similar coins, but they don't match exactly. And they were found in a different part of the world. Look at this one, for example," picking up a thick library book and opening to a marked page, "see the 'X'? Similar when turned sideways, but looking at it full on, it is a cross, not bones. Same here and here." Flipping a few more pages, "And this has a skull, but not the bones beneath it."

"So what we have could be pretty rare," Beth concluded.

"But half a coin isn't as valuable as a whole one," Lance pointed out. "Did Walt give Jeremy B. half of the only one he found or did Walt already have it with him? Where did he find it? And, most importantly, was there more? We need to find it."

Adam studied his friend. Lance seemed a lot more determined than he had been at any other time since their quest began. Determined...or desperate? He didn't want to ask in front of Beth – even though she could probably get more out of Lance than he could. "Then," Lance continued, "we also have the clue 'X. Marc the Spot', also widely used in pirate lore. Fact or fiction?"

"Well, not spelled that way, but certainly very similar," Beth replied, and then asked, "Do you think Jeremy B. was too out of his head at the end? Maybe he didn't know what he was doing."

Lance disagreed with her. "It was too deliberate. I

think he knew exactly what he was doing. He had three or four years of people not believing him. One last try? I think he would have gotten it right."

Beth gave a non-committal, "Hmmm." Her attention was on the *E-Ticket Magazine*. It was the fall 1999 issue. "This is fascinating. How come I never saw these magazines before?" Not really expecting an answer, she found the "Wings over Disneyland" page in the middle of the magazine. It was an aerial shot of the entire Park as it looked in 1964. Not being able to resist, she called, "Hey, Lance! Look at this. It's a big Pirate Ship in Fantasyland across from the Tea Cups!" She held up the pages for him to see.

"Yeah, it sure is. Say, isn't that a Keel Boat on the River there?"

Well, that didn't work out the way she had wanted it. With an unlady-like snort her mother had been trying in vain for years to get her to stop doing, she dropped the open magazine back into her lap. As she continued to study the picture, she noticed something. "Adam, this shows they had already dug out the foundation for the Pirate's ride and were doing some building in there."

He sat beside her and studied the orange-tinted photo. It was very different from the sharp digital images they were used to today. "Wow, look, it shows Nature's Wonderland and Ol' Unfaithful geyser. Also look at all the empty land outside the Park. Looks like you could see the Monorail barn from the freeway."

"Never got to see the inside of that," Beth muttered to herself.

"Sorry, sweetie," Adam said, recognizing her disappointment.

"Is there anything actually helpful to us?" Lance broke in. "I'm coming up empty here."

Beth flipped through the magazine quickly. "It is mostly about Marc Davis and his sketches for the Pirate ride. He says in 1961 or 1962 Walt mentioned he wanted to do a Pirate ride. Walt first wanted to do it as a walk-through but they decided people would stop in one place too long and the flow of foot traffic would slow down everyone within the attraction. Hey, look at this picture of the Auctioneer with Marc and Alice Davis. Look at the nose and cheekbones. The Auctioneer looks like Marc. That's funny. Back here, the magazine shows the *Wicked Wench* ship in the fight scene. Here's your cross, Adam, from those coins you showed me." Beth held the magazine up for Adam to see. "Right there on the sails."

"Look at the Captain's Quarters in this picture. I read somewhere else that map the skeleton is holding was the same one used in the movie *Treasure Island*. Wasn't that 1950? That's why it looks so old," Adam pointed out, "because that prop IS old!"

"Does it have an 'X' on it? Ooh, look at the Treasure Cave. See any of your coins in there, Lance?" She chuckled at her joke and finished looking through pages of pictures from the familiar ride. "I never got tired of that ride. I was going to work there after that last summer when the Keel Boats ended." At Adam's pat on her hand, she quickly added, "No, I'm okay now. Things happen to all of us that we don't like. We just have to go on whether we like it or not." She looked over at Lance to see if he got her point, but he was either engrossed in what he was doing or simply ignoring her. She figured it was probably the latter.

She was surprised when he challenged her. "Do you really believe that?"

Thinking about her reaction to her job loss and her blow-up at Adam, she answered truthfully, "No. But I should."

Still not looking up from what he was doing, Lance pointedly told her, "Then finish your sermon when you believe it."

Adam was staring at the two pieces of the coin – the real half piece from the clue and the cheap piece from

Tobago. He was looking at the structure of the skull on top. It was more detailed than most of the comic skulls used on pirate costumes. The captain's hat on the Auctioneer, for example, had the skull and crossbones, but the skull was flat, solid white with empty eye sockets and a vague outline of teeth. The same design was repeated in other sketches from the famous Disney animator. The coin, on the other hand, had depth to it, as though it was grinning at them, ready to talk. "Ye come seeking adventure and salty old pirates, eh?" Adam heard himself recite the spiel he had memorized from the Pirates of the Caribbean attraction.

"Adam? You all right? You look a million miles away." Beth was staring intently at Adam.

"Huh? No, just thinking. Not a million miles. More like ten actually."

"Are you thinking we should be going back to Disneyland?"

Lance was watching them now. "What are you thinking, Adam?" he asked.

Adam was frowning, lost in thought. "I don't know. A hunch? I don't know," he repeated. "Its…" he started then paused before asking, "Do you agree Walt was really interested in Pirates when all of this," indicating the coin and the research material, "was taking place?"

"Yes, it was well known he was," Lance said shortly. "What's your point? There were a lot of things going on in the same time period, but Pirates was really big. He was involved in all aspects of it, like everything else. He didn't live to see the opening of the ride, but he was sure working on it as if able to see it finished, at least in his mind."

Not liking Lance's attitude, but agreeing with what he said, Beth nodded, waiting to see where Adam was headed.

"Then there might be something in the ride we are missing. Some link to the next clue. It has to be the coin or the 'X'."

"The coin led us to Jeremy B. I don't think that has any bearing any more," Lance stated. "In all my research, I couldn't find another coin like it. I think we need to go forward with the written clue. Walt never did the same thing twice. He always went forward, not backwards."

That was the most they had gotten out of Lance in days. Beth looked to Adam for direction. He shrugged. "Well, let's try both the 'X' and the skull and crossbones. Let's see where they are located on the ride and go from there, agreed?"

They piled into Adam's Silverado and headed to Disneyland once more.

They first studied the paintings of famous pirates just inside the entrance of the Pirates of the Caribbean, which were cartoon-styled renderings. Nothing stood out to the three. The first sighting of the skull and crossbones within the ride came with the talking pirate skull above the first waterfall. The skull told them "it be too late to alter course, mateys" and to "keep a weather eye out". The rest was lost as they plunged down the fifty-two-foot drop, leveling out for a few moments within dark caverns and the sounds of water all around them. In another moment, their boat was splashing down the smaller thirty-seven-foot drop, one that was anticlimactic compared to the first drop. The first two skeletons had nothing on their hats, except for a curious seagull on one of them. In the next scene, the redheaded pirate girl in the painting that hung in the remains of a bar had a vague skull and crossbones painted onto her plumed hat. In the Captain's Quarter, the skeletal remains of the occupant in the opulent bed was only wearing a bandana, but the gold-trimmed, red velvet headboard had a large detailed skull and bones. No skull and bones were seen in the fight scene or 'dunking the mayor' scene. The auctioneer and the 'pooped pirate' by the barrel had the white flat version of the design on the hats they wore. And they found it also on the drunken pirate on the bridge and in the final shoot-out scene before riding up the last waterfall and disembarking at Lafitte's Landing.

As they walked out the exit and headed for the entry queue again, Adam wanted to know their thoughts.

Beth brought out the lack of any 'X' that she could see. "Do either of you know what that map looks like on the Captain's bed? You mentioned it was used in a movie before, Adam. Are there any pictures of it?"

"Too bad we can't just go up and look at it for a minute. That would be fun," Adam grinned, remembering his jump from the train. "We could look it up when we get back to my place, I guess. Lance, what do you think about the skull and crossbones?"

"Only that most of them look generic. Beth mentioned the Captain's Quarters which had the most elaborate skull."

"Well, that's two votes for the Captain's Quarters. Lance, you're taller than me. Maybe you can get a glimpse of the treasure map before we leave that scene."

He just nodded as they wound through the queue, silent with his own thoughts again. He didn't even acknowledge the two female Pirate-costumed cast members who were trying to say hi to him as they boarded their boat.

"Please remain seated!" was loudly broadcast as they floated into the treasure cache.

"You get that a lot, don't you, Stick?" Beth laughed, gently poking Lance in the ribs. Her smile faded as he continued in his oppressive mood. She frowned at Adam, who just shrugged and shook his head.

She tried to say something to Lance as they went through the dark tunnel leading to the ship and fort fight scene. He shushed her. Lance was listening to the ominous voice within the darkness. Beth was annoyed at Lance for the moment. She looked around the dark tunnel, what she knew was called the 'transition tunnel' which really was the section of the ride that connected the two buildings that housed the attraction.

When they emerged into the cannon fire, he apologized and explained he had been listening to the 'warnings' back in the cave. He knew most of it, but he wanted to hear the rest. "It said that we 'had seen the cursed treasure' and 'know where it be hidden'. The other voice, closely following had said an 'evil curse will strike the greedy beholders of this bewitched treasure'."

"Well, we did just leave the buried loot room," pointed out Adam.

Lance was distracted. "I know," he said curtly. He then looked away, embarrassed. "Sorry. It's just the words struck me this time, that's all." Lance paused, and then added defensively, "You asked for our thoughts."

"Did you see anything on the treasure map, by the way, before you got caught standing up in the boat?" Adam asked Lance.

He shook his head. "The edges are folded up to much and it's too far away," he said, disappointed. He ignored Adam's muttered, 'need glasses?' "We'll have to see what we can find online."

They rode around two more times. The women loaders quit casting smiles at the unresponsive Lance. Another one of them who had just come on duty had greeted him familiarly, but didn't get any kind of reply from him either.

Their results were the same after riding Pirates a total of four times: They weren't sure. Their attention was drawn mostly to the Captain's Quarters and, thanks to Lance, the warnings in the misty dark tunnel. The threesome decided to direct their research to those two places. Once those leads were exhausted, they would try again to find something else.

"Listen to this," Lance called from Adam's computer. He started reading from the website, "while Robert Louis Stevenson popularized the pirate treasure map – and its '**X** marks the spot' – in his 1883 book *Treasure Island*, he wasn't the first. Author James Fenimore Cooper's 1849 book *The Sea Lions* tells about a sailor who left behind 'two old, dirty and ragged charts'. Anyway, that must be where Walt got the idea for the map he used in his movie, and which you say he put into the Pirate ride."

"Have you found any picture of the map?" Adam wanted to know.

"No, not yet. They show the map from the book *Treasure Island*, but not from the movie. I'll keep looking, but I don't know where else to look."

Beth was staring at the picture of the Captain's Quarters in Adams *E-Ticket Magazine* again. She thought she had seen it before, not just on the ride. But where? Her postcard collection? One of her books? "Adam, I think I need to go home. I have something there that could help. I'm just not sure what or where. I may be gone a while." When Adam said that would be great, Beth looked over at Lance, wondering what might be eating at him. "Hey, Lance," she called over to him. "Do you want to come with me?"

She was disappointed by his brief, "No." She might have been able to talk to him about whatever was bothering him. Instead, she left alone.

Beth went to the second bedroom in her condo. It wasn't set up for guests. It was more like a library. Being an avid reader she shelved all her favorite books there. Some Disney collectibles from both her time working in the Park and earlier trips were showcased in a tall oak and glass cabinet. What she was looking for were her various Disney books – the souvenir hardbacks commemorating different eras, Imagineering books on concept and design, children's coloring books and comics, the 1965 set of *The Wonderful Worlds of Walt Disney*. and storybooks about Sleeping Beauty and Show White.

She first pulled out her 1995 copy of *The Nickel Tour* instead of going through her hundred individual postcards. This in-depth and detailed book had nearly every single postcard ever printed about Disneyland. More importantly to Beth, they were in chronological order and indexed in the back. It was a lot better than her vague system of filing them by different lands in folders in her filing cabinet. This book brought up only two interior shots from the Pirate ride of the Auction scene and the Jail Scene. There was also a set of twelve postcards depicting the drawings of Marc Davis, but they didn't help her.

Her Imagineering book contained mostly the new ideas going into Florida and Epcot. She couldn't find any other interior views of the ride. She thumbed through the souvenir books. She quickly tossed aside the comic books and story books. A small yellow book was almost added to the growing pile before she actually glanced at the title and cover photo. It was a 'pictorial souvenir book' called *Where in Disneyland Attractions?* She let out a whoop when the cover photo of this 1997 book showed in luxurious detail a close-up of the Captain's Quarters and its skeleton owner looking over the map Lance was trying desperately to find.

And, there on the upper right corner of the map just above the bony fingers, was a big red 'X'.

Breaking a few driving laws, Beth hurried back to Adam's apartment, the book stashed in her purse. She was met at the door by a very animated Adam.

They both said, "I found it" at the same time. "Found what?" Adam said. "Stop that!" and they both laughed at the exchange.

Beth held up her book in his face. He barely looked at it. "We are so stupid!" he exclaimed, slamming the door behind her and walking over to his desk. "Show her, Lance," as Adam held Beth in front of him by her shoulders.

"It's actually more listening," Lance pointed out. He had a website pulled up and clicked on a 'Play' button in the middle of the page. Beth could see the site was devoted to the Pirate ride.

Amazed, she listened to the entire soundtrack from the dark tunnel that had captivated Lance's attention. Then he scrolled back two pages and played the track from the talking skull over the first waterfall. Before she could say anything, he held up a finger for her to wait. He started reading from the ride description, "'the talking skull (voiced by Disney legend "X" Atencio) cautions the riders to heed his warnings. Atencio not only provided that voice, but he also wrote the entire show's script and the song "Yo Ho, A Pirate's Life for Me".' It also says he voiced part of that warning in the dark tunnel, the second part called the 'Friendly Warning'."

"Do you see?" Adam eagerly asked. "That has to be the 'X.' on the clue. The period after the letter shows it is an initial. Xavier Atencio's name was usually just portrayed by an 'X'. And, the name we have been throwing about so carelessly is also the rest of the clue."

At her blank look, he continued. "'X.' Marc the spot.' 'Marc', not Mark, or marks. Just Marc. As in Marc Davis, one of the 9 Old Men, one of the premier animators and designers! He basically designed the look for the whole ride. Look through that magazine. Almost every sketch was turned into a scene in the ride."

"Oh my word. We saw it in the Captain's Quarters over and over without really seeing it!...Oh...Oh, wait a minute. Lance? Those words in the cave? You said you kept going back to them. 'You've seen the cursed treasure. You know where it be hidden'. Xavier wrote them, right? The treasure is right next to the Captain's room. Is that too weird?"

"What are you saying? That the treasure room is THE treasure room?" Lance asked, thinking over the possibilities.

Adam paced around the room. "Brilliant!" he exclaimed, rubbing his hands together. "Absolutely brilliant! He hid it all in plain sight!"

Beth shook her head. "Wait a minute. We need to back up. It can't be. That treasure is just painted gold. It's like a huge sculpture, like bubble wrap with coins pressed in plastic, not an actual pile of stuff. Sure, some of the outer pieces are individual things, but they aren't real."

Adam pulled out the now-well worn copy of the *E-Ticket Magazine.* He bypassed the page showing the pile of treasure and turned to the middle aerial shot. He pointed to the same thing Beth had shown him earlier. "They had already excavated the area and were building parts of the ride. You worked there. Tell me, Beth, what is under Disneyland?"

When she realized what Adam was implying, her breathing became very shallow. "In that section, there are underground tunnels that lead through the different rides in New Orleans Square. Pirates, Mansion, the back road that maintenance uses behind the ride buildings." She paused. "It isn't as elaborate as the Magic Kingdom in Disneyworld where they actually built entire streets under the park where trucks and cars and employees could move from one part of the Park to the other. But in New Orleans Square, there are whitewashed corridors that have dozens of doors which open into different sections of each ride."

"What else?"

"Employee break areas, an employee restaurant, storage," she counted off, then her eyes brightened. "Storage!"

"Give the girl a cigar. Do you think Walt had access to that area?"

Beth smiled. "He designed it. He knew every inch of his Park."

Adam looked at both of them and took a deep breath. "I think we need to take a closer look at that map on the bed. I want to know what that bony finger is pointing at."

CHAPTER 15

Time to Jump Ship

MONDAY, JUNE 17TH, 2002
10:15 P.M.

"You're going to jump again?" Beth asked. "In the Pirate ride?"

Lance walked over to the window, leaving the computer for the first time in hours. "I think we all need to be there. " He turned to face them. "If this is it, we all need to be there. And be ready for whatever happens next."

Adam thought about it and agreed. "This is a lot different than hiding in a dark tunnel. Boats go by there all the time loaded with people. We have to think of the boats...."

"... and the security cameras," Beth finished for him. "There are cameras all through the ride. We need to know where they are and find a way to avoid them."

Lance looked unseeing out the window. "I can find out about the cameras. I know someone."

"What's her name?" Adam kidded, hoping to get some kind of familiar rise out of him.

"Patty," was all he answered.

After waiting a moment for some clarification, Adam rolled his eyes. "Fine. Check with your Patty. I assume she works on the ride?" Still no explanation. "See if you can pull any favors."

Thinking ahead to what they might possibly need, Beth opened the closet where Lance had told her Adam stashed his cast member costume collection. She pulled out a one-piece blue Monorail costume. There was also a complete Jungle Cruise outfit. She slowly took out an olive-colored shirt – a very familiar olive-colored shirt. "You dirty son of a…" she broke off, holding it out in front of her. "This is MY Keel Boat shirt! You had it all along?"

"Oops," Adam muttered, when he realized where she had gone. "I was going to tell you…sometime. Really!" She looked like she was ready to kill him. "You…uh, left it in wardrobe when they pulled you out and took you backstage to change. I was going to give it back to you but then I didn't see you…." He just stopped talking. The hole he was digging for himself was getting deeper.

She took it over and threw it down next to her purse. "We'll talk about that later."

"I'm sure we will," Adam mumbled to himself, edging over to the amused Lance. "Thanks for telling her about the closet, Brentwood. That helps a lot."

Lance just shrugged. "You should have told her yourself."

Taking a minute to calm down, Beth returned to his closet. "Don't you have anything from the Pirate ride?"

"Nope. Just a Star Tours jacket there in the back. Why?"

"It might be a good idea for us to be dressed sort of like a cast member working the ride. Not the hideous Capri pants and socks, but some kind of shirt that would blend in. Do you have that ugly brown vest from when you played in the band?"

Adam made a face. "That vest wasn't ugly. And, no, I don't have it any more. I think my mother burned it."

"Margaret always did have good taste," Beth smiled.

"Well, we need some kind of puffy shirt and a nametag for each of us. I stole some extra ones when I was there if you don't have any badges."

Lance could see where she was going with this. "That's a good idea, just like Adam wore all black to jump off the train, and then took off the jacket when he ran for it. We could have that crap on under our jackets until we need to jump. If we had some pirate hats on, we might not get too much attention from the other people on the boat. We could act like we're doing quality control or something. That's good, Beth. Real good," Lance commended, more animated than he had been in days.

Adam frowned. "Well, I hate to rain on your parade, but whether we look the part or not, three people jumping off a moving boat will be noticed by the other guests."

"How about if we distract them?" Lance asked

"Well, let's assume we find a good place to jump before we get to the scene we want," Adam explained. "There are the waterfalls first, then the sandy beach thing with the two skeletons, and after that, the skeleton at the helm and the bar. All those things are on the right side of the boat. The Captain's Quarters are on the left, around the corner just after the bar. We need to make sure the other people are all still looking over to the right when we get off."

"Agreed, but how?"

Adam shook his head. "Not sure. Let's work on that problem, find some clothes, and Lance can meet with his Patty. How long do you need, Lance?"

Lance gave a ghost of a smile. Patty was always happy to see him. He would have the information by tonight. "Let's say two, three days? That enough for you, Beth?"

She was lost in thought. "I can't believe we are going to jump off Pirates. This won't be easy."

"Hey, you stole a canoe, remember?"

"Yeah, but that was after dark, and nobody else was

using the River. There is a BIG difference."

"We have to do it, Beth. There's no other way."

"I know."

TUESDAY, JUNE 18TH, 2002
2:25 P.M.

Tuesday, the three were back at Adam's apartment. Beth handed Adam and Lance white, puffy sleeved shirts that laced up the front. Both guys eyed them with disdain. "Hey, you agreed it was a good idea," Beth defended herself. "I found them at that costume place on I-5. Just be glad I didn't get you the eye patches." The shirts reminded Adam of a Seinfeld episode. Beth next handed them cast member nametags that read 'Brian' for Adam and 'Mark' for Lance. Beth laughed to herself as she just realized the names. "Hey, you guys could start your own radio program," Beth said thinking about the long-running *Mark and Brian* show on the Los Angeles radio station, KLOS. The nametag she had for her shirt was 'Catie'.

The guys looked at each other, both thinking the same thing: The eye patches would have been cool.

Lance, with a sigh of resignation regarding the shirts, told them what he had found out. "Beth was right, of course. There are cameras throughout the ride. But most of them shoot from behind the boats for a short distance. There is some kind of reddish-purple light above or below each lens which provides the infrared illumination needed for the cameras to 'see' in the darkened interior of the ride. There is a bank of monitors in the dispatch tower above the place where the boats first enter the bayou from the loading dock. You can see the monitors if you look back after the boat passes under the tower. There is a Dispatch Operator who is in charge of looking over the monitors between the loadings of the boats. That person, I am told, has a priority of making sure the boats are properly loaded and everyone is seated properly. After that, he – or she – dispatches the boats which simultaneously bring up the next two boats for unloading and loading again. He or she wouldn't be watching the ride cameras unless they happen to notice something wrong, like someone taking pictures, or standing up."

"Or jumping out of a boat," Beth concluded, with Lance nodding in agreement.

"So we are screwed already with the cameras," Adam frowned.

"No, not necessarily," Lance said. "The cameras in that part of the ride shoot boats from the side as they exit the last waterfall and don't shoot them again until the boat reaches the Captain's Quarters. The next camera at that point return to the back-shoot view as the boat gets to about halfway past the scene. There seems to be a good sized dead zone."

Beth nodded. "Okay, so we now have to worry about the other people in the boat with us."

Adam took over here. "I was thinking about that and came up with a possible solution. It might be more of a problem; however, I'm not sure." He went to his desk and pulled two little firecrackers out of the top drawer.

"Aren't those illegal around here?" Beth asked with narrowed eyes.

"That's what I meant about a problem, if we get caught with them," Adam said with a little resignation. He held up one of the firecrackers and explained, "They are called 'Ladyfingers' with a waterproof fuse. I went to the store and got a cigarette lighter, too. I found that the usual Zippo or Bic lighters make too much of a loud click when you light them. Then I found this butane lighter," Adam added, pulling a thin, narrow plastic lighter from the desk drawer. "When adjusted down, the flame is really low. I think we can light it down by our feet without anyone being the wiser." He demonstrated the lighter.

The flame was barely visible and there was only a nominal sound as the wheel was turned to make the flame. "If we find we need a distraction, we can toss one of these babies onto the beach scene or the bar, or ahead of the boat into the water. Since there usually isn't much noise there, it should draw their attention…enough at least for us to jump out from the back of the boat," Adam finished.

"Won't the people in the boat wonder where it came from?"

"I don't intend to blow anything up, Beth. I think the noise will be enough. People will probably discuss it as something new on the ride they didn't see before."

"Let's hope so." Beth was getting really nervous about all this. "No other way?"

"Not that I can come up with. Lance?"

"Only that we will want to make sure one of the cameras doesn't pick up the flame," Lance said cautiously. "Any flame will light up the monitor like a 1000 watt light bulb…those cameras, being infrared, will pick up the heat signal from any sized flame and magnify it like a flash bulb going off." Lance hesitated, then added, "However, the part of the ride that we need to draw attention should be the dead zone I mentioned and shouldn't be caught by a camera…we should be okay with it. I think it will work."

The three were quiet for a moment. Then Lance said, "This is Tuesday. Beth, didn't you say it was always the slowest day at the Park? Who knows? We could have a boat all to ourselves."

"That would be nice. Oh, we do need to sit in the back row of the second boat. There won't be anyone behind us for the time it takes to wait for the second waterfall drop."

"With three of us, we should get the back row, even without requesting," Lance explained. "Remember, that row only seats three, max. We could ensure the row by requesting it at the loading dock."

"Right, Lance," Adam said. "Okay, anything else?" Adam asked looking from Lance to Beth. "You ready to do this?"

Beth nodded. Lance said, "Okay. Then let's do it."

Lance then mentioned that he forgot his outer jacket. They stopped by his place on the way to the Park. Lance told them to wait in the truck, that he would only be a minute. They thought he took an awful lot of time just to pick up a jacket. But, Lance's demeanor on his return prohibited any kidding around. Once he slid back in the cab of the Silverado, he fairly ordered Adam to "drive on".

Adam let it go. There were more important things to worry about right now. Now all they had to do was find the perfect place to jump.

TUESDAY, JUNE 18TH, 2002
5:15 P.M.

Sitting in the rear seat, their boat was propelled forward and settled into the dark bayou after leaving the loading dock and the elevated conveyor belts which launched each boat to start the ride. Lance turned and checked the dispatch tower. The woman inside was busy with the next two boats loading. He faced forward, and the three rode silently through the water and down the waterfalls. At the bottom of the second fall when everyone was looking at the sandy beach, the threesome excitedly pointed at an obvious pathway through the rocky walls illuminated by a soft blue light. It was just past an overhead waterfall and a little pool that contained remains of a wrecked boat. The pathway was on the opposite side of the beach scene which was to the right of the boat. It drew no attention of the other guests in the boat who were busy pointing out things on the beach, which included a wayward crab whose claws mechanically opened and closed and a few audio-animatronic seagulls among the two not-so-lucky pirate skeletons who were propped up against a rock mount with swords poking through their rib cages. The three friends could see that the path went straight for a few feet and then disappeared behind the white rocks. They tried to trace an imaginary path to the Captain's Quarters. What they found in the back of the Quarters on the left side, blocked by a large sea chest, was the opening of a tunnel. It wasn't very high and they would have to crawl through it, but a passageway was there. A few feet past the tunnel was the ornate bed and grisly remains.

They saw no openings in the Treasure Cache, but they did see an opening in the dark long tunnel. This opening, though, looked more like a dead end. Then they spotted an illuminated green Exit sign indicating that it was probably a place for cast members to enter the ride or, more likely, an emergency exit for guests if something happened inside the cavern through which the boats rode.

Still silent, the three looked at each other. They nodded in agreement. That was the place.

Back at the loading dock for their second trip, the cast member on load named Leslie was only too happy to seat Lance anywhere he asked when he smiled at her and made a point of calling her by her name. It was late afternoon now. People were going to dinner and lining up for the big parade down Main Street. They practically walked onto their boat.

"Hope this slim crowd keeps up," Beth whispered, leaning across in front of Adam as they sat in the last row. She was on the left side of the nearly empty boat. It was agreed that she would jump first, then Adam. Lance would follow. If there was a problem or if Lance felt he couldn't make it without detection, he would wait and follow them by taking another boat on another trip around. They hoped that would not be necessary as it would mean Beth and Adam would be stuck in an unfamiliar area of the ride for probably more than twenty minutes, the time it would take Lance to finish the ride and get back in another boat.

They didn't see Lance signal the Dispatch Operator as they floated away. There were only seven other people in their boat. Two in the front seat, three in the second seat, and two people in row three. No one had been seated in front of them. Lance had taken care of that. Patty always came through for him. He would pay her back when all of this was over. He was thinking he could afford to buy her something then.

Not knowing they had some extra time now that the following boats were being delayed by Patty, Beth found her mouth dry and her palms sweaty. They hadn't needed to take off their jackets yet. Nobody on their boat gave them a second look.

"Get ready," Adam whispered as they neared the second waterfall in the darkness. "Remember, just step up and walk quickly into the tunnel. Try not to make too much sound. I'll be right behind you." The three had previously discussed that the best way to exit the boat was to not jump but simply step from the boat onto the adjacent path that ran parallel with the boat's forward movement. Jumping from the boat might make the boat rock and draw unwanted attention from the other riders or their foot might slip off the wet boat side, even though it was layered with non-slip, textured adhesive.

As soon as they settled into the water after the fall, she edged over in her wet seat. She had her left hand on the head rail behind her, and her right hand gripping the rail in front of them. She brought her feet up under her and was in a low crouch.

"Now!" Adam whispered as he stood and helped Beth up out of the boat by holding her up at the waist until she was safely on the concrete path.

When Beth's feet were safely on the rock-like surface, she took off towards the passageway. It narrowed as it headed back, but there was still room. She could hear Adam and then Lance behind her. They moved through the passage until it forked off in two directions. The left path looked like it led directly to a black door, probably backstage where the employees would be. The right path led to the small hole in the wall they had seen on their earlier ride.

Breathing hard, they paused and took some deep breaths. "Did you hear anything behind us?" Beth asked, looking behind the two men.

Lance told her no, that nobody even looked back when she and Adam left. "The boat hardly rocked at all when you two got out. I didn't take time to look back to see if anyone noticed us, but I'm sure we are in the clear…at least for the moment."

Lance peered through the hole. "There is plenty of room behind the Captain's bed. Get behind there and wait for me. We have a little time before the next boat passes."

"Shouldn't it have come by now?"

Lance gave a brief smile. "There was a little 'delay' at the dock. Just hurry." There was always a chance one of the passengers reported the back seat was suddenly empty.

Adam went first and shoved the chest a little further forward so they could get past it. He made it to the bed and crouched out of sight. Listening for the screams from the waterfall, Beth sprinted the short distance after him. Lance had to get on his knees to be completely out of sight. "What did you do at the dock, Lance?"

"We don't have time to talk about it. Take off your jackets. I got these bandanas from Patty. Put them on. At least now we look more the part. Remember to freeze in place if we get spotted."

Lance was already standing over the bed's head-board, looking over the skeleton's bony shoulder at the map. "Don't touch it!" Beth whispered, as Lance reached over, running his fingers over the map's wording.

They heard a scream from the falls and the familiar 'whoosh' of a boat hitting the water at the bottom. "Get ready to duck back behind the bed!"

They were out of sight when the next two boats slowly passed by. Lance counted the time. "Okay, they are in the Treasure room. Go!"

The map was actually folded in half. They could see the word Indian – probably Indian Ocean. They tried seeing what was under the fold. The red 'X' didn't have any specific location that they could see. "Duck!" Lance called out in a rushed whisper.

"Already? Sheesh," Adam complained as he squatted down.

"Get off my foot, Lance!" Beth winced.

"Quit pushing!"

"Shh," Lance issued a stern warning. "This part of the ride doesn't have any noise except that harpsichord," which was playing a version of "Yo Ho, Yo Ho, a Pirate's Life For Me" in a slow, melodramatic tempo, nothing like the upbeat version in the latter part of the ride.

"Will you two knock it off?" Beth hissed.

They fell silent as Lance counted the moments. "Go."

"Where is the Captain pointing to on the map? Is that important?" Beth asked looking at the bony fingers seemingly pointing at a portion of the map, while its other hand held a large magnifying glass.

"It looks like it is in the middle of the ocean. What is that land mass there? Do you think the hand has been moved?" Lance added quickly.

"I'm sure it has been moved many times by the cleaning crew, maintenance, during ride rehabs…" Adam counted off before being cut off by the next set of screams.

"Duck!"

"This is going to take forever! Why don't we bring

the map back here?" Adam suggested.

"Shh. You aren't going to move anything!" Beth exclaimed.

"My knees hurt on these rocks."

"They aren't real rocks, Lance. Quit complaining," Adam told him sarcastically.

"But they really hurt."

"I am going to strangle both of you!" Beth whispered.

"Okay. Clear," Lance said, seeing out of the corner of the headboard and noticing the last boat passed the scene. "Go."

Lance didn't pay attention to Beth and moved the bony hand. Adam put his finger on the 'X' on the map. Beth slapped at Adam's hand when Lance again hissed, "Duck!"

They moved behind the bed as the next two boats came around the bend. Only this time something was different. A panel had slid open beneath the headboard, where the mattress would have been if it had been a real bed. The three looked at each other with surprised and excited looks. Adam was first to crawl inside the opening, closely followed by Beth. Lance got his feet inside just as the panel slid shut behind him.

"Okay, who did this?" Beth asked. "What did you touch up there?"

Lance and Adam shrugged in the darkness, neither sure if the passage opened because of Lance moving the bony hand or if it was Adam pushing on something that may have been under the map.

Lance tried to look around. "Where are we?" he asked in the near complete darkness. Only a sliver of light could be seen coming through a thin gap at the bottom of the hidden panel.

Adam had crawled forward as each person followed him in. There was still plenty of room in front of him. "Hold on a second. Don't push. Let me get my lighter."

"Sorry," she said.

"That's okay. Let me get some light in here," as he pulled the lighter from his pocket.

"Hope there's no gas down here," Lance muttered.

"Depends on what you had for lunch."

"Will you two stop it!?" Beth exclaimed, her heart beating hard in her chest.

They heard a muffled click and could see Adam adjusting the flame. More light appeared. In front of them their secret tunnel widened and kept going. Within twenty feet on the side of the tunnel they came to a handrail. His light held in front of him, Adam found a set of steps carved into the rock, sloping downwards.

"Careful," Adam cautioned. "There is a set of steps here. Hold the handrail."

As they slowly descended the stairs, they noticed the sounds of the ride didn't reach them. The way the stairs angled to the left, they figured they must be under the Treasure Cache room.

"Any light switch?" Lance wanted to know as he brought up the rear.

"Don't know if that is a good idea," Adam replied. "We don't know how close we are to a door or an exit. It might show."

Beth was awed. "We did it. We found the secret hiding place. He hid it right under the Treasure room. All those years, all those people riding it, and the treasure was right here!"

"Well, we haven't found anything yet. Keep going, Adam," Lance said, nodding ahead.

In the limited light, Adam had walked forward and came to a dead end. When he lowered the light, he then noticed that there was something in the wall. "'I found something! I think…yes, it's a handle!"

Lance took the lighter from him. "Let me see." He held the flame up and outlined the wall around the tunnel walls. "Yes, it's a door. And, it's locked. Look."

They crowded around him to see a very heavy door,

made to resemble the rock work surrounding it. The handle was a black lever-like bar that stuck out of a small hole in the heavy metal plate mounted low in the side of the door. Lance knocked on the door, not to be heard, but to feel how the door was constructed. There was almost no sound as the door was obviously extremely thick, probably made of heavy oak or mahogany. He pushed on the handle. It didn't move.

"Sounds like this door is not going anywhere," Adam said. "Look down there," he pointed to Lance who lowered the flame to where the handle protruded. "Looks like a hole for some kind of skeleton key." Lance looked closely at the little opening, hoping to see if he could see what might lie beyond the locked door.

"Can't see anything," Lance muttered, standing up. "But I think I have the key." Adam's and Beth's surprise could be seen in the dancing light of the flame.

"What do you mean?" Beth asked.

Lance reached inside his coat.

"He's got a gun!" Beth gasped as she and Adam saw the glint and barrel of what looked like a 38 caliber hand gun.

He chuckled. "Right on time, Captain Obvious. You would have disappointed me." Beth's face changed from confusion to fear as Lance's tone morphed into hateful sarcasm.

Adam moved to stand in front of Beth. "What are you doing, man? What's with the gun?"

"I'm not going to shoot you...well, not yet, anyways. Just the lock."

"That's not funny, Lance," Adam said, nervously, his hands balling into fists.

"I'm not laughing," Lance stated, unsmiling.

Beth was close to tears. "What's the matter with you, Lance? You can't do this. It's us. We're your best friends."

"Quit looking at me like that, Beth! This is hard

enough as it is."

"You fire that gun and you'll have Security on us," she pointed out, hoping in some way that he would put the gun down and give his charming smile, telling them he was just joking.

But Lance wasn't joking. And he didn't flash his devastating smile. Instead, Lance chuckled. It was an awful sound filled with anger and desperation and irony. "I *am* Security."

"What?" Beth whispered.

Now that their eyes were adjusting to the half light, they could see that Lance looked angry. "Are you more surprised that I have a gun, or that I have a job?" He shook his head. "How did you think I know so many people here? When we first came back from Missouri I was already planning ahead. You seemed happy to fly by the seat of your pants, Adam. I knew there was more at stake here than some paper stocks and nostalgic pins. And I needed a back-up plan."

"You mean 'we' needed a back-up plan, right, buddy?" Adam demanded.

"You're welcome to keep what we found so far. But this," he waved the gun towards the door, "I'm afraid I need it more than you do."

"You're rich, Lance! You have always had money. What about your new car?"

"You mean the car my father had repossessed? He hasn't been very happy with my past expenditures or my life. I was told my townhouse is next. He gave me a choice in Boston. Work for him or get cut off."

"I thought you were a trust fund brat," Adam challenged, calling Lance by the name Beth had labeled him years ago.

"Was," Lance corrected. "Yes, I was. Seems the old man can do whatever he wants with Grandfather's money. It turns out that as the three of us were flying off to Tobago, my father changed the wording of the Trust.

As the guardian of our family's estate and holdings, he said he can't support my indolent lifestyle, saying this action was for my own good." Lance paced the floor and spat out the words. "I'm broke. Except for my salary here, of course...which, Beth can attest, isn't going to make anyone rich by any means."

"Why didn't you tell us?" Beth was heartbroken. "We would have helped you… somehow."

Lance looked away from her hurt-filled eyes. He now wished she hadn't come; wished she wasn't mixed up in this. "What can I say? Embarrassment? Pride? Anger? Humiliation? Take your pick." He waved the gun in the air as he ranted. Beth flinched. He then looked down at the door. "Enough of this sentimental drivel. Once I find what's in here, and get it out, I have a feeling I will be well taken care of," Lance said smugly and added, "And I won't need any damned trust fund."

Adam edged back in front of Beth again. She wouldn't stay put. "Are you going to kill us, Lance?"

"I didn't plan on it, no. But things change," he said bitterly, "from one damn day to the next. Stand back, down the tunnel a ways. But don't try to go anywhere."

Adam and Beth moved back a few steps. Adam crouched over Beth and shielded her. Lance aimed at the handle and fired. Beth, holding her hands tightly over her ears, gave a small, terrified shriek that was absorbed into Adam's chest. With his arms tight around her, Adam felt Beth shaking like a leaf. The muffled gunshot hit straight on, making a bright momentary spark off the metal plate, but only ricocheted off. The slug buried itself into the rock wall of the tunnel a few feet in front of Adam. He looked at the mark in the wall and pulled Beth back a few more feet.

"Damn door," Lance mumbled to himself as he fired another shot which again had no effect except for another spark. This time the slug angled down into the floor where it skipped and flew past Adam and Beth. "This always worked in the movies."

Still protecting Beth, Adam snapped. "This ain't a movie, Lance. That door isn't going to be opened by bullets. That's a real gun you're holding," Adam pointed out, pleading with Lance. "And we are your real friends."

"If this was a movie, I'd have gotten the girl *and* the money by now," Lance said almost disgustedly. Lance looked down at the metal plate. "Wait, what's this?" Lance asked as he looked at the marks he left on the metal plate. He lowered the light, below the plate. There he saw, for the first time, words etched in the metal along the bottom border of the plate. Adam and Beth inched closer. Lance stood up and pointed the gun at the pair. "Don't get any ideas," he warned. He felt no satisfaction when they cowered away from the barrel aimed at them.

"Don't worry, Lance," Adam bit at him. "We aren't going to try anything. You're the one holding the gun." Adam held up his hand while keeping Beth slightly behind him with his other hand. "What's on the plate?"

Keeping the gun on Adam, Lance lowered the lighter once again. He ran his other hand over the letters, his fingers feeling the indentations formed by the letters, probably punched out by hand, one by one, using some sort of lettering chisel and hammer. The letters were not spaced evenly, and some not as deeply punched as others. But, the letters formed four unmistakable words:

'Sunnee holds the key'

Adam looked at Beth. She barely moved her head back and forth. She was still shaking, but she motioned for Adam to keep quiet. She had an idea and she desperately hoped it would work.

"What the hell does that mean?" Lance demanded, standing up looking at his two captives. The gun was now dangling in his hand. He looked at the door and the carving again, seemingly transfixed by the words. At that moment, he had forgotten Beth and Adam were even in the cavern with him.

Giving Adam another warning glance, Beth took a step forward towards the door. Getting no opposition from Lance, she knelt down next to the door and ran her fingers over the etched words. Hoping she sounded mesmerized, she whispered, "This is Indian. It has to be," she said louder, turning to look at Adam behind her. "Remember, Adam? Lillian was raised in Nez Perce country. It must be a chief or someone like that."

Lance turned on her. The gun remained pointed downward as if he didn't realize he still held it. "You sure?" he demanded.

Not lying completely, Beth answered, "Yes, I am sure. She was born in Idaho. There's a reservation there. I can't remember what it's called, but we can find out," Beth said as she stood and backed up towards Adam again.

Lance came to a decision. "Okay, we're going to get out of here. Beth, you go first. Go back up through the passage and get behind the bed and stay there. There has to be a latch on the inside to open the panel. Feel around for it. Once through, after the second boat passes, go through the little cave and wait in the passage out of sight. If you try anything, Adam will find out if he is allergic to lead administered in small doses at a high rate of speed."

"You're breaking my heart, Lance," she whispered. She wasn't aware of the tears running down her face.

"I'm sure you'll get over it. And probably a lot sooner than you should, if I remember your quote correctly, Runt."

The use of one of their old nicknames only made her tears fall faster. Adam watched helplessly as she disappeared into the darkness of the tunnel, followed closely by Lance. He could hear her fumbling to find some kind of latch that would open the secret door. When Lance moved forward, Adam knew she had found it and he silently followed them out of the quiet cavern. He hated the feeling of helplessness that hung over him.

At the fork where they had come in after jumping from the pirate boat, Lance had them turn the opposite direction and took them backstage into the employees-only area under Pirates and New Orleans Square. Lance had ordered them to carry their jackets and leave on the fake nametags. He wanted them to look like cast members going through the maze of tunnels so there would be less questions at this point. He transferred his real nametag and I.D. to the outside of his jacket, keeping his pirate shirt covered. Holding the gun hidden inside his jacket pocket, he had Adam and Beth walk in front of him through the black exit door within the ride and into the sterile white passages that snaked throughout the underground portion of the ride and served as maintenance and service corridors.

"How are we going to get back up to the surface?" Adam wanted to know.

His question seemed to confuse Lance, whose mind was already in turmoil. "What do you mean?"

Adam wanted to keep Lance talking, hoping something would jar him back to normalcy. "The waterfalls dropped us how far – forty feet underground? I just wondered how we get back up to the surface."

"Seems you don't know as much about Disneyland as you thought you did," Lance jibed him. "No wonder you couldn't figure out the simple fact that the rides in Fantasyland had moved."

Don't provoke him, Adam's mind warned. *Let him talk*. "You couldn't figure it out either." *Rats*.

Lance didn't seem to mind the retort. "We aren't underground, genius. If you'd remember the hundreds of times we had to go to New Orleans Square, you would remember we had to walk uphill to get there. The Square is thirty feet above the street level of the main entrance.

Once we went down the two waterfalls, we were back at street level."

They walked silently through the empty corridor. Signs posted on occasional doors told which attraction or shop or restaurant was on the other side. Beth was using this time to remember the maze of corridors she hadn't been in for five years. She formulated an idea and hoped it was a good one. First she needed to know where Lance was taking them.

"What are you holding?" Beth demanded when she looked back to see Lance's position.

"A little souvenir I caught the two of you stealing after I saw you jump off the boat. I'm going to turn you in to Security." He chuckled at his own cleverness. "That ought to keep you 'tied up' for quite some time. I can probably convince them to hand you over to the local police. By that time, I will be well on my way." Lance tossed the book he had grabbed in the air and caught it. It had been one of the dusty props on the dresser in the Captain's Quarters. His mood had lightened considerably. Beth had stupidly told him where to find the key to the treasure. And now he was about to rid himself of the two partners that he no longer needed.

"No fingerprints," Beth mumbled as if she were trying to tell Adam something.

"What did you say, Beth?" Lance demanded.

"Security won't hold us. There are only *your* fingerprints on that book."

"That won't matter. It will just take them even longer to figure out who did what." At her negative shake of the head, Lance realized he might be mistaken. After all, she had already had dealings with Security. Perhaps he did need some more definite proof. Nobody else had seen them jump. He smiled as he came up with a brilliant solution.

Lance suddenly yelled, "Look out!" As Adam and Beth spun around to see what happened, Lance hurled the book at her face. Beth caught it automatically before it smacked into her. Lance smirked. "Now it has your fingerprints."

"When did you become so devious?"

"About two minutes after I became desperate."

They walked along silently as they walked along through the maze of corridors. Soon they emerged into a much larger tunnel, one that appeared to be used for large trucks. Around a corner near where the large corridor open up into the back-lot area of the Park came three girls dressed for the Haunted Mansion. They were talking among themselves as they headed for their evening shift. When they saw Lance, they all squealed and clustered around him, forcing him to stop. They seemed delighted to have him all to themselves. His hand dropped into his gun pocket, but he smiled at them and called them each by name. He called for his 'friends' ahead of him to hold up and wait for him. Frowning, he realized they weren't obeying. But the three girls weren't that easy to dissuade. The tallest got in front of him, smiling invitingly at him, asking when he got off work.

During the distraction Adam and Beth kept walking slowly ahead. They looked as if they had just finished their shift and were heading back to their lockers to change clothes. Beth was whispering frantically, "Adam, we have to get away. We can't let him take us to Security. They'll remember me. It won't be pretty. Listen. We are near the end of the Jungle Cruise, near the African Veldt. Up ahead the road branches off in three directions. You take the left branch. Walk down a ways and look for a building that says 'Emporium'. You will find the door to the back of the store which is near the entrance of the Park on Main Street. Just put on your jacket and walk normally, like you know where you are going. I'll go to the right. It comes out between the tour guide queue area and the City Hall Building. We have to get to your truck and get out of here."

"Can't he have Security stop us?"

"No. He isn't going by the book."

"I don't think he cares at this point."

The girls were going to be late to their shift and were saying good-bye to Lance. They seemed intent on getting him to promise to call. Beth and Adam were about out of time. They could see the corridor branching ahead of them. Lance was starting to catch up.

"Take the book, Adam. You need to throw the book down that middle corridor as far as you can. Then start running and look for that door. He'll have to go get the book. He has to have some proof, and I probably can't outrun him without the head start."

They took another few steps and Adam heaved the book. It hit the pavement and skidded away from them. They took off running as fast as they could in the other direction. They heard Lance cursing as he went after the book. He had to retrieve it. Lance knew that much. But her tactic didn't gain them much time as Beth would have liked. They also didn't know who Lance would go after once he got the book. Knowing Adam's weakness, Lance went after Beth. However, he had to slow up for a moment when two Jungle Cruise guides walked past saying hello to him.

Not looking back and waiting for Lance's hands to grab her at any second, a breathless Beth flung herself through the Cast Member Only door. It banged open and she excused herself as she bumped into one of the tour guides. "Sorry, I'm late again!" she said as she hurried towards the souvenir stand. The guide, startled for a moment, finished her last-minute instructions to her group of guests and led them away to start their tour. Still not daring to look back, Beth hurried through the people under the entry arch and sprinted for the exits.

Lance burst through the entrance to the tour guide area moments later only to find an empty courtyard. The guide who had taken her last group into the Park was gone. Beth was out of sight. He ran out into the Town Square and looked all around for Beth among the hundreds of people milling about the area. He went through the arched opening and ran towards the main entrance, looking out past the exit turnstiles. But Lance didn't see her anywhere in the area. Drawing a deep breath, he cursed loudly. He then took the book still grasped in his hand and, with an angry yell, threw it like a discus over the Newsstand souvenir booth into the trees beyond. One startled mother passing by took notice of his nametag and turned towards the City Hall. Language like that had to be reported.

Red-faced, sweating, and uncaring of the sight he was presenting, Lance ran back through the entry arch and began a hectic search in the Town Square for Adam.

But, by this time, Adam had already crossed from the Emporium to the Disney Clothiers, Ltd. shop on the opposite side of Main Street. Walking quickly through its side door, he made his way through the large crowd getting their pictures taken with Mickey and Minnie in front of the Mad Hatter Shop. Following the general movement of people, he stayed in the middle of them all the way past the Opera House and the Bank of Main Street. Blending in with a huge family heading for the exit, he by-passed the hand stamp and headed towards the parking lot tram. And, more importantly, to find Beth.

Now the race was really on. Not only did they have to find the meaning of the clue, they now also had to outwit a frustrated and dangerous Lance.

CHAPTER 16

THE RACE IS ON!

TUESDAY, JUNE 18TH, 2002
6:10 P.M.

Adam sprinted for the Mickey and Friends Tram, hoping to see Beth waiting for him. Not finding her and not waiting to see if Lance caught up with him, he managed to jump on the tram just as it pulled away from the loading area. Ignoring the angry look of the cast member who was supposed to prevent things like that from happening, he half-stood, scanning the cars ahead to see if she was one of the other passengers. Not knowing if she had ducked down for safety, he had to resign himself to wait as they headed north to the parking structure.

After getting off the tram at the parking structure, Adam rode up the escalator to the second level, apprehensively looking across the heads of people below him for a sign of either Lance or Beth. Again, seeing neither, Adam stepped off the escalator and jogged down the parking isles to find his vehicle. As he approached where his truck was parked, his step slowed. He looked anxiously around for either Beth or Lance. He gave a sigh of relief when Beth softly called his name from a few cars away.

Beth came out from between two cars, first looking around then running up to Adam. Adam could feel her heart pounding as he pulled her in for a quick hug.

"We need to get out of here," he told her, taking Beth's arms off his neck, even though he didn't want the hug to end. "Lance won't have a car since we all came together. We might gain a little time while he has to call a cab."

"What are we going to do, Adam?" Beth sounded miserable. Her affection for Lance, his betrayal, and the fact that all this was killing her was there in her voice. She had never felt so much conflict.

Adam wasn't unaffected by all this, either. To have what he thought was his best friend pull a gun on him — and on Beth — was far beyond anything he had ever had to deal with before. "Don't know, sweetie, I just don't know," Adam said as he unlocked the passenger door and helped Beth in. "All I know is we need to get out of here as fast as we can." He climbed into the truck and started the engine. Neither said a word as Adam concentrated on exiting the parking structure. It was always busy with cars coming and going, excited kids darting away from their parents so they could get to Mickey faster. Upset kids being dragged kicking and screaming back to their cars to go home and other people could be seen wandering down the center of the aisle trying to locate their car, hoping they were on the right level.

Adam drove straight to Beth's condo. "I think you need to pack a few things," Adam told her as he pulled up in front of her house.

Beth stayed in the car for a moment. She turned to Adam and touched his hand so he would stay there too. "Adam, the information I gave Lance wasn't real. We don't actually need to go to Idaho. I mean, Lillian was born in Idaho, but I have no idea what 'Sunnee' refers to. I don't think the clue has anything to do with the Nez Perce."

"I know. I wasn't planning on jumping on a plane," Adam replied, letting go of her touch and opening his door. As he walked around to her side, he held her door open as she swung her legs out of the seat. He continued, "I just feel that you shouldn't stay here alone. Lance is, well, unpredictable right now, to say the least. It might not be safe," Adam added as he closed the door to his truck.

It crushed him to see her eyes fill with tears. She didn't argue, but went straight to her bedroom and pulled out a carry-on she hardly ever used. Adam followed, advising her not to take anything that Lance would notice was missing. Then he changed his mind. "No, make it look like you have indeed left for a trip. If Lance comes here, I think we need to make him believe we took your interpretation of the clue and headed to Idaho."

"You think he will break into my house!?" She sounded shocked. Lance was pretty nonchalant about personal boundaries. But, going through her stuff? Then another thought hit her. "What about my car? Do you think he will take my Bird?"

Adam stopped her from running out to her garage. "Listen, I'll padlock the garage so he can't get in or drive out. I don't think he is interested in your car. All he wants is whatever treasure he thinks Walt left. Personally, I doubt there is anything that has the kind of value Lance is thinking of, considering the items Walt has left behind so far. But, I'm not going to take any chances," Adam said as he looked towards the garage. "I think I have a pretty sturdy lock in my toolbox." Adam stopped next to Beth. He took her by her arms, making her look at him. "Look at me, Beth. I know you're upset. I am too. But, you are more important than that car and more important than any treasure we might find… I want you safe. All right?"

She could see his feelings for her in his eyes. He hadn't looked at her that way in a long time. Beth felt something inside her, an emotion she had not felt in a long, long time. She just nodded.

While Adam secured her garage, Beth finished throwing some clothes into the bag. Glancing in the extra bedroom, she decided she didn't need any of her books. Adam had a better collection of research books. There wasn't anything of use on her computer to worry about. The kitchen...all her food, there was nothing she could do about that.

She indicated the pirate shirt she was wearing. "What about this? Should I leave it?"

Adam thought for a minute. "No, we will probably need them again once we figure out the key clue. Just grab another jacket and a hat."

Within ten minutes they were back in Adam's truck. Beth took a last look at her place and hoped it would be fine whenever she got back. Sighing, she turned to Adam. "Adam? I am confused about one point."

He managed a smile. "Only one?"

"Well," she admitted, "a lot of points, but I'll get to Lance later."

"What is your one point?"

Beth frowned and sorted out her thoughts. They were so jumbled she had a difficult time focusing. "It's about Walt and his diary. We know he was on Tobago in 1960, right? But the point that keeps bothering me is that the Pirate ride wasn't talked about until, what? 1961 or 1962? How could he possibly have left that clue with Jeremy B. in 1960?"

Adam had been checking his rearview mirror constantly. Then, remembering he didn't know what Lance would be driving now, he stopped himself. He didn't want Beth any more nervous than she already was. "I thought about that, too. But, think about Disneyland for a minute."

"Which part?" Beth gave a little laugh.

"The part back in the early planning stages. I read that Walt had been thinking about his family park sometime in the early 1940's when he would take his daughters to a merry-go-round and he would have to sit and watch them with little to do than to eat popcorn and watch the girls having fun... The idea was just in his head, growing as the years went by. He mentioned it later on, but was either busy with other projects and movies or was met with criticism. I think it might have been the same with the Pirate ride. He could have been thinking about it for years before he told any of his Imagineers about it."

Beth was silent for a minute, thinking about what he said. "That's possible. But the clue pointed directly to Marc Davis and Xavier Atencio. There was no team for Pirates yet. How would he know who would work on it?"

Stopped at a red light, Adam turned to face her. "Marc Davis had been with Walt for a long time at that point; Walt knew what Marc was capable of doing. Once Walt did announce he wanted to build a Pirate attraction, he could have given Marc a drawing of the coin he had and told him to work it into the design. Same with Xavier. He was an artist for the studio for almost thirty years. Walt could easily have told him the exact words he wanted to use on the ride. Walt was the boss. You know he would have made sure that what he wanted was there in the final product." Adam paused for a moment. "It wouldn't surprise me that Walt left specific instructions that either have been destroyed or lost. Instructions that could have been clearly followed by Davis, X. or anyone else Walt may have trusted."

Beth was silent as they continued on their way. It made sense. It did fit in with what she knew about Walt Disney. "Too bad Walt didn't live to see the opening of Pirates...or any of the additions made to Disneyland that he had planned before his death. He would have been so proud of what they did," she commented as they turned onto Adam's street.

Adam pulled into his parking spot at the apartments. He just nodded his agreement as they headed for his place.

When Adam started throwing some of his clothes into a gym bag, Beth became confused. "Oh. I thought we were going to stay here."

He looked at her with a sly grin. "As much as I would like to have you here with me, it isn't safe here either. We need to find someplace else to stay. Help me go through these research papers. See if there is anything that might help us with the clue."

Beth sat on the sofa, taking up some of the papers with shaking hands. She really couldn't concentrate. Her mind was going over and over what had happened with Lance. When she thought about Adam snapping closed the lock onto her garage door, she gave a startled gasp when something else came into her mind. "Adam! Where are the diary and all the animation cels you found??" She could see they weren't on his desk where he had shown them to her.

Adam looked up from his computer and the information he was transferring to a diskette. He planned on clearing his hard drive of anything useful. "Don't worry. I put them back in my safe yesterday. I started getting nervous with them just lying around here from day one. Even *before* Lance started going screwy."

Relieved, she went back to the notes littered throughout the room. "Your handwriting is as bad as it ever was. From what I can tell, I really don't see anything that could help. Should I throw them out?"

"No, no, leave them scattered around like they were. Lance still has a key, unfortunately. Grab up that big book there about Walt and we need to leave. I have the computer cleared," as he ran his fingers through his hair, looking around. He was frustrated. This was his home; he didn't like to run. He wanted to face that son of a ….he wanted to have it out with Lance once and for all. If he didn't have Beth to protect, he would do just that. But, he did have her, thank god, he smiled to himself. And he had to make sure he didn't do anything to screw it up again like he did five years ago.

"So where are we going? A motel?"

"Wow. Two offers in one day! I'm deeply touched,

sweetheart."

Beth gave him "The Look". He chuckled at her expression and merged onto the 91 Freeway and headed east. When the 91 Freeway came up, he took the northbound ramp heading towards Yorba Linda.

"You're going to pull your parents into this?" Beth was surprised as she realized where they were headed.

Adam was a little more concerned than he let on. He wasn't sure at all that going to his parents was a good idea. But, he didn't have time to come up a lot of different options from which to choose. If he did figure out something better later, they could move out. "Well, they adore you. Always did. For some reason," he added under his breath, knowing full well she could hear him.

She sniffed. "At least they have good taste. Didn't they…uh, like any of the other girls you brought home lately?" She tried to make it sound as if she didn't care. But deep down, she was anxious to know and being just plain nosey. He had acted like he didn't have a girlfriend when they were on Tobago and he had been considerate and attentive lately. But on Tobago, they had been in a wildly romantic location and had been all alone. Now they were still partners in this treasure hunt. He hadn't talked much about his personal life other than his construction company. It wouldn't hurt to find out who else was in his life.

"So, are you asking if I am seeing anyone?" he asked, keeping his eyes on the freeway traffic.

"Oh, well, no…" she broke off, embarrassed he had seen right through her. She should have known.

Hiding his smile by checking the side mirror, he knew exactly how to answer her. He had been planning on just that question coming up at some point, and he was ready. Solemnly, he said, "You know, Beth, we have known each other for a long time. If you want to know something, just ask. You don't need to beat around the bush."

Not even recognizing her own speech, she walked right into it. "Okay, fine. Are you dating anyone?"

"None of your business." He didn't know how he managed not to laugh. He could see her turning red. Apparently she had just remembered the words she had thrown at him at the car show.

To break the silence that was growing uneasily since his joke, he asked her something about Disneyland. "Tell me something, Beth. I don't understand how Lance could actually hold down a job at Disneyland. He's always been with me since we found the diary. Either we were following up the clues, or we were researching them. I don't see when he ever could have been on the job."

"You missed your exit," she pointed to the freeway sign as they barreled past it.

"I know a short cut. And how do you know which exit to take? They moved since we were... since you last... oh hell. They moved," he just finished, not wanting to bring up their past and his hand in its termination.

Beth just smiled. "I like their new house. The view is amazing."

His eyes narrowed at her. "When were you here?"

"Apparently when you were off 'minding your own business'."

Damn if she didn't always get the last word! "One for you," he muttered, taking the next off ramp and heading away from the freeway. "So, what about Lance?"

She thought a while before answering. "He would have to be on a part time basis, even in Security. Part Time employees have a more flexible work schedule. I was Full Time, but even my hours varied depending on when the Keel Boats would be running. Let me you ask this: Who made all the arrangements for your trips?"

Adam answered immediately, "Lance did it all."

"And you were together every day."

"Yes....Well, no, now that I think about it. There were always a few open days before we would fly out. I figured it was because of the timing for the flights we had to take."

Beth didn't think so. "Lance could have had to work on those days to meet his time requirements. And, on some days with you and later with me, too, he could have been on the late shift and not gotten off until really late."

Adam pulled over in front of a neat, trim two-story house, white with blue shutters. "That might explain why he fell asleep so much on the sofa."

"I thought he always did that." Beth looked at the peaceful house and wondered if they should be here. "Do you think this is a good idea, Adam, really? I really like your parents."

He helped her out of the cab of the truck. "I do, too, Beth. They're my parents." He pulled their bags out of the truck's bed. "We'll have to explain some of it, but they don't know about any treasure or what we have been searching for."

"Won't be easy," Beth brought out. "It is so unlike Lance. Without a full explanation, they might not understand."

"I don't understand either, so we will be even." Adam led her up the walk. There was a huge pot of pink flowers hanging on the porch. Adam hadn't seen them before.

"Oh, the fuchsias are doing great!" Beth exclaimed touching the petals as Adam reached for the bell, still wondering how Beth knew so much. He hadn't been gone from her life that long, had he?

Margaret and John were delighted to see them. They were even more delighted to see them together; yet they were puzzled by the bags in Adam's hand. Adam gave them a quick hug and asked his dad to come outside with him. Margaret took Beth back to the kitchen where she was fixing lunch.

"Sorry we didn't call ahead. This was kind of impromptu."

Margaret could tell Beth was upset by something. Her eyes looked miserable, despite her smile and attempt to talk normally. Margaret just hoped Adam hadn't done something stupid again. "That's all right, dear. You know you are welcome here any time. Help me cut up these tomatoes." Beth would talk when she was ready; Margaret just bided her time.

Adam surprised his dad by asking if he could park his truck in his parent's garage. "I just need to get it off the street, Dad."

As they walked towards the back of the house, his dad asked, "You haven't gone and done something boneheaded again, have you?"

Adam stopped short. "What do you mean 'again'? What have I ever done that was boneheaded?"

His dad just looked at him.

"Okay, fine. There have been one or two things… But no, it isn't that. I'd rather tell you and Mom together."

"You in trouble?"

Adam watched the garage door slide soundlessly up its tracks and disappear overhead. "Depends on how you define 'trouble', but maybe. Yes. I need Beth to be safe." Adam's blue eyes were a mirror image of his father's as they stood in the shade of the garage looking at each other. "I can't tell you all the particulars right now, but it involves Lance too."

His father's eyebrows shot up at that. "Lance? That boy's never been a lick of trouble since we've known him. You two fighting over Beth?" he asked with a chuckle. *Now that would be interesting*, he decided.

"Beth?" It took Adam a minute to understand what he meant. "No, it's not like that. She never liked him that way for some reason. Every other woman sure did."

Both men stood shaking their heads slowly side to side, same expression of disbelief on their faces.

"Let me pull my truck out. Maybe by that time you'll

decide what to tell me." John's pickup roared to life and he backed down the driveway, pulling over to the side so Adam could park inside the garage. 'Michaels Construction' was still stenciled on the doors of his F250.

"We might need to borrow Mom's Audi," Adam told him when John walked back to his side.

"That's up to your mother. So, you going to tell me or make me guess some more?" John asked, not unkindly as he leaned against the garage wall. Adam usually was forthright with them. This hesitancy was unusual. But, he had Beth with him again, and now there was a problem with Lance – two people he knew Adam liked better than all the rest of his friends. If Adam's silence was unusual, then the problem must be as well. John wouldn't push. "So, how are you doing with my company? Have any customers left?" he kidded as Adam led him inside the house after the Silverado was hidden in the garage.

Adam knew full well his dad kept up with Michaels Construction since he retired. The foreman Scott had worked for John a lot longer than Adam had. Their golf games every Sunday were for more than just golf. However, John would not butt in. Adam knew when the company was turned over to him, it was his. But he also knew John was up on current developments, too, and ready with any advice Adam might care to ask of him. "Yeah, we're going mainly into trailer park repairs now."

His dad groaned as if in pain. "Now that's cruel, boy, just plain cruel!" He put a fond arm around Adam's shoulders. They were smiling as they walked into the kitchen.

Beth looked more relaxed as she set the table. She caught the look of 'I don't know either' that was exchanged between John and Margaret and started to feel guilty. Adam motioned her to come back to the kitchen. He took one of the chrome bar stools at the kitchen island. Margaret swatted his hand away from the salad.

"I thought you wanted me to eat my vegetables," he

joked with his mom.

"Yes, but at the table, not with your fingers. Really, Beth, I did raise him better than that."

Beth smiled at the interplay. "You should have seen what he did with mashed potatoes in his apartment."

"Now don't go telling tales, Beth," Adam warned, "or I'll have to tell her about that mess you left in your kitchen."

"Three dishes in the sink do not constitute a 'mess'."

Margaret smiled to herself listening to them banter back and forth. It seemed like Adam was doing the first sensible thing in five years. Lord, she didn't know how that boy could be so dense sometimes.

During lunch Adam told them they had hit a snag with their project. Since his parents didn't know about his trips to Missouri or Tobago – at least he didn't think they knew – he left that aspect out. He said there had been a major disagreement with Lance over the direction the work was taking, and that Lance didn't take it very well. Adam threw in Lance's conflict with his own parents saying it just added to Lance's bad feelings. After stumbling around with the explanation for a few more minutes, Adam just stopped talking and pushed his food around on his plate. Beth's look of misery had returned.

John carefully wiped his mouth with his napkin and folded it on the table. "Well, Adam. That was interesting. There seem to be some holes big enough to walk an elephant through..." He held up a hand to stop Adam's protest. "But I understand there is something going on you don't like, it involves you two and Lance, and you can't tell us the particulars right now. Correct?"

Beth and Adam just nodded.

The parents exchanged a look with each other. Margaret nodded to John. He continued. "We trust both of you, and we know when you want to fill us in you will." John paused then asked with a conspirator's whisper, "It's not illegal, is it?"

Adam and Beth both started to shake their heads no, then stopped and looked at each other, dumbfounded. What Lance and Adam had done in San Francisco was considered outside of legal. But they had promised not to do that again. So, what about the other things? Was it considered illegal to jump off the rides and take something hidden for forty years? They were just following the clues as they found them. Right? Lance pulled a gun. That was illegal, wasn't it? But they didn't have a gun - Lance did.

At their perplexed look, his dad sighed. "Okay, then. I take it you don't know at this point? Are you putting your mother in danger, Adam?"

"No! Well, I don't think so. There was the gun…"

"Adam!" "What gun?" "Who has a gun?" poured out from both of his parents.

"Okay," Adam held up a hand. He took a deep breath. They were still staring at him. "Okay," he started again. "Lance is very upset because his father cut him off and is no longer giving him any money."

"Always thought he should have a job," John muttered and was kicked under the table by Margaret. "Well, a man should work."

"Lance does have a job a Disneyland…"

"A real job," John snorted, and then realized what he had said. "No disrespect, Beth."

"He works for Security," Adam tried to continue.

John looked relieved, "Then that would explain the gun."

"Dad, he pulled it on us. Beth and me."

"What did you do, son?"

Adam rolled his eyes. "We didn't do anything. Lance wanted something he thought we had, or would have…" He was talking in riddles again and all of them were getting frustrated. "Let's just say that Lance isn't his usual charming self any more. He's changed in the past few weeks. Pulling that gun shows he is desperate.

I needed to get Beth out of her place, and I don't feel my apartment is safe, either. That's why I brought her here. We need to lay low while we finish our project. Once that is over, we can fill in the elephant holes for you. We promise."

John and Margaret engaged in that silent communication long-married people always manage. "Of course you can stay here. I don't know what we'll do if Lance shows up, but if he pulls a gun, I'm getting out my crowbar."

"I don't think it will come to that, but thank you. We would like the use of your computer upstairs, if we can. I also don't want to be leaving anything out downstairs to reveal that Beth and I are here. I'd rather it look like we are out of town."

The rest of lunch remained uneaten, so Adam and Beth cleared the table and loaded the dishwasher. Margaret took Beth upstairs to get her bedroom ready, and then joined Adam and John out on the back patio. Adam looked out over the valley; the view was incredible and the breeze up here was better than where Adam lived. Adam relaxed in one of the recliners, and for a moment, they enjoyed the peace and quiet.

"Dad, can you take over at work for me for a few days at least? Scott has it all in hand, but I have had to leave a lot of responsibility on him lately."

John was glad to be invited back to the business. The growing darkness hid the excitement in his eyes. "Sure, no problem, Adam. I'd enjoy seeing the crew again."

"Uh huh." Adam wasn't fooled for a minute. "Don't go rearranging the files again. Took me months to get them straightened out."

"Hey, my system worked for me for twenty years."

"Yeah, that was the problem," Adam snorted. "You hadn't updated it in twenty years!"

Margaret stepped in to avert the same good-natured

argument they had had since Adam took over the business four years ago. "Adam, you had better take good care of that sweet girl up there."

"Why? Don't want to lose your insider information for the sales at Anne's?" he joked.

She was not amused. "From what you've managed to <u>not</u> tell us, this doesn't sound like a joking matter, Adam. I mean it."

"Yeah, Mom, I will," Adam told her, properly chastised. "If she'll let me."

There he goes being dense again, Margaret sighed. *Any fool could tell Beth adored him...any fool except for Adam.*

"I'll take care of Lance if he shows up here," John promised him. Then he added, "You just finish whatever the hell it is you are working on." John paused and added with a frown, "And, if it is illegal, you'd better have a damn good reason for doing it."

Adam just nodded. He knew he and Beth had to finish finding the treasure...if there really was an actual treasure to be found. And he knew they had to do it as quickly as they could.

TUESDAY, JUNE 18TH, 2002
10:15 P.M.

Lance was exhausted. His rage had increased when he realized he was stuck at Disneyland without a car, and now had lost both Beth and Adam. He knew it was fruitless to go to the parking structure. They would be long gone by now – not that he could have possibly walked up to them and charmingly asked them for a lift to his place.

The high emotions, the constant travel, and working all times in-between had taken their toll on him. When the taxi dropped him off, he thought about driving straight to the airport and getting on the next plane to Idaho. He stood on his doorstep for a five full minutes, just staring over at his garage. His new Mercedes was gone, but his old stand-by, a 1989 Jaguar VandenPlas sat there waiting. *One up on you, Father*, he numbly thought. He finally headed inside his townhouse and went straight to the bar. He poured the last of his Oban Single Malt, no ice. Sitting at his computer he pulled up his favorite travel website and booked a flight for the next morning to Lewiston, Idaho. It was the closest airport he could find near the Nez Perce Reservation in the northwestern portion of Idaho. Further investigation revealed a one-hour drive to the tribe headquarters. Might as well start at the beginning, he thought. He vaguely congratulated himself on not going straight to the airport. The flight didn't leave until 10:35 in the morning. The drive to the airport tonight would have been too much for him. Also, there would have been the problem with airport security and his gun.

He pulled the silver handgun out of his jacket pocket and put it on the desk next to his computer. Staring at it, he cursed the Fates for putting him in the predicament he was in. He cursed his father for taking away the only lifestyle he had ever known. He cursed Adam for wanting a third of the treasure. He cursed Beth for meddling and involving herself in something in which she didn't belong. He cursed Adam again for bringing her in – ignoring the fact that it was he himself who had suggested her. He quickly ran out of people to blame. It wasn't his fault he liked the taste of silver spoons.

The Scotch was taking its toll on his already-tired body. His fingers were idle on the keyboard of his computer. He knew he should start his research on 'Sunnee' and get a head start on tomorrow. Well, not tomorrow. For some reason, a plane took all day to get from California to Idaho. He wouldn't get in to Lewiston until 6:40 p.m. He'd have to get a motel room and get a fresh start on Thursday. His flight home was on Saturday. That should give him plenty of time before Adam and Beth showed up. They were probably still cowering in fear in some closet somewhere…

He stumbled to his bedroom and fell onto the bed. The combination of Scotch and fatigue put him to sleep within minutes.

The alarm, which he didn't remember setting, jolted Lance awake in the morning. Still numb and with a pounding headache, he showered but didn't bother shaving. He threw some clothes in a carry-on and jammed his laptop computer on top of the clothes. He didn't like the look of his red-rimmed eyes, but figured he could sleep some more on the plane. He just hoped flying coach would be comfortable enough to allow it. He took some cash out of the dwindling supply in his hidden wall safe and put the gun inside on the shelf before closing the thick door.

The hour-long drive to the airport was uneventful. He tried to pass the time by trying to regain his anger and irritation with his situation. But he was just too tired. *Probably having to fly coach will summons it back*, he told himself with a ghost of a smile.

He walked to his boarding gate oblivious as usual to the longing stares and smiles following his every step. His unshaven face and finger-combed hair presented an unkempt, totally sexy sight to many young ladies as he passed them. Had he been himself, he would have had plenty of company to pass the time waiting for his flight.

But he wasn't himself. He was determined in his goal to find the treasure. He had one object in mind. He was tired beyond belief. And, he was miserable.

After the tenth fruitless glance out the upper story window of his parents home at every passing car, Adam finally relaxed and concentrated on their search for 'Sunnee'. Adam was again going through the book he brought on Walt's life and work. Beth researched the word on the computer search engines. She found over 25,000 entries. Groaning at that discovery, she dug in.

She found it had to do with:

1. a location in Thailand
2. a type of Muslim
3. part of a work by Alfred Lloyd Tennyson
4. a girl's name meaning warmth, strength, even temperament, born during summer
5. an exotic plant,
              and,
6. many, many different people from photographers to artists to classmates searching for others from their school.

She decided to skip the links dealing with Muslims and having to read the Qur'an since she knew Walt was not part of the Islam faith. Adam looked over when he heard her chuckling to herself, but didn't want to break her concentration.

Beth pulled up a few of the Thailand links, but found them to be too far-fetched in regard to Disney and his life. She took a needed break and asked Adam if he was interested in going to Thailand to investigate in person the search result. She got a non-committal grunt as Adam was deep in his own thoughts. *Quit goofing around, get back to work*, she told herself.

The poem by Tennyson was interesting. But, other than the "sometimes my heart is like an island" clue they had solved, she didn't consider Walt as very poetic. Artistic, yes. Driven, yes. Far-sighted, yes. But poetic? She didn't think so.

She gave a sigh that Tennyson hadn't provided a clue, and started on the list of artists and photographers.

Maybe she would find a link to Walt through their words or work. She pulled up the first name on page three of the searches.

Adam hadn't heard what Beth had said. He was reading through the extensive work on Walt's life and achievements. The book was over seven hundred pages, filled with references to just about everything involving Walt and his studios. That same book had helped when he and Lance had gone off to St. Louis and Marceline. He hoped it would help again. Of course, he had first checked the index in the back to see if there was a listing for 'Sunnee', but no such luck. He would have to do it the hard way. Page by page.

Margaret brought them some lunch after they failed to come downstairs at noon. She was surprised it was so quiet in her study. Usually those two were laughing and kidding with each other. *Even more so when Lance had been involved*, she sighed to herself. The part about Lance bothered her a lot. If there had ever been someone who had been born under a gilded star, it had to be Lance. She had never heard a cross word from him. His manners had been impeccable. He had the 'look' of someone with money, but had never acted that way. He was never one to flaunt his wealth. But if someone needed something, Lance would be the first one to provide it. Charming. Graceful. Handsome as hell. No, this was very hard for Margaret to comprehend. Knowing Beth as well as she did, Margaret knew it was killing her. Adam? Adam made friends for life. He chose carefully and he chose well. With the exception of his dumb-as-a-brick mess-up with Beth, he kept his friends. Thank goodness his renewed relationship with Beth seemed to be getting straightened out.

Margaret was politely thanked for lunch and despite her stalling, she couldn't see what they were working on. Oh, she knew it had to still be something to do with Disneyland, but could not for the life of her come up with anything that would be so important, so vital that it would be life-altering for someone like Lance. It just didn't make sense. And when she was politely thanked again for lunch, she took her leave and left them alone.

"**Y**ou have anything, Adam?" Beth sounded far away. Adam brought his word-weary eyes off the book and looked around for her. The computer chair was empty. She was stretched out on the sofa, her feet just inches from the chair in which he sat. He wondered how long she had been there.

Beth repeated her query at the questioning look on his face. Her voice sounded so tired. He shook his head. They had been working at it all day. "You?"

She sighed. "Nope. But I did find some fascinating photos."

"Of Walt?"

Adam sounded so hopeful she was sorry she brought it up. "No, sorry. Just one of the photographers with only one name. She does excellent work. People, animals, landscapes. A little bit of everything. Interesting website."

"Glad you are enjoying yourself," he commented dryly.

She didn't like the sound of that. "Hey, we have been at it all day! I am on page twenty-one of the search engine, I'll have you know. 25,000 entries, Adam, 25,000 entries for 'Sunnee'. My eyes were starting to cross."

He was instantly remorseful. "I know. I know. I'm sorry. I haven't found any reference at all. Lots of interesting facts I will probably need at my next Mouse Adventure race…if I ever do another race, but nothing that we need now."

She looked thoughtful. "Who will be your running partner this fall…if you decide to race again?"

Adam was about to automatically say, "Lance" since they had run the last four races together. But, unless some miracle happened, it didn't look like that would be the case ever again. He realized how upset he was over the loss of his friend. He had Beth scoot over on the sofa and lay down beside her. It felt good to relax. She immediately curled into his side and put her head on his chest. He stroked her hair while they both thought about Lance.

"Where do you think he is by now?" she asked in a quiet voice.

Adam gave the start of a chuckle. The situation with Lance was both funny and sad. "Probably half way to Idaho. When he didn't turn up here looking for us, I figured he would head there."

Beth thought that was probably true. "You don't think he researched it first like we are doing?"

"I don't know. If he did, he wouldn't be on his way to Idaho." He moved his hand and stroked her back. "That was pretty quick thinking of yours in that cave. How did you remember Lillian was born there?"

"You aren't the only one who knows Disney trivia." The rubbing on her back felt good. She would be asleep soon if she stopped talking. "It just popped in my head. I wasn't sure if he would buy it. He seemed pretty....I guess desperate is the best word I can come up with." She broke off a minute. "Adam? Do you think he would have shot us?" That part had really scared her.

He held her closer. When Lance had fired that first shot at the door, he really did think it was possible. Now, with time and distance, he wasn't sure. He hoped not. "I don't think so, sweetie. He had to know, deep down somewhere, we were his friends. I don't think so," he repeated quietly, and hoped he was right.

They lay there quietly, enjoying the warmth of contact and the respite from their work. John came in a few minutes later.

"So, this is how the younger generation gets work done. No wonder the country is going to...."

"Dad!" Adam broke in. "Sheesh. We're just taking a break." Beth tried to sit up, but he wouldn't let her. She pulled a hair out of the nape of his neck. "Ouch! Fine," and released her. She looked embarrassed to be caught in that position by his father – who actually thought it was cute.

"You two ready to come to dinner?" John asked, amused by Beth's discomfiture and Adam rubbing his sore neck.

"Dinner? We just had lunch," Adam said, then looked over to the digital clock next to the computer on the desk. "Oh, man, it's 7:00. How did that happen? Beth, are you hungry?"

She was already out the door to go help Margaret.

"You two find anything, besides time to snuggle?" John wanted to know, his eyes twinkling.

"Nothing wrong with a good snuggle." Adam refused to be baited. He knew his dad adored Beth. "And, no, we haven't found anything yet. How is Scott doing with the Anderson project?"

They walked down the stairs towards the dinner table. "It's going well. I took care of that miscalculation in the French doors you had done. No big deal."

"What miscalculation…." Adam started.

His mom cut him off. "No work arguments at my dinner table. I had enough of that for twenty years."

John threw a smug smile at Adam and carved a slice off the roast. Adam let him have his moment. He knew dinner wouldn't last forever.

WEDNESDAY, JUNE 19TH, 2002
2:11 A.M.

Adam was dreaming of a tropical paradise and a tropical umbrella drink singing him a song. He didn't know that song, but was fascinated by the drink singing to him. "Adam? Adam?" He smiled in his sleep as Beth suddenly entered the dream and danced with the umbrella. Then the umbrella shoved him…

"Adam! Wake up! I found it!" Beth shoved him again and he bolted upright, instantly awake. The blanket fell off his bare chest.

"What? Beth?" He smiled, seeing her standing there next to his bed. "Is this invitation number three? You know, third time is a charm…" he broke off being cute by her hands on her hips, not the inviting pose Adam had in mind.

"My word, is that all you think about?"

"I'm a guy."

"Yes you are, and you are really good at it," she shot back. She slapped his hand away as he reached for her. "Didn't you hear what I said?"

"I couldn't hear you over the singing drink…Never mind. What did you tell me?"

"I said I found it! I found Sunnee."

He glanced at the clock beside his bed. It was 2 a.m. "What are you doing up? I thought you went to bed hours ago."

"I did, but couldn't sleep. Aren't you coming to see what I found?" He could tell she was really excited.

He threw back the covers. She glanced down. "You'd better put on a robe, Adam. This is your parent's house."

"Fine," he said resignedly. He grabbed his jeans instead of a robe and tugged them on over his sagging boxers. "What did you find?"

She took his hand and pulled him into Margaret's office. She pointed at the screen and he sat down and started to read. "Oh my god. You found it! I don't believe it. Who would have thought of something like that! This is… this is…" he broke off, sitting back in the chair where his excitement suddenly changed to confusion. "This is really odd. Now what do we do?"

Beth just shook her head. She was stuck on that point too. For what she had found was that Sunnee was…

The family dog.

CHAPTER 17

1927

The Tudor style house on Lyric Avenue was finished. He had chosen the Silver Lake District right next to the Los Feliz hills. It wasn't a huge house, but it was home, their first real house. Now he wanted a dog.

He was gone a lot, working late at the nearby studio – that was certainly nothing new. Lillian's mother had moved in with them to help ward off the loneliness Lillian faced with his long hours at work. Sometimes he would be gone all night, working so late it was easier to sleep at the studio. He sympathized with Lillian's feelings, but work was work.

As the holiday season approached, he prodded her about getting a dog. However, Lillian would have none of it. A dog in her new house? Dog hair all over, the mess, the dog smells. Still, Walt kept after her. He loved dogs. He finally asked her, if she had to choose, what kind would she want? It came up that chow dogs didn't shed, had no fleas, and very little odor. If she had to choose, it would probably be a dog like that.

The very next day Walt went to a kennel and found a chow pup about eight weeks old. He would leave it in the kennel since it was still about a month before the

Christmas holiday. The day before Christmas, he brought the dog over to his brother Roy's house next door. Finding a big hatbox, he decorated it with a fancy ribbon.

The family was all together with women were busy cooking. Walt had his niece bring in the big, wiggling hatbox and put it, unnoticed, under the tree. Walt's niece began to hand out the presents. She placed the large box in her aunt's lap.

It was not the reaction he had hoped for. Lillian didn't like anybody – not even Walt – picking out her hats for her. "Oh, you didn't!" she exclaimed. Shaking her head, she started undoing the huge ribbon on top. When the box jumped in her lap, she gave a little shriek. But when she opened the box, a fuzzy, black-nosed face peeped out of the box. It was love at first sight. The imagined hat fiasco was forgotten.

That scene was so special to Walt that decades later in 1955, the scene was used in the animated feature *Lady and the Tramp*.

The dog became a constant companion. When the family went out for ice cream, Walt would get one for the dog and feed it to her on the sidewalk outside. They named her

Sunnee.

WEDNESDAY, JUNE 19TH, 2002
2:18 P.M.

Lance drove through the green rolling hills of the Nez Perce reservation. It was beautiful country. The reservation sat on 770,000 acres filled with prairies, rivers and canyons. The Clearwater River cut through the land. He had learned that much during a quick look through a guidebook at the airport the night before. It wasn't much information, he reminded to himself, certainly different than the trips he had taken with Adam. Even as each clue was subject to subterfuge, subtlety, and obscure references, he and Adam would have had pages of information by now; streets, landmarks, buildings, people. This time, he just had a name and a vague location. He should have forced Beth….He rolled down the window of his rental for two reasons: To attempt to alleviate a strong smell of cigarettes from a previous driver, and to let the fresh air blow on his flushed face. Within that warm summer breeze, he tried to make himself forget his friends – his former friends, he amended. He was in control. He could do this without their help. He was as competent as they were.

He was alone.

It was not a good feeling for someone as gregarious as Lance. His sharp anger hadn't returned even as he tried to recapture it, to let it flow through him; perhaps a justification for his actions. When crammed in coach on the airplane, sleeping in a dingy motel room reeking of tobacco and god-knows-what-else, eating watery scrambled eggs and cold toast for breakfast, driving a piece of crap car, nothing worked to intensify his anger.

He looked over the plains as he drove the fifty miles to the reservation headquarters. He could see mile after mile of waving blue horizons. Unknown to Lance, the blue shimmer was the Camas flower with beautiful vivid blue spiky petals on a tall green stalk dancing with the subtle breeze that swept through the surrounding plains. The bulb had been a food staple for the inhabitants of the area. Lewis and Clark had even eaten it when they had passed through. *Beautiful sight*, thought Lance. The view out the windows of his car probably helping stifle any anger he wanted to feel.

He pulled into the well-kept parking lot and got out into the heat of the day. There were a few other cars already there. He walked into the wooden building and glanced around at the artifacts depicting the history of the Nez Perce. Under normal circumstances he would have loved to study them more closely. But these weren't normal circumstances. He had to find this 'Sunnee' person and get the answer to the clue.

Lance was greeted warmly by a tribal representative, a dark-skinned native who worked in the Nez Perce historical museum and who nametag identified him as 'volunteer Mitch Longtree'. After Mitch asked Lance if there was something he could answer for him, Lance smiled at him with a self-depreciating grin that opened more doors than a master key. Lance then explained he was searching for a person who might have been important about forty years ago. He wondered if they could possibly help him search records, or if they knew of a great chief named Sunnee. He even tried different pronunciations of the word: Soon'ee, or Sunny, or Sun Nee'.

Mitch looked at him funny, but tried his best to recall anyone by that name. There was a little girl named Sunny, but they wouldn't tell him where she lived. Lance was sure that wasn't what he wanted anyway; she was too young and didn't seem to Lance to fit the clue.

He explained a little more. This person might have been involved with Walt Disney a long time ago. Walt's wife, Lillian Bounds, had been born in the area. Could there be a connection, please?

"Why didn't you say so in the first place?" Mitch asked with a smile. "Mrs. Disney was born back in the town of Lapwai, thirty-five miles north. Just follow the road you came in on."

He graciously thanked Mitch and took a last look at the picture of Chief Joseph. Maybe he would have a little more time to learn more of the Nez Perce history after his drive into Lapwai.

He drove north on the 95 highway, retracing his route. In the distance after the fields of Camas ended, the hills were a dusky blue, inviting the explorer to come search there. Another kind of riches lie hidden out there – the history and culture of a proud people.

If Lance had taken the time, he would have learned

the Nez Perce tribe had even bred their own horse. The tribe began a breeding program in 1995 by crossbreeding the Appaloosa and a Central Asian breed called Akhal-Teke. It was called the Nez Perce Horse. The tradition of selected breeding and horsemanship of the Nez Perce had been destroyed in the 19th century. They had since reclaimed the honor.

He found the courthouse in Lapwai. This town of just over a thousand people was the seat of government of the Nez Perce Indian Reservation. The records he would need should be here. Again he was met with friendly warmth and this time he began with the Disney family connection. Yes, the records state she was born here in 1898. It was just an outpost then. At that time, Lewiston, only twelve miles away, was accessible only by ferry over the Clearwater River, wasn't that interesting, sir? Lance gave only a passing interest to the history of the town and its accessibility. He needed different information.

Lance returned to the subject of a Chief Sunnee or some other important person living at that time by that name. The blank looks he had been continually receiving were starting to discourage him, making him think twice about the clue and Beth's interpretation of it. Lance learned that there was nobody associated with the Nez Perce named Sunnee who would have been used by Walt for such an important clue. He hoped to be mistaken, or that he had misunderstood the name.

He bit back the curse that was on his lips and asked where he might plug in his computer. He didn't want to go back to the awful motel room. He was directed to the public library in town.

After having a quick lunch, he did what he realized he should have done before he ever rushed onto a plane and flown for two and a half hours to Idaho – with a five hour layover in Boise, no less! *Could have walked there quicker than that*. He found a well-worn school desk with short walled partitions between other desks, and started researching the name "Sunnee" in the cool, air-conditioned – and nearly unoccupied – library of Lapwai.

WEDNESDAY, JUNE 19TH, 2002
10:10 A.M.

"How in the world do you research a dog, Adam?" Beth was getting flustered. "This was a beloved family pet. How could a dog have the key?"

After the initial discovery by Beth, both she and Adam became frustrated locating any additional information and the connection between the dog and the key they were searching for. In addition, both were fighting sleep deprivation and fatigue. By 3:30 that morning, the two had finally curled up on the sofa and dozed off with no real answer.

Adam had been the first to awaken at 9:30 in the morning. Looking over at Beth, still fast asleep, Adam moved the comforter over her then walked into the adjoining bathroom to take a shower. When he came back in the room, Beth had already gotten up. Adam saw the clothes she had fallen asleep in neatly folded on the reading chair and Beth was wearing one of his mother's guest robes. With a cup of coffee in one hand, she stood looking over the computer monitor that she had been using the night before.

"Good morning, Beth," Adam greeted her when she didn't notice that he came back into the room. He had wrapped a towel around his waist and was drying his hair with another.

Beth looked up, eyeing the towel-clad Adam with an appraised raised eyebrow. "Good morning back. Leave me any hot water?" she asked, taking a sip of coffee to mask her purely female reaction to the sight before her.

"Plenty," Adam answered, excited to get started on finding more out about their Sunnee lead. "I almost woke you to see if you wanted to save water," he commented with a sly grin.

Beth stood there silent, a momentary pause that indicated consideration. She set her coffee mug down on the desk and brushed past Adam on her way into the bathroom. As she passed him, Adam thought he heard her whisper something like, "next time."

When Beth had showered and put on some fresh clothes, she returned to the couch. "I don't get it, Adam," she admitted, still no closer to understanding the connection to Sunnee and their quest.

Adam didn't understand it either. They had watched *Lady and the Tramp* together with his parents and a lot of popcorn. Other than the hatbox scene described in a website, there was nothing in the movie that seemed to be of any help. "Sunnee was a chow. I didn't notice any chows in the movie. Is the clue that the dog was a chow, or just that it was a dog? Or is it that particular dog? I wonder where Sunnee was buried?"

Beth was shocked. "Adam! We aren't going to dig up a dog! That's awful!"

"Well, the clue says 'Sunnee Holds the Key'. Maybe it was on his – or her – collar or something. We don't really know if it was male or female, do we?" Adam asked, spreading his arms apart. He then put his hand in his pockets. "Hey, maybe it is some kind of doggie jewelry."

"I really don't think so," Beth disagreed. "Based on the keyhole in that door, I would say it would have to be a pretty big key." She paused, then added, "That is if Walt even means a key in the literal sense."

"I know! It was a tattoo Walt had put on the dog, then the coat grew over it and hid it," Adam joked.

Beth laughed at that. "Only way that would work is if Walt had the dog stuffed after he died. The tattoo would be long gone by now."

"Like Trigger, Roy Roger's horse," Adam played

along. "Wonder where the dog would be? Think they would let us shave ol' Sunnee?"

She threw a pillow at him. "Poor dog. You'd better just let Sunnee rest in peace!"

Adam clutched the pillow and joined her on the sofa. He really hadn't been serious. She was a lot more fun to work with than Lance, and certainly a heck of a lot more fun to look at, Adam thought looking at Beth. Not wanting his mind to start thinking about Lance, he thought out loud about the dog. "So, is it the dog or the chow or the key she is supposed to have? Walt always loved dogs. Maybe this points to some other dog we are supposed to find."

Beth remembered some of her other findings. "Well, there were some standard poodles later in their family. One of them, I think named Lady, was a frequent visitor to the studio. There was even a blanket for her in Walt's office. He was crushed when she died."

"So you think it might be pointing at 'a' dog, not 'the' dog Sunnee?"

"Hey, I am still new at this clue-finding stuff. My specialty is Disneyland," she reminded him, knowing that was why he called her in the first place.

Adam stood and paced around the room, taking the little pillow with him. He just nodded. "It might be Disneyland still, considering it was Walt's true pride and joy. How many dogs are there?"

"Six," she said immediately, hiding a grin.

He was impressed by her quick response. "Really? Wow. How in the world…"

"I don't know!" she exclaimed, laughing at his expression. "I just made that up. You seemed to want a number."

He threw the pillow back. "Well, since it is all we have to work on right now, let's list what we know." He took up a pen and paper and looked at her expectantly.

She shrugged. "Okay, dogs are as good a place to

start as any." Beth stopped and thought for a moment. "Hey, good thing we don't have to figure how many mice are in the Park!"

"Yeah," Adam agreed. "Heck, there are probably tens of thousands of Mickey Mouse depictions throughout the Park, not even counting all the souvenirs there," Adam figured.

Beth and Adam were silent for a moment while both of them thought the number of dogs that could be in Disneyland. Beth broke the silence. "We already saw Nana in the Peter Pan Flight. There used to be a dog in each scene of the Carousel of Progress, but that's in Florida now. Goofy is a dog, sort of. Pluto. The gravedigger's scared dog in the Haunted Mansion...I always feel sorry for that dog. He didn't ask to be there…" She broke off when he looked at her funny. "Fine. You name some."

"Isn't there a dog at the Friendly Indian Village in Frontierland?"

"Yes, it was part of my Keel Boat spiel. The little boy he is with is fishing in the River."

"Oh, and there is the dog kennel just outside the main entrance. There would be keys for the cages," he pointed out.

"There are some dogs inside Pirates. I always liked the one singing with the Pirates right before the burning town scene. Are there any in Splash Mountain?"

Adam had to shrug. "I don't know. I don't ride that enough to know. Somebody I was with didn't like to get her hair wet…." He broke off, looking pointedly at Beth.

That surprised her. "You haven't ridden it in five years? Didn't you go back to the Park more often than that?"

"Only to get ready for the Mouse Adventure race. We would do a quick run through the Park and familiarize ourselves with what had changed since the last time we did the race."

Beth just said, "Hmm," and let it go for now. "What

about Storybook Land? Any dogs there?"

"If there were, they were too small to be seen by the human eye. And I ain't riding it again to find out!"

"Then, I think we have our dog list. I can't think of any other ride that would have been there in the 1960's. Can you?"

"Nope." He suddenly grinned at her.

Wary, she asked, "What?"

"Looks like somebody is going to have to ride Splash Mountain."

"I could sit and wait while you go on it."

"No, no. Two sets of eyes are better than one!"

"Great," she mumbled. She wasn't looking forward to it.

THURSDAY, JUNE 20TH, 2002
11:25 A.M.

The next day, back at Disneyland, Adam and Beth checked the dog kennel first. Other than two miserable lonely dogs extremely happy to see them, there was nothing to find. It was just a kennel. Air-conditioned, but still a kennel.

Adam took their annual passports and got Fast-Passes for Splash Mountain. It was Thursday and there were more people in the Park than on Mondays, Tuesdays, or Wednesdays. The FastPass would probably save them close to an hour wait time. "Let's ride the Mark Twain around while we wait for our pass time to come up. Okay? We can check that dog near the village."

Beth agreed, biting down the nostalgia that overcame her whenever she got near "her" River and the sights that were so familiar to her. Adam understood better this time. When he had first called her to meet him at the Park, he simply didn't think of the memories it would bring up – memories of him or those of her favorite job.

He rubbed her arm as they retraced their route, walking along the River of America towards the Mark Twain landing. They could see the Columbia Sailing Ship loading, so they didn't have to hurry.

"You want something to eat?" Adam asked, realizing it was nearly noon.

Her nose wrinkled. "I'd rather wait until after Splash Mountain. I don't like the drop at the end."

"Aww, it's only fifty-two feet long."

"At forty miles per hour," she added in an undertone.

They were standing on the top third deck of the Mark Twain as they slowly made their way around Tom Sawyer's Island. The big paddlewheel made a soothing, rhythmic *swoosh, swoosh, swoosh* in the water as its slow rotation pushed the big white steamboat around the island.

"I miss the Burning Settler's Cabin," she sighed. "It always looked so cool to see the flames shooting out of the roof. And Uncle Jed with the arrow sticking out of his chest. 'And there's Uncle Jed out in the front yard wearing his new 'Arrow' shirt. Oh my, it looks like the Indians gave Uncle Jed a 'house warming'," she quoted from her old spiel. Beth paused for a moment, thinking back. "It looks so plain now."

"When we ran the Mouse race, we had to ride the canoes and go through Keel Boat Rapids. We had to make our own 'white water rapids' with our paddles. The ducks sure didn't like it," Adam remembered.

"There's our dog," she pointed off to the left. On a protruding log, a little boy was squatting down, looking into the River to see if there was anything in his fish trap. The shaggy white dog slowly wagged his tail.

Adam studied it for a minute as they sailed past. "Well, the only way to know if there was something on the end of that fishing line would be to get a canoe and check it out. Want to 'borrow' another canoe?"

She gave a grimace. "Let's just put that plan on hold as a back-up, okay?"

It was another few minutes before they were back at the loading dock. They headed for Splash Mountain. Beth was not what you would call 'excited' about the ride.

As they floated and bumped around through the different scenes, Beth told herself it wasn't that bad. Every time their log was captured in a gate and raised to a higher level, she told herself it wasn't that bad. It was right before they got to the drop, in the few remaining moments of peace that she remembered something.

"Adam?"

He was sitting in the seat right behind her. "Yes?" He was really enjoying the ride.

"I thought of something. Splash Mountain wasn't built then. We didn't have to ride…." Her last words were cut off by her piercing scream as they plunged down the steep flume. A wave of water crashed over them at the bottom.

"Woo hoo!" Adam yelled. "I'm soaked!"

"Did you hear what I said before the drop?"

"Oh, yeah, I heard it."

She wiped the water out of her eyes. "Well?"

"I guess you didn't hear me over your screaming. You scream like a girl, you know."

She actually growled at him. "Well?"

"I said 'yes, I know that. I just wanted to ride it again!"

Adam had become saavy enough in the past few weeks to hit Splash Mountain's exit gate running.

After lunch at the Blue Bayou (Adam felt he had better treat Beth to something really special), they rechecked their dog list. Adam crossed off 'Splash Mountain' and ignored her glare. "Haunted Mansion?"

"Walt started on it in 1961 and they had planned on

opening it to the public in 1963. But, after the work with the World's Fair in New York in 1964 and then Walt's death in 1966, the Imagineers pushed it back until 1969," Beth filled in. "The entire attraction had changed significantly since the beginning conceptions."

"Didn't they build the mansion but it sat unused for a number of years?" Adam asked, thinking back to something he had read.

"Yes. I read that too," Beth told him, taking a bite of her Chicken Cordon Bleu. After swallowing and taking a sip of her Mint Julep she added, "I believe building the ride created problems, and additional costs that they weren't willing to spend just yet. And I also heard – but don't know it if is true – that when they did open the ride, someone had a heart attack and died while on the ride. I think they revamped the ride after that too."

Adam looked thoughtful, then crossed it off their list. "That doesn't sound too promising for what we need. Carousel of Progress was in Disneyland in 1964 after it finished at the World's Fair. Unless you are up for a quick trip to Walt Disney World in Florida, we can leave that for later, too."

Smiling, Beth remembered, "Wow, I haven't been there since the 1999 Intercontinental Canoe Races. My team didn't do well; their river is so much longer. I still have the special pin we were awarded."

"So, that leaves Goofy, Pluto, and Pirates, right?"

She took another sip of her drink. "You have the list."

He caught her tone and wondered if taking her on Splash Mountain would fit on his dad's list of 'bone-headed things'. Probably. He chose to ignore the thought for now. "Let's go on Pirates again. See if there are more than just the two dogs we know about, okay?"

After lunch and after a short wait in the queue area, Adam and Beth boarded a boat on Pirates of the Caribbean, both thinking back just a few days ago that Lance had pulled a gun on them. Both pushed the thought out of their heads and focused on locating dogs on the ride.

After the ride, they sat on a bench in front of Pirates facing the river. Adam jotted down note in the notepad he had brought. In his limited penmanship, Adam read off the locations of the dogs they found in the ride: They found a dog singing with the pirates, a dog barking at the girl hiding in the barrel, and a dog holding the key to the jail cell. Adam read off the three locations again. When he read the third one again, they stared at each other.

No, that can't be it. It's right out in the open. What kind of key was it? Isn't there a lock on the jail cell?

But.....

The map with the 'X' had been in plain sight under the big skull and crossbones on the Captain's bed matching the clue Walt had left on the coin.

They found the secret door under the Treasure Cache.

Hidden in plain sight.

Brilliant. Adam and Beth stared out over the sea of people and the Rivers of America at Tom Sawyer's Island. Both of them were completely unmindful to their surroundings…and both only focused on one thing:

They needed to see that key again.

Beth pulled out her digital camera and flashed several pictures of the dog as they went past it again. "No flash photography, please" came over the hidden speakers, and a few of the other passengers in their boat who now had little white dots dancing in their vision glared at her. She didn't care.

Within the mouth of the smiling dog was indeed a large round ring, holding a large, black key.

It was a skeleton key.

They were silent as they headed back to Adam's parents house in Yorba Linda. Silent, thoughtful, and extremely excited. The key had to be the clue. The dog wasn't a chow. It looked like a mutt with shaggy white fur with large black spots on its coat, and it was holding a key.

They printed copies of Beth's photos of the dog and the key. She managed to get it from three angles without too much distortion – straight on, side view, and from the back.

Adam asked the question they had both been pondering: "How do we get the key?"

"Well, as much as we would like to, we can't grab it as we sail past it. It is probably locked in the mouth pretty tightly." She paced the floor of Margaret's office. "Any way to get a copy made of it from pictures?"

Adam took the pictures up again and studied them. "Nice idea, but I don't think we could get the correct measurements. Skeleton keys were pretty exact."

"Want to try?"

He shrugged. "I would need to have a blank key. Something that old isn't just laying around. My locksmith might be able to do it, but he would have to have a blank. That could take a long time to find. We'd have to search antique stores…" he broke off. He didn't think that was the answer. He had something else in mind. "You up for a midnight raid?"

"What?" Beth sounded astonished. "What do you mean?"

He threw himself on the sofa, staring at her while he worked it out verbally. "Say, for instance, we go back to our little secret cave right before the Park closes. We jump when it is really slow. We lay low inside the cave until everybody is gone. The cameras will be off and no one should be around. We walk down to the dog, borrow the key, and bring it back to see if it fits the lock. Whether or not it works, we take it back to the dog and no one is the wiser."

"Cleaning crews."

"What time do they go through the ride?"

Beth didn't know. "I never got to work the ride. Maintenance crews might be in if there is a problem. We might have to lay low a long time. Then, we have to get out, with or without the treasure." Beth then added as an afterthought, "Adam, what if there is just another clue behind that door?"

"Then we will follow it, I guess," Adam said, shrugging his shoulders. "But, you know, Beth, I have a feeling that this might be the last clue and beyond that door…" Adam trailed off.

"Well, let's worry about that later," Beth said. "Let's open the door first."

"I guess we can't go walking through the same corridor Lance took us through carrying something."

She gave a little laugh. "Well, we could try it, but I don't see it working very well."

"How about this? We stay in the cave overnight. When the first boatloads of people go through, we pretend we are cast members doing ride check, or something like that, and jump into the boat. Ask them how their day is going. Stuff like that. Think that might work?"

Beth slowly nodded. "I like that. We have the clothes. Quality Control. But what if we had something large to carry out? Something bigger than what you have found so far?"

"I guess I can bring my backpack and hope for the best."

"Your Pirate backpack, right?" she smiled.

"So, do you want to ride together, or in separate boats?"

"Separate boats, I think," Beth decided. "We'd better have a good dinner. It will be a while before we see the light of day again."

Adam thought about Security and grimaced. "Don't say it like that. Let's just hope our luck holds out."

The Park stayed open until 11 p.m. that night. Main

Street was lit with thousands of tiny white sparkle lights in the trees. The water and light spectacle Fantasmic was over and the majority of the crowds were surging towards the exits. Beth took Adam's hand as they strolled through Adventureland. They could hear the double shot of the revolver the Jungle Cruise skippers used to 'scare the charging hippos in the trees. You never know when they might jump'. They decided to go right to Pirates and see how long the lines were. There were just a few guests filing through. The cast members were tired after a busy day.

Beth was allowed to have the back seat alone in the second boat. Adam followed her a minute or two later. The other passengers were more up front and didn't seem too concerned with either the ride or the other riders. Beth was unnoticed as she made her jump and hid behind the white rock walls. Heart pounding, she realized these stunts never got any easier. She held her breath at every sound, startled when Adam came around the corner to join her.

"Anyone see you?" she whispered.

"I don't think so. They all looked pretty sleepy. You?"

She just shrugged. "Behind the bed after the next two boats?"

Adam just nodded and put his arms around her to calm her. He was nervous too. This wasn't a sure-fire plan of his. He could see some 'elephant holes', as his dad had called them. But, they had to try. At least there wasn't a gun pointed at them. That much was a relief.

The second boat went by and they crawled behind the bed. Two more boats, and they were at the map. Beth moved the bony hand and Adam pushed where he thought he had before. Going behind, they were shocked to see the panel had not opened. "What did you do?"

"I think it is what didn't I do....Let's try again....Now."

Beth moved the hand back and Adam touched different places on the map, including the red '**X**'. This time, the door opened and they sighed with relief as they crawled through. Adam lit the small Maglight he had hidden in the backpack and they made their way down the flight of stairs carved out of the fake rock.

They flashed the light over the carved door and the floor around it. Nothing looked moved or altered in any way. They surmised Lance had not been back. They half expected to see the remains of a crowbar or sledge hammer attack on the door.

"Now we wait." Adam shook out a small flannel blanket near a wall so they would have some back rest. The two sat down next to each other. The concrete surface was hard on their rears. "What time do you figure we should try going out?" Adam asked as Beth cuddled up close to him.

He could feel Beth shake her head against his shoulder. "Not sure. Depends on where Pirates is on the cleaning and maintenance list. I would give it a good three hours. If they had any big maintenance things to do, they would have the ride closed for a few days and do it all at once. Since that isn't the case now, it might just be light cleaning, taking trash out of the water, and a quick check on the flume, the audio-animatronics and the sets."

As they settled next to each other, enjoying the warmth and familiarity, Adam brought up something that had been bothering him. "Maybe you can help me figure this out, Beth: How come our secret access panel was never discovered? It's been like thirty-five years. The map had to have been moved. The covering stuff on the bed was probably changed or cleaned. How come nobody found this cavern?"

Beth was silent for a moment. "Yeah, I thought about that, too. There are probably lots of hidden places in Disneyland that only certain people know about. But this one?" She shook her head again. "Only thing I could come up with is the location of the little door. It is behind the huge headboard. From all the pictures we have seen, the bed is in the same place. It hasn't moved. It is possible the door could have been opening and closing every time someone did something to the bed. But it wouldn't have been seen because it is hidden in a place no one would go. We were back there and we didn't see the door until it was actually open."

"I guess you could be right." Adam's arm around her shoulder pulled her a little closer. "You bring any cards?" he asked.

"Oh! I didn't even think of anything like that! What are we going to do for at least three hours?"

"Well, I guess Strip Poker is out of the running."

"I don't think that ever was *in* the running," Beth said with a light laugh. She pictured the two of them getting caught in the latter stages of strip poker.

If anything, the banter helped relieve some of the nervousness. She still expected a side panel to slide up and they would be exposed to the utility corridor running next to them, marched off to Security, and thrown in jail. *Okay, that last part didn't help my nerves*, she decided.

The minutes ticked slowly by. The noise of the crackers Adam brought to munch on sounded overloud in the quiet cavern. His offer for her to 'try and get some sleep' went nowhere. She was too wound up. Adam had told her he would go for the key and she would just wait there for him. It didn't help that he added, "If I don't come back within a reasonable period of time, just leave as we planned in the morning and get out of here. You know where the truck is parked on the side street." She nodded. The side street idea had been good. A car left overnight in the parking structure risked being towed away. The surrounding motels and restaurants didn't allow non-customers to park, either. They had to walk all the way in from one of the back streets behind the Disneyland Hotel, but it was worth it, they both decided.

"Is it time?" she asked as Adam got up and prepared

to leave. Her heart started pounding again.

"I'm going up for a listen. If I hear anyone working, I'll come back down. Don't worry, sweetheart. We'll be fine." He gave her a hug and a lingering kiss before grabbing the handrail to go back up.

The door panel slid silently open when Adam pushed on the lever just inside the secret passage. The darkness that greeted Adam was a welcome thing, hopefully meaning that no one was working in that area. Still, he crouched behind the headboard and waited, listening.

The animation of the ride had been turned off, as had the running water. It was eerily quiet. He thought about all those people who thought it would be so cool to walk around the Pirate ride when no one else was there. They would be surprised at how spooky and 'wrong' it felt.

He continued to wait, probably a good five minutes, letting his ears become accustomed to the silence. An occasional drip of water could be heard, but nothing else. He walked to the edge of the scene and looked both ways. Darkness greeted him. He didn't want to chance the cast member pathways in the back of the rocks, so he worked his way next to the water flume. When he ran out of walkway, he took off his shoes and socks and waded through the two-foot deep water that was perfectly flat with no boats or pumps moving it. He decided to keep to the water and not leave wet footprints as he went through the silent gun battle scene and the Dunking the Mayor. The Mayor had been left in the down position. He smiled and wondered how long he could hold his breath. Adam thought it was kind of like a wax museum that looked so authentic you wondered if the figures were *really* made of wax. The burning town didn't look quite so bad without the flames shooting up. He found himself daydreaming about the eeriness of the motionless figures and almost walked into two women of the cleaning crew finishing up in the Jail Scene. He slowly eased back in the water and sank down in the water until his head was out of sight from where they were working. He heard them stop talking and knew they were looking in his direction. He held his breath and waited as the water soaked into every inch of his clothes. Damn, he hadn't figured on that. He would be a mess in the morning. After a couple of moments, the women went back to their work and their animated chatter. They moved on to the pirates in the final ammo scene and Adam waited where he was, water lapping around under his chin. *Glad I took my shoes off*, he silently chided himself as he clutched them to his submerged chest.

The women seemed to take forever on that last scene in the ride. What were they doing? Sewing new outfits for the pirates?? Okay, calm down, he told himself. Nothing you can do, except look like a floating head when the first boat comes through in the morning...

It was finally quiet. The cleaning crew had gone out one of the doors hidden behind the burning timbers. He waited another two or three minutes to make sure they didn't come back. Silence.

He stood up from his crouched position and eased his sore legs. He waded his way to the waiting dog. "Hello, Sunnee," he greeted quietly as he reached for the key. He was too short. He had no choice but to get up on the walkway and risk the water run-off being seen. He figured a wet butt print was better than two footprints, so he sat on the edge as near as he could get to the silent dog and leaned backwards towards the dog.

He gave a small tug on the key, hoping a piercing alarm wouldn't go off. He eased from his ready-to-run tenseness when nothing happened. No alarm, and no key. Sunnee didn't want to let go. He had to turn around and get up on his knees to work the key ring out of the dog's mouth. Hoping he wouldn't have to pull the faithful dog's animated head off, he felt around in its grinning mouth. He found there was a hook hidden on dog's tongue. Relieved, he twisted the hook and the key nearly fell into Adam's hand. He breathed a sigh as he had been holding his breath. Before he turned to head back to Beth, he gave Sunnee a pat on the head.

With the key in hand, he started back to the Captain's Quarters, hoping Beth was still undiscovered. Since he was already wet, he kept to the water. He would have to use Beth's blanket to wipe up the trail of water he would leave going back to the hidden cavern. Not a good time to leave a red-flag trail, he decided.

When Beth heard the hidden panel slide open, her heart started pounding even as she knew it had to be Adam. In her nervousness, Beth flashed her light directly into his eyes when he came down the stairs. "Adam! You're all wet!"

"And blind, Captain," he remarked dryly as he could only see a white light in front of his eyes now. "Thanks."

Beth muttered an apology of sorts. "You were gone a long time. Why are you all wet? What happened?"

He told her the story and then went out to wipe up the water quickly. When he came back, she was staring at the key. "You didn't try it yet?"

She shook her head and handed it back to him. "You should do it. You've been working on this a long time."

Adam handed Beth his flashlight and took another out of his backpack. "Hold your light on the door," Adam told her. He then looked through the dim light into Beth's eyes.

"Excited?" he asked.

"Excited. Scared. Nervous."

She shone her light on the ancient door, finding the opening for the key in the heavy metal plate; two silver marks where the plate was permanently scarred by two bullets. Adam licked his dry lips – the only part of him that was dry – and aimed the key.

His hand jumped when Beth suddenly asked, "Does

it fit?"

"Geez, you scared me!" Adam said, his hand shaking with the key just short of the keyhole.

The key slid easily into the lock. He gave a tentative turn to the left and nothing happened. A turn to the right and they could hear the tumblers fall into place. A low sounding "click" could be heard behind the metal casing that held the key inside the door.

Hands shaking, Adam tugged on the door that probably hadn't been opened in forty years.

It creaked open, surprisingly easy on the brass hinges that were on the inside part of the door. A musky, dank smell poured out and dissipated. But, instead of another deep cavern of a room like they were expecting, this space was about the size of a closet. After shining their light around the cobwebbed interior, they fastened the beam on the one object sitting on the floor of that closet.

With a quiet determination, Adam started pulling the top off a beat-up wooden crate marked "Props".

Pants legs rolled up as high as he could, Adam made his way back to the dog to return the key. The dog had held the key faithfully for forty years and it had to be returned.

Adam dried off as best he could after he made sure his footprints were gone from around the Captain's Bed. They waited behind the huge headrest when they heard the first screams of people coming down the waterfalls. Another day was at hand.

Now they had to get out.

Their jackets were pushed on top of the stuffed backpack. They had on their pirate shirts and bandanas, the fake nametags in place. Adam just wished Beth didn't look so worried. Her eyes looked terrified.

This time they didn't want secrecy. They had to get on a boat and sit before the first camera picked them up.

And make sure the other passengers believed they were working on the ride.

"Always look like you know what you are doing. People will believe you." Lance's words came back to them. The words brought a sense of loss regarding their friend, but also a realization it was good advice.

"You first," Adam gave her a little shove.

"Don't push me! I'm going, I'm going," she muttered. She thought she heard him add a quiet, "I love you," but she was already walking towards the boats.

You work here. You belong here. You are Quality Control. You are dead meat, her mind just couldn't help adding that last part.

Back straight, Beth smiled at the startled people as she stepped out of the walkway. She pointed at the first boat, "Any room?" She waved at a little boy who seemed shocked that a pirate girl was talking to them. She pointed at the second boat. "I'll catch the next one, thanks!"

She lightly jumped into the empty fourth row, grabbed the head rail for stability and sat quickly. Those in the front rows turned to look at her. "Hi, there! Don't mind me. Quality Control. I need to check the stabilizers now and then. Wouldn't you think they would have the guys doing this, wouldn't you? But, no! They have *me* jumping into boats. So, how is your day going so far? Having fun?" She couldn't stop her chatter. Either that or she would start shaking. "How many rides have you been on so far? Remember, don't try this at home" she laughed to the people behind her. She could see everyone relax, and hoped they couldn't see her heart pounding against her nametag. She removed the bandana and pretended to fix her hair as they went up the waterfall. The nametag was also stashed into a pocket and she tucked the laces from her blouse inside the best she could. Exiting with everyone else, she headed for the sunlight outside and didn't look back. She headed slowly through Adventureland, resisting the urge to run as fast as she could. Directing her steps to the Monorail, she hoped Adam was right behind her.

Waiting in the Monorail Station looking out over the silent, empty Submarine Lagoon, Beth waited and waited. The monorail Big Red had come and gone. The next, Monorail Blue, was winding its way around the overhead track. She gasped when a hand was put on her shoulder.

"It's me!" Adam whispered.

She gave him a bear hug, her hands brushing against the heavy backpack. "You're all right! You look awful."

In the light of day, he did look awful. Unshaven, his clothes wrinkled from being soaked and drying on his body, eyes haunted, movements jerky. "I feel awful. And wonderful. And still nervous," he quietly told her. "I'm pretty sure it went all right, but I'll feel better when we are in my truck and heading away from here." He tugged his baseball cap a little lower.

They moved into the middle of all the people waiting for the Monorail as it silently slid into the station. Beth held her questions until they were seated and pulling away from Tomorrowland. The Monorail slipped higher, banked right, and carried them over the berm that separated the reality of life outside the Park from the fantasy inside. The monorail sped up and traveled parallel to Harbor Boulevard, a good twenty-five feet above the cars below, until it turned right again and headed across the short-term parking lot and towards Downtown Disney. They looked down into the new California Adventure that had opened a little more than a year earlier. It was built on what used to be the original parking lot. Within a couple of minutes they came to a smooth stop at the Downtown Disney Monorail Station near the Disneyland Hotel. Glancing quickly around, Adam and Beth didn't see anyone who looked like Security officers waiting. Trying to look like any other tourist, they ambled down the staircase and even had their hand stamped at the exit.

"What do you mean you are 'pretty sure' it went all right?" Beth asked at the first moment she could. There were people everywhere that early in the morning.

Adam groaned and shifted the backpack a little higher. "I missed the next boat. It was too full," he told her. "The reaction to me being there seemed, well, suspicious. I guess I didn't look 'pirate' enough. I thought one guy in particular was going to yell his bloody head off when I jumped in next to him. I had to start talking real fast."

"What did you tell him? I did the 'Quality Control' thing and asked how their day was going."

"I didn't think that was going to work with him. He wanted to know about the backpack. It almost threw me off-balance when I jumped. Plus, it made a clanking noise when I hit the seat. I had to tell him I was Maintenance and complained about the heavy tools they gave us. He asked why I didn't work at night like everyone else."

Beth laughed. "Good question."

"Yeah. He had everyone staring at me. I told them I needed to check out the waterfall at the end and that it could only be tested with a boatload of people. That made some of them nervous."

"Well, duh. That chain-drive at the end makes a lot of people nervous. I always expect to plunge backwards myself."

Adam nodded. "Well, as soon as we got to it, they all turned and looked at me. I guess they wanted to know if we were going to make it all the way up. I gave them all a thumbs-up and said to 'listen to how smooth it is. Perfect'. They all turned their heads to listen to the motor. Then they all nodded wisely, like they had it all worked out."

"How about your friend?"

"He had to agree with them, or look stupid." Adam smiled at her. "Like we've been told, act like you know what you are doing and people will believe you."

Still walking slowly but steadily, they traveled past the Rainforest Café and turned right as if they were going to their car in the Downtown Disney lot. Walking purposely through that area, they exited the Disney property and made their way to Adam's truck that, thankfully, hadn't been towed away.

It wasn't until they were heading down Harbor Boulevard towards the 91 Freeway that they finally took a normal breath.

They had done it!

CHAPTER 18

WALT'S TREASURE

FRIDAY, JUNE 21ST, 2002
9:38 A.M.

Margaret heard her front door open and went to investigate. She looked at the ragged appearance of her son and Beth and swallowed her first question of 'where have you two been all night!?' Beth looked exhausted and Adam looked like he had gone swimming in his clothes – his *pirate* clothes? She bit back her second question.

"Dad here?" Adam asked, looking towards the back of the house and ignoring the questions that he could see in his mother's worried eyes.

Margaret shook her head. "No, he is on the Anderson job this morning. A couple of the subcontractors are starting today." She expected some spark of interest, but he looked too preoccupied, too tired. "You okay, honey?" she asked Beth. *That was a safe enough question.*

Beth had slumped on the sofa. She could see Margaret eyeing her puffy pirate shirt that somewhat matched Adam's. Explanations would come later. As tired as she felt, it would be much later. "We didn't get any sleep last night." *Okay, probably not the best thing to say*, as Margaret's eyebrows shot up. "We were at the Park," Beth added.

That didn't help either. "All night? Some kind of pirate party?" Margaret smiled and threw up her hands. "Don't mind me. Why don't you go on upstairs and take a shower and maybe get some rest. We'll have something to eat once you're back downstairs."

"Thanks, Mom," as Adam turned and headed for the stairs; Beth on his heels.

Margaret wondered about the black backpack that was sagging between Adam's shoulders. It looked very heavy.

Adam paused at the door of the bedroom Beth was using. "Shower or nap or open the pack?"

"Yes," she answered with a tired smile.

Adam rubbed the back of his neck. "I guess the adrenaline wore off on the drive over here. I'm exhausted, too." He dropped the backpack next to her bed. "Go ahead with your shower, take a nap, and I'll be back in a couple of hours."

"You're leaving?!" Beth was surprised. She figured he would want to see the treasure he had worked so long and hard to get.

Adam looked away from the backpack. He had waited this long. It would be here when he got back. "Yes, Captain," he said with a small smile, "I want to check our places just to make sure everything is all right. Can I have your key?"

As she found it in her purse, she asked, "What if Lance is there waiting?"

Adam doubted it, but told her, "I'll have to deal with him if and when it happens. But, I think it will be all right. Go take a shower before you fall down."

Beth knew he didn't want her along in case Lance did show up, but she was too tired to argue this time. She went into his arms for a hug. He smelled like chlorine…and something else. "I think they must heavily chlorinate the water in Pirates. You smell like a bottle of Clorox!" Beth remarked, pulling a little away but keeping her arms around Adam. "I think you should take a shower."

"Is that an invitation? My, you've been giving me lots of them lately."

Beth kissed his neck and pulled away, sitting on the bed. "Men," she laughed, shaking her head. *Maybe someday,* Beth thought to herself as she thought about the idea. "Get out of here so I can get some sleep." As he lifted a hand for a quick wave, she added quietly, "You be careful, you hear?"

"Yes, dear."

"And, Adam?"

"Hmmm?"

"Change your shirt."

Beth rolled over and snuggled into her pillow. Adam looked down. "Shirt? Oh." He went to his room and pulled off his puffy pirate shirt.

Beth was still asleep when Adam got back. He slipped her keys quietly into her purse and contemplated lying down next to her. She had been so worn out from both their exertions and the strain that he decided to let her be. As he turned to leave, he was surprised to hear a small voice ask, "Everything okay?"

He looked at Beth lying on the bed and saw her big brown eyes watching him. "Thought you were asleep."

"I was, but you came stomping into the room rattling my keys around. Who can sleep through that?" she smiled.

He crouched down next to the bed and stroked her hair. "Sorry. I tried to be quiet."

She closed her eyes at the soft touch on her hair. She would fall asleep again if he kept that up. "Everything okay?" she asked again.

He nodded. "Our places look just the same as when we left. I didn't see any signs of anyone being there."

Her eyes were sad. "Where do you think he is?"

Adam didn't have to ask who 'he' was. He stood up from his position on the floor and sat next to her on the bed. "I've been thinking about him, too. If he planned his trip like he usually did – and there's no reason to think he wouldn't – he is probably still in Idaho. I guess he will be there at least until tomorrow or Saturday. But, I have no way of knowing."

"You think he'll figure out the clue and come looking for us?"

Adam's heart lurched when she voiced her fear. How could he protect her from a distraught, desperate man with a gun? "Come here," he offered, holding out his hand.

Beth sat up and went into his arms for the comfort he offered. She could feel his heart pounding. She felt him take a deep breath before answering her. He finally said, "I don't know what he will do. You know how intelligent Lance is. I was surprised he fell for your trick in the first place. But, yes, I think he will figure out the clue eventually and go check the hidden cave. If he still works for Security, he'll have easier access than we did, that's for sure."

"You think?" she kidded, trying to lighten the dark mood she had inadvertently set.

"We'll just have to play it by ear. I miss him too," Adam added quietly, resting his chin on top of her head.

"What about your parents?"

Adam had just started to kiss her neck. "I don't miss them at all…"

She laughed and pushed him away – even though his kisses felt *really* good. "No! That's not what I meant and you know it!...Adam, you're going to have to stop kissing me if we are going to have any type of intelligent conversation."

"The art of conversation is highly overrated…And besides, I have five years to make up for." He resisted her efforts to get up off his lap.

Beth settled back in his arms when she realized she wasn't going anywhere. In-between his kisses, she asked again, "So, what do we tell your parents?"

"That I'm making up very well."

"You are impossible!" she exclaimed and poked him not so gently in the ribs, knowing how ticklish he was.

"Okay, okay!" he conceded, "you win. Get up."

Beth wasn't sure she just had a victory since she had been enjoying his kisses very much. He felt her hesitancy and gave her a knowing smile. As she plopped down on the floor next to the backpack, she mumbled, "You are just plain evil, Adam Michaels!"

He slid down next to her. "And, you, Beth Roberts, are just plain adorable."

"Riffraff," she muttered under her breath.

Adam was surprised. She had never played that game with him. Only Lance. "Touchy," he shot back at her with a grin.

"Carouser."

"Shorty."

"Tease."

"So, how come you never did this with me before," Adam wanted to know.

"You aren't very good at it."

"What?!"

"Oh, come on. 'Touchy' and 'Shorty'? Sheesh," she said, pulling the backpack between them, hiding the laughter in her eyes.

Adam folded his arms. "What's wrong with 'Touchy' and 'Shorty'? What did you want? Frigid?"

Her head shot up. "Excuse me?" she demanded.

Oops, crap. Back peddle, Adam, back peddle. "I…I was just trying something Lance would have said. Sorry…I…oh, crap. Just open the pack."

Beth bent her head and looked at the zipper. She could barely keep from laughing. *Oh, Adam! You are adorable!* "Gosh, this is heavy."

"Tell me about it. I had to jump into the Pirate boat with that on my back! Almost landed like an overturned turtle."

"Still can't believe we did that," as she pulled out some black jewelry-sized boxes, nine by twelve manila envelopes that felt like they were stiffened with cardboard inserts, and yellowed regular legal size envelopes. There was some kind of heavy gray metal box in the bottom of the pack. She pushed the pack back over to Adam to let him lift the box out. As he did that, she started opening the black boxes.

After the first one, she gave a little cry and quickly opened the matching second one. "Oh, look, Adam! Matching his and hers Mickey Mouse watches! They are stamped 'Walt Disney Enterprises'! They have to be from the 1930's! How cute! Look at the old design of Mickey. They look brand new."

The first yellowed envelope contained four unused admission tickets for the opening day of Disneyland, dated July 17, 1955. There was a handwritten note from Walt that said, "I know it is too late to use these, but thought you would like to see what the real ones looked like! See you at the Park. Walt". Beth knew Walt was referring to all the counterfeit entry tickets that had been printed and the thousands of extra people who had flooded into Disneyland on Opening Day. It had been a disaster from everybody's standpoint.

The second envelope contained a check filled out and signed by Walt himself. It was a cancelled check for $5000 and the memo on the bottom said 'first payment for Disneyland'.

Inside the manila envelope that Beth opened first were two documents. As she read her eyes opened wider. She had always wanted one of these, but never figured she would be able to afford it: There were two Honorary Lifetime Memberships to Club 33 – the exclusive private club located over the Pirates of the Caribbean ride that had only a limited membership. Beth knew it would include automatic entry into both Parks, free parking, and, as she read the wordage, it also included the cost of all the meals for up to six guests. She held back her squeal of delight. She wasn't sure how all this was going to be divided up yet. But, she was definitely getting a dinner there and soon!

Smiling to herself, she opened the other large yellow envelope. There were four documents inside, all matching. Printed on the top of the documents was a picture of the Mark Twain that looked like it was taken off an etching. There was fancy scrollwork and cursive lettering. She hadn't seen papers like this before, and wasn't sure what they were. "Adam? What are these?" She handed them over to Adam, not noticing his blanched face. She turned her attention back to the Club 33 memberships.

Adam licked his dry lips and looked over the paperwork. He was a little dazed. It took a minute before he could figure them out. They were similar to the Santa Fe Railroad certificates he and Lance had gotten in Marceline. When he looked up at her expectant face, she attributed his pale appearance to this latest find. He was having difficulty breathing normally. His eyes were wide and excited. And his face had lost his normal healthy look. "These are stock certificates," he hoarsely explained. "We are owners of four thousand shares of stock in Disneyland."

Beth broadly grinned at that. "Wow! We own part of Disneyland?"

He handed the certificates back to Beth and just mutely nodded.

"I didn't realize opening the treasures was this exciting!" Beth exclaimed. "Is this how you felt every time you found one of the capsules?"

Adam didn't answer her. He was staring down at the closed metal box at his feet. It was an ugly little box that was eighteen inches long and about ten inches wide and deep. There were no markings of any kind on the outside that would indicate either the origin of the rusted box or the contents. But, it wasn't the box that caused his current condition. It was what he had found inside that had stunned him.

He pushed the box over the carpet closer to Beth. At her questioning look, he said very quietly, "Open it."

Beth was very eager. She had really enjoyed opening each envelope and box and discovering what was inside. She simply figured Adam realized that and wanted her to open the next 'present' from Walt. "What is it? A model of one of the ride cars? Oh! I know! It's a piece of the Matterhorn!" Adam remained silent as she opened the stiff lid. The rust had penetrated the old hinges and the lid stuck halfway up. Beth let out a whoosh of breath and her hands started shaking. She slowly reached for one of the objects in the box and brought it up to her face.

It was a solid gold coin stamped with the skull and crossbones design for which they had searched high and low inside the Pirate ride. It matched the half pendant they had taken to Tobago. Only this one was whole; the edges worn from time and elements; the Latin lettering on the back a mixture of bold and worn off.

Tearing her eyes from the gold coin, she looked at Adam's face. He just slowly nodded to her. She dropped her eyes back to the chest and to the hundred identical coins that lay there. She ran her fingers through the coins, feeling the cold metal slip past her fingers and hearing them clink together with a sound that only gold makes. She then noticed there were other types of coins mixed in. Some had a cross and a crown embossed on them. Some had a noble-looking face in profile. Some were smaller than the one she handled. But, each and every one of them looked to be solid gold.

She looked back at Adam. Before she could say anything, he held up something she hadn't seen. He must have taken it out of the chest before passing it over to her. He held it up on the index finger of his right hand. Dangling off a thick black string, swinging slowly back and forth, was a little pouch. It was black, about four inches wide and about five inches deep. The rough fabric might have been some type of canvas, but it was difficult to tell. It had obviously been hand-sewn.

Beth just looked at the little bag swinging in front of him. She was suddenly having as much trouble breathing as Adam was. "Oh, Adam," she whispered. "What are we going to do? This is incredible!"

He just shook his head side to side. He was overwhelmed. He held the dangling bag out to her, indicating she was supposed to take it.

She licked her lips and took the string off his finger, holding his now-empty hand for a minute. He didn't know if it was for strength or for support or just for the simple human touch. He watched as she pulled open the drawstring closure at the top of the bag. She visibly paled when she peered inside the bag.

Opening her left hand and cupping it in front of her, she tilted the little black bag and poured.

Into her hand flowed a sparkling rainbow of gems. There were blues, reds, pinks, yellows and greens. There were round ones and rectangular ones. There were some that were flat-bottomed and had a domed top. Sapphires. Rubies. Diamonds. Emeralds. Still on her knees Beth went over to where the sun came shining through the window and held her hand in the beam of bright light. The sparkle and glare from the stones hurt her eyes as they sent myriads of colored spots dancing through the room.

"Oh, Adam!" she gasped. "How could he leave so much? I don't understand." With her hands shaking, she carefully poured the stones back into the dark bag. She laid the bag gently on top of the coins, and lightly smoothed the old fabric with her fingers, forgetting the jostling they must have received when Adam was getting them out of the Pirate cave.

"I don't understand either....Even though...." He broke off, unsure.

"What?"

"This might possibly explain the huge expansion Disneyland underwent early on. Then there were the Florida properties. Walt probably took items from this treasure chest, sold what he needed when he needed it, and then left the rest. The family never wanted for anything. I can only imagine he went back only as he needed to...to finance his dreams and ideas. I can also guess he added the other items, such as the watches and the certificates, as time went on, as well. Maybe those items were included to connect the treasure specifically to him." Adam just quit talking and shrugged. There had been no explanations left with the treasures other than the note with the Opening Day tickets. All they had was the diary. 'Remember me' Walt had written.

They would never forget.

When dinner was finished, Adam and Beth had his parents return to the table after it had been cleared. They knew it was time for explanations.

Adam had taken the diary out of his safe when he had checked on his apartment. He now put it on the table in front of him. The backpack was on the floor between his chair and Beth's. He asked them to please let him tell the story all the way through without interruptions and then ask questions, if they had any. He faintly smiled at the last part. How could they not have questions? Hell, he still had them himself.

It took an hour for him to recapture the past eight and a half weeks. He could see his parents holding back comments and questions. Their faces registered the surprise and, in some cases, the shock at what the searchers had done and what they had found. When Adam was through, he brought out the certificates, the watches, and the tickets they had just found and laid them out over the table. When he set the beat-up chest on the table, his dad set the stock certificates he had been examining back on the table and pressed his lips together. He hadn't been allowed to talk yet.

Adam opened the lid so it faced his parents. They were totally shocked. His dad reached across the table, then stopped his hand and looked at questioningly Adam. When Adam wordlessly nodded, John took a couple of the gold coins and handed one to Margaret. "My god!" he muttered.

They looked to Adam for more of an explanation. He held up the black pouch and then opened it, spilling the gemstones into his shaking hand. It didn't get any easier no matter how many times he looked at them and told himself they were his. Theirs.

Margaret gasped and stood from her chair. It almost fell over in her haste. She had always loved gemstones. Rubies were her favorite. She looked at the large stones in Adam's palm and picked out a squarish ruby. It was over half an inch wide and almost as deep. Holding it up to the light she muttered, "It looks flawless." She looked back at Adam's hand, still held outright with the gems slightly shaking side to side. "It looks like the Seven Dwarfs mine! Adam, this is incredible. Oh, are we allowed to talk now?" she looked back at John, suddenly confused.

Adam gave a nervous laugh. "Yes, of course you are. I…I don't know what to make of this. Beth and I are about ready to jump out of our skins. I don't even know where to start."

Margaret started talking in her nervous excitement. "I don't know anything about the gold coins. But I know a little about the gems. You'll need to have the stones appraised. I don't know enough about them to help you in that area. You might look online first to get some idea on what they are worth." She glanced at John, not sure she should continue, but did anyway, "There is a website I like that has stones like these. You can measure yours to find their size and then compare with what they have listed. It's called awesomegems. There are also a lot of pages with information about each type of stone. Maybe they can recommend where to take them to be appraised."

She broke off when John was looking at her strangely. "And how do you know so much about this, Missy? Hmmm?"

She gave him a wide guilty smile. "I...I did a little shopping with them. Really helpful people," she stammered to a stop.

"What did you get?" John sighed.

Margaret looked at Beth where she knew she would get more support. "Remember that wonderful Princess Di cocktail ring I had made? The oval blue sapphire surrounded by diamonds? It was from them."

"Oh, I love that ring!" Beth exclaimed. Then she glanced at the look on John's face and started fiddling with the stock certificates instead of talking any more.

John cleared his throat and broke the silent tension that had been mounting. There were more important matters to discuss than his wife's ring. "Well, Adam, I can't approve of everything you did to reach your goal. But, I understand why you had to do it. I think you know the seriousness if you had been caught."

Adam silently nodded. It still turned his stomach to think what might have happened to him and Lance.

"There is one point I wonder if you have thought about yet. Your life is now officially changed forever," his dad declared. "Do you two realize that?"

Both Adam and Beth nodded. How could it not be changed? It wasn't just the dollar figure on what was setting on the table in front of them, either. With the treasure came responsibility – responsibility to use it and to use it wisely. They both understood. With each passing moment the understanding was sinking in deeper and deeper.

"You are a grown man, so I won't give you my advice. Unless, of course, you ask for it," he added with a grin. "Then your mother and I will be more than happy to do what we can. You know that. Do you have any plans already, or is it too soon?"

Beth just shrugged and looked at Adam. It was his treasure. She didn't know where she figured into the mix. That gorgeous blue sapphire would be nice…

Adam looked at the treasure chest and then shut the lid. The stones had already been put back in their little bag. "Well, I've thought of a few things I want to do. I do want to do something for the school in Marceline and for the little girl, Mandy who helped us. I don't know what yet, but I'll think of something." He didn't know what else to say. His thoughts were all scrambled. Pay off his student loan. Pay off his parent's mortgage. Pay off Beth's car and his truck. Set up a trust fund. Maybe a scholarship. Maybe he could bring Mandy and her family and some friends of hers out to stay at the Disneyland Hotel and give them a nice vacation at the Park….

"Well, there is one thing I know I am *definitely* going to do," Adam said, standing. There were three pairs of wide, expectant, excited, concerned eyes staring at him.

"What's that?" his dad wanted to know, curious as to what was going through his son's head right now.

"I'm taking all of you to Club 33 for dinner tonight!"

They all let out a cheer and released some of the tension by dancing around the room like five-year olds at a party.

"What time do you want to go?" John asked.

"How about around 6:00? Time enough for all of you to get ready?"

"Oh, I don't know what to wear!" Margaret claimed.

"How about your Princess Di ring?" John muttered as he went to the stairs to change.

Listening to his dad's advice, Adam had sent in three of each type of stone. He called them his inheritance from a beloved uncle. The website Margaret had recommended gave the location and the contact person of the laboratory who specialized in grading and appraising world-class gemstones. Adam would receive certificates on authenticity and approximate value of each of the stones he sent in.

It was four weeks before the gemstones got back from the lab in New York.

Adam did some of his own research during those four weeks. He read up on rubies, sapphire, emeralds and diamonds so he might understand the wordage of the certificates when he got them back.

Even then, he was unprepared for what he was told.

SATURDAY, DECEMBER 6TH, 2003
1:45 P.M.

Adam stood on a ridge feeling the cool wind blow into his back. Below him was a gently sloping hillside of green grass and flagstone walkways bordered by flowerbeds of hardy marigolds in gold and yellow and carefully pruned evergreen shrubs. Here and there were topiaries of Mickey and Minnie, Dumbo and Donald. A gazebo had been built in one corner of the yard and dark wood benches arranged at various vantage points. At the bottom of the hill was a slow moving river surrounded by trees and carefully placed boulders. Further on, beyond the property, loomed the San Gabriel Mountains, their peaks powdered white from the first snowfall of the year.

Behind Adam was a house. It was French in style, two stories, with a second fireplace in the master bedroom suite. There was a long driveway leading from the main road to this house. The driveway was bordered by trees that would someday fill in and form a green canopy under which to drive. The rose garden off to the side was barren of any color this late in the year. But, when spring came in a couple of months, there would be roses in every color of the rainbow.

Sitting next to Adam was a huge Golden Retriever. She nudged her head under Adam's hand and pushed upwards so he would start petting her again. Then she saw a flash of gray move across the yard, and she was off in a golden burst of speed. She hadn't caught a squirrel yet, but that didn't stop her from trying. Adam looked over at the commotion as the squirrel wisely went up a tree. Adam called her back. "Sunnee, heel!" Sunnee looked at Adam, then she looked up at the tree, then she looked back at Adam. With her version of a doggie sigh, she came reluctantly back to Adam's side. However, she still watched that tree.

Adam had bought one hundred acres here in Yorba Linda. He had gotten out of the remodel work and decided to build spec homes. Each home would be on a five-acre parcel. Each would be unique. This was the first home he had built, and he was tremendously proud of it.

For months Adam had worked on this house, doing most of the work himself with his subcontractors. What he couldn't or wouldn't do – like the electrical – he contracted out and oversaw the work. Other than the crews, he kept the project to himself. Nobody else had seen it yet.

There was only one thing wrong with this house. It wasn't a problem with the heating or the air; the plumbing was fine. The design of the house allowed for flow of movement and had no wasted space. He had worked with a designer on the interior. The chimneys both worked well.

No, the one thing wrong had nothing to do with the design or the mechanics of it. It was a fine house with five bedrooms, four bathrooms, walk-in closets, and a soft oak kitchen. It was a home for a family. Adam himself had just moved in about a month ago. But, he was alone. Well, there was Sunnee. But she was usually busy with the ongoing squirrel situation.

Yes, that was the one problem – Adam was here in this large house all by himself, so far. This was going to end today. Adam had sent out one invitation. It only contained an address and the time to come, nothing else. And, as he looked at his watch, he expected to hear a car at any moment. Turning from the view of the river, he walked back to the house whistling for Sunnee as he walked. The dog would come, eventually.

And so would Beth. Beth would be arriving at any moment and Adam was excited to see her. In the year and a half since their treasure hunt ended, they had continued to see each other. They gradually regained the relationship they had had before that day long ago when she gotten fired from Disneyland. They had rebuilt their relationship and expanded it. He wanted her to be the first to see his home.

Beth had been busy too. They had approached Disneyland with an offer: Disneyland would get – on loan – the pieces from their collection that held the most interest from a historical and collector vantage point. Such as the first nametag, the cancelled check, the matching watches, some of the cels never before seen, the original opening day tickets, and handwritten notes. In exchange for the exhibit, Beth would get her old job back. Considering her beloved ride was no longer in existence, she would get the job of her choice – for as long as she wanted, with the option to switch and train on other attractions, whether it would be a Jungle Cruise skipper or a Monorail pilot. She had been very busy at the Park and extremely happy. The offer was working well for both Disneyland and Beth.

Now Beth was on her way to an unknown address

somewhere near the Michaels' home, but in an undeveloped section. She had programmed the address into the navigation system of her new Grand Cherokee Limited and was following the turns as instructed. When she was told she 'had arrived at the destination', she saw a long driveway and an incredibly green lawn stretching into the distance. She pulled to a stop in front of a beautiful house. She could tell it was new from the size of the plants around the house and the fresh paint and trim.

The front door opened and Adam stepped out, closely followed by the biggest Golden Retriever she had ever seen.

Tail waving, the dog gave a deep, half-hearted 'woof' and then greeted her like a long lost friend.

"He's beautiful!" Beth exclaimed, stepping out of the Jeep.

"She," Adam corrected with a grin.

"She? What are you feeding her? Steroids?"

"Nope, just a big girl. Say hello to Sunnee."

Beth started laughing and got on her knees in front of the dog. She had a difficult time getting her arms around the wriggling mass of gold hair. "Perfect name, Adam."

"Yeah. I thought so, too. Every home should have a dog."

"So, is this your first spec home?" Beth looked around and liked what she could see so far. "This is so exciting, Adam!"

Adam took her arm and walked her through the front door. "Living room." She could see a nice fire burning in the fireplace, its white marble mantelpiece glowing in the light. Before she could enjoy the warmth or the surroundings, he tugged her through to the next room. "Dining room." She barely had time to look at the crystal chandelier hanging from the white ceiling medallion before he took her out the French doors. "Back yard."

"Gosh, Adam," she laughed as he dragged her along

the freshly laid sod lawn. "I hope you give a better tour for prospective buyers. They might want to spend a little more time looking at it."

"I wanted you to see the view before it got too dark," was his explanation.

"It's two in the afternoon."

"Obviously, Captain. I wanted you to see the river."

"I like rivers," she replied as they got to the top of the crest. "In fact, some of my favorite….." Whatever she was going to say died on her lips as she looked down at the river below. Yes, there was a river, but Adam had added to it, trenching out a side river that curled around a familiar shaped island. It was created to look just like Tom Sawyer's Island in Frontierland, complete with a settler's cabin – not burning – and a log fort, a barrel bridge, and some teepees and even a canoe. There was also a wooden dock made out of logs. But Beth didn't notice the fort or the cabin or the dock. She was looking at what was bobbing in the water, tied to that dock by its rudder and bow.

It was the Bertha Mae, one of Beth's keelboats from Disneyland.

There were tears running down Beth's face as she stood there, staring. "How did you find her, Adam?" she whispered. "She was sold."

"I found the blueprints online and built her myself. She…."

Adam found he was talking to himself. Beth had taken off, running down the hill with a happy Sunnee barking at her heels. She came to a halt on the dock and just stood staring at her boat. The Bertha Mae was even painted a soft blue. Beth stepped up on the narrow deck that was just above the dock; she ran a hand over the shutters nailed open next to the two openings on either side. There were benches inside the cabin just like before. Hanging from the inside roof were two old-fashioned metal lamps. Walking forward, Beth ran her hand along the side of the boat – fearing if she didn't touch it, it would vanish. There was the little bench built for two out front. She walked back and wiped the tears off her face. Stepping aboard, she found the control panel and the red-tipped throttle. There were the stairs and handrails leading up to the benches on the top. "Slide all the way down. Slide on down. No, keep sliding. It's the only way we keep the seats clean." She saw the speaker mounted on the tall mast that held a Disney flag, and found the switch on the control panel to activate it. She flipped the switch and banjo music poured out of the squeaky speaker. "Now sit back and enjoy some of that deeeelightful banjo pickin' music guaranteed to make the next few minutes fly by like hours." She leaned back against the rudder that arched over the back of the boat. It felt just right.

She looked to see Adam watching her from the dock. He looked extremely pleased with himself. She flew off the boat and into his arms. "Oh, Adam, thank you! I've never received a more perfect present!"

He enjoyed the hug. "I'm glad you like it. It wasn't easy finding some of the engine parts."

Her head snapped up. "Engine parts? You mean the Bertha Mae runs?"

"What good would it be if it didn't, sweetheart?"

He had to hang on to her to keep her from jumping back on the boat and taking off. She broke away from his kiss and thought of something and asked, "Why did you build my keelboat at a spec home? What am I going to do with her?"

Adam laughed and leaned back to look into her face. "Who said this was a spec home?"

"You did."

"No, I didn't."

"Well, then, what did you say?"

"I didn't say anything."

Beth looked even more confused. "Then whose

house is it?"

Adam had his hand in his pocket as he answered her. "Mine. Do you like it?"

"You built yourself a house and you didn't tell me?"

He smiled at the look in her eyes. "Now, if I had told you it wouldn't be a surprise, would it? Do you like it?" he repeated more gently this time.

She looked at Adam. "It's perfect."

"So, you do like it."

She just nodded.

Adam waited a long moment before he asked his next question. "Do you think you could live here?"

"With you?"

"Well, and Sunnee," who at that moment was pushing his leg with her nose.

"Oh, well, if Sunnee is going to be here, I might think about it," Beth said shyly.

Adam brought his hand out of his pocket and looked down at his closed fist. "Do you remember on the flight to Tobago when I told you the reason you had fallen into the River that awful day? You asked me why I did what I did in arranging it."

"You never told me why."

Adam licked his dry lips. "I know. I asked you to trust me; that I would tell you later."

Beth gave him a small smile. "Is this later enough?"

"Yeah, it's later enough. Come sit with me up here." He led the way up the stairs to the top deck of the keelboat and they sat facing each other, knees touching. Adam leaned forward and took her right hand with his left. "You do know I'm sorry for how that day turned out, right?"

Beth nodded, but was silent. This had bothered her for six years and she was anxious to hear what he would say.

"I had a plan for that day. Randy did as I asked him

to and you fell in, as you were supposed to. I jumped in, like I was supposed to. But, then the Suit showed up and you were hauled off. That wasn't supposed to happen."

"My shirt coming off?" she asked, her cheeks red with the memory.

"That wasn't supposed to happen either." Adam was going to add 'that was a bonus for me', but wisely didn't say that out loud. "Something different was supposed to happen that day, and I have regretted it for six years."

"What was it?"

Without taking his eyes off her face, Adam held up a ring that had been hidden in his right hand. It had a sparkling princess cut cornflower blue Ceylon sapphire in the middle, surrounded by pave diamonds. Each corner of the mount had another blue sapphire. There were alternating diamonds and blue sapphires down the band on three sides in an intricate filigree pattern. Beth's mouth fell open. "I was going to ask you something," Adam was almost whispering now. "Maybe I went about it the wrong way, but I had wanted to make that day memorable. I knew how much you loved your keel boats, so I wanted to ask you to marry me with the keel boats in the mix somehow. I guess I didn't think it through very well."

He watched a tear run down the side of her face. He hadn't even seen her tear up. "Oh, Adam."

Was that a yes? Are those happy tears? Why is she just sitting there? Did he forget something? Adam had never proposed before, so he didn't know exactly what was supposed to happen. "Am I supposed to get down on one knee?"

She wiped her eyes and laughed. "If you do that up here, we might just keel over and somebody might get keeled…and I don't want that to happen before I say yes."

He slipped the ring on her outstretched finger and then moved over to the seat next to her. Taking her in his arms, he sealed their promise with a kiss.

EPILOGUE

LAPWAI LIBRARY, NEZ PERCE COUNTY, IDAHO

WEDNESDAY, JUNE 19TH, 2002
5:50 P.M.

Lance stared at the computer screen. His worn-out, tired mind just couldn't grasp the answer that was right there in front of him. He scrolled to the top of the information page. He scrolled down. He even brought up another link. It said the same thing.

Beth lied.

That was his first coherent thought. Beth lied. His Beth, his dear, sweet Beth had lied. In the face of their great discovery, at the moment of truth, she lied to him.

Lance's second coherent thought added the fact that he had pointed a gun at them and indicated he might have to shoot them…

Oh god. He dropped his head onto his arms next to the computer. He thought over the entire journey with Adam, and later with Beth. He thought about the diary and the flights to Missouri – all three of them – and to Tobago; he thought about pouring over the clues and books and the excitement they had shared when they figured out where they had to go. He thought about all the planning Walt had put into the search and the treasures they had found – and that he, Lance, had so flippantly given to Adam and Beth.

He must have dozed off. Not surprising with all the strain he had put himself through lately. His laptop computer screen had switched to his screensaver. He lifted his eyes to the narrow sandy beach of Barcolet Bay. What a beautiful island it had been. Lance believed now that it had been the most significant of their finds. And, it had been the most significant for Beth and Adam. He remembered the sight of her legs swinging slowly off the side of Adam's beach chair, the murmur of their low voices. Adam had been forgiven.

Would he ever be forgiven?

Lance moved his mouse and the beauty of Barcolet Bay vanished and the original screen page returned. Somewhat refreshed by his nap, he reread the information. Then he went back to the first reference work he had found and reread that as well.

All their travel. All their research. All their plans and efforts. And it all came down to this: a dog.

They broke into a warehouse and rappelled down ropes. They dug up Walt's tree. They risked life and limb in a condemned building. They jumped off a moving train… *Okay, it was a slow moving train, but, still, it was a train*. They pretended to be filmmakers. They dove shark-infested waters…*Okay, they were fairly harmless sharks.* They jumped off of the Pirate boat with other people around… And it all comes down to a dog!

Lance sat back in the padded library chair, his fingers steepled in front of his face. He stared at the blinking cursor next to the description of the family Christmas and the puppy present Walt gave to Lillian.

The chuckle out of his lips surprised Lance. He ran his fingers through his messy hair and shook his head. He must be really tired…There was that sound again. It was another laugh.

A dog! He felt the corners of his mouth turn upwards. Beth sent him to the middle of the Indian reservation. Did she know then that it was a dog? He doubted it, but still giggled at the thought of what she did. Brilliant. She was simply brilliant.

Here he was, in a small town, in a small library, hundreds of miles away, and he was stuck here until tomorrow. Oh, god, it was a dog!

He started to laugh again. The librarian instinctively looked over to shush him, but, there was no one else there. He seemed to be enjoying himself now. He had looked so glum when he came in...

Lance wasn't aware of her scrutiny. His head was back on the chair and he was holding his stomach. He got to a point now where he couldn't stop laughing. He saw Beth's face as she looked in awe at the etched words on the door below Pirates and then as she told him it was an Indian word and Lillian had been born in Nez Perce country. And he believed her and jumped on an airplane. Oh, god! He couldn't stop laughing.

He laughed at Beth; he laughed at himself; he laughed at the fuzzy puppy that started this insane hilarity. He wiped the tears that formed at the corners of his eyes before they rolled into his ears again. He laughed until his stomach ached and his jaws hurt. He thought about San Francisco and his joke on Adam with the missing clue. Adam had been livid. He laughed harder still.

As with a good crying jag, Lance's laughing jag eventually wore out. And it left Lance exhausted. He closed the lid of his computer with a soft click. Head back, his stomach still lurching with infrequent giggle spasms, he closed his eyes. Then, leaning forward, he rested his head on the lid of his closed laptop.

The last thought he had before he fell asleep in the library was, "I am such an idiot."

At the now-strange silence, the librarian padded over to where Lance slept. She didn't usually allow such behavior, but, she couldn't remember the last time she had heard anyone laugh so hard. She wondered what it had been about. She normally would have awakened the sleeper and had him go elsewhere. This was a library, after all. But, he looked so peaceful, his head lying on his computer as if it were a pillow. The worry lines she had seen in his forehead were erased in his sleep. She didn't have the heart to awaken him.

He slept undisturbed for three hours.

JULY 27TH, 2002
11:30 P.M.

Dressed in the blue pants, white shirt, and blue rimmed, flat-topped white hat of his Security uniform, Lance and his partner did their final sweep of Critter Country and New Orleans Square. They checked the restrooms and stores for anyone trying to sneak a night in Disneyland. Shining their flashlights over the canoe dock and the hidden recesses of the dismantled Country Bear show, they found no one hiding.

It was 11:30 p.m. Saturday night. The Park had officially closed at 11:00, but if anyone had still been in line for an attraction, they were allowed to ride. There were a few regular Park attendees who liked to be the 'last one out of the Park' and they were currently in the far corner of Fantasyland, drawing out their slow exit as long as they could. Some of the shops on Main Street were still ringing up last minute souvenir sales and the stroller rental facility was busy with their hundreds of returned strollers and power scooters.

His partner's walkie-talkie buzzed and he was told to go to a possible problem at Big Thunder Mountain. With a 'see you later, Lance', his partner strolled off as Lance continued his final sweep. Lance walked through the ride queue for Splash Mountain and checked with the Ghostess at the Haunted Mansion that the ride's exit was all clear. He wandered through the quaint streets of New Orleans Square. All the shops were closed with various managers closing out registers behind locked entrances. He checked the courtyard off Royal Street. It was always a popular place both for lovers and hiders. He found neither.

Speaking into his walkie-talkie, he checked in with Central and gave his all-clear report. When he got back his "roger-out" he was officially off-duty and through for the night. Lance nodded politely to the last of the cast members as they tiredly said 'good night' and headed backstage to their lockers, showers, and street clothes, before they headed home.

Lance paused as he walked past the entry to Pirates of the Caribbean. *It's right there*, he told himself. *You have to go look*. He shook his head 'no' and headed for the path round the Treehouse. In front of the Jungle Cruise he stopped and looked back towards New Orleans Square.

"I have to do it," he said out loud. He turned back towards the Treehouse and entered the Cast Member Only door that was off the left side of the Pirate entrance and below the staircase that went up to the Disney Gallery Collector's Room.

His soft-soled shoes made no sound as he walked through the bright white corridor. He was all alone. The ride operators had long gone. The maintenance crews didn't begin their work until the Park was completely cleared out of guests. He found the door he wanted and stepped from white bare walls into a rocky cavern. He wouldn't think about that day when he forced Adam and Beth down that corridor at gunpoint. He only thought about the little hidden cave and a dog.

With no need for secrecy he walked up to the skeleton sitting in the Captain's Quarters bed. He didn't know for sure who did what on that fateful day when they had discovered the hidden passage. He moved the bony hand and checked the door. The passage was still closed. He went back and put his hand on the map as he tried to remember what Adam had done. The door didn't open. He returned to the bed one more time and put his finger on the red **X** on the map. In the silence of the cavern he could hear the little door glide open.

Lance used his security flashlight to light his way down the carved steps. Just as he suspected, the heavy wooden door was closed as he shown his flashlight over it. He read the words again and couldn't help but chuckle. As he was shaking his head over the irony, his beam of light showed that the door now had a gap between it and the rockwork door jam. It had been closed tightly the last time he had been there. *No way*, Lance thought as he reached forward and pulled on the door. It swung outward, its heavy weight swinging with only a little sound upon its hinges.

Damn! They did it! He smiled and almost gave a victory shout as he pulled the door fully open. He was surprised, as Adam had been before him, that the room was so small. The flashlight beam did a quick tour of the walls and ceiling and then focused on the scattered pieces of wood spread haphazardly in the center of the floor.

Crouching down, Lance lifted the pieces of what had to have been a wooden crate. He found one board with a faded stenciled 'Props' off to the side. The top and sides of the crate had been torn off and whatever had been inside was now gone.

"Damn. They did it," Lance repeated out loud, standing up while still shining his flashlight over the broken crate.

The reality hit Lance as he piled the pieces of wood off to the side. Adam and Beth had figured out the clue – whatever it meant – and had somehow come back and opened the door. They had taken whatever it was that had been hidden. "Damn," he repeated, the sound reverberating off the concrete walls around him.

Well, he had the crate, he smiled glumly to himself. He figured he might as well put all the wood in the same place, so he tilted what had been the base of the crate to lean it against the side wall with the other wood. He was just about to leave when he noticed something odd about the floor under the crate.

"What have we here?" he muttered to himself. Crouching down again and shining his light on it, it looked like some kind of button recessed into the fake rock floor. It had been hidden and protected by the crate. Lance could tell by looking at the dust marks surrounding the wood that Adam hadn't moved the base of the crate and therefore wouldn't have seen the depression underneath. Figuring he had nothing to lose, Lance pressed on the rock-colored button.

Nothing happened. Lance pushed on it again. Nothing.

"Figures," he grumbled, standing.

He was just about to leave when he felt a faint rumble beneath his feet and heard the sound of gears turning - gears that hadn't been used in a long time and needing a little grease. Wary, Lance slowly backed out of the little closet, unsure of what was happening. After a moment, the rumble stopped. As he waited, the back wall of the little closet began to slide sideways. As he shone his light on the wall, he watched it disappear completely into the hidden recesses of the cavern.

Lance moved forward again, careful not to step on the hidden button on the floor. He peered into the opening and saw that it was another room, larger even than the cavern in which they found the locked door. From where he stood he could see a dim white glow and a flashing red light emanating from inside.

Wide-eyed, Lance took a step inside the new room. He thought for a moment then glanced at the crate; he grabbed the rectangular bottom section of the broken crate and set it into the opening of the sliding wall to possibly halt the movement of the wall in case it tried to close. He wasn't sure how much strength was left in a forty-year old piece of wood, but it might buy him some time to get out should something make the wall close. He didn't want to discover that the door might somehow unlock only from the other side. The thought of being trapped down here made Lance break out in a cold sweat.

His flashlight wasn't needed. There were low wattage lighting units in the ceiling of the chamber, many of which looked as if they had burned out. Lance assumed the opening of the door had tripped some switch to turn the lights on. The remaining few lights provided illumination enough for Lance to recognize that a large machine of some sort was inside the room; listening for a moment, Lance could hear the machine making a soft humming sound. There were tubes and conduits coming in and out of the machine with panels of switches and levers mounted on the front side facing Lance. Every few seconds another sound could be heard: The release of air emanated from somewhere on the side of the machine. He looked around each side of the structure before locating where the soft *sh sh sh* sound was coming from. A wispy vapor exhaled out of a pipe located near the bottom of the machine. The emitted mist flowed eerily along the floor before dissipating completely.

Following the various tubes emerging from the machine, Lance spotted at least a dozen large cylinder tanks against a dark wall to which the maze of pipes were connected. Each tank stood about five feet tall, each at least a foot in diameter. They looked to Lance to be oversized scuba diving tanks. On each cylinder, a series of valves and pressure gauges were attached to a complex-looking array of brass connecting fittings. Lance looked at one of the tanks and wiped some dust off a metal label adhered to the side of the tank. The label read "Liquid Nitrogen". On another tank, Lance saw the word "Oxygen" printed in yellow letters across the top near the pressure gauges.

Lance shook his head, confused by the number of tanks and their contents.

Near the top of the large machine that was surrounded by the various cylinders was a small window that was fogged over. The window, about eight inches in diameter, was illuminated every few seconds by the slow, blinking red light that was located somewhere inside the mist-covered glass window. On then off. On then off. The cadence of the blinking light was almost hypnotic. Lance vaguely wondered how long that light had been blinking as he looked over the obviously functional machine. Being somewhat familiar now with the machinery of Disneyland and some of the attractions, Lance could tell this wasn't part of the Pirate ride, or the neighboring Indiana Jones ride, or the Jungle Cruise. This machine was not as sophisticated as the state-of-the-art technology that operated within the Park. It not only looked very old, but a layer of dust had accumulated on every flat surface visible making the equipment appear to not have been serviced or worked on in decades. Had this been a long-forgotten ride component, some sort of fog machine, Lance wondered.

Lance walked around each side of the unit. It was rectangular in shape, about ten feet long, five feet tall, and about four feet wide; it resembled a refrigerator lying on its side. The box-like machine took up half the back portion of the room. It was pushed up near the row of cylinder tanks lining the back wall.

He decided the window with the red light was the only 'entry' point. Why else have a window? It reminded him of a space capsule; a little like what he remembered NASA's first manned Mercury capsule looked like, with a small, very thick glass window, just like the one in front of him with its red light blinking inside.

He glanced around the otherwise empty room; the walls were bare on any charts, instructions, or specifications. A piece of yellow paper lying on the floor next to the side wall caught his eye. Picking it up, Lance quickly recognized it as a page torn out of the diary making his heart skip a beat. There was a cracked, yellowed piece of adhesive tape on the top edge. He turned the paper over and read the words: **Push Here**. There were no other instructions or indication of where "here" was. Lance turned and looked over the machine's array of buttons and levers.

Lance's heart was pounding as he walked over to the machine. The note had to have fallen off one of the panels. But which one? He used his flashlight for more illumination. Being careful not to touch any switch or lever, in fear of causing some catastrophe, he tried to find the remains of the sticky tape somewhere on the panel.

He felt along the bottom of various buttons until he felt the traces of adhesive near a button off to the side of all the main panels. It was a round black button which didn't look very special, except for being by itself. What would happen if he were to Push Here, Lance wondered, lifting his hand over the black button.

His fingers lingered over the top of the button for a deciding moment then suddenly pulled his hand away. He didn't know what was in the machine. What could possibly be hidden under Disneyland that needed to be protected by all that technology? He thought he should at least determine the contents of the machine or figure out what it was there for.

Lance walked slowly over to the foggy window. He ran his tongue over his suddenly-dry lips. His heart rate hadn't returned to normal. As he raised his sleeved arm towards the window, his heart pounded into his throat. He had never understood that terminology before. Now he understood the phrase and the feeling.

He slowly wiped the condensation off the round window. Taking a deep breath, he looked inside. At first he couldn't make out any recognizable shape or structure.

The red light was off and the inside of the machine was as dark as night. Then, suddenly, with a foreboding pre-monition, Lance looked away from the window. He looked all around the room. Why are there tanks of liquid nitrogen and oxygen in the room? Why did the machine and equipment look so old?

As the red light that illuminated the window blinked on, Lance looked into the glass again only to see his reflection within the wet surface. In the blur of the glass, his eyes and face were red from the light as he tried to see inside. The red light blinked off and the fog that had covered the glass before quickly returned as the ice-cold temperature within the machine caused the moisture within the room to condensate over the glass window. Lance felt his heart pounding in his ears; he felt his breath catch in his lungs. When he finally took a breath, it clouded in front of him in a ghost-like apparition as he leaned in over the machine, looking into the round window. Before the red light illuminated the opening again, Lance quickly wiped the glass with the sleeve of his uniform.

The red light flicked on and before it could fog over again, Lance looked in. He again saw his blurred reflection. Before the red light blinked off, Lance leaned in closer. Dust in the room made Lance blink twice. It was then that Lance choked out a scream.

The image inside the glass window – inside the machine – didn't blink at all. For inside the window was a man.

Lance took a step back as he forced his breathing to return to normal. In those few, still moments, a sudden calmness and awareness settled over him. He thought of Adam and Beth, the clues and the diary, the history of the man they had learned so much about; a man that had one of the most profound effects on the world of entertainment and beyond.

And now that man was only inches away.

Lance clasped his fingers behind his head and looked up at one of the remaining lit bulbs hanging over his head. He could only think of one thing:

"Holy crap."

–THE END–

References & Quiz

Many of you may be interested in the MouseAdventure quest that is featured at the start of this novel. MouseAdventure is an actual event that takes place at the Disneyland Resort twice a year. It is put on by MousePlanet and you can check out their website at mouseplanet.com/mouseadventure

This website is full of fun and helpful facts about the Disneyland Resort and Walt Disney World. The Mouse-Adventure will be in Walt Disney World for the first time in November 2009.

The quests Adam and Lance attempt to finish are similar to actual quests that are featured in these races. With the exception of one answer – the number of pillows in Walt's apartment (just say 5) – the quests Adam and Lance ran are accurate and can be completed if desired. The answers are provided below, should you wish to check your own!

Enjoy!

Quest 1 – Canoe Quest

How many seats in a canoe?   12
How many riders can a canoe hold? 20
The canoes have been in how many different lands since
    they started running? 3
                             Total: 35
Name the different lands: Frontierland, Bear Country,

Critter Country

QUEST 2 – MULTIPLE CHOICE

1. In Critter Country, which wooden animal can
   NOT be found?
   a. Tortoise
   b. Porcupine
   <u>c. Coyote</u>
   d. Moose

2. How many rubies are on the Golden Horseshoe sign?
   a. 39
   <u>b. 40</u>
   c. 41
   d. 42

3. As you sail through the Bayou, what creature do you see?
   a. Possum
   b. Swamp Cat
   c. Raccoon
   <u>d. Alligator</u>

4. What two animals did the Pirates NOT set free?
   a. Cat and Dog
   <u>b. Duck and Geese</u>
   c. Donkey and Chickens
   d. Pigs and Parrots

5. What do the Pirates offer the dog for the key?
   <u>a. Bone, Rope, Mug</u>
   b. Mug, Ball, Bone
   c. Bone, Cat, Rope
   d. Ball, Rope, Meat

6. What is Indy's truck license plate?
   a. THX1168

b. NDYJNS
c. <u>WH11204</u>

7. Which bad end does not come to those who stare
   at Mara?

   a. Eaten by rats
   <u>b. Stung by scorpion</u>
   c. Impaled on stakes
   d. Bitten by snake

8. Which pair has wandered into Adventureland?

   a. Snow White & Prince Charming
   b. Bernard & Bianca
   c. Buzz & Woody
   <u>d. Mrs. Potts & Chip</u>

QUEST 3 – HORSING AROUND

Name the horse from each of these movies:
1. Sleeping Beauty - - Samson
2. Hercules - - Pegasus
3. Mulan - - Khan
4. Beauty & the Beast - - Phillipe
5. Cinderella - - Major
6. Aristocats - - Frou Frou
7. Mr. Toad - - Cyril Proudbottom

Bonus: Name the lead horse on the Carrousel: Jingles
Bonus: How many horses are on the Carrousel: 72

QUEST 4 – ALL JUMBLED UP

Unscramble the mixed up attractions:
1. rigid handlebar tour - - Big Thunder Railroad
2. landslide radio yarn - - Disneyland Railroad
3. troll was dismal - - It's a Small World
4. yell troll joy - - Jolly Trolley

5. sure uncle jig - - Jungle Cruise

6. faint scam - - Fantasmic

7. ten inhuman soda - - Haunted Mansion

8. briar soot rot - - Astro Orbitor

9. trust sora - - Star Tours

10. mansion teacup - - Space Mountain

11. dinnertime cook hat - - Enchanted Tiki Room

12. repeat bicarbonate fish - - Pirates of the Caribbean

13. sandy door millennia - - Disneyland Monorail

14. teamwork trivia barn - - Mark Twain Riverboat

QUEST 5 – THE ROAD RALLY

Total up the following:

1. Address of Pieces of Eight Shop: 25

2. Number of pillows in Walt's Apartment: 5

3. Number of Teacups: 18

4. Number of Fire Engines: 2

5. Number of Flying Elephants: 16

6. Number of Astro Orbitor Rockets: 12

7. Maximum number of guests in a StarSpeeder: 40

8. Number of seats around the large dining table in the main dining room at 33 Royal Street: 8

9. Number of stairs in the flight of steps around the golden elevator: 24

Total: 150

ABOUT THE AUTHORS

NANCY TEMPLE RODRIGUE

Nancy has been an avid Disney fan ever since she was 6 years old and went to Disneyland for the first time with her family. She has been writing stories most of her life and attempted her first novel back in 1989. Those who know Nancy well will remember her Star Trek years! HIDDEN MICKEY is her first published work.

While she grew up in Modesto, California, she lives with her husband Russ in a small town called Lompoc, California, surrounded by the beautiful wine region called the Santa Rita Hills. Russ is also a Disney fan who grew up in Anaheim. His first visit to Disneyland was in August of 1955. They enjoy showing their award-winning 1957 T-Bird and 1923 T-Bucket in local car shows. More than likely, Nancy is probably busy planning her next trip to Disneyland.

Nancy and her co-author Dave have been good friends since 1981 when they first met at Disneyland.

Please visit the website at:
http://HIDDENMICKEYBOOK.COM

Join the Hidden Mickey fan club:
http://HIDDENMICKEYBOOK.COM/fanclub

(*please turn to next page*)

DAVID W. SMITH

Having worked at Disneyland in the late 1970's, Dave experienced first-hand the inner workings of the park and the many wonderful inspirations that were cultivated within the mind of Walt Disney. Dave always felt a special connection to Disneyland, growing up just a couple miles south of the park in Garden Grove and seeing it evolve and grow to what we now recognize as the world-wide destination resort it has become. Dave believes everyone who has ever had a dream can relate to Walt Disney's own dreams of "doing the impossible." While most of us never fulfill our dreams to the extent Walt did, we all can imagine just how he must have felt walking down Main Street, USA of Disneyland, taking in all that he had done. However, while most of us would have felt a sense of accomplishment, knowing Walt as we know him today, he, most likely, would have been thinking of something new or doing something better…instead of being satisfied his success. His saying, "Keep moving forward" certainly kindles this spirit!

Dave Smith is the author of two top-selling tennis instructional books, TENNIS MASTERY and COACHING MASTERY and is the Senior Editor of the world's top-rated tennis website, TennisOne.com. While Dave has published more than 100 tennis articles over the past 8 years, HIDDEN MICKEY is his first venture into writing novels. Dave has been a featured speaker at various tennis conferences, clubs and workshops. He owns Top Notch Tennis Academy in St. George, Utah.

Dave has been married for 20 years to Dr. Kerri N. Smith and has two children, Kyla Marie who is ten and Keaton Bruce who is six.